BY THE AUTHOR OF

Undercover

Room 9

SOLEDAD
SANTIAGO

Room
9

A PERFECT CRIME BOOK

DOUBLEDAY

NEW YORK

LONDON

TORONTO

SYDNEY

AUCKLAND

A Perfect Crime Book
PUBLISHED BY DOUBLEDAY
a division of
Bantam Doubleday Dell Publishing Group, Inc.
666 Fifth Avenue New York, New York 10103

DOUBLEDAY is a trademark of Doubleday, a division of Bantam
Doubleday Dell Publishing Group, Inc.

Book design by Anne Ling

Grateful acknowledgment is made for permission to reprint two lines
from the musical *Les Misérables*, © Alain Boublil Music Ltd. From the
song "Who Am I" by Alain Boublil and Claude-Michel Schonberg.

Library of Congress Cataloging-in-Publication Data

Santiago, Soledad.
    Room 9 / by Soledad Santiago. —1st ed.
        p.   cm.
    "Perfect Crime."
    "A Perfect Crime book"—T.p. verso.
    I. Title. II. Title: Room Nine
    PPS3569.A5455R6 1992
    813'.54—dc20   91-12007
                                                        CIP

ISBN 0-385-42123-0
Copyright © 1992 by Soledad Santiago

To my mother, G. E. Vural,
whose dedication to the children of India
taught me that each of us
can choose to make a difference.

And to Eric Simon for help beyond measure.

ACKNOWLEDGMENTS

Special thanks to:

Rhoda Golden of the N.Y. State Commission on Government Integrity for inspiration.

Joan Westmeyer, Joan Cannon and Chris Plummer for endless hours of proofreading.

Peter Bloch for encouragement from the beginning.

Kate Miciak, my editor, for knowing there is blood in stones.

Leyla Rocio, my daughter, whose flamenco heart gives me courage.

Rocky Taino, my son, for telling me all about Joey.

The strongest Poison ever
  known
Came from Caesar's Laurel
  Crown.

WILLIAM BLAKE, "AUGURIES OF INNOCENCE"

Whoever tells the truth is chased out of nine villages.

ANONYMOUS, TURKISH PROVERB

Room 9

PROLOGUE

The man didn't scream; he didn't flail his arms. He just sailed downward like a rag doll in designer pajamas. Some of the busy shoppers below saw him and began to scream. He didn't hear them. He was falling fast.

On the sidewalk a toddler in a stroller sucked her fingers hungrily. The earth rose up and slapped the man with its vast indifferent palm. The child disappeared. Only a few inches away, the mother stood untouched. Her heart cracked like an egg and everything in it that was good spilled at her feet. The child lay broken beneath the man. Then, from the blurry edge of consciousness, the mother heard sirens and a Christmas carol.

The police and EMS personnel arrived within moments and almost simultaneously. The man lay mutilated beyond recognition. While the EMS attendants prepared to scrape him up, Officers Olson and Jefferson began to canvass the building from which the shoppers had seen the man fall. They were the ideal team for a job like this, foot soldiers who had worked together so long they operated without having to speak. Olson was a heavyset man in his late forties, as white as they come. Jefferson was younger, leaner, and black. Neither of them had ever made it out of "the sack." Meaning they were perennial bluecoats.

The team began on the twentieth floor. When they reached the twenty-third floor, they found a whimpering woman huddled behind an unlocked door.

"Ma'am . . . ma'am."

She looked up at the two blue uniforms. "My husband," she whispered. "My husband." Her face was wet with tears.

Officer Olson squatted down beside her. "We're here to help you, lady." Then he took her hands and pulled her to her feet. She tottered as if drunk. He walked her to the couch.

Jefferson said, "She's in shock. Get the medics over here."

As Olson called for backup Jefferson looked around. The mirrored modular living room was elegant to a fault, no knickknacks, nothing personal. The master bedroom, decorated in simple black and white, was designer all the way. Then there was a boy's bedroom with handcrafted wooden furniture—a captain's bed, a desk, a bookshelf holding several baseball trophies, an array of Heavy Metal posters. Jefferson wandered into the study, which was cozy and casually expensive. One wall was covered in pictures and plaques. To his surprise, he was familiar with a lot of the faces.

They were famous faces. Not Hollywood but politics—a young Senator Kennedy, Governor Rockefeller, Governors Carey and Cuomo, former Mayor Koch, the current police commissioner, Kavanaugh, and the current mayor, Kenneth Nicosea. In each photograph, in slightly different poses, stood the same tall, lean, elegant man. He was the only person on the wall who aged. In the earlier pictures his hair was sandy and his face unlined. In the more recent pictures, his hair had gone silver, the face was still young, but the eyes were somehow murkier. All the pictures were in matching neat black frames. Jefferson stepped in for a closer look. He pushed his cap back and called his partner. He didn't have to say anything, the pictures said it all.

"Holy shit," Olson said. "Holy shit. We'd better call the brass."

Ten minutes later Police Commissioner Kavanaugh called Deputy Mayor Brogan at home. In another five minutes, Mayor Nicosea's hot line rang in Gracie Mansion. Seven minutes after that the mayor called Ron Hunter, his press secretary. It was 9:29 P.M.

"Isenberg just killed himself. The asshole jumped from a balcony and crushed some kid when he landed. This is bad, this is very bad, this is bad press," the mayor said.

"Thank God it's past the six o'clock. We need a statement, we need it fast. I'll get the commissioner to block the area off so there's no visuals."

"Brogan did that already."

"You should have fired Isenberg six months ago," Ron Hunter said.

"How could I? He was with me from the beginning."

But City Hall was in luck. Two hours later, and long before the morning editions, a fire in a brand-new homeless shelter in Brooklyn knocked Deputy Mayor Isenberg's suicide off the front pages with fabulous copy and visuals. In preparation for an election year, the administration had closed most of its welfare hotels. The homeless had been relocated to newly constructed temporary shelters mostly in the outer boroughs just in time for a lot of Thanksgiving publicity. Only two weeks later, a shelter in Queens had gone up in flames. Fortunately for the mayor, no one had died in either fire.

Isenberg's suicide still got plenty of ink. Not since Queens borough president Donald Manes, had a New York City public official committed suicide. The fact that Isenberg had been the administrator of the emergency temporary shelter construction program seemed like an odd coincidence. None of the papers even mentioned it.

1

C ity Hall stood pretty as a palace in a shroud of falling snow. Out front the Christmas tree was lit. I recall being blinded by snow that turned to water at my feet. She was up there, the veiled lady they call Justice, standing over the clock with the Roman numerals, holding the sword and scale. That day she was invisible. I blamed the storm.

I climbed the wide sweep of stair and walked between the Greek columns into the limestone portico. There were five doors. Only one opened. Visitors were often confused, but I had opened that door a thousand times before. The winter wind swirled snow around the marble steps. A cop opened the door for me.

Inside, the lobby was warm and brightly lit. A handful of reporters clustered around a City Council member. Beyond, in the rotunda, a class of schoolchildren flocked together in their Sunday best. The children ogled like noisy tourists in a church. Like all the other visitors, they prayed for a glimpse of His Honor, the mayor. I felt it too—that illusion that I had entered the perfection of an ancient temple, a heartbeat at its mysterious center.

The guard at the metal detector winked at me as I walked through. He didn't ask me to place my bag on the X-ray conveyor belt. He never did. As I headed for the mayor's office Ron Hunter, the mayor's press secretary, crossed the hall in front of me. Ron was the youngest, best looking of the mayor's advisers. A former Pulitzer Prize–winning reporter on a midwestern daily, he wasn't much liked by the New York press corps. Despite his arrogance, I had the feeling the mayor didn't really confide in him. For one thing, he was the mayor's third press secretary in as many terms. He had come aboard after the last election, just like me. The mayor's reputation was that it took him at least a decade before he actually trusted somebody. I had defied all that. In terms of the trust I had earned, my rise had been meteoric. Hunter resented me accordingly. He routinely passed by me without seeing me. In the City Hall caste system, I was beneath him, a shadow. He was a professional, I was merely support staff.

Mayor Nicosea was seated at his Louis XV mahogany desk flipping through the clips. He never actually read the newspapers. The press office clipped the important stories of the day and Xeroxed them for him. That way his fingers didn't get dirty with newsprint and his mind didn't get cluttered with stories his trusted advisers felt he had no need to see. He didn't look up. I studied the top of his head, which, except for one small spot, was still rich with dark brown hair. He was in his shirt sleeves.

I said, "I'm terribly sorry," and began unbuttoning my coat. "Trouble with the trains."

"You need to take travel time into account," he growled, reaching for the coffee someone else had obviously brought him. When I didn't answer, he did look at me. The handsome features were chiseled into a new unhappy configuration. The gray eyes were murky, as if someone had reached far down into a once-clear pool and stirred up some ancient mud. I was waiting for him to say something about Jason's funeral, which was only a few hours away.

He asked, "What's going on out there?"

Except for the occasional press event, he hadn't ridden a subway in at least a decade.

"The protestors stopped traffic at the Brooklyn Bridge and all trains coming in from Brooklyn were delayed by about two hours."

He didn't ask what was I doing in Brooklyn now that I had moved to SoHo. I had moved, but my son, Joey, was still staying with my mother until I got our new place together. I had been so homesick for Joey that I had been going back to Bath Beach almost every night.

"Maybe it's not so bad," the mayor said. "It diverts attention from last night's fire."

I just shrugged and spread my hands. Then I added, "They want their special prosecutor."

The unblinking elders looked down from their frames on the wall.

"I can't go against my own police department," he said, as if the cops were all that stood between us and the abyss.

I took off my coat. "I guess not."

Through the window behind his head I could see Broadway, the subway stop, and the twentieth century.

He got to his feet. "I'm just about to start a press conference," he said. "A press conference on my appeal to Washington for aid to the homeless. Senator Cleghorn and the human-resources commissioner are waiting for me in Brogan's office." Brogan was the first deputy mayor. Like former Deputy Mayor Isenberg, Brogan had been with the mayor from the beginning. Until six months ago Nicosea didn't make a move without Isenberg and Brogan. Then Isenberg had been expelled from the inner circle. They hadn't taken his title or his salary away, just his office and his job. Now he was dead.

The mayor said, "Why don't you get settled in and then join us in the Blue Room?"

The Blue Room was tucked in the corner of the executive wing.

It was a large stately room where the mayor held his press conferences. The Blue Room had a counterpart at the other end of the building in the legislative wing—Room Nine. It didn't compare in size or opulence and no one guarded its door. But without Room Nine the Blue Room was a theater without an audience. All the reporters who covered the City Hall beat were based in Room Nine.

It was odd that the mayor had invited me to the Blue Room. He never invited me to press conferences. Administrative assistants don't go to the Blue Room. It was reserved for Brahmin, royalty, the upper crust. Assistants like me stood guard outside to make sure no riffraff got in. Nicosea stood up and played with the knot in his red tie. "Coming?"

It was his first press conference since the fire and Jason's suicide. I shook my head. Some snow hit the rug beneath my feet and disappeared. "I have to check your calls first. I'll step in later."

He put on his jacket and checked the alignment of his cuffs. I headed down the hall to the receptionist's station in front of Deputy Mayor Brogan's office and asked, "How are the calls this morning?"

It was barely nine o'clock, but Velma the receptionist looked as wilted and ruffled as if she had already put in a full day. "Everybody wants details about Isenberg and about the relocations after last night's fire. Some of them want reactions to the protest. I just keep referring them to the press office. The mayor has calls from agency heads and even the governor's office, but he hasn't gotten around to returning any."

I turned and climbed the step that led to the first deputy mayor's office. Every pane on the French door was covered with Christmas cards. Inside, sounds of the press conference mingled with the muffled sounds of the rest of the city. I edged up to the side door and cracked it ajar. The mayor was leaning on the podium with the bemused expression of a borscht-belt comedian. He had finished his presentation and was feeling for audience reaction. He was flanked by the senator, the commissioner, and the deputy commissioner—a white man, a black man, and a woman who looked like a man. The rest of the room was all city government types and press. In the back, five cameras, four cameramen, and a camerawoman stood on a platform. Cameras were rolling. Below them, sound people fidgeted with battery packs and cassettes.

"Mr. Mayor, political pundits are saying that your efforts in Washington are doomed—that you've been in office too long, that your administration is emasculated. Your temporary shelter program for the homeless is literally going up in flames. How do you respond to that?"

The mayor's forehead glistened. "Let's face it, a lot of people hate these shelters. We have a crazy arsonist out there. But we can't give up. We've done more than any other city in the nation. Let's get a context here. The homeless crisis is national and we've got to take the battle to Washington."

"What about the fire in Queens only two weeks after you opened the new shelter system and now this week's fire in Brooklyn? That's two shelter fires in a month. Do we have a pattern?"

"It's too early to tell. The fire department is still investigating. The first fire was clearly arson."

"Is the police department close to an arrest?" another reporter called out.

The mayor's frustration knotted my stomach. It was as if we were connected by an invisible cord—an umbilicus. When he squirmed, I cringed. I took a deep breath, and he tried again.

"I can't comment on that. But I can say that when we catch the arsonist, he'll be prosecuted to the full extent of the law."

"Why not build permanent housing?"

The mayor shook his head as if he were speaking to a stupid, wayward child. "We would all like that. I would like that too. But I'm the mayor and I have to be more responsible. I have to take a broader view." He reached across the podium toward the press corps with outstretched arms and open palms. "Look, I'm being up-front about this. If this city tried to house every homeless family, we would go broke. And how would the taxpayers feel about that?"

"What are the exact statistics on injuries, hospitalizations, and relocations?"

"I can't give you the numbers here and now. We're in the middle of a crisis and we're not collecting numbers. We're trying to help *people.* I know that five people are in the burn unit. Two from the first fire and three from last night. I went to see them early this morning."

"What will happen to the families that have been returned to the hotel system?"

"Obviously returning these families to the New Fairfield is a temporary solution. Currently, the other shelters in the temporary system are full. That's why we're going to Washington. The federal government has to step in."

First Deputy Mayor Brogan, always the elegant intellect, stooped to whisper in the mayor's ear. The mayor nodded and continued. "Another question?"

"Any topic? What about Isenberg?"

The mayor's face turned red but he betrayed no discernible emotion. I felt my own blood rushing. He said, "Jason Isenberg was a distinguished public servant. Many of you will recall that he pulled New York City through the water crisis a few years ago and he personally pulled our shelter program together. His death is a great tragedy."

"Why do you think he did it? Was his recent demotion a factor?" The voice cut like a jeer.

The mayor's blush deepened but his expression remained unchanged. "Look, I am not going to engage in this kind of specious discussion. I refuse to tarnish Jason Isenberg's many years of fine public service with speculation. Next."

"What about the child who died? Is the city planning to make reparations?"

Now the mayor did look shocked. Such a thing had never occurred to him. But not wanting to sound callous, he nodded bravely and gave a stock answer. "We're looking into that."

The reporters knew they had him now. The questions got tougher. "Mr. Mayor, protestors stopped commuter traffic from Brooklyn into Manhattan for two hours this morning because you have ignored their call for a special prosecutor. Five black men have died in police custody since September and this city's black leadership is interpreting your lack of action as racism. How do you respond to that?"

"That's ridiculous and anybody who knows me knows better. I will not be intimidated into action."

"Mr. Mayor, is Internal Affairs making any progress in its investigation into police brutality in black communities?"

"Obviously, I can't comment on an investigation in progress. But I am calling for a halt to the protests. Give the system time to work."

"Mr. Mayor, the black leadership says they'll protest until they get a special prosecutor. What do you say to that?"

"I've answered this question more than once. At this point there's no need for a special prosecutor. And let me add that our men in blue risk their lives every day out there in the streets and—"

"The charge is that the New York force is racist, that the cop in the street is racist. How do you respond to that?"

The mayor's anguish was turning into anger. "I responded to that earlier. The charge is ridiculous. How can you generalize like that? We have some very brave men and women out there."

"How do you explain the five deaths?"

"Give the process time to work."

"Answer the question, just answer the question."

The mayor's eyes found me. Even before he spoke, I knew what was coming.

"Right here in this room," he said, "we have living proof of the sacrifices our men in blue make. We have a woman here who paid the ultimate price for her husband's courage and dedication to the people of this city—Marie Terranova. I'm sure you'll remember this city's pain and horror three years ago when Officer Terranova was killed."

He didn't mention that Joe was shot by another cop, a fed.

The klieg lights turned in my direction. They blinded me. The heat burned my flesh. Damn! Was he that desperate? Did he have to throw me to the wolves? I felt their eyes eating at me. When I was able to focus, I was looking at Hunter across the room. The press secretary was enjoying my misery. Or maybe he was just glad to see the mayor off the hook.

Brogan tilted his head ever so slightly. The mayor's bodyguards began to move. The mayor took his cue. "All right, fellas, that's it, we're headed for a ribbon cutting on Staten Island."

The human triangle that surrounded the mayor sliced through the crowd with Darnell Smalls, the mayor's personal bodyguard, at the lead. Smalls was chocolate brown and gorgeous. Hunter and Brogan completed the triangle. The reporter from the *Guardian*, the communist paper, called after Nicosea: "Mr. Mayor, Mr. Mayor, is it true the FBI was investigating Isenberg?"

Nobody paid him any mind. As the triangle passed me the mayor said, "I'm going to need you at Isenberg's service." Then he was gone.

What was he going to need next, blood? It was years since I had been a professional widow, and I wasn't about to pick up the veil again. Not for the force. Not even for the mayor himself. I exited with the press corps and went to my office to bury my doubts in my paperwork.

It was almost noon before the mayor returned. We disposed of fifteen items on the "must do" list I had prepared for him. Then we had time for some calls before heading uptown for the funeral. As I dialed for him he stood by the window, the public persona gone, face flushed, hands thrust deep into his pockets, so transparently anxious that I felt sorry for him. I thought about the kindness he had showed me three years ago when I needed work in order to avoid going crazy. Even now, he always gave me flowers on Secretary's Day and time off when Joey had special occasions at school. I felt bad that I had been angry with him at all. After all, he was under attack so often, he had to be slippery sometimes. He sheepishly studied his wet wing tips. I studied him. Then the other line rang. I picked up. A desperate sound came from the receiver.

The call was from the New Fairfield. Somehow somebody's grandmother had gotten the mayor's private line and knew it. The voice was broken by anguished sobs. Her panic was so loud I knew he heard it too.

I put my hand over the receiver. "This woman says her daughter's about to kill her grandchild."

"How did she get this line?"

"She wants to talk to you."

"She can't," he said matter-of-factly, thumbing through some papers. "Switch her over to the press office."

"This woman is desperate."

"Look, are you a psychiatrist?"

I shook my head foolishly.

"Refer her to the press office," he repeated.

"The press office?" I wanted to say those jerks don't have an ounce of compassion among them. But I just said, "Why?"

"They know all the help hot lines available and they can get the cops over there."

"Ma'am—" I could hear her crying and a commotion in the background.

"Please," she said. "Please, you've got to help us. My daughter's always been a good mother. But we got no food for the baby and she just snapped."

I clutched the receiver, locked eye to eye with Nicosea. "Switch it now," he ordered.

"Ma'am, I'm going to switch you to another line where you can get help."

"Oh no," she sobbed, "please . . . I've already been switched six times."

"C'mon," Nicosea said, "we haven't got all day."

I hit the button and switched her over to Hunter's secretary. I had handled a lot of calls in my time, kept a lot of riffraff away from him, even helped a lot of people by referring them to the right person, but that day was different. For a while it was cold and silent between us. I couldn't look at him. What was happening to me? Was it Jason's suicide?

"You're losing perspective," he said quietly without looking up. "You have to know what you can do and what you can't."

I nodded. He was probably right. All the problems in the world seemed to converge right here on City Hall. And who was I to judge? Still, as soon as I could, I went back to my office and called 911 just to make sure the cops were alerted. Again I passed Hunter in the hallway. He stopped and actually spoke to me. "You'll be riding in the mayor's car," he said.

I felt my shock rise to my face. He smiled, saccharine and deadly. "To the funeral," he said.

I nodded. He turned to sashay up the hall in his slightly pigeon-toed way.

All over the building, senior staffers had pulled rank to get the late lunch shift. Everybody wanted to be seen at the funeral. A lot of people had driven to work for the occasion. They could offer rides to whomever they wanted to be seen with. Because I was the mayor's assistant, everyone invited me. In the women's room, secretaries from the legislative wing, the executive wing, and the press office were fixing their faces for the funeral.

"Marie, I brought my car today. Do you want to ride with us?"

I stepped up to the mirror. "Thanks, Patty, but I'll be going with the mayor."

Patty laughed. "Well excuuuse me." The other women giggled. Some of the eyes in the mirror were full of envy. I studied myself. In my simple black suit, I was totally appropriate. I touched up my eyes with shadow, my cheeks with blush, and my lips with lipstick that looked like no lipstick at all. The mirror told me I was thirty-eight and starting to look like my mother.

Ten minutes later, I sat sandwiched between Hunter and the mayor. The three of us were a tight fit in the backseat of the mayor's Lincoln Continental. Both men balanced their open brief-cases on their knees. The mayor was reading his correspondence. Hunter was reading a complicated Freedom of Information Law request for the computer tapes of several city agencies. There was a deafening absence of conversation.

After a while the mayor took off his reading glasses and stared out the window. He sighed. He rubbed his hand over his bald spot. Was it growing? He sighed again. Finally he said, "That press conference was vicious. I shouldn't have let you talk me into it, Ron. I don't want any more press conferences until this Isenberg thing blows over."

"You mean cancel tomorrow's ten A.M.?" Hunter tried desperately to catch the mayor's eyes.

The mayor played with his cuff links. "It was a mistake. I looked bad."

"You didn't look bad. Canceling a press conference will look bad. It looks like you have something to hide."

The mayor gave Hunter an evil stare. "I don't see the need to subject myself to that kind of abuse. The press is going wild, they're not sticking to the rules. They're asking any goddamn thing they feel like asking. Weren't you listening? Didn't you hear those questions?"

"I thought you handled them very well, Ken."

For a few blocks they stayed in a tight-lipped silence. Then Hunter tried again. "Tomorrow will be good for you. You've drafted legislation with two black congressmen. You're going to have a black sponsor in the House. The protests are very visual, they're getting a lot of electronic coverage, and you need to counteract that with some positive exposure with blacks."

"Who's going to cover an announcement about new legislation?" the mayor whined. The prospect of facing an empty Blue Room was clearly more humiliating than facing a room full of hostile questions.

"They'll come," Hunter promised. "I guarantee you the press will come."

"Television?"

"Yes, television."

The mayor studied the streetlights, from which soot-soiled Christmas tree ornaments hung heavy with snow. "Of course," he said, "of course they'll come. They'll come to lynch me."

Another brutal silence fell until we reached Fourteenth Street. Then Hunter looked at his watch. "Do you want to go over the details of the funeral?"

The mayor snapped his briefcase shut and wrapped his arms over the expensive leather. I pushed my knees closer together and studied my lap. Hunter began: "Here's the thing . . . it's a tragedy, Jason Isenberg was a good public servant and a friend, you feel just terrible for the family, you can't speculate on what happened. Stay close to the widow as you're leaving the funeral home, that way no reporter can ask you anything offensive. . . . There'll be no press at the cemetery. It's gonna be one of those Orthodox deals, so you're going to have to shovel some dirt down onto the coffin, the oldest son will hand you the shovel after the family members have each dumped a load . . . then the rabbi will slash the lapels of their suits with a razor blade and they'll rip them."

The mayor looked mournfully at his impeccably tailored lapel.

"Just the immediate family," Hunter said reassuringly, "and then it will be over. Have you read over your remarks?"

The mayor didn't answer. He studied the city outside his tinted bulletproof window. On the street, snow was turning to slush.

Finally he said, "I don't know if I should be doing this."

"You're committed, the family asked that you speak. It means a lot to them. You have nothing to lose."

The mayor rubbed his palm over the leather in his lap. "How's it gonna look to the press . . . me being that close to them."

"It's a humanitarian gesture. If you had turned them down, it might have gotten out, and that would look worse."

The mayor put his glasses back on, opened his briefcase, and pulled out some three-by-fives. He shuffled them before beginning to read. His voice, thick with emotion, paused in all the right places. All the while, Hunter's eyes were intently glued to the mayor's lips. I remembered spoon-feeding Joey when he was an infant. Hunter's lips twitched in sync with the mayor's. I saw my own mouth open every time I offered the spoon to Joey. When the mayor finished, Hunter sighed. "Wonderful."

The mayor removed his glasses from his nose, wiped them with the clean white hanky he always had in his back pocket, and placed them in their case. Hunter watched intently. Finally the mayor placed the three-by-fives in his pocket and said, "I think I'll ad-lib."

"A lot of work went into those remarks," Hunter said plaintively, and I felt his muscles tighten too, but the mayor didn't respond. Then the mayor reached into his inside jacket pocket and produced a miniature notepad. "Now, Marie," he said.

Even though I couldn't move, I came to attention.

"Take care of this for me after the funeral, will you?" It sounded like a question but it wasn't. He handed me the little pad. I opened it close to my chest so Hunter couldn't read over my shoulder. It was a list of names that started with the mayor's wife and kids and ended with the Gracie Mansion cook and me. Hunter wasn't on it.

"About the same amount as last year?" I asked, meaning how much should I spend but not wanting to be direct in front of Hunter.

The mayor played with the knot on his tie then winked at me. "I trust your judgment."

I nodded proudly. Even though I was a little tired of being the mayor's personal errand boy—not to mention I had just finished his wife's Christmas shopping—I relished Hunter's distress. He might be the public alter ego, but on the inside he would never get this close.

When the car reached Seventy-sixth Street, it slowed. The block was already lined with limousines and Lincoln Continentals. Camera crews and reporters clustered at the entrance to the chapel. The driver double-parked and waited for his instructions.

"Why don't you go first, we'll come later," Hunter gallantly volunteered. "You don't need your press secretary at your side when you step into the funeral home."

The mayor turned to me. "Let's go, Marie."

Hunter sank down in his seat. The driver got out and opened the car door for the mayor. I slid out too. Reporters came running.

"Mr. Mayor, Mr. Mayor!"

But the mayor just shook his head sadly as if to say, "Not now, fellas," and we stepped into the cool silence of the Riverside Memorial Chapel. Surrounded by City Hall types, we took the elevator to the second floor. At the mayor's elbow I was getting a lot of respectful looks. But as soon as the elevator door opened there was Hunter looking like he had taken the steps two at a time. He whisked the willing mayor away.

I stood alone in the crush of mourners that filled the anteroom. I saw only backs until the mayor approached the widow and the crowd in front of me parted. I couldn't hear what he was saying, but when he shifted position, I saw her pale face. As I approached she became strangely familiar. She was much younger than Jason, about my age. Her eyes were large, very large, but the pupils were just slits and there was a slowness about her that suggested she was heavily sedated. My lungs locked and I had difficulty getting air. At first I thought it was the dress. I had a cheaper version of that dress in my closet. The mayor took the widow's hand and offered condolences I couldn't hear. Then it was my turn.

I stared at the dress with its expensive jacket. The jacket had been ripped through to its lining. The purple silk of the lining lay across her breast like a wound. I just stood there and whispered, "I'm sorry."

She looked up at me and said, "I know."

I heard a sound in my head then, like the first note of taps. Mercifully, the crowd moved me forward into the large chapel and I lost myself in the back. The chapel was unadorned—no stained-glass windows, no candles, no smiling saints, no flowers by the coffin. I sat down in a pew in which you could not kneel for prayer, and closed my eyes. I heard the low whispers of the pols and smelled the many varieties of their gaudy cologne.

The mayor and Hunter sat up front with the family. Behind them were several rows of commissioners, deputy commissioners, a few state officials, agency heads, and the press. Even the retired party boss, Vic Milano, was there in the same row with Howard Mendelssohn, the mayor's father-in-law. Irish and African-American commissioners were particularly well represented because the service was a photo opportunity to reach the Jewish vote. All the way in front, the closed coffin beckoned to me like an ungodly altar.

When everyone had settled into the pews, the rabbi began in Hebrew. I couldn't understand what he was saying, but the words reached like a primal incantation deep into my guilt. Like all the other hypocrites gathered here, I had abandoned Jason when he was relegated to the basement. His office had disappeared from the main floor over a weekend. In the six months since that had happened, I had not even bothered to try to find out why he had fallen so quickly out of favor. Overnight, he had become a City Hall untouchable. His ostracism had been complete and final. Just being seen with him was bad news. And all of it unspoken.

After the rabbi finished his chant he introduced the mayor. Sorrowfully, the mayor rose. He passed by the coffin and climbed the steps to the podium. Then, without his cue cards, he repeated the speech Hunter had written for him almost verbatim. His voice resonated with emotion and caught in all the right places. The mayor had a phenomenal memory for lines and his delivery was impeccable too.

When the mayor returned to his seat, Jason's older brother spoke briefly. After that Jason's fourteen-year-old son got up. His young skin seemed stretched over an ancient mask of pain. When he attempted to speak, the corners of his lips twitched with the fierce effort to control his sobs. He tried again, his boyish voice breaking between syllables. I thought of my own twelve-year-old son, who had been only nine when he saluted his father's coffin, and the air seemed to leave the chapel. The boy's voice cracked, "What can a son say when he loses his father?" His eyes rested on the white pine coffin. "Dad, I love you . . . you were a great dad."

Even the hardest of pols shifted uncomfortably in their suits. Mendelssohn put a hand gently on Nicosea's shoulder.

"What I wanted to say was"—the boy's eyes never left the coffin—"good-bye, Dad, I love you, Dad, and I know you didn't mean to hurt anybody."

Jason Jr. returned to sit at his mother's side. The rabbi began again to chant in Hebrew. Although the words were foreign, the meaning was clear. He was talking to God, lamenting an eternal story of human frailty and mortality. The widow sat erect and dignified. No tears fell from her eyes. I watched the boy, the smallest, saddest person in the room.

The coffin seemed luminous. It was just a rectangular wooden box, unvarnished and undecorated. I recalled Jason's mysterious fall from grace and saw him standing there at the foot of City Hall's basement stairs, forlorn as a kid without friends. Then I imagined Jason falling those twenty-three stories. I imagined the cops scraping up his remains, the blood, the shattered bones, and it was as if I could see through that simple pine coffin to the faceless monstrosity inside, grinning at this collection of hypocrites. Death had restored Jason to power for one last moment.

Suddenly the simplicity of the chapel and that plain wooden box seemed barbaric. My angry heart wandered back.

It was a sumptuous Catholic funeral at St. Anthony's in Little Italy. Hundreds of candles flickered and the prism of my tears cast rainbows over the dark and cavernous church. The polyurethane coffin was steel blue; the lining, white satin and velvet. The sweet smell of incense burned at my nostrils as the compassionate saints looked down through the old stained-glass windows. The Madonna herself stood holding the Child, the serpent pinned under her foot. It wasn't until I raised my head and saw Him on the cross, His head hanging, the crown of thorns heavy, the nails cutting through His hands and feet, that I began silently to scream. I knelt beside my husband. I touched my husband's hands, cold as plastic. He wore a new uniform; you couldn't see the bullet through his heart. On my tongue I tasted the smell of the sweet, turgid flowers, and when I touched my lips to his, my husband, there was no warmth, no breath. His lips were dead. My husband. I started to wail then, just rock and wail. The fancy coffin, the American flag, the mayor, and all the police brass in the city were no help—no help at all.

I wiped my tears and returned to the funeral of the moment. In the back of my head I heard that note again. The beginning of taps. I watched as four men carried the simple coffin down the aisle. The service was over. The mourners began swiftly to exit. The pols were pew-hopping the way they table-hopped at political dinners. A lot of them were rushing to stay close to the widow. They knew the camera crews would catch her on the way out, so if they were near her, they would appear on the six o'clock news and maybe make hard copy too. I let them all pass me by.

When I got up, I stepped into the aisle on a leg that had fallen asleep. I stumbled and thought I would fall, but a strong hand grabbed my elbow. I turned to look up and my heart jumped. I managed a nod. He stood behind me, young but not too young, short but not too short, beautiful but not too beautiful, and his eyes, his eyes, his eyes were Joe's eyes. I sat down again. I figured I was hallucinating.

"Are you all right?" he asked with an odd little accent.

I nodded thank you, and mercifully he kept going.

I sat there for a long time feeling the texture of the emptiness that filled me. Then I headed for Bloomingdale's.

2

I was sitting at my desk with coffee and a hangover reading the *Daily News*, when Larry Pierce, the *Dispatch*'s City Hall Bureau chief, poked his head into my office. A tall, elegant black man, Pierce was the best-dressed reporter on the political beat. On the job he always went politely for the jugular. Behind him entered the eyes from the funeral. I brought my cup to my lips and struggled to wake up. Larry smiled and said, "This is Marie, the mayor's mother."

I tried to return the smile but the corners of my mouth resisted. "Please, Larry, I'm old but not that old."

They continued standing there. The eyes taking me in.

"Can I offer you some coffee?"

Larry shook his head. "No thanks, I just came by to introduce you to someone. Raul Vega, meet Marie Terranova, the mayor's administrative assistant. Anyone who's worked here for ten minutes knows Marie's his right hand."

I said, "Larry is prone to exaggeration."

"Raul just joined our Room Nine staff. He's from the *Miami Herald.*"

Raul stretched his hand out; I held it for a moment. "Nice to meet you," he said.

"Welcome to City Hall," I answered. But I didn't mean it. I hadn't planned on seeing those eyes again. They made me nervous.

The newspaper in front of me was open to page three. I had already flipped past the cover photo of the mayor and the widow exiting from Riverside Chapel. A little hammer was tapping a tuneless rhythm in my brain.

Raul Vega said, "We've met, in a way. The mayor introduced you at yesterday's press conference." I hadn't seen him there, and mercifully he didn't mention seeing me at the memorial service.

"Raul made a name for himself in Miami, he covered the mob, the big drug busts, you name it. He gave Edna Buchanan a run for her money. Now he's interested in doing some tamer stuff."

I was about to ask Larry since when he considered New York politics tame when the newspaper on the desk grabbed my eye. The headline read, NEW FAIRFIELD NIGHTMARE: MOTHER KILLS INFANT AND SELF. There was a three-column picture. Two bumpy plastic sheets on a sidewalk. One bump was tiny. I felt the blood leave my face. Larry and Raul were looking down at the paper too.

Larry said, "Raul's only been with us forty-eight hours and he's already landed on page three."

I looked up at Raul and then back down at the article that carried his byline. Considering the topic, I didn't know if I should congratulate him or not. I said, "I haven't read the story yet."

Raul said, "The dead woman's mother said that she personally pleaded with the mayor for assistance, but the press office denies it."

I was beginning to wonder if this visit was casual after all.

I studied Larry's expression closely. He had been at City Hall longer than I had, and we both knew the rules. Reporters were supposed to grill the press office, not staffers like me. Larry smiled tentatively, almost as if he too had been taken by surprise.

Raul asked, "You would know if someone spoke to the mayor, wouldn't you?"

Larry winked at me. "Marie knows Hizzoner better than he knows himself."

Raul seemed to be looking into the back of my skull where all the answers were. I rubbed my hand over my eyes. The paper said that the grandmother lay sedated in Bellevue. That probably meant a straitjacket and padded cell.

"If the borough presidents would let the mayor build more shelters, people wouldn't be going crazy in these hotels," I said by way of answer.

"You'd know, wouldn't you?" Raul persisted.

I shook my head and studied his beautiful face. The son of a bitch wouldn't back off, so I offered the truth that hid the lie. "No," I said. "No, she didn't talk to him."

"Raul won the Miami Press Club Award," Larry said.

"I can see why, but next time you have a question take it to Hunter or one of his deputies. There's five of them."

Larry punched Raul playfully in the arm. "The lady's right."

Then he turned to Raul, who was still staring at me. "Let's make the rounds?"

I watched them walk away, both with that cocky reporter's gait that says, "I'm a cop with brains. My press pass is as powerful as any badge. Mess with me, I dare you." I wondered how long it would be before competition between the two of them heated up. Then I closed the newspaper in front of me.

It wasn't long before I felt compelled to open the paper again. The photograph of two plastic-covered lumps on the sidewalk whispered their accusation. I heard the old woman's desperate plea. I should have done something. But what? Here I was, power-less at the center of power. Could I have convinced Nicosea to talk to her? Would it have made a difference? The intercom buzzed. It was Hizzoner.

"Marie, I'm in Brogan's office. He's conducting a meeting in my office. Let's do the gifts. There're no other holes in my schedule."

I closed the newspaper. "Be right there."

Under my desk were all the shopping bags from Bloomingdale's and an assortment of wrapping paper. I took the bags and headed for the deputy mayor's office. With its French doors and chandelier, it was my favorite office in the building. Inside, Brogan's desk was up a step like an altar. When I walked in, the mayor rubbed his hands together like a kid who's found a prize. "Let's see. How did I do?"

I locked the door behind me and placed the gifts on the desk. He seemed pleased. "Let's wrap them together," he said.

"You have time?"

When had he ever had time for something as mundane as this?

He shrugged. "Not really, but let's do it."

Then, as I cut the paper, I had to say it. "There's a new man," I said, "a new man in Room Nine."

The mere mention of Room Nine flushed his face. His relationship with the press was decidedly love/hate. He was acerbic and accessible. They liked matching wits with him. But deep down, he hated them. They couldn't be trusted. A lot of them were to the left of center. The mayor handed me the first present. "Another wise-ass?"

I placed the gift on the paper. "He's pretty aggressive."

"They're all after the Pulitzer," the mayor said as he watched me fold the paper.

"You know that woman did throw the baby out the window and then she jumped herself," I said.

He cut some tape from the dispenser and together we wrapped golden angels around a perfume called Poison. He said softly, "It's one thing to kill yourself . . . but an innocent child?"

"They were starving. She was desperate. I guess she snapped."

He cut some more tape. "Look, you've been through a lot. Could you see yourself throwing your kid out the window?"

I said, "I think it's different when despair is all you've ever known."

"You can defend her if you want to, but some of these people are just beyond help."

I took a piece of tape from one of his fingers. "Did you see the byline?"

He shook his head.

"It's the new guy, Raul something. He's from Miami. He asked me if the woman had talked to you."

"Doesn't this asshole know he's supposed to go through the press office? What did you say?"

I placed a crimson bow on the first gift, set it aside, and started cutting another piece of paper. It said, "Noel, God Rest Ye Merry Gentlemen and Peace and Goodwill Toward All Men." His anxiety was palpable. I let him stew. Finally I said, "I told the truth. She didn't talk to you."

"These goddamn crusaders," he said. "If they can save the world, why don't they?"

Then his mood seemed to change. He reached into his pocket; his grin became mischievous. There was a small Tiffany box in his hand. He put it into my hand. "Open this."

I opened it slowly. He had actually taken the time to shop for me. An elegant gold-and-diamond collar pin lay on the deep blue velvet. My hands were shaking. I didn't know what to feel. I said, "It's beautiful but you shouldn't have."

"I had it made a while ago. Do you really like it?"

No man had ever bought me anything this expensive.

"How could I not?" I said, but my throat tightened. It was a gift I should have gotten from a lover, not from him. "You actually had this made?"

"It was before all this." He waved his arms as if the mess of Jason's suicide hung in the air around us. Then as he placed the pin on my lapel I could contain my questions no longer. I opened my mouth to break the unwritten rule, the rule passed down from special assistant to special assistant, from staffer to staffer. *Never ask more than you're told to ask.*

"What really happened to Jason?"

He hesitated only a moment before answering. "Jason had cancer, I guess it will surface in the papers any day now."

"He didn't look sick."

"It was early, but I guess he couldn't stand the idea of what might happen to him."

I fingered my brooch. "Then it wasn't because he was shot down."

The packages were almost done. The mayor folded the remaining wrapping paper. "That was a long time ago, at least a year . . ."

"Six months," I corrected him. Then I asked the question I had not dared to ask six months ago. "Why? Why exactly did Jason get shot down?"

The mayor walked over to the portrait of Peter Stuyvesant, the first governor of New York, and searched for dust on the gold leaf frame. "Jason had some very serious problems. . . . Look," he added without turning. "This can't come out."

I just stood there. We'd worked closely together for three years. How could he even think that I might betray his confidence? Then, as I shoved the wrapped packages back into my shopping bags, he said, "Jason was an addict."

I was confused. Jason had been a health nut.

"Twelve years ago Jason took a big salary cut and left an executive position with my father-in-law's bank to manage my first mayoral campaign. After that he grew to be my right hand."

Outside, shoppers sloshed through the snow. The mayor continued, "But when Jason turned forty, something happened to him. He started to gamble. He was always slinking off someplace to gamble. It was getting harder and harder to hide. But I just couldn't bring myself to fire him, not after all those years."

I remember the way he turned to me. One eyebrow twitched, then settled. "I hate to ask this but I have to, Marie. You cared about Jason, so I know you will want to help."

He took a set of keys from Brogan's desk drawer. I was surprised that the drawer wasn't locked. He said, "The things in Jason's office need to be boxed, and it has to be done by someone I trust."

I put the scissors back into my shopping bag. He went on.

"We're old-school, you and I. We play by the old rules." Gently, he placed the key in my palm and closed my fingers around it. "Just put the stuff in boxes."

"And then what?"

The mayor shrugged. "Don't worry about that. You box, Brogan will analyze. His thinking is that we need to know what's in there in case we get any FOIL requests. Better not to be taken by surprise."

"You're not expecting that, are you? Why would anyone make a Freedom of Information request for Jason's files? What would be the point?"

The mayor thrust his hands into his pockets, tucked his chin, and talked to his chest. "There's nothing more tempting to those journalistic ghouls than a dead man's grave. Christ, he can't even defend himself. Jason will get a lot of ink for a while. They'll probably do his sex life, and when they stumble into his gambling, they're going to want to see his financial disclosure statements. Let's hope he's clean. And don't forget he administered the shelter program and now the shelters are burning."

The mayor paused to let the next few words sink in. "Jason could tip the election."

Could Jason reach from the grave and cost us the election? Was that a possibility? The mayor was shooting for an unprecedented fourth term. The odds were against him. Could he be out of a job next November? If he was out, I was out. Suddenly November seemed like tomorrow.

"It's Christmas Eve," I said. "Can it wait till next week?"

He looked unhappy. "I guess it'll have to," he said, "but don't wait too long."

That night I was the last to leave City Hall. The snow was falling fast and hard. During the day an odd gathering of protestors had surrounded City Hall. The homeless had arrived with blankets and shopping carts. They had already divided City Hall Park into neat little squares. Some had laid out their blankets, others their cardboard boxes. One woman sat next to a house made of two shopping carts connected by green plastic garbage bags. Next to her stood several brands of cleaning fluid in plastic bottles. Another woman sat in the dark, sewing rags together.

Several men were constructing a roof by suspending pieces of plastic between park benches. One mournful, raggedy group hung a string of multicolored lights on a naked tree. Except for their hacking coughs, they were a silent crowd.

On Broadway some young black protestors were break-dancing to rap music while waiting for the special prosecutor they might never get. They had dropped their protest signs; their slogans melted into the slush. The backbone of the protest had gone home for Christmas; only the determined and the dopers with their small-time pushers remained. They had no Christmas to go to. Both crowds were being watched by some sad-faced cops who weren't going to get home in time to trim the tree.

The snow was deep but there was a well-worn path from City Hall to the subway. I followed it, looking forward to seeing my son's face, but cursing myself because once again I was going to be late. My way out of the City Hall area was blocked by a horse. When I got around it, I saw Raul Vega. He was talking to a cop. In one hand he held one of those skinny pads reporters carry, with the other he held the horse's reins. He was wearing a short brown leather jacket and khaki pants that fit just right. I was hoping he wouldn't see me when he did. He let go of the horse abruptly; it skitted back and neighed. The animal's breath rose between us like steam. A bluecoat moved one of the wooden horses that fenced off City Hall and let me out. "Merry Christmas," he said.

Vega followed. I walked a little faster. Down on the subway steps, he caught up with me. "Rough night?" he asked. I didn't bother to answer.

"What is it about me that irritates you so?" He offered a quirky little smile.

I stopped to look at him and to remind myself that he was from Room Nine and it would pay to be civil.

"It's not you," I said. "It's Christmas."

"I know what you mean," he said.

I pulled a token from my coat pocket and continued down the stairs. On the platform I realized the trip home could take hours. People carrying packages were stockpiled as if they had been waiting for days. I decided to call Joey and tell him I'd be late. The phone on the platform was out of order. I went back up.

Four people were ahead of me waiting to use the one working
phone on the block. As I stood there the snow settled on me like a
blanket. Finally it was my turn. I pulled my gloves off with my teeth
and put my quarter in the telephone slot. My mother picked up on
the third ring.

"Pronto." Fifty years in America and she still sounded like
Sicily.

"Mom, the trains are really bad again tonight. I'm going to be
very late. Can I talk to Joey?"

"That job . . ." My mother's voice trailed off, the recrimina-
tions so old they no longer had to be put into words.

"Mom, let me talk to Joe."

"He's out now."

"I just want to tell him I'm on my way."

The phone went dead. Punishment, I suppose, for not having
landed a second husband. I studied the receiver for a moment then
slammed it down hard as a curse. I headed back to the dark mouth
of the subway. Raul Vega was standing there. "Going to Brooklyn?" he asked.

When I didn't answer, he said, "I live in Brooklyn too."

"What part?"

"The Slope."

"No good, I'm in Bath Beach."

"Doesn't matter. We could take the bridge and you'd get home
in forty-five minutes instead of at midnight."

"It's Christmas Eve, don't you have plans?"

"Yeah, my plan is to get home."

I thought about that crowd down there on the platform and
Joey's disappointed face if I didn't get home soon.

"Where's your car?"

"Right there." He pointed to the City Hall lot.

"Let's go."

To get to his car we passed the homeless shantytown. Old men
and women warmed their hands over a garbage-can fire; the reflection of the flames streaked their miserable faces with an eerie light.
Their accusing eyes followed us.

Raul said, "Jesus, it's really true, this city has no heart."

I took the word *city* to mean "mayor" and was personally offended. "It's not just New York," I said. "It's all over America. This country has a big deficit."

He shook his head. "You can say that again."

The car was a little red, dented Honda that was covered in snow.

"Get in," he said, and opened the passenger side.

Then, while I was safely in the car, he struggled with bare fingers to remove the encrusted ice from his windshield. The ice seemed to cut into his flesh. His face twisted in pain. When he got in, he brought the chill air with him. "Goddamn it," he said. "Goddamn it, I hate the cold."

Snow sparkled in his hair; his brows and lashes were silver. I wanted to laugh but I didn't. He fought with the ignition for a while. It coughed but that was all. *"Carajo,"* he said, *"carajo."* His brown skin was copper from the cold. Finally the ignition caught and the car started. We plowed our way through the deepening snow to the barricades, where he produced his press pass, and we exited City Hall Park. When we finally hit Broadway, he turned to me. He looked awfully young. He said, "I don't see how you fit with that crowd."

"I don't see what you mean."

In the car five minutes and it was already cat and mouse.

"Where's your ego, your hunger for power?"

"I don't like politicians," I snapped. But it was the wrong answer.

"Is that politicians in general or the one you work for?"

"Is there any heat in this car?"

He chuckled. "Yeah, there's heat," he said. "Heat under your collar." Then he reached over and pulled a switch. "I just wanted the engine to heat up so the air wouldn't come out cold."

"Where are you from?" I asked just to let him know I knew he was a foreigner.

He slid his eyes over toward me. "Where do you think?"

I said, "Puerto Rico," even though I knew if he was from Miami, he was probably Cuban.

"I'm Cuban," he said. "But I suppose it's all the same to you."

I didn't answer. He headed for the Brooklyn Bridge.

"Where am I taking you?"

"Bath Beach. You take the BQE south onto the Gowanus, stay left until you hit the Belt Parkway, and take that to the Bay Parkway exit. Is this wrecking your Christmas Eve?"

He took his eyes off the road for a moment. "Not really. I haven't been in town long enough to have any plans."

I studied his profile carefully. He added, "Christmas is seldom fun."

On the windshield snowflakes dissolved into water. Finally I asked, "How old were you when you left your country?"

The car skidded and he loosened his grip on the wheel to let it realign. "Two," he said.

"So how come you have an accent?"

He offered a deep sexy laugh. "I suppose I cultivate it. I don't want to get too assimilated. Or maybe it's because I grew up in Little Havana with my grandparents and they speak no English."

For a moment he reminded me of my mother—in the country for five decades, but never sure she wanted to be a part of it. Joe and I had wanted to be American and not much else.

The Brooklyn Bridge rose ahead of us like a cathedral. Night and snow were falling all around. I was watching his beautiful profile as he concentrated on the road, and for some reason I began to talk. In the warm sanctuary of his car I told him about Joe, about our love, and how he was killed three years ago in early December. He led me on, sometimes with a gentle question, or just a nod or a sound that said "I'm with you, I'm listening." When I had finished, he said, "I knew all that, I knew when I first looked into those big sad eyes of yours at the funeral."

"So you do remember?"

"Sure I remember. You seemed very upset. Did you know Isenberg well?"

"Not really. I did work for him for a few months when I first got to City Hall. He was a very charming man."

"A genius, they say."

Already I regretted talking. The conversation was taking a turn down a path I couldn't pursue. So I just said, "Nobody ever really knows what's going on inside someone else."

"You don't really believe that," he said. "What would be the point if we never understand each other?"

As he said that he was already turning onto my mother's block. "We're down there on the right." I pointed out into the frozen Brooklyn night. A heavy snow was falling. It was almost eight o'clock and the street was deserted. Everyone was at home celebrating Christmas Eve. He pulled up in front of my mother's small wooden house. We sat there listening to the click, click, click of the windshield wipers.

Through my mother's lace living-room curtains, I could see the Christmas tree and the multicolored lights flashing off in groups of three and four. As we sat there in silence the sound of the wipers seemed to get louder and louder. He reached forward and turned them off. The world outside the windshield began quickly to disappear. He turned toward me. "Can I see you again?"

In the reflection of the snow on the windshield, his pupils were silver. I pulled my coat up around my ears, preparing for the cold outside. He shifted in his seat and his unbuttoned coat fell back, revealing thighs that strained against khaki pants. He massaged the steering wheel steadily. My panty hose was starting to itch. Now that we were parked, I noticed that he smelled faintly of citrus.

I said, "I don't call giving someone a ride home seeing them." But my voice was cracking.

He shook his head. "Semantics. All right then, may I take you out sometime, dinner, a movie?"

"I'm too old to date. I have a twelve-year-old son and I'm a widow."

"I know that. But you can't stay in mourning forever."

That cut pretty deep.

"Look," I said, "a relationship with you would be a conflict of interest."

He raised a sarcastic eyebrow. "Now who's jumping to fourth gear? I said dinner, a movie. I never used the word *relationship*. Besides, where's the conflict of interest?"

He was getting me mad. "I'm the mayor's administrative assistant and you're a reporter. What do you call that?"

"You don't work in the press office, you're a secretary."

"I'm not a secretary." A lump was tightening my throat. "I'm more than that, I'm the special assistant to the mayor and my job means everything to me."

He stopped playing with the wheel. "You gonna marry your job, make love to it, hold it in your arms at night?"

I slapped him then, just like that, without premeditation. It was as if my arm moved before my brain did. He sat there holding his cheek, looking at me in the most surprised and stupid way. As soon as I had done it I couldn't believe that I had done it. He couldn't believe it either.

"Is this a psychotic break or are you just nuts?" But his eyes were laughing.

I don't know why I didn't get out of the car. I just sat there pulling on my coat, speechless with rage. He rubbed his cheek, then put a finger in his mouth. "No blood," he said.

Finally I said, "Look, I'm sorry, but you're very insulting."

"Don't you think you're just a little oversensitive about that job of yours?"

The way that he said it made me laugh.

"I'm really sorry," I said. "I guess I spoiled your Christmas Eve. It's eight o'clock already."

"I told you, I haven't been in town long enough to have plans."

I was watching Joey, his face pressed against my mother's window, his breath creating a circle of uneven condensation.

"Why don't you come in and eat with my family?" Even as I said it I was surprised.

"I'd be extraneous."

"Not at all," I said, picturing my mother and all the others studying this young handsome reporter, wondering if we were in the sack together. The thought of upsetting them like that was suddenly very appealing. "Not at all," I repeated. "There's so many people in there they won't even notice one more, and I'll feel better if you let me make it up to you."

"Lots of food," he said, rubbing his hands together.

"Yeah, more food than decent conversation."

He laughed. "You're on."

We raced each other through the knee-high snow toward the house. I stopped to kiss Joey's smile in the window. We scrinched our faces and rubbed noses through the pane. Then Joey came to open the door.

"Mom, Mom, you made it!"

He let me kiss him, but when I tried to nibble his cheek, he turned away. Then he looked at Raul.

"This is my friend Raul. He works in City Hall and he just came to New York from Miami, so I invited him over to enjoy Christmas Eve with us."

Christmas tree lights reflected in Joey's eyes. "Does Grandma know?"

Suddenly I had second thoughts. My mother was about as friendly to strangers as a mongoose to a snake. I said, "No, we just met." Joey rolled his eyes at me. We stared at each other trying to figure out what to do with our guest. Except for the lights on the tree, it was dark in the living room. We could hear the party in the back of the house. The fragrance of cinnamon and wine mingled with the scent of pine needles.

I was still trying to get my boots off when Joey took Raul to meet the others. Joey was half as tall as Raul. He had gotten taller without my noticing.

I studied the coats on the rack trying to figure out who was in the house. I counted Zi Jeannie, my mom's youngest sister. She was fifteen years younger than Mom and only seven years older than me. There was Jeannie's daughter Lilly, her husband Robert, a cop, and their three-year-old daughter, Gloria. Like my mother, both Jeannie and Lilly were stay-at-home wives. Then there were Jeannie's teenagers: Vinnie, a seventeen-year-old punk, and Barbara, a nineteen-year-old college student who was sure to break the mold. I liked Barbara a lot. Then there was Mom's older brother, Big Vinnie. His wife had long since died and his kids had scattered; one was in Florida and one had married a Jewish guy from Forest Hills and never came home anymore. Big Vinnie was a truck driver, but the word was that he was "connected."

I didn't have to see the scene inside to know what it looked like. The men and boys would be playing cards for small stakes. The females were hard at work putting finishing touches on the Christmas feast. I followed the smell of garlic and basil to the back of the house and found everyone positioned just as they were in memory. Only it wasn't like it used to be when the family was bigger and the house was full of kids, their eyes wide with wonder, stuffing their faces with every finger, asking every ten minutes when they could open their presents. Now, except for Joey and Gloria, the kids in the house were teenagers, and they both looked ready to keel over from boredom.

My mother, apron over her Christmas dress, was bent over the sink. Aunt Jeannie was standing next to her holding an empty serving bowl. Gloria sat on the floor ripping into a box of Perugina chocolates. Big Vinnie, Robert, and Vinnie Jr. were playing cards. Barbara was rocking in the rocking chair, watching the card game. Raul and Joey were sitting at the table, which was set but empty, talking. Nobody looked up. Normally, Joey's attention would be all mine. I stood there feeling uncomfortably like a ghost. My mother poured angel-hair pasta into a colander to let the water run off. Without turning around, she asked, "Who is the stranger?" in Italian.

I was embarrassed. I didn't say anything.

"Where's he from?" Again in Italian.

"He works in City Hall, he's from Miami, he's Cuban, and Mama, they understand Italian pretty good."

Raul and Joey looked up from their conversation, both obviously amused by my discomfort. It's pretty hard to disguise the words *Miami, City Hall,* and *Cubano.*

"He's Mom's friend, and mine," Joey said in English. "And he plays basketball."

Joey and his father had played basketball a lot. I wondered if Joey remembered.

"Can I help?" I asked my mother.

"Give your friend something to drink."

Joey jumped up. "I'll do it. What would you like?"

Then, as he rattled off the choices, I went around the room and kissed everybody on the cheek. Whenever I kissed my mother, she'd push me away with a curse, *"Disgraciata."* She never did have much faith in me, and now I'd brought a Cuban to the house. I wondered how old Raul was. He had to be younger than me. Was it obvious? I kissed Mama on the back of the neck. Her hands were occupied, so there wasn't a thing she could do. She said, "You're late. You're always the last one."

"I had to finish something for the mayor," I said, just because I knew it would irritate her.

She dumped the pasta into the empty bowl in Aunt Jeannie's hands. Jeannie was forty-five, but with my mom she acted like she was still six, like Mama was her mama.

"Maybe when you live in Manhattan, you can get home better hours," my mother said. She was still sour about my recent move to SoHo. "Maybe then you see your boy more too." She twisted the knife of guilt.

"Who's the guy?" Aunt Jeannie wanted to know. Steam from the bowl in her hands rose up, seeming to melt her painted face. Aunt Jeannie wore a ton of makeup.

"He's just somebody from work who gave me a ride," I said.

"He's cute." Jeannie carried the pasta over to the table.

"Is he white?" my mother demanded under her breath.

I snarled back, *"Sì, Mama, sì."*

Ever since Joe's partner had been a black man, and we had become best friends with his family, Mama didn't trust me. I picked up an empty bowl. Mama said, "Why don't you meet a nice Italian boy?" I was thirty-eight and she still wanted me to meet a boy. She poured clam sauce into the bowl in my hands. The sauce was so hot, for a split second I imagined it falling into my lap and burning everything "down there." Mama would like that. "I'm not seeing him, Mama, so what are you worried about?"

She licked the wooden spoon and headed over to the sink. As she turned on the faucet she slid an evil eye over her shoulder. "You blind, you know that. You so-o-o smart, City Hall big shot. But you see nothing."

She raised her wet hands in frustration, then brought them down and dried them on her apron. A lock of very white hair fell forward over her wrinkled face, and at that moment I forgot all the years of conflict between us and hungered for her as passionately as when she had me at her breast. I embraced her round little body. She was soft and warm. "Mama, let's have a good time."

"Okay, *figlia.*" She patted my behind. "Let's eat."

When we got to the table, she glared at Joey, who was still sitting next to Raul. Joey pretended not to notice. Finally she said, "Joey, you sit by me."

Joey looked at me.

"Joey, you sit by me," she repeated, patting the chair next to her.

"I like it here," Joey said.

Mama shot me a venomous sideways glance. I tried that same look on Joey. He grinned and didn't budge. Everybody else was busy getting comfortable in their seats. Finally I said, "Let him sit where he wants, Mama."

"He sit next to me like always."

"He's fine where he is," I said, taking the chair next to her. Aunt Jeannie sat down on Raul's other side. He looked at me and shook his head ever so slightly.

I concentrated on the food—clear broth, antipasto, followed by spaghetti prepared several different ways, stuffed calamari, fried shrimp, fillets, smelts, mussels, pots of steamed broccoli and peas and onions. In the wide center of the table stood the red wine, the Parmesan, the ricotta, and the crusty Italian bread we ate with everything. For a while we were absorbed in passing the various dishes around and filling our plates. Then Big Vinnie asked Raul if it was true that all the dope in New York City came from Miami. After that, everyone speculated about the Super Bowl.

Even when I was married, I hadn't liked sports because they took Joe away from me. Still, I had tried to understand. But now I was sitting across from my little man, and it was clear that in sports he and Raul had found a common interest. I was beginning to wonder if inviting this guy had been a mistake when he reached his fork across the table and stole a few strands of spaghetti from my plate.

"What's your opinion, lonely lady?" There was a sparkle in Raul's eyes that said he was completely at home.

"Yeah, Mom, do you think the champ's new wife is going to ruin him for the ring?"

Raul winked at Joey. My teeth bit into a mussel and I decided to go along. "You mean like Samson and Delilah?"

"Good analogy," Raul said, smiling at Joey.

"She's gonna mess him up," Joey said very seriously. He was ready to drop me from the conversation so he could reclaim Raul's total attention. But Raul's eyes were on mine.

"You like my mom," Joey finally said, and got both our attention.

"Yeah, I do," Raul said, stuffing a forkful of arugula into his mouth, "but she doesn't believe me."

I was beginning to see it just wasn't possible to ruffle this guy.

The conversation turned to my job. Working for the mayor was like working for a celebrity, and whenever the family got together, eventually the attention would turn to me for the inside scoop. Vinnie would ask why the trains weren't running on time, why the garbage wasn't being picked up, or why crack dealers were taking over the city. When he got tired of the easy questions, he'd ask me when I was going to find another man and be a real woman again.

I was watching Raul and Joey, hoping nothing humiliating would come at me from Vinnie's end of the table, when Vinnie started talking with his mouth full.

"You knew that Isenberg, didn't you?"

Raul was still talking to Joey. He didn't look up.

"Not too well, Vinnie."

"You think there was something corrupt going on there, and he had to take himself out?" Vinnie asked while shoving some garlic bread into his mouth.

I bit my cheek. I had never mentioned that the guy sitting across the table from me was a reporter. Vinnie rattled on, not meaning any harm. I said, "No, nothing like that, Vinnie."

"Look at that Manes, he killed himself because he got into one too many shady deals."

"C'mon, Vinnie, he was under investigation. This was nothing like that."

Raul's ears were getting bigger by the moment. I figured I had no choice but to answer Vinnie truthfully.

"Isenberg had terminal cancer. . . . You're gonna see that in the papers soon."

Vinnie shoved a smelt between his teeth and grunted in satisfaction. He had gotten the inside story. Raul didn't react at all. It was as if I had said nothing new. Had he known or was he just that cool?

"The one I feel sorry for is Esther," Vinnie started again. "After all that bouncing around when she married him she musta thought her life was settled. Money, power, everything."

I didn't know what he was talking about.

Aunt Jeannie said, "Which Esther? We don't know any Esther."

"Esther Mauselli?"

And then I remembered. Esther and I had been in high school together. She was a pretty girl but always an outsider. Her father was Italian but her mother was Jewish. I remembered Esther mostly because a lot of kids had always been jealous of her: she got more presents than anyone else in school because her family celebrated Christmas and Hanukkah. But then in our senior year, her family left the neighborhood, and I never saw her again.

Raul was watching me. I said, "I didn't know she was married to Isenberg." In the three years I had known Jason, I had never met his wife. Her picture had been on his desk, but I hadn't made the connection. Now I knew why the widow's face had been so familiar.

"It's gonna be tough for her to collect the insurance because he killed himself," Vinnie said.

"Blood money," my mother snapped, and for a few minutes everybody was silent. Vinnie was always putting his foot in somebody's mouth. The whole family knew that for three years now I had been putting Joe's death benefits in the bank because I didn't want to touch blood money. But just last month I had decided to leave Brooklyn, and I had taken that money and bought a co-op in SoHo. My mother had prayed for me, but she hadn't forgiven me, and in our family everybody respected my mother's grudges. Raul, who couldn't know why talk had come to a dead halt, brought it back to life by complimenting my mother's cooking.

After eating for several hours we went to midnight mass. My mother did her best to be civil to Raul, and I appreciated that. In church Joey stood between Raul and me holding hands with us both. The church was only half-full but the Gregorian chants rose to the rafters, and a thousand candles flickered. Joey's face shone, his eyes sparkled. I hadn't seen him this happy in a long time. When mass was over, we left my mother and the others chatting with the other worshipers. On the way back to the house Joey fell asleep in the backseat of the car.

"Don't wake him up. Let me carry him in for you," Raul said.

"He's kind of big for that."

"Let him be a child tonight," Raul said softly, and my son, half-awake, crawled into his arms.

Once Joey was upstairs, Raul and I stood whispering in front of the Christmas tree. My mother and the others hadn't returned from church yet. The lights were going on and off in Raul's eyes and the scent of the evergreen wrapped itself around us. "I'd like to kiss you good night, but I'm not sure about that mean right hand of yours."

I folded my arms behind my back and offered him my face. He stepped in close. Then I tasted him. His lips were soft and sweet with anise. My heart danced. Since Joe, no man had tasted good to me. I said, "Joey really likes you."

"I'd like to take him out sometime to a ballgame or a fight."

"Something macho."

"It's hard to be more macho than you," he whispered, and touched his cheek where I had slapped him earlier.

"Do you forgive me?"

"Absolutely," he said, and then he reached into his back pocket and handed me his business card.

It rested between my fingers like a slice of red light. Then it turned green. It read, "Raul Vega, staff reporter, the *Miami Herald.*" The past was covered with a felt pen. He had crossed out the *Miami Herald* and substituted the *New York Dispatch.* There were two phone numbers and an address, also written in by hand.

"Just in case you ever need me," he said.

"What are you going to do about what you heard at the dinner table?"

"What? The wife?"

"No, the cancer."

"I guess I'll read it in the paper like everybody else."

I took another kiss. Then I led him to the door.

"See you at City Hall," he said.

I watched him walk through the snow to his car and day-dreamed about forgetting the conflict of interest and robbing the cradle. As he drove off I decided that it was impossible. I climbed the stairs and sat at the edge of Joey's bed watching him sleep. When I finally tried to take his shoes off, he woke up. "Did Raul leave?"

I nodded. "It's late, Joey."

He looked disappointed. I listened to the wind wrap itself around the house and heard the others come in. Joey sat up; for a while he studied the world outside the window. It had stopped snowing. He turned and threw himself into my embrace like he used to when he was little.

"Mom, let's put our coats on and go for a walk in the snow."

The snow under our feet made a soft crunching sound; behind us our footsteps formed a parallel trail. Joey slipped his hand into mine. At the end of the block, he stopped. As ice water seeped into my shoes I felt his warm hand in mine. I looked down through the falling flakes into the sweetness of his young face. He was so beautiful I had to look away. The stars over Brooklyn burned bright and pure.

"Recognize any constellations?" I asked.

"That's the Big Dipper." He pointed to a cluster of stars. "See, like a pot with a handle."

At first I didn't see, but then I did.

"Joey, do you know that some of those stars we see aren't even there anymore? They burned out thousands of years ago. That's how big the universe is, the light is still traveling and the star is gone."

Joey sighed. "I know that, Mom. Everybody who ever went to science class knows that. But what does it mean?"

"I guess it means we don't always see things as they are."

"Like what?"

"Well, like you and Grandma. You think because she's always bugging you, she hates you. But really she loves you. Grandma probably loves you more than anything else on earth."

"Then why is she so mean to me?"

"She's old, she thinks things are supposed to be a certain way, and she can't understand anything else."

"That's not what I think, Mom. I think Grandma loves me so much because I remind her of Dad, and then she hates me for the same reason. And I'm sick of it. I don't wanna live with Grandma anymore. When can I come to Manhattan?"

"Soon, Sonny Boy, soon," and I pulled his cap over his eyes.

He stopped to fix his cap. We were under a street lamp and around us a halo of light sparkled like diamonds on the snow. Beyond the light, everything was dark and shadowed. "Mom, I don't wanna hurt your feelings, but could you stop calling me Sonny Boy?"

We had walked in a circle and were back at my mother's house. I rummaged in my purse for my house keys. Instead, I found the keys to Jason's office that the mayor had given me. As I continued to search I asked, "What should I call you?"

"Just call me Joey or Joe."

I kissed him on the forehead but there was a lump in my throat. He was growing up too soon. I didn't know that earlier in the day, at City Hall, I had stepped onto the path that would pull us apart.

3

I followed the echo of my own footsteps to Jason's door. It wasn't locked and I went in. The cramped room was cold and its dank smells were laced in mold. Rusted grates covered small windows that were eye level with the ground behind City Hall. I telephoned Maintenance to request twenty cardboard boxes. Then, as I returned the receiver to its cradle, Jason's favorite painting seemed to come to life. Hung behind his desk, a whole village danced frantically between two gods—good and evil. In Indonesia this dance is an annual event. Jason had often spoken of it. Wind tossed the snow above and feet passed by, casting brief shadows on the wall.

I tried to open the top drawer of a file cabinet, but it was locked. I tried a few other drawers; nothing opened. I had already given up, deciding to search for a key, when a drawer just slid open. Inside lay a canister of tobacco and a pipe. As I pushed the drawer shut something behind it caught my eye and I felt a chill. I thought I saw Jason himself, hiding in the shadows of the room. When I turned, it was his trench coat on a rack. It stood in front of an old shower stall that hadn't been used since Mayor Lindsay.

As the mournful wind whistled above I walked over to the coat and put my hands into its pockets. From the cloth came the whisper of his smell and I felt an envelope. In it was an airline ticket from Miami to the Bahamas dated the day of his death. Feeling I had trespassed on secrets of the coffin itself, I replaced the envelope in his pocket. What was I doing here? Should I just tell the mayor I was too busy? Then someone else would do the job, and I didn't want that. The mayor trusted me and I wanted to keep it that way. I folded the coat over my arm and took it upstairs.

That night after work, I took the coat and a pound of mandel brot to Jason's shiva. I stood in front of the unlocked door of the penthouse apartment knowing that I was supposed to let myself in. The coat grew heavier in my arms. I pulled the cloth to my face, and I could smell Jason, his pipe tobacco and the musky after-shave. I stepped in. There was a mirrored armoire in the vestibule and I gave myself a glance. My heart knocked. I had no reflection. From the rooms beyond I heard fragments of conversation, a long sigh, and an occasional laugh that self-consciously swallowed itself. As I studied the sheet that covered the mirror a middle-aged woman stepped into the hallway. I reached wordlessly toward her with the cookies.

"Thank you," she said. "I'm Jason's sister Hannah."

I offered my name and that I worked at City Hall. I felt her stiffen. I added, "I'm an old friend of Esther's. Could I see her?"

"She's in the living room."

"I'm not sure she'll remember me. It's been a long time."

A pool of paraffin had formed at the base of a very large candle. Sheets billowed from the mirrored walls they covered and the mourners sat like nomads in a tent, focusing on Esther, who was stationary as a lizard. She wore the same clothes she had worn at her husband's funeral, the woundlike rip on her lapel wider and deeper. Her eyes were slits, either from drugs or tears or both. Every mourner told a story and the words crystallized to form a wall against the endless silence that is death. Esther's attention flickered whenever she wandered into the wasteland of her private grief. I waited until she looked up at the coat and invited me into the study.

Even in his absence Jason filled this room completely—his pipe racks and pipes, the soft leather recliner with his slippers waiting, framed academic degrees, citations, and a wall of photographs that defined a life and a career in public service. She walked up to that wall and, while looking at me, used a finger to touch the frames until she reached a space where there was nothing. The space was very obvious, very white.

"I miss Jason," she said hoarsely, and took the coat from my arms as if it were the corpse itself. I thought about mentioning the ticket in the pocket but didn't. Instead, I imagined Jason's last trip, which, according to the papers, had been taken from the balcony that was attached to this room.

"Did you know Jason well?" she asked.

"I worked for him for a short time when I came to City Hall." Her green eyes went gray like the ocean under clouds. If she remembered me, she didn't say so.

"I'll be packing Jason's files and things, and I wondered what you want me to do with the personal items."

"I know you," she said. "I had forgotten all about you. Now here we are so many years later with so much in common."

Suddenly she seemed full of a venomous energy that made her hardly recognizable as the wilted woman who sat by the melting candle. She took a white handkerchief from her pocket, pulled at it, and said, "The city took both our husbands."

I watched her manicured fingernails rip at the cloth that wouldn't rip and felt my compassion drain like blood from a cut. She said, "Our boys are about the same age."

"Joey," I said, "is twelve," because I knew her son was four-teen.

"You love him more than anything in life, don't you?"

I nodded.

She reached into Jason's pocket, and if she felt the envelope, she didn't show it. With her other hand she pointed across the room to a line of fruit baskets. "Some fruit?"

"No thanks."

The harsh reflection of the overhead light on the cellophane made the fruit underneath look plastic. Most of the condolence cards attached to the baskets were signed by the hypocrites at City Hall. The cellophane protested as she ripped a card from its Scotch tape moorings. She studied the card for a moment, then it slipped from her fingers and fell to the floor. I picked it up for her. She didn't take it right away. She didn't take it until I had time to read the oddly brutal inscription: "The greatest griefs are those we cause ourselves."

When she took it back, she said, "We really should renew our friendship."

She hugged me as if we were back in the locker room at half-time, readying our pom-poms to cheer for Brooklyn High. Then, abruptly, she turned and left the room. I stood for another moment surrounded by Jason, his scent, the carefully chosen objects that defined this room. Then I left. Later, I realized that Esther had said nothing about what she wanted me to do with Jason's things.

It was New Year's Eve day when I finally began to pack the contents of Jason's office. Joey was with me because he was on vacation. We came in late after a big breakfast at Ellen's Café across from City Hall. Ellen's was like a downtown Carnegie Deli. Instead of pictures of actors, a whole wall was covered with pictures of politicians posing with Ellen, a former Miss Subways. While I began clearing my desk, Joey made the mandatory pot of coffee I kept in my office. He counted and measured spoonfuls of coffee, then let the coffee fall into the filter. His scowl said he wanted to talk, but the words weren't coming.

"Is something bothering you, Joey?"

"Do you have to know everything, Mom?"

"I'm just asking."

When the water began dripping through the percolator, he finally said, "I'm sick of Brooklyn."

"I know, I got tired of it too. But you'll be in Manhattan soon."

"It's not Brooklyn that bothers me, it's Grandma. She's like a witch. She won't leave me alone. Why can't I come to live with you?"

"I told you. I want you to finish the school year where you are . . . and Grandma takes good care of you."

"I don't want to live with Grandma. I want to be with you."

"I want to be with you too, Joey, but sometimes we have to wait for what we want. We can't always have it right away."

As he turned away to hide his tears his voice broke. "Why didn't you wait until school was over to move? Why didn't you wait for me?"

He began to pour himself a cup of coffee.

"Stop that."

"I'm old enough to live away from you, I'm old enough to drink coffee."

He brought the cup to his lips as deliberately as if it were hemlock. I felt guilty and angry at the same time. Even though he was wrong, maybe he was right. I'd bought my loft in downtown Manhattan on impulse. After that my mother made life so unpleasant that I moved out before I was really ready. Now the loft was unfurnished and Joey was in the middle of a school year. When Joey finally put the cup down, I didn't know whether to smack him or hug him. I pulled him to me. His dark hair tickled my nose.

"We're gonna have a new life, Joey," I said. "You've got to give it time. It won't be that much longer."

"It feels like forever."

"Let's go upstairs and see Willie Mays's bat."

We were standing in the rotunda at the foot of the stairs to the second floor when Raul stepped through the metal detector. Joey ran to his side. At that moment Hunter stepped out of the press office. He looked at Joey and Raul, then grimaced at me. In my head I did a nervous little shuffle between Joey's pleasure and Hunter's disapproval.

"What are you doing in this dump?" Raul asked Joey.

"Beats school."

Raul laughed. "I'll bet." Then he just looked at me.

I said, "He's on vacation."

Something uncoiled in my belly, circled my spine, then dipped deeper down. My temperature rose, and fearing the heat would show in my eyes, I raised them to the oculus above and studied the dust trembling in a shaft of winter light. When I looked at Raul again, he was admiring the perfect curve of the rotunda steps.

"These were the first stairs in America without visible supports, and the city officials were afraid to climb them. When President Lincoln was assassinated, he was laid in state up there."

"What's 'in state'?" Joey asked.

I said, "It means his coffin stood up there."

Raul's words echoed from the marble as he said, "Because he was born in a log cabin and became president, Lincoln was a hero to poor people. They came from everywhere just to get a look at him. After the real people climbed those steps, the politicians finally had the guts to do it too."

I said, "We're on our way to see the baseball exhibit."

Raul ruffled Joey's hair. "See you later, champ. If you get bored with your mom, come and see me in Room Nine."

Raul walked away. Joey said, "Your face is all red, Mom. Are you okay?"

I yanked his hand and pulled him up the stairs to see that goddamn baseball bat.

After that we went down to the basement. Joey ran his finger along the chipped walls, skipping ahead of me humming a tune I knew, but couldn't name. As I unlocked Jason's door cool air crawled under it and circled my feet. Inside, it was dark until Joey found the light switch. The snow-crusted windows mirrored the empty cardboard boxes that were stacked in the center of the room.

"You pack what's in the desk while I pack the files," I told Joey, and we both went to work.

"There's nothing in here, Mom, just sugar and soy sauce," he reported. Then, as he reached down into the second drawer, he produced a bunch of blue chips. "Hey, poker chips."

"Just drop them in the box."

"What about these, Mom?" He picked up one of the three pictures of Jason and his son.

"Wrap those in paper towels," I said, "so the glass won't break." Just as I said that a picture slipped through his fingers and glass shattered on the floor. Before I could tell him not to, Joey kneeled to pick up the glass, cut himself, and began to bleed. I grabbed his finger and sucked. He pulled back. "Mom, please, it's not a snakebite."

I was crouched next to him when I saw the picture behind the picture. Without thinking, I pulled it from the frame, ripped it in half, and tossed it into the wastebasket with the rest of the broken glass. While I was doing that, Joey made one more discovery.

"Look how weird this calendar is."

It was a desk calendar, the kind you use year after year simply by changing the pages. Besides the day's date, every right-hand page had a three-month calendar on it. I saw what Joey meant. Jason had circled many dates all through the calendar, always on the three-month projections, not on the actual day-to-day calendar.

"It's like a code or something," Joey said. There was a long pause during which we just looked at each other, suspended like creatures in water that is freezing fast.

"Is this the dead guy's office?" my son asked.

I put the calendar in the box with the pictures and the plastic poker chips. Except for one chip. One chip I put into my pocket.

"Take this box up to my office and then go run some cold water over your finger."

"Then can I watch TV with the cops?"

"Sure."

It took me about an hour to move the contents of the files into the cardboard boxes. Then I taped the boxes shut and left them to be picked up by Maintenance. They had instructions to deliver everything to Brogan's office. I locked the door behind me and headed for the catacomblike space where City Hall's cops were headquartered. Joey wasn't there. I went upstairs. Joey wasn't in my office either. I went to the Governors' Room and the baseball exhibit, the Board of Estimate chambers, and finally, when there was nowhere else to go, I went to Room Nine.

There are more than twenty-five rooms in City Hall but few are as feared and revered as Room Nine. For generations this twenty-eight-by-eighteen-foot chamber has housed the City Hall press corps, which these days numbers almost twenty people, six of them women. I stepped in. Eight reporters sat at wall-to-wall desks that were barely visible under an avalanche of old newspapers, news releases, and half-empty coffee cups. A city councilman tiptoed over telephone wires that covered the floor like coiled snakes. Except for a hostile glance from the reporters who were working at their computer terminals, nobody paid him much mind. Raul was sitting next to a six-inch stack of newspapers, whispering into the telephone.

"Has anybody seen my son, Joey?"

Raul looked up but he didn't say anything.

The *New York Post* bureau chief poked his head out from behind a paper. "Well, I'll be damned, the mountain came to Muhammad. This is an all-time first. The Italian iceberg never meets with the press."

"Don't be silly," I said. "It's just that I'm on the other side of the hall."

"And we all know Marie likes to keep her lines clearly drawn," one of the women reporters said, putting her feet up on the desk. She'd taken her boots off and her socks were blood-red.

"I take it that means you haven't seen Joey."

Nobody bothered to answer. I left, silently marveling that this surly bunch had more power than the mayor himself. They are the clearinghouse. Most of what New Yorkers know about their government comes out of Room Nine. Small wonder that the mayor didn't trust this bloodthirsty crowd.

I was about to step back into my office when I noticed that Brogan's door was ajar. I poked my head in. Joey was at the computer.

"What are you doing? That's the deputy mayor's computer."

"He's not here, Mom."

"Still, you don't belong here. What are you doing?"

Joey pointed at the desk calendar next to the computer. It was Jason's. "I'm trying to break this code. I think it's a simple binary."

"What code, Joey? There's no code."

I grabbed the calendar.

"Aw, Mom, c'mon, please. I've already fed in January to June. But the last two months have the most numbers."

"Joey, if you're at that computer when Brogan walks in, I could lose my job. Now turn it off and let's get out of here."

He got up reluctantly and followed me back to my office. I dropped the calendar into the box under my desk. Fortunately, the day was almost over. But not for Joey. While I was in the women's room cleaning the coffeepot, Joey went to Room Nine and brought Raul back to my office.

"I hear you're on your way to another illustrious family get-together," Raul said.

Did he have to know my New Year's plans revolved around children and ancient relatives?

"It's nice for the kids," I said.

"No, it's not, it's boring," Joey said as he packed his bulging book bag. And then, ignoring me, he accepted Raul's invitation to dinner.

The crowd at Victor's Café on Fifty-second Street was festive. We sat in the sidewalk café under hanging plants and our feet rested on terra-cotta tiles. Walls of glass separated us from the winter outside. Passersby hunched their shoulders up around their ears and small white clouds escaped from their mouths, in conversations we couldn't hear. From the menu we picked yellow rice with black beans, shrimp *al ajillo*, *ropa vieja*, fried sweet bananas, marinated steak smothered in onions, and *chicharones* as an appetizer. Joey ordered a pitcher of Coke and Raul one of sangria. A guitar player moved among the tables, playing requests. I watched his fingers cajole the strings and sucked on a thin slice of orange. Joey's face lit up as he and Raul resumed their sports talk. And for the first time in a long time, I relaxed.

A clown on the sidewalk outside with a painted tear showed us his painted smile through the window. On the pane, our faces reflected over his and over the six multicolored balls he juggled.

"Can I give him something?" Joey asked.

Raul gave Joey a dollar and Joey ran outside. Behind me, the music came closer. I turned back into the room.

"Un canción para la señora?"

"Gimme a request, lassie," Raul teased.

I had two choices in my head—"Guantanamera" and "La Cucaracha." So rather than admit my total ignorance of his culture, I let him choose.

"How about 'Cuando Caliente el Sol,' " Raul said, and filled my glass for the second time. The waiter brought the appetizer, a dish of sausages in a red oil that was still crackling. Raul rubbed his hands together, skewered a piece of the sausage, then put it in my mouth. It was chewy, spicy, and delicious. After a while it lay like an ember in the bottom of my tummy.

We were drinking and grinning at each other, and during the chorus Raul leaned over and translated into my ear—a line about palpitating hearts, soft lips, and hot bodies on the beach. I put a piece of sausage in his mouth just to shut him up. Under the table I wiggled out of my boots.

Raul leaned in closer. "I'm really hungry now, are you?"

His eyes were hot and promising. Then Joey came back and the food arrived. As we ate, Raul talked about the small island country where he was born, ninety miles from Key West at the tip of the United States. "It's like a Garden of Eden, but ever since Castro, the United States won't sell Cuba a hat pin."

"Why do they need hat pins?" Joey asked.

I almost choked on a sweet banana. "You're pro-Castro?"

I had the hots for a Cuban communist based in Room Nine?

He said, "My father was a doctor and my parents disappeared during the revolution. My grandparents hate Castro as if he were the devil incarnate."

That didn't answer my question, so I framed it again. "What about you?"

Raul raised his glass to toast me. "I'm a journalist. I'm pro the truth, wherever it lies."

"Does the truth lie?" Joey asked.

Raul looked at me as if he could see my thoughts and said softly, "Sometimes the truth is the best lie."

I tried not to think about all the white lies that hung like invisible cobwebs around City Hall. I especially tried to forget that I had already lied to Raul. I thought of it as an omission rather than a lie. He raised his glass, and the taste of lemon and butter mingled on my tongue.

Then as our glasses touched, Raul said, "In the interest of truth . . . the Isenberg cancer story is going to hit the papers tomorrow."

"You wrote the story!"

"No," he said, "my byline isn't on it."

I broke a piece of bread with both hands. Did I look stupid? "You could have tipped somebody else off, it's a chit you could cash in later."

"Oh," he said, "is that how it works?"

Nothing was going down my throat. I stopped eating. Then he ended my misery with a smile that was condescending even as it was kind. "Everybody's got the story. It was officially released by the City Hall press office."

"Hunter."

"Yes, Hunter."

I touched his cheek because I couldn't quite bring myself to actually apologize for my evil thoughts.

"Are you gonna stay with us? You can sleep in my mom's bed if you want to," Joey said.

My cheeks grew hot as I searched for a comeback I couldn't find. Was I that transparent? Then Raul diplomatically raised his glass in a toast to Joey. "I like you too, champ."

When Joey and I touched glasses, his lips smiled but his eyes spoke of a deeper longing. He missed his dad. And for his pain, I loved him all the more.

When we finished eating, we headed for Times Square to watch the electric "apple" fall. The air was thin and cold as a veil of ice and the roar of the crowd carried all the way from Times Square to Fiftieth Street.

"It's too late," I said. "We'll never get there now. All the side streets are barricaded."

"Wanna bet?" Raul called over his shoulder as he dashed into a liquor store for a bottle of champagne. Then he took us both by the hand and we began to run. Despite the cold, the streets were like a walking cocktail party. People rushed by, toasting us with whatever they carried in their brown paper bags. At Forty-fifth Street the barricades began. Cops were everywhere, on foot, mounted, and in cars. The noise was deafening.

Raul ducked under a barricade, taking Joey with him. A cop stopped him. "Hey, buddy, you can't go through. . . ."

Raul reached into a pocket and produced his press pass—a laminated card with his picture, the name of his paper, and a stenciled police seal. "I'm with the *Dispatch*," he told the cop, "and this is my family."

He might as well have said he was the police commissioner. The big cop stepped back. "Okay, no problem. Let 'em through. He's press."

The word went on down the line. One flash of his press pass, and we were allowed through. The crowd locked outside the barricades stared at us enviously. Joey beamed. When we got to Times Square, Raul led us to 1576 Broadway, directly across from the big billboard and the apple. We took the elevator to the third floor and then climbed a ladder to the roof.

The electricity of the crowd crackled in the air, and it seemed as though we were on top of the world. At its edges the roof inclined slightly upward, so you could safely approach the edge and watch the apple above. It glowed red and bright, high up in the night. I thought about the millions of people across the country glued to their TV sets waiting like we were waiting, full of hopes for the New Year, and tears stung my eyes. I held tightly on to Joey's coat to make sure he didn't slip away from me. Then a long sigh of pleasure from below told us that the apple had begun its descent. The crowd went crazy with joy. People jumped, screamed, blew whistles, clapped, laughed, and cheered. Raul popped the cork and champagne spilled onto the snow-encrusted roof. Joey's voice cracked as he yelled with the crowd. Raul and I drank from the bottle. I grabbed my screaming son and kissed him. Then as the apple hit bottom and the New Year began, I kissed Raul hot and full on the mouth. He was surprised, but not that much. Only ten minutes later, the people were all gone. We walked through the garbage-littered streets to Raul's car and headed back to Brooklyn.

Joey and I sat in the backseat together. We played word games and punch buggy, and somewhere after the Brooklyn Bridge we both dozed off. When we got to my mother's, Raul woke me up. With his hand on my knee, he said, "We could carry him in and go to my place."

If I said yes, it meant yes all the way. What other reason would I have for going to his place at 2:00 A.M. in the freezing cold? Hands back on the steering wheel, he looked over his shoulder to raise a scheming eyebrow. I sat up, shifted Joey's weight, and stared at Raul so goddamn hard he turned away. We both sat studying our laps until my eyes met his in the rearview mirror. "Quietly," I said, "so we don't wake my mother."

We carried Joey in and ran back to the car. The night was bitter. We were both shivering.

"We'll have heat back on in a second," he said, turning the key in the ignition. The engine came on smooth and fast. There was no traffic on the street at all. It seemed as if we were the only man and woman on earth. We were very, very quiet and I got very, very nervous. He was suddenly shy and that comforted me. We took refuge in small talk about City Hall, about Brooklyn, about anything at all.

I felt a giddiness inside that I hadn't felt since high school. Since Joe's death loneliness had driven me into one man's arms. It had been no good and I had pretended it had never happened. This was different. I wanted Raul. So I remember being afraid.

We crossed the Verrazano Bridge and headed for Staten Island.

"I thought you said you lived in Brooklyn?"

"If I had told you the truth on Christmas Eve, you wouldn't have let me give you a ride."

"You lied to me?"

"I did it for you. If you had known I was going out of my way, you wouldn't have let me take you home."

I accepted that answer but maybe I shouldn't have.

His apartment was in a two-family home and had its own entrance. In the little foyer I caught our reflections in a gold-framed

mirror. We looked rosy-cheeked and impossibly young. In the mirror I watched as he unwrapped me from my coat.

I followed him inside. We were in a large kitchen with an excep-
tional collection of spices, immaculate marble counters, and a
black-and-white-checkered linoleum floor.

"Get us something to drink," he said, pointing to the refrigerator. "I'll start a fire."

I took a bottle of wine from the refrigerator. He stepped down
into the sunken living room. Instead of a couch there were pillows
on the carpeted floor. He knelt by the empty fireplace and stirred
some ashes. Then he crumpled a few pages of the *Dispatch* and lit
them. The print flashed into flame and he said, "That's what this
paper does best."

"Isn't that a poor attitude to have about your job?"

"It's not the attitude I have toward journalism," he said, "just
toward those who abuse it."

He used a pair of iron tongs to shift a log into the fire. At the
kitchen counter I inched my behind up onto the soft cushion of a
long-legged stool. My toes rested comfortably on a chrome bar
across the bottom.

I was tempted to say that I was beginning to have my own
doubts about City Hall, but I decided not to. As they yielded to
the fire the logs spoke in a low comforting crackle and I could
smell their pungent sap.

I sat there studying my toes. When I looked at him again, the
fire was big. Its glow cast shadows that played with his high cheekbones, and colored his black hair purple. I watched his hands as he
shifted the logs, his long elegant fingers vibrating in the flames,
and I wanted him so much my insides trembled.

I tried to see through him, through flesh and bone to the heart.
He must have felt my scrutiny because he turned to say, "Don't.
Don't look at me like that. I'm not Jack the Ripper."

I got up. Under my feet the black and white floor became a
gigantic chessboard. I had lived my whole life inside those lines—
playing by the rules—good daughter, good wife, good mother,
good worker. I moved a foot forward and inched out of a square.
Now I was at the edge of a precipice. Terror welled up and through
me in a powerful rush. I stepped on a line and walked it like a

tightrope. The chessboard began to spin. It opened like Alice's rabbit hole and I slid in. I laughed. I laughed so hard I didn't see him walk over to me. I didn't know he was there until I felt his warm hands on my back.

4

He kissed my laughing mouth. His hands searched for my flesh, but I was buried in layers and layers of clothing. The burning logs smelled like smoky incense. My breath was tight. He wet my dry mouth.

He pulled me into the living room, down onto the pillows, and then on top of him. His fingers wandered under my sweater. As I slid slowly up and down on him I felt him hard against my belly. "Yes," he whispered, "yes." And as I tasted red wine and sweet bananas in his languid kisses I slipped gradually out of the layers of my clothing. Then when I was naked, I felt him strain toward me through his clothes.

"Help me take my shirt off," he said, and with trembling fingers I did.

"Talk to me. Tell me what you like." He nibbled my neck. "This?"

I didn't know what to say. Joe had never asked me that.

"This?" He put his hot mouth around a nipple.

I moaned but I couldn't talk.

"Please," he said. "Please, please."

Except for the wind of my breath, I was silent.

"Do you want me to tell you what I like?"

"Yes," I said, "yes."

He unbuckled his belt and extricated his penis. I went down. It touched my cheek, erect, purple, a heart on a stalk. A drop of moisture glistened there.

I took him into my mouth. I felt the tender skin of the head close, very close to my teeth. He moaned and pushed deeper into my throat. I brought his pants down to his knees. He kicked them off. Then as he gently caressed the hair on my head his breathing grew fast and shallow. After a while he cajoled me up. "Come here."

I felt the texture of skin on skin, the hardness of him. With his legs he separated mine. His face slid down my body. He laid his cheek on my naked stomach and sucked on my belly button. Then he slid farther down, all the way down to my knees. Down there, he planted some kisses. His hot breath made my skin feel cool. Slowly, he moved up, slowly. Slow kisses, slow hands on my inner thighs. Then, with his fingers, he opened my lips. I sat up. "What are you doing?"

His slightly Oriental eyes smiled wickedly. "Looking for my honey."

He put his tongue in there. I tried to pull away. He looked up. "Marie," he said. "Relax."

His hair was wild, his chin wet. I let myself fall back on the bed. His tongue moved sweetly, knowingly, in me. I played with his hair and my legs opened wider. His moans vibrated through me. I grabbed his head with the soft flesh of my thighs and found his rhythm. He licked me like an animal licks itself.

My head thrashed left, then right. Inside, I began to quake. The sounds that came from me begged for mercy. He cupped my ass and forced me to stay with him. His mouth got hot, very hot. I melted into his pleasure and my own. He drank me until I unfolded like ripples from a pebble and sank deep into myself. I was down in a well and the surface of the water closed above me like glass. I convulsed and cried like I was going to die. When I stopped, I heard the steady crackling of the fire in the fireplace. Then I pulled him up. His face glistened with my juice. He smelled like me; I tore into his mouth with mine and tasted myself.

He took the cheeks of my ass in his hands and every muscle in his body tensed. With a low groan that made me tremble, he slid into me, slowly. His face said that he was perched on the line where pleasure is so intense it's almost pain.

He was skilled, very skilled. My breaths came faster, shallower, I could feel my breasts swelling. He lifted my legs to get in deeper. He grabbed me by the back of the neck and rotated his hips. "You're mine, hear. I'm gonna make you mine. Say you're mine. Say it."

"Yes," I whispered, "yes," and felt myself open and close around him.

"*Mine*, say it."

I listened for the rhythm of him in my womb and felt him tapping, tapping at its mouth. "Yours," I said. "Yours."

"Tell me . . . tell me. Tell me never to stop."

"Don't . . . don't . . . don't stop ever."

We lay for a long time breathing together, our bodies intertwined, still one, and then he shifted his weight off me. I was staring at the ceiling when I heard him ask, "Have you been with anyone since your husband?"

There was that one, but rather than say, I turned away. He propped himself up on an elbow but then he let the question go.

When I woke up, it was almost dawn. He was snoring slightly. I had to get home. A guilt with teeth was gnawing at my throat. I tiptoed around like a thief. If I made it home before anyone woke up, I could pretend last night never happened. In the fireplace only ashes remained.

The sky over Staten Island was gray with the first light of day. My ears ached from the brutal cold. Where the hell was I going to get a cab? I pulled my coat up around my face. The salty smell of sex surrounded me; deep inside I felt the bruises of his insistent touch. The wind beat against my forehead, my temples throbbed. I was about to turn back when I heard a sound like twenty cherry bombs going off at once. A pink stain smeared the sky. I heard screams, and then I stepped into a nightmare.

A blast had shattered the first-floor windows of the big building, where wild red flames seemed to eat the air as screaming women and children ran barefoot in the icy slush. I began to run. I ran to the corner phone booth. With trembling fingers, I called 911 and the Red Cross. Already the multiplying flames had created a false and deadly dawn. A scorching heat that singed my face rolled down the block. I stood there with the receiver in my hand, not knowing what else to do. I decided to call Brogan. A machine answered. I tried Hunter. Another machine. In desperation, I broke all protocol and called Gracie Mansion. Whoever picked up didn't want to wake the mayor. But I insisted. An angry Nicosea came on the line. I begged him to come quickly to Staten Island.

"Look, Marie, that's a decision for the pros."

"I tried to reach Hunter and Brogan."

"Someone's on the other line. Hold on."

He put me on hold. The cold winter air had become weirdly tropical and smoky. My eyes hurt. I realized then that this building consumed in flames was the Donovan, one of the new shelters that had opened with such fanfare Thanksgiving week. When the mayor came back on the line, I tried to tell him. He said, "That's Hunter. We're on top of it. Thanks. Go home where you belong, Marie. What the hell are you doing in front of that hellhole at this hour anyway?"

"I . . . I . . ." I couldn't possibly answer that question.

"Go home, Marie. You've got the Christmas crazies again. It happens every year."

"Not every year." I wanted to scream at him: *"Not every year, just since Joe's death.*" But I said nothing, and anyway the line was already dead.

I don't know why I did what I did next, but I did it. I dug in my purse for Raul's card and I called him.

"Hello." His voice was so deep with sleep I didn't recognize it.

"I'm sorry, I guess I misdialed—"

"You didn't misdial," he said, coming awake. "Where are you? Why did you leave?"

I couldn't explain leaving but I told him about the fire. "Be right there," he said, and hung up.

The police and fire departments were arriving. Screaming sirens magnified the other screams, the human screams. Adults and children, desperate to escape the flames, pushed onto the already crowded fire escapes. Just as two police cars pulled up, a man jumped from a window. He landed with a sickening sound like a giant water balloon bursting. As more people clambered downward, another explosion happened somewhere inside the building. Bodies flew to the pavement below like rag dolls, and then the fire escape itself just slid off the building.

A barefoot boy wearing an adult's undershirt and nothing more ran howling through the snow. I opened my arms and he came to me. I wrapped my coat around him and his long thin shrieks broke into sobs. As he huddled inside my coat his pain became mine and it paralyzed me. Then I saw Raul talking feverishly into the corner pay phone. With the boy in my arms I hobbled toward Raul.

"I've just given you the description . . . look it up in the clips . . . find out how many rooms, how many people are supposed to be in there . . . yeah . . . yeah . . . I'll call you back with quotes."

He hung up and turned to me, his face flushed. The flames were so intense now they made a whipping sound. The chrome of the phone booth and Raul's pupils glowed red. "Thanks," he said, "this is a real break."

"What happened in there?" he asked the boy in my arms.

The world was crumbling around us and he wanted a quote from a child. The boy shuddered.

"Why not ask him how much it hurts?" Then I took my bundle

and ran to the first-aid team that was just arriving. The boy's hands and feet were covered in blisters where the fire had eaten at his flesh. I held him as a nurse injected him with a tranquilizer; the light left his eyes and he slipped into the refuge of oblivion.

For the next few hours I helped the Red Cross process survivors for relocation. My lungs ached from breathing smoke. I fought the urge to vomit as the smell of roasted human flesh overwhelmed me. All around us burn victims waited for medical attention. Those for whom all hope was gone lay twisted in fetal positions—fists clenched, arms raised, knees bent, as if they had died fighting the flames. Others were hidden under plastic sheets, their blood seeping into slush and filthy snow.

In the icy cold of dawn we served coffee and tea. We distributed blankets to shuddering survivors who waited to be processed for relocation. Most stood there in stunned silence; some wept. We filled out a form on each survivor. The shelter had been populated mostly by single mothers and their children, a few elderly couples, and a collection of junkies, crack heads, and winos. A lot of the people had third-degree burns from running back into the flames to rescue others.

The last person I processed was a fragile old man with a limp. He walked with a cane and had a Boston accent. His translucent skin seemed stretched directly over his skeleton; his hollow, wild, gray eyes stared at the carnage. Tears ran down his cheeks as he wrapped his gnarled fingers around a Styrofoam cup. I asked him his name and age.

"Every nation has the government it deserves," he said. I asked his name again. "You know," he said, "these shelters are purgatory on earth, purgatory with no reprieve. I'm holding a press conference soon."

"Tell me your name, that's all I'm asking."

"No one should be in government who can't earn more in the private sector."

"I really need to know your name."

He stood up and waved the cane he was carrying around in the air. "I'm the three-legged beast," he whispered hoarsely, "but you . . . you are blind, blind as a larva in a cocoon."

He came very close to me. The smell was terrible. As if he

already had died. He touched my forehead with his dirty thumb. "Here," he said. "Here, I will open this third eye of consciousness." He kept rubbing his finger on my forehead. I was too tired to evade him. "Ah yes," he said, "I see it. I see it. You will escape the cocoon, but not without pain."

Because I was already in pain I just sat there watching him, this greasy, defeated prophet waving his cane in the air as if the right constellation of moves would bring water from a stone, hope from the heavens, or just plain change something.

"You're not making any sense," I said wearily.

That seemed to calm him. "Well," he said, "my dear, it's a riddle . . . to solve it you must apply yourself."

I showed him the form I was trying to fill out. The things it asked were simple. Name, age, location of family, if any. He took the pen from my hand and carefully wrote, "THADDEUS FINX, 62." I thanked him. "Now I can process you for relocation."

"I've seen the fires begin, you know, all of them; as destiny would have it, I saw the beginning of each. There is no arsonist."

As he stood there, on that battlefield of agony, he seemed almost transparent, an astral projection or a figment of my own imagination.

"The lies transformed from thought to deed become monsters that devour us," he told me. "Devour us in flames." I put the paper that was his passport to another purgatory into his spidery hand, hoping to be rid of him. The look in his eye was not gratitude or relief but something else. "You will remember me," he said, "when you are ready to solve the riddle."

"Perfection of means and confusion of goals," he mumbled as he hobbled off. "Tell that to the mayor."

My eyes burned, my throat scratched. I hadn't seen Raul in hours. Now that the fire was out, a thick pall of smoke rose from the remains of the shelter. I covered my face with my hands and sat there trying not to cry, when I heard a familiar voice, tense and urgent.

"We have a situation here. A situation that is potentially very embarrassing to this administration. This is the third shelter fire since the cold hit, each of these fires took place in a new facility, and the reporters are going to try and goad you into anything they can get. The question may seem innocent, but believe me, once they've twisted your words, it could cost you your job."

I peeked around the truck. Hunter was talking to two men I recognized from their City Hall visits—the police department's press secretary, Jim Mulligan, and the fire department's press secretary, Dave Bigelow. Two career civil servants whose brains were alcohol mush. Just then Raul approached them. Sweat and soot covered his face. There was a terrible anger in his eyes.

"Why haven't we seen Hizzoner this morning?" he asked.

Hunter regarded him impassively. Even though it was barely daylight, he was impeccably dressed in brown wool slacks, a beige turtleneck, and a camel-hair coat. "We have a perfectly competent personnel on the scene," Hunter said. "The mayor has personally authorized the Human Resources Department to make emergency payments to these families before the day is out. He's already left town to be the leadoff witness before the Federal Housing Committee in Washington in the morning. That was previously scheduled."

"Do you have any idea how the fire began?" Raul asked Bigelow.

Bigelow was a big beefy guy who had put in his time as a firefighter before taking a desk job. He shoved his hands into his pockets and talked out of the side of his mouth. "Well, we know that fire burns up and out, that's how fire burns, we can tell when it's accelerated, fire leaves a signature. We can tell a lot . . . but now is too soon. I can't comment now."

"When will you have an answer?" Raul's frustration was obvious.

"We're assessing the situation now."

Hunter stepped forward. "The fire does seem to fit the pattern of the other two."

Bigelow swallowed his surprise, Raul hid his anger, and I hid myself. I knew the mayor wasn't scheduled to leave town for several hours yet.

5

"My understanding is that you called the Red Cross to the scene."

"Yes, I did," I said proudly, "and they did a great job."

"Well, it looks lousy. The mayor wanted his own Department of Human Services to relocate those families and you prevented that."

"What's the difference as long as the people got helped?"

"There's a big difference," Hunter said. "It's one of perception. We've already had two fires, the perpetrator hasn't been caught yet, this time six people were killed. It looks bad, it just looks bad. At least you could have let us clean up our own mess. It would have played better on the tube."

"I wasn't thinking about the press, I was thinking about the people."

"Well, Marie, you've made my point for me. We have to be rational now. Bad enough six people died. We can't do anything about that. But by bringing in the Red Cross instead of our own people, you hurt the mayor personally."

Hunter twisted the knife with the precision of his Ivy League arrogance. Like the others at City Hall, he knew my pride was rooted in my efficiency and my loyalty to the mayor. But now I stood under the unsupported staircase as he added insult to injury. "What exactly," he asked, "is your relationship to Raul Vega?"

"None. There's no relationship."

"Vega seems to be very close to your son. He was the first reporter at the fire. In fact, the only one to make the morning papers. You didn't by any chance call him too?"

My courage ebbed away. I said, "You're insulting me now," but as I turned to climb the stairs the weakness of my response echoed in every click of my heels. I had not intended to climb those stairs, I had no reason to be on the second floor, but I couldn't turn around and risk bumping into Hunter again. I walked over to the City Council chamber. Through the windows in the double doors, I could see that the room was empty. I stepped inside.

It was a magnificent room, almost like a chapel, golden curtains, a painting on the ceiling and two inscriptions. "Government of the people, by the people, for the people" and "Equal justice for men of all persuasions." Women were not mentioned. I studied the portrait of George Washington standing next to his horse's rump. After wondering about the painter's message, I went back downstairs to my office.

I reached under my desk, took the box I had filled with Jason's things into my arms, and went to see Deputy Mayor Brogan. Hunter's words kept revolving in my head: *What exactly is your relationship to Raul Vega?* I had in mind to cover myself with a little power play of my own. As I opened his door Brogan looked up over his bifocals. "What do you have there, Marie?"

I clutched the box that was the proof of my loyalty and held it as if it were a lot heavier than it was. "These are the personal effects," I said, "the personal effects from Jason's office."

Brogan took the glasses off his nose. Even when he was seated, his size was imposing. "Well done, Marie. But I don't need to see them. Messenger the box to the widow with a personal note of condolence. You know what to say."

He returned his eyes to the papers on his desk, as if to say this conversation is terminated. I sat down. "I'd like to speak with you, to speak with you if you have a minute."

"I have a mountain of paperwork here, Marie. . . ."

"I don't want to take this to the mayor."

Now I had his attention. Brogan came around the desk and placed his bulk in the chair next to me. He wasn't just tall, he was heavy. "Let's have it, Marie."

Now I wasn't sure where to start. I shifted the box in my lap. Finally I said, "I want to protect the mayor, so I don't want to involve him, but I thought someone should know so we don't wind up in another public embarrassment."

"Have you talked to Hunter?"

"Hunter doesn't take me seriously."

Brogan nodded. "He can be abrasive. But you see, his arrogance keeps the press in line."

My lips were chapped; in my head I saw pictures of bubbling, charred human flesh.

"I was at the shelter fire New Year's Eve. I happened to be in the area. I'm sure you'll be hearing about it because Hunter is furious with me for calling the Red Cross."

"You did that?"

"Yes."

He took his glasses off again and began to polish them with a handkerchief. He held the lenses up to study them. With my teeth I pulled some skin from my lower lip. Finally he said, "Well, you're to be commended," and put his glasses back on. "Hunter doesn't deal in substance; I do. Talk to me."

"One of the shelter's residents claims he saw all three fires start. He said he might go to the press."

Brogan leaned forward. Behind his glasses his eyes narrowed.

"He said he knew what was really going on and that it's not arson."

"Was this man a former fireman; I mean does he have any expertise in the field?"

"No . . . he's an old wino."

Brogan sighed impatiently and leaned back in his chair. "Marie, I think you're worrying too much. The fire department will sort it out, I'm sure."

"What if they don't want to know? What if there were violations they should have known about and now they're covering their tracks?"

"Why would you say a thing like that? Why would you even think it?"

Time opened like a trapdoor and I was back in my first moment in City Hall three years earlier. I had come seeking the truth behind Joe's crazy death. I felt that I was looking into a pit deeper than the grave and then I heard Brogan's soothing voice: "Marie," he said, "let me confide in you. The mayor has already asked the Department of Investigations to look into these fires. We should have some answers soon."

The past retreated. Brogan returned to his desk, which stood one step up like an altar. I got to my feet, still holding the box.

"On another topic, Marie, someone was working on my computer on New Year's Day. They left a document of only numbers on the screen. Almost like a game. The computer was on throughout the holiday. I thought perhaps since you're across the hall, you might have seen something."

In the space between seconds I wondered if I should tell.

"It was Joey, my son. He's a computer buff and he was playing games with Jason's calendar. I'm very, very sorry. I stopped him as soon as I noticed, but I guess in my rush to get him out of your office, I forgot to tell him to turn the computer off."

I touched the golden doorknob; a blue spark shot from my fingers. Brogan said, "What calendar?"

"His desk calendar. It's in the box."

I was halfway out the door when he called me back. "By the way, Marie, that homeless man you talked to, do you know where he went? DOI might be interested."

"I think all the men went to the shelter on the Bowery. His name was Finx."

Brogan came down the step again. He put his hands on the box and eased it from my grip. "On second thought," he said, "on second thought, maybe I should take this to the widow myself. It might be a meaningful gesture."

I left feeling reaffirmed. I had gotten rid of the box without having to see Esther again and Brogan was happy with me. When I returned to my office, Jason's villagers danced on my floor. Someone had stood the painting against the wall opposite my desk. I knelt for a closer look and noticed for the first time that the villagers wore masks. The intercom buzzed. It was Hizzoner.

When I stepped into his office, Nicosea didn't look up. His complexion was ashy, his fingernails bitten to the quick. When did he chew at himself like that, at home at night, alone in the dark? I had never seen him take so much as a nibble. "I have the need for . . ." he said. "I'm going to work through lunch, the need for a yogurt."

"Anything else?"

He shook his head.

There was a long line in the deli across the street from City Hall. I was reading the label on Hizzoner's yogurt when somebody else's conversation drifted to my ears. "He's ethnocentric, that's what he is, ethnocentric."

"So he has a chip on his handsome shoulder. But when it comes to women, he's eclectic. He changes women like you change underwear, that's what I hear. He was involved with one of the editors at the *Herald,* that's what I hear, and she's one of the reasons he left."

"You have your ear so far to the ground, you're underground. How do you know all this?"

The two voices shared a dirty laugh.

"I happen to have a friend, a friend at the *Herald.*"

The *Herald!* Did she mean the *Miami Herald?* I looked up. On line, a few people ahead of me, were two of Hunter's deputies. Pam Muccio and Elaine McCarthy. They were both young, svelte, and blond. Hunter hired only women, attractive women. They never lasted long and rumor had it that some of them were close, very close, to the press. I clutched my yogurt enviously. Suddenly shopping for the mayor was humiliating. Nobody would ever ask them to go fetch.

"I'm going to do lunch with him," Pam said.

"Do lunch or do him?"

There was a bitter taste in my mouth. Was it because they were discussing Raul as if he were a piece of meat? Or was it because he sounded like a willing piece? How long before she landed him in the sack? I cursed myself for having fallen into his well-rehearsed trap. I paid my money and returned to City Hall.

The mayor was still at his desk. He didn't look up when I walked in. I put the plastic spoon on top of the napkin and took the yogurt out of the bag. He picked the spoon up and flexed it between his fingers. The plastic bent and then it snapped. Half the spoon flew across the room. He scowled. Fortunately, there was a collection of spoons in his drawer.

I knew that he was still angry that I had called him that morning of the fire, and I wanted to make peace, so as I handed him another spoon I said, "I'm sorry about the other morning."

"It's naive of you to expect me to solve every problem in this city personally."

"It's just that I know how hard you've worked to get these shelters built. So I thought . . ."

He got up and headed for the window. With one hand on the blue velvet drapes he studied the protestors camped outside and shook his head in disbelief.

"The crazies," he said. "The crazies are trying to drive me out of office . . . and now you want to blame me for the way the world is too."

"I finished packing Jason's files and things," I said by way of atoning.

"Oh."

"Yes. Brogan has everything. His people have the files and he's bringing the widow the personal effects himself."

"Brogan?" he said as if he had never heard the name before.

"What are they going to do with the files?"

He shrugged and pulled on the curtain cord as frantically as if it were a noose. "Study them, I guess. Reallocate Jason's responsibilities. Not that there was much."

"What was Jason doing those last six months?"

He brought a hand to his face, and for a moment I thought I would actually see him bite a fingernail. But the hand stayed lost in the air. "I really don't know. I just didn't want to put him out in the street, so Brogan gave him something to do. I don't know exactly what it was, something ceremonial, I think. A minority talent bank, or something."

"You can't blame yourself," I said. "Nobody can stop a suicide but the victim."

He didn't say anything. He just peeked out at the homeless encampment that had become his permanent view. I brought his yogurt to him, spoon and all.

Out there in City Hall Park the world seemed to be a traveling circus of paupers. The homeless in their layers of rags wandered among tents, cardboard-box homes, clotheslines, and garbage-can fires. From any window you could see a broken human being standing in the knee-high snow chastising an invisible companion.

"Hunter was right," the mayor said. "I should have had these nut cases locked up when they first showed up here. Now they've dug in and it's gonna be a battle. If they don't go away soon, I'm going to be as crazy as they are."

He dipped his spoon into his yogurt and searched for the fruit on the bottom. "This will be your first election with me, Marie. It's brutal, always brutal. This Jason thing has really gotten to you."

"I'll be okay. But what about you? Why put yourself through it? Why not go into the private sector and take me with you?"

His eyes narrowed as if I had spoken treason. He stirred his yogurt some more and returned himself to the center of the universe. "You know a better man for this job?"

"Of course not. There's nobody like you."

He turned to face me. In his eyes I saw something fractured but unyielding. "Marie," he said, "please, Marie, do me a great favor. Don't let the pressure get to you. We're a great team."

I felt so powerful when he said that. As if I were the mayor too. I wasn't professional staff, but more than any of the others, I was his other half. I controlled his schedule. I protected him. Together we played good cop, bad cop. I decided when he had time to see someone or do something and when he didn't. Actually, he decided but we both pretended that I decided. I was his cover. We were a team.

That evening as I left work I passed Hunter on the City Hall steps. He was chatting with two of his deputies, the same two from the deli. "There goes the new human-rights commissioner," he said sarcastically, loud enough for me to hear. The two women laughed.

Instead of taking the plowed path that was protected by police barricades, I chose to walk through the homeless encampment. They came toward me with their open palms. I dug in my pockets for change and gave away a few quarters. But I didn't have enough change to fill all the outstretched hands. So I put my head down and pretended not to see. An old woman stepped in front of me. "Got a cigarette, honey?"

"I don't smoke."

She called me a cunt and a few other things. My blood pounded in my head. Was the mayor right after all? Were these people just nuts?

I sought refuge in a newsstand by the subway.

"Good evening." The young Pakistani inside the stand smiled at me. "You have been having a good day?"

"Yes," I lied. "How about you?"

"I do not wish to complain," he said, "but these people, they are very much hurting my business."

I bought a candy bar and nodded, thinking that his complaint was the mayor's complaint. The homeless were bad business.

Rather than going to the loft and continue unpacking I took the subway home to Brooklyn. When I got there, I went around the back of the house to enter from the kitchen door. As I trekked through the snow I saw my mother at the stove and Joey at the kitchen table bent over his homework. I tapped on the door. Joey jumped up. When I first stepped into the room, it seemed warm and peaceful.

"Mom! Mom! What are you doing here?"

My mother turned. "Joey, you sit. You suppose finish you work."

To me she said, "You home?"

I took off my coat and left my boots at the door. Barefoot, I went to the sink to wash my hands. Then I sat down across from Joey in the spot my father had vacated twenty years ago. My mother's evil look said that I was a curse on her—a widow daughter who refused to remarry. When I sat in my father's spot, it was that much worse. She looked like she wanted to spit out a heavy burden, but then she swallowed whatever it was and turned back to the stove. "You eat?"

"No, Mama, I didn't."

So she fed me; she served me like a wife serves a husband. She didn't sit down with me like she used to before I bought the loft, but she didn't leave either. In little ways she made it clear that this was her home and that I had achieved the status of a visitor. When Joey finished his homework and went upstairs to shower and change into his pj's, my mother placed a cup of coffee on the table before me. As its pungent, familiar aroma rose she sat across from me and played with her apron.

"You no like?"

I took a sip and nodded. *"Molto bene."*

Then she came to the point. "When you take Joey?"

Over the edge of the cup I studied her accusing eyes and felt like a murderer. "Soon, Mama, he's not happy and the schools aren't safe."

"You come home. Joey, he go Catholic school."

"I can't, Mama. It's three years since . . . since . . . It's time for me to start a new life. I'm too old to live with my mother."

"In the old country *il fanciullo non di lasca la familia,* don't leave home unless get married."

"This isn't the old country, Mom."

I stood up, leaving the cup half-full, and went to her. As something bitter threatened to rise from the back of my throat I put my arms around her. "Mama, I'm not leaving you. We'll see each other. You'll see Joey."

She sat rigid. "Empty house. *Fra poco saro morto.* Soon I gonna be dead."

"Oh, Mama."

To escape her, I went to the window in the kitchen door. Outside, the brittle branches of the naked winter trees shivered as if spring would never come again. When I couldn't stand the silence between us anymore, I went upstairs.

Joey rocked at the edge of his bed as impatiently as a traveler in a waiting room. Posters of his basketball heroes covered the wall and his YMCA trophies lined the bookshelf.

"I hate my school and I'm not going back there."

I sat down next to him on the bed. "What happened?"

"I'm sick of it, that's what."

He gave me that same accusing look my mother had just given me. I tucked him in, thinking how much easier life had been before he had a mind of his own.

Later, as I lay in my old room studying the fading pattern on the wallpaper, Esther Isenberg called. She sounded as if we had remained friends all these years, as if nothing had ever changed— as if Jason had never lived and died. "Let's take the boys skating in Central Park on Sunday. Jazz and I are desperate for some air."

"Who?"

"My son, Jason Junior. We call him Jazz."

Before me in the shadows I saw the sad young face speaking of his love for his dead father. "Sure. That'll be fine."

After I hung up, I wondered about Esther. It hadn't occurred to me yet that in her despair she was dangerous.

6

We saw them approaching through the trees. Esther was wearing a mink jacket and sunglasses and Jason Jr. wore a cap that hid his eyes. Although they walked next to each other, each seemed alone. She was carrying a large package. Joey grabbed my sleeve; the skates that hung over his shoulder slammed into mine.

"This isn't going to be fun, Mom."

I took his hand and squeezed it. "It will be okay."

"Good, cuz I'm not ready for anything heavy."

"It won't get heavy," I said, and waved at Esther. When the four of us reached each other, she hugged me in a perfunctory way. Her perfume was sweet and rich. "I'm so glad you could make it," she said. "Jazz and I really needed to get out of the house."

Jazz looked even more pale and thin than he had at his father's funeral. He was a young Jason but somehow he seemed very, very old and cold as a plastic doll. His eyes were lifeless and shallow as glass. Joey didn't like him much.

"This is for you, Joey." Esther handed Joey the package she carried. He took it reluctantly. We all sat down on an empty bench under a leafless tree and watched Joey unwrap. Inside was a scarf.

"Hey, just like yours." He pointed without enthusiasm at Jazz.

"Oh, how nice," I chimed in.

And with a little prodding from Esther, Joey wrapped it around his neck. Then, when we got ready to skate, I realized that Esther had not brought any skates.

"Should we wait in the restaurant while the boys skate?" I asked.

Joey's face soured as if he had just swallowed a slice of lemon and Esther shook her head. "No, go ahead and skate awhile."

Joey, Jazz, and I laced our skates in silence. When Jazz took off his gloves, I shuddered. Many tiny scabs seemed to move like insects over the back of his hands. Joey noticed too. Neither of us said anything.

Joey pulled on my arms. "C'mon, Mom, I wanna see if you remember how."

I followed him to the ice. The bare black arms of the winter trees glistened in coats of ice. Between the short gasps of our breathing, I heard our skates scraping the ice. Above us both the sun and the moon were pale fingerprints on the sky. Our circles progressed to figure eights, which Joey said represented infinity. The place where he and I would be the same age. At the edge of the ice Jazz watched us, his sad face obscured by the angle of his cap. Esther was hidden in her mink cocoon.

"I feel sorry for them," Joey said.

I knew that meant he was ready to skate with Jazz.

I joined Esther and we sat watching the boys skate. In their matching scarves they looked like brothers. I sat unlacing my skates, waiting for her to pick the place where our conversation would begin.

As I wriggled my toes and pulled one skate off, she asked, "Remember Jack Engstrom?"

In my head I could find no memory of Jack Engstrom. So I said, "No, who is he?"

Her chest heaved in a dry laugh and the mink shimmered on her like a second skin. "You never did sleep with him, did you? And he was something too."

The picture popped. Engstrom, his thick legs, thick neck, deep-set black eyes, and full lips always twisted in a smirk. He had been captain of our football team and by definition the most desirable male in our high school. Esther and I had both wanted him but I had landed him, though not for long. When our relationship didn't progress below the waist, he demanded his ring back. Then he was Esther's steady date. I searched for her eyes, but in her dark sunglasses, I could see only my own reflection. I saw myself in miniature, superimposed on the ice in front of us. I felt a jealousy so deep that it was physical. I rolled my scratchy socks one into the other and tried to pretend I didn't feel what I was feeling. But with the certainty of those who have known us when we were young, she touched the very thing I was trying to deny.

"You always were such a goody two-shoes," she said, "and I was such a tramp." She pulled her mink collar up around her face. I looked down at my simple wool coat, feeling the best had passed me by.

"I was always jealous of you," she said. "You always did everything right."

The sun slanted between us, almost blinding me. "C'mon, Esther, you got all the guys."

"Well, you were such a saint."

For a while neither of us said anything. If she only knew. Around us the city rose quiet as a graveyard. Finally she raised her shoulders and let them fall. "What good did it do you? Life still cheated you."

I felt cold and hungry, so I got up. As we walked to the restaurant I asked her a simple question. I knew it was more difficult than anything she had asked me. Was I asking because I wanted to know or because it was an easy revenge? I asked, "What happened to Jason? What really happened?"

From under her sunglasses a tear snuck onto her cheek. Then she said, "Jason was the best thing that ever happened to me. He wasn't judgmental. He didn't care about my past, we had a great life together. But when they moved him to the basement, everything changed."

At our feet in the snow lay the shadow of a human being, which as children we called an angel. In the play of the sun on the snow I saw Jason as I had last seen him, the day he died, stooped and defeated, gray eyes inscrutable as stones underwater, standing in front of his beloved Indonesian villagers. I heard her say, "City Hall is a nest of vipers. Get out before they turn on you."

Our feet trampled the shadow of the angel and I added, "But isn't it true that he was a compulsive gambler?"

"That was no big deal, it was recreational. He had it under control."

I wanted to say, "That's not what the mayor told me." But I didn't. I couldn't bring him into it. She must have seen the skepticism in my eyes because she said, "Sex became Jason's addiction. That's what that airline ticket to the Bahamas was about."

I said, "The one in his raincoat."

She nodded. The boys circled back in our direction.

"Jason was seeing another woman. He would invent these business trips to visit potential city contractors. I knew he had no responsibility for contracts anymore. It was his way of trying to restore some sense of power to himself. I understood, God knows I did enough of that in high school. Sex for ego building. He would have gotten over it . . . Laetitia Hadley . . . a goddamn social director at the Paradise Cove on Paradise Island."

A slight breeze rustled the brittle branches. Slivers of ice fell at our feet.

"Why did he kill himself? Was it really the cancer? He looked so well."

She stopped walking and she took off her glasses. Her eyes were empty. "I don't know," she said. "I really don't know."

By the time Joey and I headed back to the loft I was exhausted. Dozens of ads offered meaningless remedies for the emptiness I felt —makeup, dating services, trashy novels, even an astrologer. I sat next to Joey on the subway pretending we were just a mother and child on a Sunday afternoon but thinking that he was the only one who filled the empty places in my heart. He said, "Jazz is weird, real weird."

"What do you mean?"

"Promise you won't flip out."

I squinted at him.

"Promise."

"Okay, I promise."

"He's a walking drugstore. He had marijuana and crack and some crazy stuff called unknown on him."

"Did you—"

"C'mon, Mom, gimme a break."

"But he offered it to you, didn't he?"

Joey shrank into himself. "I shouldn't have told you. You're not gonna tell his mother, are you?"

I bit my lip and stared at my feet, fighting the impulse to rip Esther's gift from his neck. Instead I shifted my anger to the graffiti whizzing by in the tunnel. What kind of lunatic would risk his life to write his name where no one cared to read it? About five minutes later, I said, "We won't see them again."

Joey looked at me as if he wished I would grow up and shrugged. "They're your friends, Mom."

Back at the loft Joey and I made hot chocolate and I vowed to forget about Esther and her troubled son. The loft, which had once been a candle factory, was a big, high-ceilinged, empty space lined with tall windows. A kitchen area had been built with brand-new counters and appliances. The wooden floor had just been laid and polished. So far I had just bought dishes, kitchen appliances, a futon, and some small potted trees. Joey got a huge kick out of the fact that we now had our own indoor yard. We skated the floor in our socks then sat on a window ledge sipping the dark sweet chocolate. We were just deciding we needed some walls when the phone rang. Joey picked up. He chatted for a while in low familiar tones before handing me the phone.

Raul said, "Sounds like you guys had a great day together."

I didn't know how much I had missed him until I heard his voice. "Yes, we did." I wondered whether Joey had told him about Esther and Jazz.

Raul said, "My trial time at the *Dispatch* is over and I'm going to Miami tomorrow to tie up a few loose ends. Come with me."

"What?"

"You heard me. It's a chance for us to spend some time together away from all this conflict-of-interest bullshit."

"Miami? You *are* crazy."

"Don't you want to know what the attraction is before you give up on us?"

"Where would we stay?"

"A hotel on the beach, a night in Little Havana. Wherever we want."

"I don't know. I don't know if I can get off—"

"That job is a perennial excuse. Think about it and I'll call you tomorrow."

He hung up first. Joey was walking the imaginary line where my wall would be when he said, "I think you should go."

"You were eavesdropping."

He raised an eyebrow and aged thirty years. "Let's just say I couldn't help but overhear."

When I caught up with Raul at the airport, he was already on the boarding line. He was wearing jeans, a gray turtleneck, and a leather jacket. He looked very young. I was out of breath from rushing.

"You just made it," he said. "I thought you were going to stand me up."

Feeling like a teenager in a tryst, I said, "I had a lot of stuff to wrap up at work."

We didn't talk much until we had settled into our seats. I watched him buckle his seat belt before buckling my own, and I was so nervous we might as well have been launching for Mars.

"This will be my final break with Miami," he said as we began coasting down the runway.

"You can never make a final break from your hometown," I said, thinking about my mother and Brooklyn.

"Miami is my hometown but it isn't. Cuba is my real home."

The plane strained forward and up, and I felt the relief of knowing that the takeoff was behind us.

"Do you want to go back?"

"That's not exactly an option."

"I was asking about your feelings, not your options."

That stopped the conversation. He was silent. The plane kept climbing. Another man who couldn't talk about his feelings. But then he said, "Part of what attracts me to you is that you seem so rooted. As rooted as a tree."

Was that a compliment or an insult? "Rooted in what?"

I was thinking sand, shifting sand, but he said, "Tradition . . . your motherhood, your loyalty, your Italianness. You're rooted in all that."

"What's so attractive about that? A lot of those so-called roots are shackles."

"There you are, starry-eyed in a nest of vipers."

That was the second time that week I had heard City Hall called a nest of vipers. First Esther, now him.

"Nicosea's no viper. He's one of the best mayors New York's ever had. He pulled the city out of economic chaos."

"The changing economy pulled the city out. Nicosea looks good in a suit. He's all front. A former thespian."

"He's stopped corporate flight, lowered the dropout rate, economic development is up, unemployment down."

"And he's been good to you."

"As a matter of fact he has. He gave me a high-level job when I hadn't worked in years."

"Ever question his motivation?"

"No; no, I haven't. What're you driving at?"

"Nothing, I'm not driving at anything."

I looked out at banks of cauliflower clouds. "Are you implying that I'm naive or that I'm stupid?"

He pushed his seat back and stretched. "Neither. Don't project your insecurities onto me. I'm just saying you weren't meant to spend your life as a secretary."

I was tired of explaining to this guy that I wasn't a secretary. So I just said, "Let's get off this topic. I thought we left New York to get off this topic."

After that I pretended to fall asleep, and then I actually did. When I woke up, I had my head on his shoulder and my mouth was hanging open. He smiled and touched my cheek. "These heavy political discussions just knock you out, huh?"

The flight attendant preempted my reply. "Ladies and gentlemen, we are descending into Miami International Airport. Please remain seated until the plane comes to a complete halt. When you deplane please remember your hand luggage and thank you for . . ."

"Deplane . . . deplane . . . Americans have a knack for bastardizing the language that is unparalleled in the Western world."

I didn't say anything. What lunacy had possessed me to think that I would enjoy a weekend with this arrogant asshole? Outside the window the Everglades slipped under us. I thought about the reptiles hidden in the tall straw grass. Then the whitewashed high-rise skyline of Miami rose against the brilliant aquamarine of Biscayne Bay. Maybe it wouldn't be so bad after all.

The landing was clean and smooth. The airport itself was much easier to navigate than any of New York City's airports. Ten minutes later we had our luggage. I followed him to the car rental lot. The warm Miami air embraced me and I felt that I had left January behind. We didn't talk much as he piled our luggage into the car he had rented. We were still quiet as he followed a maze of streets out of the airport. In a few minutes we were on a huge expressway that led to a network of expressways. Then downtown Miami appeared. It looked brand new. A purple line of neon ran in the air above the streets.

"That's the people mover," he said proudly.

"It seems more modern than New York."

"Well, New York will be a nice town if they ever finish it"—he chuckled—"but Miami is something else. A child of the sixties."

He found a Spanish station on the radio and began rocking in his seat. "Calle Ocho, here we come." His cynicism seemed to lift, and his mood became festive. The bumper sticker on the car in front of us read: "Will the last American to leave Dade County please bring the flag?"

"Where are we staying?"

"At my grandparents' house in downtown south Miami where I grew up."

"I thought—"

He cut me off. "It's empty now."

As we entered Miami's Cuban section the streets became livelier, full of people and sidewalk cafés. Raul sang with the radio. His grandparents' house was in the heart of Little Havana. On the side streets off Calle Ocho, I saw many shrines on the front lawns of neat little houses. There were even shrines at gas stations. The Holy Mother was everywhere.

"Your people are more Italian than the Italians."

He bristled at the comparison just as my mother would have. "We weren't raised by the Irish Catholics, so we don't embrace the bitter cup like you Italian-Americans."

"What do you mean?"

"We're not ashamed of our bodies. We're not guilty about our pleasures. That's what separates the real Italians from the Italian-Americans."

"The *real* Italians?"

"You know what I mean."

He was right about the Irish priests but I didn't want to admit it, so I said, "These days my parish priest is from Trinidad."

He laughed. I pointed out a plaster saint on somebody's lawn.

"Saint Lazarus is one of my people's favorites because of his spectacular ability to endure poverty and pain," he said.

"Oh . . . *la miseria,*" I said, "self-denial." How well I knew it.

He said, "That kind of resignation doesn't fit too well with my politics."

We passed a monument dedicated to the Cubans who died in the Bay of Pigs disaster. "I call that the monument to American ambivalence," he said. His look challenged me to contradict him. I kept quiet because I didn't want to start an argument.

His grandparents' home was set back from the street. On the immaculate lawn, the Virgin stood in a shrine surrounded by plastic gladiolas. The pink stucco, Spanish-style house was protected by an ornate network of wrought-iron gates. A small bakery next door advertised *pan y dulces.*

Inside, the house was completely furnished but aggressively unoccupied. It looked like it had been cleaned and dusted just yesterday. The red velvet living-room set was covered in plastic and a Madonna in sapphire-blue robes stood in a niche in the wall. Raul listened as if expecting his grandmother to come down the stairs. We walked through the house together, our footsteps absorbed by the rugs. He took my hand and held it tightly. In the silence I thought I could hear his heart beat.

"You miss them, don't you?"

Without his cynicism he was lost, so he pretended he hadn't heard me. I could feel him reaching for a past he couldn't return to. I stepped up to the altar and lit the candle in the glass cup, just like the candles in St. Anthony's.

"You light candles for the dead," he said. "We light them for protection."

He was wrong but I crossed myself and didn't contradict him. Now that he had brought me here, he seemed intent on emphasizing our differences. He was shutting me out, like a child disguising need with hostility. The tropical night pushed at the shutters and I asked him to show me the house.

The house was full of ghosts—his grandparents, his parents, Cuba itself, the ghosts of his childhood. We went from room to room and they seemed to stand around us, between us, breathing our air. There were many pictures of his parents in Cuba. In several his mother was pregnant. Many of the pictures were taken on a hacienda overlooking the ocean. There were pictures of him too. Brand new, just born, in the arms of adoring family members, a big family with people of all shades, brown, black, white.

There was one picture that particularly mesmerized me. He was in the arms of his grandmother. She was still young; her big black eyes looked straight at me.

"She was a very strong woman," Raul said. "She worked in the tobacco fields from the time she was eight years old; when she was fifteen, she married my grandfather. His family had money. They had six children . . . all killed by Castro's revolution. They were already sixty when they came here and started over with nothing. They built that bakery next door."

I studied his grandmother's kindly wrinkled face. It reminded me of my grandmother's face. My grandmother whom I had never met. My grandmother, born in the heat of the Mezzogorno, pushed into an arranged marriage before she was fifteen. My grandmother, keeper of the village dream book, a dictionary of symbols that helped the women to interpret and share their dreams. I told him that his grandmother reminded me of mine.

"You want us to be the same," he said, "but we're not. Our histories are different."

"Different but the same," I said, leading him to the bed where I knew we would find common, if not higher, ground.

When I fell asleep that night, I was content. Deep in my sleep a buried memory came to life.

Joe was sitting at our kitchen table in his undercover clothes. He looked as slimy as a junkie. In front of him were scrambled eggs and burned toast. He was looking up at me as if we had never met before. I sat down across from him to try one more time. My anger had kept me awake most of the night; I knew I looked like hell and sounded worse. "Joe, talk to me. What's wrong? What's going on with you?"

"Nothing," he snapped. "I told you, I can't talk about it."

"Something's wrong. Is it the job? You don't talk to me. You don't touch me."

He stuck a fork into his eggs. They were wet at the center. He pushed his plate away in disgust. "Jesus, I can't even get a decent meal anymore."

He got up and headed for the door. I picked the plate up and hurled it after him.

"I'm your wife, not your maid!"

I missed. The plate shattered against the wall; the eggs slid to the floor. He didn't look back. The next time I saw him was in the morgue.

My heart rattled at the gates of my chest. I lay there like a prisoner. Across the room in a vanity mirror I saw the pale light of the reflected moon. When I walked over, my feet didn't feel the floor. I sat down and began to brush my hair with the heavy silver brush that must have belonged to Raul's grandmother. A hundred strokes. My arms got tired, and then I saw them. The hands of the grandmothers, Raul's and mine, kneading dough. The dough became a larva. It had my face. I was in agony. The grandmothers smiled. I looked into myself and the head that came out of me was my own, full grown. And then I really woke up—to the sweet comforting smell of rising bread.

Without disturbing Raul, I left the house for the bakery next door. As the baker handed me the warm loaf he said, "You are with Raul?" He was a tiny man with small hands like a woman's and deep black eyes.

I nodded.

"He ask me last week to clean house for you, your visit. Is good?"

I ripped a piece of bread and bit into it. "Very good." It was like Italian bread but softer. Then it hit me.

"Last week? He asked you last week?"

"Yes." The baker nodded with a smile. "Last week."

"How could that be?" I asked rhetorically. "He didn't invite me until two days ago."

"Ahhh"—the baker laughed—"he like to plan, Raul, he always plan ahead."

When I got back to the house, Raul was up, but I kept my little encounter to myself. I figured I was there for fun and it didn't matter that he was—so to speak—so cocksure of himself. We had breakfast and then he left me to my own devices. He had to pay a visit to the *Herald* and he had errands to run. My day was luxurious. I spent the day reading a treasure I had spent a long time finding, *Una Donna* by Siberla Aleramo. Many people considered it the first feminist novel. It was dark by the time Raul returned.

We strolled down Calle Ocho looking for a snack. Christmas lights still flashed in store windows. Furniture store after furniture store displayed chrome, Formica, plastic, matching sets for every room in the house, all on layaway. Jewelry-store windows offered gold and silver chains, initial rings, and religious medallions. Raul steered me into a little restaurant with a long window across from a pocket park. Old men in guayaberas sat drinking *café con leche*, playing dominoes, and talking in Spanish. The mix of chatter, laughter, and the rich smell of strong coffee conspired to make me feel that I was in the Little Italy of my childhood. I realized that if I kept my mouth shut, I could fit right in. I sat down by the window, and across the street I saw a guy who seemed much too small for his seersucker suit pull a fedora down over his eyes and step into the circle of light under a lamppost as if waiting to be spotted. He seemed to look straight at us. Then he walked into the park.

"Do me a favor, honey. . . ."

I was about to say "don't call me honey," but Raul was getting up, "Order us coffee and I'll be right back."

I thought he was going to the men's room but he left the restaurant and ran across the street to the park. I sat there wondering who was crazier, him or me. When the waitress came, I asked for two coffees.

"American?" she asked.

I nodded.

I had finished my coffee, and fifteen minutes had passed before Raul finally returned. He made a lot of noise sitting down. Then he measured spoonful after spoonful of sugar into his cold coffee. I wasn't about to help him by saying anything. Instead I wondered what the hell I was doing in this city of strangers. He brought his cup to his lips and grimaced. Then he put it down and signaled the waitress with two fingers. *"Dos con leche y dos flan,"* he called out.

When all those diversions were exhausted, he tapped his fingers on the tabletop and said, "Maybe I shouldn't have brought you down here after all."

"Who was that?"

He made a show of deciding whether or not to answer me. Finally he said, "That was one of my oldest and best sources. I wouldn't have won my award without him. The FBI caught him in a major dope deal a few years ago and he's been a part-time informant ever since."

"What did he want?"

"Money."

At the table next to us an old waiter sliced some Cuban bread. He put the slices on something that looked like an iron. As he squeezed the iron down I heard the bread sizzle.

"Smells good," Raul said. "When we leave here, I'm going to eat you till you melt."

"Good try, Vega, but not very sophisticated. I'd rather you answered my question."

The waitress brought us two cups of hot milk and a pot of coffee that was as strong as expresso. Raul poured the milk into our cups and the coffee into the milk. "It's just that I don't want to put you in jeopardy," he said.

I listened to the medley of conversations around us and understood nothing. I studied his beautiful dark eyes for a clue.

"You look like you belong here," he said.

I sipped the coffee and relaxed a little. "Aw c'mon, tell me," I coaxed. "What did you get for your money?"

The waitress brought two caramel desserts. Raul stirred his coffee religiously. This time there was no sugar in it.

As I tasted my custard Raul said, "According to my source, Isenberg was involved in a cocaine cartel. He came down here once a month to make a pickup."

The caramel melted on my tongue; it was incredibly sweet. I said, "You're out of your mind."

He sipped his coffee calmly and didn't even bother to respond.

"You came down here to see your *snitch?*"

"That was a part of it."

Rather than explode right there on the spot, I got up and walked out.

When he caught up with me, I was standing in front of a store that was wrapped around a corner. Inside looking out at us and larger than life were a lineup of plaster saints, a black Madonna, Christ on the cross, a brass Buddha, and a very large red and white circle—yin and yang. I was studying the sign that said the saints were purchasable in small monthly installments when his reflection appeared on the pane. He put his hands on my shoulders. I shook him off. "You brought me down here to chase Isenberg stories?"

"I brought you down here to be with you. Is it my fault you work in a corrupt administration?"

"It isn't corrupt for you to have a hidden agenda?"

"I didn't mean to hurt you," Raul said. "Sometimes I'm just clumsy."

"Nicosea's not corrupt. I'd stake my life on that."

"I don't know yet. I don't know if he's corrupt or if he just looks the other way."

I started around the corner. He stayed where he was. Now he stood there in the lineup next to Christ. The crown of thorns was sharp and vicious. I said, "Your snitch is crazy. I knew Jason. Jason would never be involved with anything so sleazy."

"According to the grapevine, he was, Marie."

"Look—your friend is wrong. Jason did come down here a lot but it was for a different reason."

"What?"

"It was personal."

"Personal like getting rich off other people's misery?"

"No, personal like a mistress, a girlfriend."

Even through the store's two windows, I could see his eyes light up.

"Are you sure?"

I was so intent on proving my point that I just walked into his trap. "I was cleaning up his office and I found a ticket from Miami to the Bahamas. I brought it to his wife and she told me about a woman named Laetitia Hadley, she's a social director at the Paradise Cove on Paradise Island."

I said that and immediately wished I hadn't. I started walking again. He called after me, "She lied to you. She's part of the cover-up."

"You're crazy!" I yelled back. When I turned, the black Madonna's serene, sad eyes seemed to follow me. Under the street lamp Raul's skin was golden. I asked, "What's to cover up?"

He came toward me, hands in his pockets. "Isenberg held the key to this administration's dirty secrets," Raul said. "And everybody wants to make sure they die with him."

"That's crazy. This isn't Watergate. Besides, if there was a cover-up, I'd know, I'd be a part of it—"

I stopped midsentence.

"My thoughts exactly . . . and my advice to you is get out, Marie. You're low man on the totem pole and that makes you the ideal scapegoat."

"Now I know you're nuts. I'm not important enough for that. I don't have that kind of power."

"You worked for Isenberg. Go to the Department of Investigations. Go before City Hall sets you up to take the fall."

What kind of ploy was this? Didn't he know New York politics? I laughed. "The DOI works for the mayor."

"Then tell *me.*"

The cat was out of the bag. He was ravenous for a story.

"I have nothing to hide. I don't know anything!"

"You probably know more than you think you know."

I knew more than I was saying. I knew about the gambling and he obviously didn't. I thought about the chips Joey had found in Jason's desk, the chips with Paradise Cove printed on them. I still had one in my purse. If I tracked that chip to its origin, Raul could see he was wrong, once and for all. It would mean he would learn Jason had been a gambler and a womanizer, but even that was better than what Raul was thinking now.

The Madonna looked tenderly at the child in her arms. I thought about Jason's son, his sad eyes. I said, "Let's go to the Bahamas." Then my hand jumped to cover my mouth as if trying to shove the words back in.

"You mean that?"

I nodded, but my fingers were still over my mouth. As we stepped into the yellow haze of a street lamp our shadows stretched in front of us. They got longer and longer until they slipped under us and were gone.

"What if I'm right?" he said. "What if Isenberg was up to his ass in corruption?"

Now our shadows were short and fat and followed us. I said, "You're wrong and I'm going to prove it to you."

Paradise Island was like a Garden of Eden with tropical vegetation in endless shades of green, a flawless blue sky, and a sun that played on the ocean. Paradise Cove turned out to be an old British villa nestled against the ocean with bungalows on the beach. As the concierge handed Raul our key I asked about the social director. "Miss Hadley is off today," he said, "but she'll be back to lead the social activities bright and early tomorrow morning."

A valet in a flowered shirt carried our luggage down a path to the beach, where a bungalow stood hidden in a coconut grove. It had a thatched roof like a hut but inside it was all luxury. A wall-to-ceiling window looked out at the beach and the ocean that ran to the edge of the sky. Raul tipped the valet and then we both just stood there in pure awe.

"Isenberg knew how to live," he said.

"Is that supposed to be funny?" I snapped, standing there angry and confused.

He turned to place his suitcase on the bed. "I just meant it's beautiful."

I fought the urge to cry.

"What's wrong?" he asked, changing into his bathing suit.

"This," I said. "This is all wrong."

"I'm going for a swim," he said without bothering to challenge me.

I sat down on the bed wondering if Jason had ever stayed in this bungalow. The summer turned to winter and I shivered. I hated Jason for his selfishness. I hated him for killing himself. And I hated myself for this foolish adventure. After a while I put on my bathing suit and went outside.

I placed my towel on the sand and lay there with my eyes closed. Above me, the fronds of the palms clicked musically against each other. The rush of the ocean toward the shore was tempered by a shimmering heat. I stroked the sand with my fingers.

A shadow passed over me. "You're going to burn," Raul said. Drops of the cool ocean dripped from his skin onto mine. I opened my eyes. He knelt on the sand. Then his fingers pushed my bathing suit aside.

"You can't do that here."

"There's nobody, just us. That's what these places are made for."

His cool tongue came into me. The waves pounded the shore and receded only to return. Somewhere a rooster crowed. I got up and ran into the water. He lay down on the beach. We stayed away from each other until the day was gone and the palms turned lavender. That evening we danced in the nightclub like strangers who had just met. That night we tore into each other with the kind of gusto only hostile lovers seem to manage.

The next morning before Raul woke up, I went up to the main building. In the dining room breakfast was being served, but I wasn't ready to eat. I went down to the pool. A small, athletic woman was examining some tennis rackets. Her skin was a rich mahogany and her short woolly hair was cut in an elegant square top. She wore a gleaming white tennis outfit and Rayban sunglasses. As I sat down she looked up and smiled.

"Good morning, I'm Laetitia Hadley. Do you want to sign up for tennis?"

My heart began to pound. I wanted to get away from her. "I've never been near a tennis court. I play Ping-Pong."

I heard my own nervous laughter.

"Are you here by yourself?"

"Yes," I lied.

"Well, maybe we can remedy that," she said. "I could find another Ping-Pong player and perhaps seat you with someone at lunch."

I wondered if she had accommodated Jason this way.

"Oh, that's okay."

"Have you had breakfast?"

She had a slight British accent. I shook my head.

"Actually, we could play now. It's not good to play after you eat."

I don't know why I got up and followed her to the atrium, but I did. "You'll probably beat the pants off me," she said with a bright smile. "I don't play much Ping-Pong."

The Ping-Pong table stood in a luscious jungle. Parrots, parakeets, and lovebirds sat like blossoms in the foliage. We tossed a coin. My serve. For a while we hit the ball back and forth amiably. "You're good at this," she said.

"We had a table at home when I was a kid."

"Where are you from?"

"New York City. What about you?"

"I'm from here," she said.

"Married?" I asked, slicing the ball.

"No." She hit it back.

I listened to the tap, tap, tap of the ball and then I heard myself say, "Did you love him?"

The lovebird made a sound like a pigeon. "I beg your pardon?" She smiled quizzically. I sliced the ball hard. She missed. We stood on either side of the long green table, silently staring. Under that finishing-school veneer, she was a tough cookie. I took a stupid gamble, one that I hadn't planned on. I said, "I'm Esther Isenberg."

She served the ball back to me without stepping into my trap. I said, "I loved him very much."

She kept her eye on the ball. "What is it you want from me?"

"I just want to know what your relationship was. How often did you see each other? When did you meet?"

"Why?"

"There seems to be so much about my husband I didn't know —I thought you might help me. Did he give you his real name?"

"Of course he did."

"And did you get him into the gambling?"

She caught the ball in her hand and stopped the game. "He was the gambler. I don't gamble. I never even set foot in the casino."

When she served again, it was with a new aggressiveness. I returned her serve, and when the ball seemed to have taken on a rhythm of its own, I apologized. "I didn't mean to attack you. It's just that I kind of blame his suicide on all those gambling losses."

This time she missed the ball and her surprise was transparent. "Losses? Jason was great at the tables. I don't ever remember him really losing."

I put my paddle down. There was no point in trying to serve again. For a moment it was as if I actually were Esther, looking for answers I couldn't find. Confused and hurt, I excused myself from the game. Laetitia Hadley just stood there, the lovebirds around her still cooing, and watched me walk away. I retreated to the bungalow. Raul was still asleep. I sat down on the bed trying to make sense out of what Laetitia Hadley had told me. Did everyone have a different version of who this man had been? Raul stirred. His eyes opened. He looked at me and smiled. "Hey, early bird."

"I did a stupid thing just now."

"You got out of bed?"

"No, I met Laetitia Hadley and I pretended to be Esther Isenberg."

He sat up. "What happened?"

"She believed me and she basically confirmed the affair."

He ran a hand through his hair. "Jesus, who's the reporter here?"

If I hadn't been so nervous, I would have laughed. Instead I said, "So you see, your source is wrong."

"My source is rarely wrong."

"But she confirmed it."

"So Isenberg fucked around. What does that prove?"

"It proves he came down here to see her."

If I could convince him, maybe I would believe it myself.

"It doesn't prove much of anything," he said.

"This trip was for nothing?"

He got up and studied the surf as it came and went. "Last night was *nada*, huh?"

"You know what I mean!"

He turned back to me. He was naked and sad and young. He spread his hands in a kind of plea. "Let's do what we said we were going to do. Let's forget all that and enjoy ourselves. We only have one more day."

So we made a truce and then we went out to play. We rented two mopeds, we explored the island, we ate by the sea, we laughed, and we forgot all about Jason. But that night when Raul insisted on a trip to the casino, Jason's ghost joined us again.

We stood at the top of the long stairway down into the plush casino. It was small and classy. The walls were a rich mahogany and the carpets pool-table green—no one-armed bandits, just baccarat, blackjack, and roulette. The silence that enveloped the players was punctuated by the ritual of the games of chance—cards moving in fast hands, the spin of the roulette wheel, the click, click, click of the ball as it landed on a number. Every few moments, a croupier's stage whisper resounded across the room, *"Mesdames et messieurs, faites vos jeux,"* and then *"rien va plus."* I watched the backs of the players. They stood like wax mannequins removed from the rush of time. In the far corner of the room, behind bars, stood the cashier's window.

The cocktail dress Raul and I had selected that afternoon in the hotel boutique was designed to raise and expose my cleavage. Raul stood at my elbow in his rented tux, as chic a man as I had ever seen. I studied his sash and the frills on his very white shirt, thinking what fun it would be to strip him. "You're gonna lose money here," I whispered.

His eyes dropped to my half-naked breasts. He cleared his throat and touched that stupid bow around his neck. "I know when to stop."

I fought the urge to giggle and lost. My breasts trembled. He wet his lips. I felt wild and sexy the way I had always imagined Esther to be. As he surreptitiously patted my ass I descended into the pit. Raul followed.

We wandered among the tables until he sat down to play. Raul entered the fellowship of the game. For him time stopped too. I watched the grim faces of the players. Then I got bored. I began to wander from table to table. In my bag I had Jason's chip. Every once in a while a man's back, his neck looked like Jason's. When I saw Raul again, he had moved to a new game.

I headed for the bar. I inched up on the bar stool next to a perfect stranger. To sit, I had to slide the tight material of my dress halfway up my thighs. Before I could order, the stranger next to me got the bartender's attention. "A glass of champagne for the lady."

He turned to me. He was an older black man, elegant, silver-haired, and very sexy. Two glasses of champagne arrived in crystal flutes. My stranger toasted me. I took a long cool sip.

"It's wonderful," I said.

"Not bad."

Four drinks and three strangers later, I saw Raul's angry eyes in front of me in the tinted mirror. He was watching me jealously. And then it came over me again. That crazy urge. A new stranger had just bought me a drink. I told him that my ex-husband and I were big fans of Paradise Island. I added that ultimately Paradise had lost its allure because my husband had become a compulsive gambler whereas for me it was purely recreational.

"People do get hooked," my stranger said.

"You know, you haven't even told me your name."

For a second he looked uncomfortable and then he made one up. "David," he said. "David Braithwaite. And you?"

"Esther," I said. "Esther Isenberg."

"Oh," he said, and for a moment I thought he had read about the suicide. "Your ex was a regular here."

In the mirror Raul watched. I lifted my glass. "Here's to recreation."

There were several calculated possibilities in my tone. He shrugged. "I guess losing can be addictive too."

"What do you mean?"

"Your ex. I never saw him win."

I pursed my lips as if to a bitter revelation, but really I was trying to swallow my surprise. The stranger was getting ready to order another glass for me when I slid casually off the stool, as casually as was possible in that snakeskin of a cocktail dress.

"You're leaving?"

I smiled. "To lick my wounds."

In the mirror I could see Raul timing his exit to mine.

"Don't you think you were enjoying that a little too much?" he demanded as we left the casino.

"Jealous?"

"Very funny. How does it feel to unleash that wild woman living in your skin?"

The silver path of the moon on the ocean looked solid enough to step on. I felt a dizzying lightness beyond the weight of all my memories.

"Your friend Isenberg used to lose big at the tables," he said.

I glared at him. I was tipsy. In the moonlight his angry eyes were frightening.

"That's not what Ms. Hadley said." My words were angry and slurred.

"Oh . . ."

"She said he *always* won."

"You never mentioned that this morning," he said so softly that it was menacing.

"I forgot."

"I see."

The fingertips of the waves erased our footsteps behind us. I said, "I didn't know you suspected Jason of being a gambler."

"Where did you get your suspicions?"

I shrugged. We walked in silence until Raul said, "Hadley wouldn't know. Employees aren't allowed in the casino."

"According to her, Jason always had plenty of cash when he came back out. She said he was good at the tables."

Raul bent down to take his shoes off. When he stood up again, he said, "There's only one way both versions could be true—only one way he could have lost and won at the same time."

"What's that?"

"He always brought a pocketful of chips with him. It's a money-laundering technique, not even very original. Somebody was paying him off—paying him off in chips. He'd cash them in and take his laundered money home."

"Wouldn't the casino notice that?"

"Did you see that teller's window?"

Yes, I had seen it.

He said, "People buy chips there and they cash them in. The teller doesn't communicate with the croupiers. The chips are money. The teller doesn't care how or where you got them. He just cashes them in when you bring them to him."

On the shimmering water I saw that pile of chips Joey had found in Jason's desk drawer. We had reached our cove. I took my shoes off, unzipped my flimsy dress, and ran into the water. In the moonlight I saw Raul, his face in shadow, walking along the shore, his tuxedo like a straitjacket. I let the waves beach me. Still wet, I slipped into my dress and led him back to the bungalow.

He came to me on his knees. I wrapped my legs completely around his back, he stuck his tongue down my throat, and that was that. It was everything a night in the tropics should be. The ocean whispered incessantly. But I never did tell him that he was right.

7

Kennedy Airport was cold, drab, and endless. I carried my hand luggage. The jacket I was wearing was a useless rag. The cold had gotten colder, or it felt that way. Raul walked next to me but seemed far away. I had planned to say good-bye in a casual but final way. But in his silence he had beaten me to the punch. We negotiated our way through the multinational crowd, following signs to our luggage. An alcoholic, would-be bellhop stepped in front of Raul. "Nice jacket, *hermano*, looks expensive, you making the lady carry her own bag."

On Raul's neck some veins popped up. "Back off, man," he said. "The lady's carrying her bag because she wants to."

The hustler was young but very dejected. His face folded in despair. All the love in the world could never fix him. He opened his palm and brought his misery menacingly close to Raul. "C'mon, you're not like these white folks. You understand what can happen to a man." He put his hand on Raul's shoulder and breathed in his face. Raul removed the hand. "Don't do that. Don't touch me, man."

I looked around, suddenly very conscious of our fellow passengers. Next to us a young mother struggled with a toddler who was using every limb to try to escape her grip. In front of us were the mix of wealthy WASPs and Jews who had spent their Christmas vacations in Florida. The conveyor belt ran empty.

I foraged in my pocketbook for money and extricated a dollar bill, which I held toward the man.

"I can't get no food with that."

I found another dollar. He took it grudgingly and turned to the nearest foreign couple.

Raul's lips were tight; an angry blush had turned his cinnamon skin copper. He ignored me and studied the entrance to the conveyor belt with religious intensity. Finally I asked, "What are you so mad about?"

"You shouldn't have done that."

I shrugged. "Is it a big deal?"

"No, of course it's not a big deal. It's your money. But you shouldn't have encouraged that Puerto Rican bastard."

As he said the word *Puerto Rican* he looked at me as if I were an insect. An Italian insect.

"Well, well," I said. "Under that thin humanist veneer beats a heart full of prejudice."

"He's not a bastard because he's Puerto Rican, he's a bastard who happens to be Puerto Rican."

I gave up talking to him. He was too good with words and no rationalization was beyond him. I couldn't wait to get away from him.

Because cabs were scarce, we wound up sharing. It was about five in the afternoon by the time we got out of the airport. On

either side of the Brooklyn-Queens Expressway, Queens seemed
dead. There were no people in the streets. Raul borrowed the
driver's *Dispatch.* The six victims of the Donovan fire had been
buried yesterday. The mayor had attended the funeral service.

"Very slick," Raul said. "They managed to bury all these people at once so that it's a one-shot story."

He handed me the paper. I studied the photo spread of six
closed coffins being carried from St. Patrick's Cathedral. They
were draped in flowers. It looked like more money had been spent
on this funeral than the deceased had seen in any given year of life.
Just then we passed a graveyard. It stretched on and on.

"When Joey was little, we used to hold our breaths every time
we passed a graveyard so none of the spirits could get in," I said.

"You're so sentimental about that kid."

I gave him a look that could have cut the hide of an armadillo.

"Don't get me wrong," Raul said. "He's a great kid, but he's
gonna grow up and then where will you be?"

I stared resolutely out at the tombstones and kept my thoughts
to myself. I had had a man. A real man. Not him.

He looked at me like a gypsy reading a palm. "Yeah, well," he
said. "Dead people are always easier to love. The longer they're
dead the more perfect they get."

It was rush hour and traffic was slow. I watched strangers heading to unknown destinations feeling the frustration of being stuck
here with him when things between us were already over.

"You can let me off after the bridge," he told the driver. "That
way you can take the FDR straight to Brooklyn."

As we came to the end of the bridge, traffic came to a complete
halt. Now that we were motionless, the silence between us grew
thicker. We were on the Manhattan-bound lane of the lower level
of the Queensboro Bridge. At first I thought there must be an
accident on the road ahead of us. But when we inched ahead a bit
more, I saw the signs: NO JUSTICE NO PEACE . . . HOW MANY MORE?
. . . UNITED THE PEOPLE WILL NEVER BE DEFEATED. Then I saw the
camera crews and finally the small knot of dark-skinned demonstrators. They had joined hands to form a human barricade and
they were chanting "Death in the cell . . . How many more . . .
How many more before justice?" Their breath frosted in the air. It

was another demonstration for the special prosecutor. Cops in riot gear were trying to move the demonstrators without inciting a riot. This was midtown and the crowd knew it. The cops couldn't afford to crack any heads in midtown. The demonstrators wouldn't be moved.

Raul leaned forward. I could feel him coming to life. "Hey, buddy, could you open the trunk?"

As the driver got out Raul reached into his pocket and pulled out two twenties, which he folded into my hand. "I'm gonna check this out," he said.

I studied the bills in my hand. Then I grabbed his face and bit his lip in a cruel farewell. He yelped. I stuffed the bills into his shirt pocket. As I watched him walk off in search of his story I felt a mix of emotions I couldn't name. Whatever it was, it was over.

The cab just sat there, trapped in unyielding traffic, buffeted by the shouts of the demonstrators. After a while I started to chat with the driver. He had a very heavy Russian accent.

"You must like the freedom in America," I said.

"Freedom! Freedom. I am working six days, fifteen hours every day, paying more than hundred dollars for rent cab. No time, no time to be freedom."

"But it's better here, isn't it?"

"Better. What better? No time for eat, drink, talk with friends."

He stared at the demonstration in disgust. Reporters postured for the crowd, the crowd and the cops postured for the cameras.

"I lose money now," he said. "This freedom is expensive." We sat there for a long time. Leaflets fluttered under the traffic. Then, as the last of the reporters wrapped up, the crowd ambled away. They climbed back into the buses that had brought them. Once the cameras were gone, there was no point in staying. I thought about Hunter sitting in front of his four television monitors assessing the damage. I imagined the mayor in his Louis XV chair— alone, fearing that his days in power were numbered. It was like coming home to a war zone.

Once on the FDR Drive, we really started to move. An early-winter night had fallen over the city. In the darkness, its electricity, that mysterious energy, was even more palpable. We passed the

Wall Street towers that cradled City Hall and the Twin Towers that had once housed the offices of the state government in New York City. But the World Trade Center had become too expensive for government, and all the state's agencies, the Department of Labor, even the attorney general, had moved out. Only the governor's office remained high on the fifty-fifth floor, surrounded by brokerage firms and international banks.

When the cab finally stopped in front of my mother's house, I was relieved to be back on familiar turf. I grabbed my bag and headed for the back of the house. Through the living-room window I saw my mother's face lit by the glow of the television. The wooden house was so flimsy I could hear the demonstrators chanting on the six o'clock news, "No justice no peace."

My mother got up and changed the channel. "A single parrot caused the death of a million chickens in California. . . . People will continue to smuggle exotic birds until there are no exotic birds left."

Through the window of the kitchen door I could see Joey doing his homework. I tapped my nails on the pane, and he turned to let me in.

"Mom! Mom! I didn't expect to see you tonight."

I ran my fingers through his hair. "How's it going?"

My mother hobbled into the doorway. "This trip," she said, "what it was really?"

"Just a trip, Mama," I said. "Just a trip," and I headed for the staircase.

"You not gonna take you coat off?" She pointed indignantly at the closet, but I continued up the stairs.

"The Cuban, how old he is?"

That last question made me stop. "Who cares?"

She bowed her head as if a great weight had just fallen on her and wrung her hands in her apron. "Why you don't find a nice Italian boy?"

I clutched the banister as I had so often as a girl, but now I was a middle-aged woman and weary of her criticism. "Mama, I'm thirty-eight years old and I don't want an Italian boy. I don't want any boy, I want a man."

Her face wrinkled into a little prune and her mouth twitched. "This man only want one thing."

"Mom, what he wants I want. Can you get that through your head?"

I listened to the thump thump thump of my suitcase as Joey dragged it up the stairs ahead of me, and regretted my words. Joey turned and crossed his eyes at her.

"You stoppa that, somebody gonna slappa you and you gonna stay that way."

"Grandma, how many superstitions do you have room for in your head?"

My mother stood at the foot of the stairs wiping her hands on her apron, scowling up at Joey as if he were the devil's disciple. My teeth were chattering. Upstairs, I followed the dark hallway to my old room. My suitcase was on the floor. Joey, his arms folded over his chest, stood petulantly like a good imitation of my mother.

"I gotta get me away from her, Mom. You gotta get me away from her."

I lifted my suitcase up onto the bed. "C'mon, Joey, she loves you and she's good to you. Why do you have to be mean to her?"

"You tell me to think for myself and then you want me to swallow Grandma's shit with a smile."

"Don't curse."

"Are you gonna take your coat off?"

I stepped into the dark of the closet and the wire hangers tinkled against each other. Joey paced through the shadows of the room.

"You gonna marry him?" he demanded.

I hung up my coat, wishing I had never been to Miami. "I don't know, Joey, I don't think so."

"Why not? He's nice. He likes you and we could all live together in Manhattan."

I stood for a moment in the deep closet. The closet smelled of mothballs and cedar. I watched as Joey talked with his arms and hands, passing through the shadows in the room, reminding me more and more of his father. He wanted to know what Grandma had meant when she said Raul only wanted one thing. And what had I meant when I said I wanted it too? When I refused to talk about it, he turned his anger back to my mother.

"Grandma's unconstitutional. She frisked me and she didn't have probable cause."

I stepped back into the room. "What did Grandma find when she frisked you?"

"Dad's Swiss army knife . . . the one you gave me."

"Why take that out of the house?"

"Protection."

"From who?"

"The kids in school . . . and after school."

"That's crazy, Joe."

"Mom, you're not a man. You don't understand. Everybody carries weapons. You want me to get killed?"

Why was he torturing me like this?

"Don't even talk like that, Joey, please."

He picked his book bag up from the floor. It was sliced like a venetian blind. Through it, I could see the light from the lamp.

"What's that?"

He came up to me, opened his mouth, stuck his tongue out, and just stood there.

"Cut it out, Joe."

I unlocked my suitcase.

"They carry razor blades on their tongues," he said.

"Who?"

"Single-edged . . . I'm lucky I'm not dead."

"What are you talking about?"

"The kids from the shelter are stalking me because I had a fight with one of them. Mom, they travel in packs, they don't travel alone. They tried to get me at the bus stop. I'm lucky the book bag is all they got."

I stood there paralyzed by fear. One of the new shelters was a few blocks from my mother's house. The community had objected loudly—too many homeless families in one place, no services, kids running wild. But the shelter had been built anyway. The mayor had said the services would come later. I, of course, had supported him.

"That's why I need the knife," Joey said, dangling the book bag in front of me like a skeleton.

"A weapon you don't know how to use is worse than no weapon at all. They'll take it from you and use it against you."

"I'll learn how to use it." He walked out.

I called after him, "Joey! Joey, I forbid you to take that knife out of this house."

My mother sat at the kitchen table over a cup of coffee, smoking a Camel and wearing the new version of the same flowered smock she had been wearing since 1970. She had never smoked a cigarette until my father died of lung cancer. Then she picked up his last unfinished pack of Camels and became a devotee. Now she sat there pulling tobacco strands from her lower lip like a sailor looking for a fight. On the stove the cannelloni was still warm. I served myself. Joey's homework was still on the table. I glanced at it. The math was new math and Chinese to me. The social studies was no different than it had been twenty-five years ago. I went to the refrigerator, took some ricotta, and plopped a generous spoonful onto my pasta. Joey came in and sat at the table with us. He said, "I'm sorry, Mom."

My mouth was full. "Let's talk about it later, Joey."

"Mom, I got the best grade in the class on my science test."

"That's wonderful, Joey."

"Can I get a snake, Mom? The science teacher has one and he wants to give it away. I got first choice because I'm the best in the class."

"I don't know, Joey."

My mother looked up. *"Il serpente e un animale bruto*—very low *animale* . . . dirty."

"That's not true, they're clean and they don't eat much."

"What do you feed them?"

"Mice."

I swallowed a mouthful of soft squishy ricotta. "Aw, Joey, that's disgusting."

"No it's not, Mom. It's the balance of nature."

My mother said, "Is bad . . . evil I no have in my house."

"So are you gonna marry him?"

I watched my mother's face. Was she hearing this? "C'mon, Joey—we've had this conversation."

"So can I have the snake?"

"Could you keep it in the basement?"

My mother got up and hobbled to the stove. Joey took a long black rope from his pocket and put it around his neck. It just hung there. Then it undulated slightly. My mother screamed.

"*Madonna* . . . you bad, Joey . . . you very bad."

He smiled wickedly. "It's just a black racer. It's harmless."

Joey got up and walked out. My mother began to weep. I went to her and took her little round body in my arms. She sobbed, "He's bad boy. He need a man control him. You too much City Hall, who cares City Hall, City Hall mess up *familia*, you no home. You see what happen. He's bad."

I hated it when she called him bad. But this was no time for a confrontation. So I just held her. After a few minutes, I heard Joey puttering in the basement. When Mama was peacefully in front of the television again, I went downstairs. The snake was in an empty fish tank, skinny except for a lump in the middle.

"I just fed it," he said. "It only eats once a week."

We stood there watching it together. It lay as still as a rock. I couldn't see any eyes.

"This snake is harmless," he said. "Grandma's ignorant."

"I know," I said. "It's bedtime."

He looked at his Swatch. "It's only nine-thirty."

"Yeah, but you're gonna need some time to get ready."

"I don't need a bath. What about the snake? Can I keep it?"

"It looks like you already have it." I tapped the glass just so Joey would know I wasn't scared.

As I headed up the wooden basement steps I looked down at him standing in the corner, his snake on the workbench, his father's tools hanging on pegboards all around him. "Do you want me to tuck you in later?"

"I'm too old to be tucked in."

"I love you, Joey."

He looked up into the slice of light that came through the half-open kitchen door. "I'm sorry, Mom."

"What for?"

"You know how some people don't know how to say good-bye, so they start a fight?"

"Uh-huh, yeah. Are you mad that I went away?"

He stroked his snake. "I guess."

While Joey took his shower I called Esther. There was no answer.

8

Snow surrounded the old man like a clean white halo, and his gray eyes sparkled out of the darkness of his face as if he knew me. He leaned on a cane and was standing as close to City Hall as you could get and still stay behind the police barricades. Near him a trio of women warmed themselves by a garbage-can fire. They all wore layers of rags, their feet and heads wrapped in plastic. The old man stood staring at the fire as if he would rather freeze to death than go near it. That was when I remembered him. He seemed even more frail than he had the morning of the shelter fire.

"Hey, miss . . . miss . . ." He hobbled toward me, and the three women came my way too. Even in the bitter cold, the stench of unwashed human flesh was nauseating.

"Divine providence," he said, "that we should find you just when we need you."

The woman next to him nodded in a toothless grin. On her head she wore a turban of green plastic from which protruded strands of matted white hair. "God bless you," she said, "for helping us."

"We were just discussing the vagaries of politics and how the man at the top is often insulated from reality. You work here, do you?"

I nodded. Behind him City Hall looked like Versailles, but smaller.

"We need a message delivered to the mayor so he can spare himself and us too. Can you arrange an audience?" the old man asked.

I was about to explain the impossibility of that when the mayor's Lincoln Continental pulled past us to the foot of City Hall's steps. We all stared at the tinted windows. At the top of the steps Hunter and Raul stepped onto the portico. The mayor got out of the car. The old man's face lit with hope. "Serendipity," he cried, and rushed the barricade. "Your Honor, Your Honor!" He hobbled toward the mayor, flourishing his cane. The three women followed. So did I.

"Your Honor," the three grandmothers chimed. "Your Honor."

The mayor began to climb the ice-slick steps. The old man rushed to catch up. "Your Honor, Your Honor, if we can't speak with you, we must tell the press."

Now the mayor turned to look. Just then the old man tripped and fell up the steps, knocking the mayor down. The old man landed spread eagle over the mayor.

Raul ran down the steps to the mayor, and Hunter ran back inside. The old man was trying to get up off the mayor. "I'm sorry, Your Honor, my apologies," he kept saying.

Raul helped the old man up. As he made it to his feet he flailed his cane in the air. "Don't." He looked down at the mayor on the steps and his voice rang out in the icy stillness. "Don't turn your back. Someday you could be me."

Raul extended an arm to the mayor, who got to his feet, brushed himself off, and continued resolutely up the steps. The old man followed, still waving his cane. Hunter came running down the stairs with two cops making a beeline for the old man. The cops lunged toward him and caught him by the cane. As they did, the old man staggered and fell again, pulling them both down with him. I suppressed a laugh and then I saw that the old man was hurt. His mouth and nose were bleeding. "Your Honor . . . Your Honor . . . some vital information, Your Honor," he cried weakly.

The cops picked themselves and the old man up. They tossed the frail collection of bones into the back of the squad car and sped away. No sirens. The mayor caught his breath while leaning on a Corinthian column.

"A comment, Your Honor?" Raul shouted.

"You must be kidding, Vega," Hunter snapped as the head of security hustled the mayor into the sanctity of City Hall. I was still standing there with the trio of homeless grandmothers when Hunter came down the steps again. "Still agitating?" he asked sharply.

"Don't talk to her like that. She just wants to help," one of the old women admonished. I just stood there like Lot's wife turned to salt. "Nice tan," Hunter added as he turned to go back inside.

I stood for a moment longer, shuddering among the homeless and then I followed him up the icy steps. When I got inside, Raul was nowhere around. Hunter was standing by the door talking to the chief of security. I stepped past them and was about to pass through the metal detector when the cop on duty stopped me.

"Miss Terranova, you're going to have to put that purse on the conveyor belt," he said.

No one had ever questioned my purse before.

"You think I'm carrying a bomb?"

He smiled sheepishly. "Just following orders, ma'am."

Hunter stepped up behind me and walked through the metal

detector, briefcase in hand. No questions asked. I watched my pocketbook disappear behind some rubber strands. Hunter studied the skeletons inside.

"So where'd you go?" he asked.

"The Islands," I said, and grabbed my bag. Then, as I rushed away from him, I contemplated the worst-case scenario. The one I had been sure wouldn't happen. Could I have been spotted with Raul?

"Hey, look who's back!" Velma, the receptionist, stood hands on hips outside the door to my office. As I pulled my gloves off I tried to remember the "I'm in charge" routine I usually used for this part of the day. The girls from the steno pool were making coffee. Velma had this gleam in her eye that said she knew I had finally gotten laid. After I took my coat off and hung it on the rack with all the others, I went to my office, sat behind my desk, and tried to settle in. I had been away only four days, yet I felt like an impostor. I was sipping coffee and opening the mail when the mayor buzzed.

I grabbed a pad and pencil and headed for his office. He sat behind his desk in a very official pose and that look on his face as if a stranger had just opened the door. Or was I simply projecting my guilt?

He brought a hand to his cheek and I noticed that his fingernails were at the quick now. "A lot happened while you were away," he said accusingly. He didn't mention the incident on the steps and neither did I.

I sat down across from him, put my pad on my knee, and showed concern. "It was only two working days."

"Hunter says you were out there with that crazy old man just now."

"That old man was at the shelter fire. I told Brogan about that old man."

He got up, leaned against the wall, and put his thumbs into his belt hooks. "I could have been killed."

"I think he was just trying to tell you something."

"I can't listen to every fanatic in this city. I have to govern, for Chrissakes. I put more money into shelters than any other mayor in the country. I built them faster than government ever builds anything. For God's sake, in this city it takes six years of red tape to cut the ribbon on a school and I built those goddamn shelters in two years . . . and now some lunatic is trying to burn them all down and it's my fault!"

I sat rigidly in the ornate chair, afraid to say too much. Hunter had obviously been hard at work during my absence. I wanted to talk about Florida. To tell him what I had learned about Jason. But I knew if I did that, I'd be out on my ass. In City Hall bad news was always kept from the mayor. Nicosea fondled the miniature golden lion on the handle of his letter opener. I just sat there. The longer he whined, the more treacherous and somehow personally responsible for his misery I felt.

"So what happened to the old guy?" he finally asked.

"I don't know. The police took him away."

He sighed. "Good thing there weren't too many press hounds around. He'll get a disorderly conduct and a good meal. Those people belong in institutions anyway."

I didn't disagree.

"Take a letter," he said, and began wandering around the room, staring out the window, dusting the picture frames with his fingers as he always did while dictating. After the letter he told me he didn't want to be disturbed for the next few hours. I went back to my desk, and the phone began to ring incessantly.

For the next hour I made excuses for him and put everybody off. As I did that I began to remember who I was and to feel calmer. Then the mayor's wife called. I buzzed him just to give him the option. He said, "Not now, Marie. I don't feel up to it."

I covered for him. I said that he was in a meeting.

Half an hour later his father-in-law called. Again I buzzed the mayor.

"I thought I told you I didn't want to be disturbed."

"Yes, Your Honor, but it's Mr. Mendelssohn. I thought you'd want to know."

The pause on the other end was audible. "All right, put him through."

Mendelssohn always got through. Raul walked in. We hadn't spoken since the trip. I didn't want him in my office. I said, "Please take your questions to the press office."

"Is that by way of hello or do you have amnesia?"

He was smooth, cold as ice, but I heard the hurt deep down. I attacked before taking any time to notice how that gratified me.

"Leave me alone. This is dangerous."

"Dangerous how?" He leaned back as if struck by an absurdity. "For whom?"

"For me. It doesn't look right."

"You're paranoid," he said, and added, "I want to talk to you about Florida."

"I can't talk to you now."

"When? When can you talk?"

"Not now!"

Hizzoner's button lit up on the console on my desk and the telephone buzzed. I picked up. "Be right in."

Raul leaned across the desk, bringing his anger in closer. He wanted me to meet his eyes but I wouldn't. Instead I remained seated and stared resolutely at his crotch.

"When? When can we talk?"

I heard Nicosea's door into my office open. The door was behind me, Raul and the other door, in front. There was a powerful static in the air between us—so powerful the mayor must have felt it too. We stared at each other, the three of us, each from a different spot on the triangle. "Marie, did you hear me buzz?"

"Yes, sir. I did."

Raul's eyes said that he was wondering if there was anything between the mayor and me. Anything nonprofessional. Anything sexual. The mayor's eye caught mine. There was a look there for which I had absolutely no interpretation. This man I thought I knew so well, this man had a look in his eyes I had never seen before. As the moment crystallized there between the three of us I knew what it was—terror—pure, sheer, raw, utterly infantile terror. It didn't take him but a fraction of a second to recover, and as he stepped back into his own office he said to Raul, "Go back to Room Nine where you belong."

Raul smiled broadly. "Said the fly to the spider. It's always worth a try."

The mayor's knuckles went white and I saw his lips stretch thin, very thin. "What did you say?"

"*Nada,* sir, *nada.*"

I followed the mayor, notepad and pencil in hand, without so much as a backward glance at Raul.

As the mayor sat down behind his desk he said, "He's new. He was on the steps, wasn't he?"

"Yes."

"Is he the one you mentioned to me before?"

I was confused. I couldn't remember what he was referring to.

"From the *Miami Herald,*" he added.

"Yes." I nodded, vaguely remembering Raul's first day at City Hall. Had it only been three weeks ago?

"Ready to work now?"

I nodded and began shuffling the papers on my lap. I read him the list of letters he had to answer, papers he had to sign, so he could choose which to do now. He dictated a few responses and the others he left to me to write and sign.

It was several hours later as I was using the auto stamp—a stamp with a facsimile of the mayor's signature on it—that Brogan strolled in. He was so tall I had to crane my neck to look up at him. "Need Hizzoner?" I asked.

Brogan was one of three people who could always get in to see the mayor—the other two were Hunter and Mendelssohn. Not that Mendelssohn came around much. Otherwise the door remained closed unless you were on the schedule. Brogan fingered the oversized red calendar book I kept on the corner of my oversized desk. He ran his palm over the leather surface, then casually picked it up and leafed through it—like shuffling cards—not slow enough to see anything.

"These are sensitive times," he said, edging one cheek of his formidable derriere onto the corner of my desk. "Sensitive times, Marie, and we have to be conscious of that."

"You mean what happened on the steps?"

"What happened on the steps, Marie?"

"This morning . . . on the steps."

"Oh that," he said. "That was nothing, but I'm concerned about you."

Now he put both cheeks on the corner of my desk and continued to toy with the big red schedule book. "A reporter has been asking about you, Marie."

I tried not to let the instant quality of my panic rise to my face and eyes. "About me?"

I don't know why I knew it would be Raul, but I knew.

"You remember the call from the welfare hotel . . . the infanticide?"

"The grandmother . . . the suicide." I nodded as casually as possible, but my lips were dry.

"Yes, the phone call to the mayor you told Vega never happened."

"Yes."

"Well, he says he has evidence it did—did happen."

"The mayor never spoke to her," I said.

"But the call came through on his private line, didn't it?"

"Yes, it did."

"And you never gave it to the mayor. Instead you called 911."

I stood up. "He didn't want it."

"Marie, you shouldn't take unilateral action. I've told you that before. You should have asked the mayor."

"I did. I did ask the mayor."

"Look," Brogan said, "that's beside the point now. Just don't talk to Vega. Don't talk to him at all and don't talk to anyone else from Room Nine. This could be some sort of trap, and we want to protect you."

And then casually, ever so casually, he headed for the door, the schedule book still in his hands. Like leaving the chapel with the Bible.

"My book." I pointed. After all, it was my job to keep and disseminate the schedule.

"Oh," he said. "Oh, I think my office will handle the schedule for a while. There's so much going on right now, so many ridiculous requests to be put on his schedule that an additional buffer would be helpful for now."

And with that he walked out the door and took the most important part of my job with him. I didn't react because I couldn't. I had no one to complain to. Certainly not the mayor. That was never done. For the next hour things were so quiet I thought the city outside had disappeared. Or forgotten me. The phone didn't ring once. I thought about Jason, about the lethal silence of the fall from grace. Then Brogan stepped in again.

"By the way," he said casually, "I forgot to mention, Hizzoner also asked that for now, his calls be routed through my office, so I've told the switchboard."

"Why?"

"Well, to shield you, Marie. We have to be extra careful for a while."

As he stood in the doorway two maintenance men came in. One was reading something. "This slip says you want this picture hung up. Do you care where?"

I shook my head. My voice seemed stuck somewhere in my throat. In my turmoil I didn't even see Brogan leave. The maintenance men drove two nails into the wall and hung the picture across from my desk. Then they left too. The villagers in the painting seemed to grimace at me, their wild feet constantly moving. I noticed some drummers I hadn't seen before. In the back of my head I heard the drums beat, but in my office it was deadly silent. In two strokes Brogan had cut the heart out of my job.

That night I was on the path behind City Hall when I saw Raul coming toward me. Before I could decide what to do, he was next to me. "Sneaking around corners?" he asked.

Just then the back door to City Hall opened, and the same two maintenance men came out carrying three cardboard boxes—the boxes I had packed in Jason's office. My handwriting was on them. I ripped my eyes from the boxes to meet his. It was a very blue evening and the homeless had already started lighting their candles. Every night they had some kind of vigil. They began as soon as darkness fell, and now, in the deepest part of winter, darkness fell early. I watched the candles reflect in Raul's pupils, and from the corner of my eyes I saw the maintenance men climb down City Hall's backstairs, carrying the boxes.

I wanted to ask Raul if it were true. Was he asking the press office about me? But I didn't dare. He said, "Word is Channel Four is breaking a big Isenberg story tonight. Something hot, something completely new."

The maintenance men passed right next to us. I could smell the cardboard. I could feel Jason. I jammed my hands into my pockets and started to walk. Raul kept pace.

"I wanna work this story like everybody else and I'm holding back because of you, Marie."

I didn't say anything. The walkway ahead of us was empty, the snow shoveled neatly aside; behind us were the homeless in their vigil. The maintenance men carried the boxes into the Boss Tweed courthouse behind City Hall. Again through the back door. I wondered what Raul knew that he wasn't telling me. But that night I saw no point in trying to hold him back. Besides, how long would that last?

He leaned into me. "Be careful, Marie. This is bigger than either of us suspected."

For a moment I thought we were back in Miami and he was talking about us, the relationship, the feelings. Then I knew he meant the politics, whatever dirty secret lay behind Jason's suicide.

"Do what you have to do," I said. "But leave me out of it."

By now we were in front of the bronze statue of the founder of the *New York Tribune*, Horace Greeley. He towered over us in his fringed upholstered chair, a newspaper resting casually on his knee. For some reason we both stared down at the inscription beneath the statue. I knew that Greeley was a famous newspaper man back in the 1800s but the plaque read, "Near this spot stood the *New York World* whose publisher Joseph Pulitzer upheld the highest traditions of American journalism." Softly, Raul read the last line out loud: " 'An immigrant who rose to fame and fortune and never in the process lost the common touch.' "

I looked up at Greeley. He had a beard and looked kind of messy. Raul looked across at Park Row, where every great newspaper in the city had been housed at the turn of the century, and said, "Your guy has lost the common touch. He wants to stay in power no matter what the cost."

I stepped down into the mouth of the subway. A man was leaning into the wall, a stream of his urine spattered from step to step. As I tiptoed around it Raul called after me. "Be careful," he said. "Call me if you want."

The platform was crowded. The train didn't come. My coat weighed me down. I began to sweat, dizzy with fatigue. Finally I stepped to the edge to see if the train was coming. Two points of stationary light stood deep in the darkness of the tunnel. The lights shot forward and began to move. The impatient crowd hovered all around me at the platform's edge. I felt a hand on my back and something pushed me forward, hard. The train was seconds away. I saw myself down on the tracks, myself—pieces of me —arms, legs, severed head, and hands. A hand held me from my fall. Metal ground into metal and the train stopped. The electronic doors opened and the people rushed by. I turned to see the face of my savior. He seemed to pulsate there in a hard hat and baseball jacket. I wanted to thank him and searched his eyes for a place to begin. But they were cold and empty and knocked the gratitude right out of me. "Watch it," he said. "Not good to go too close to the edge."

I stumbled onto the train, collapsed in a seat, and watched the stations blur past. I felt as disconnected and disoriented as I had after Joe's death—but this time there was no knot of pain around my heart and no rage ready to explode. This time I felt nothing, a terrifying nothingness inside of me. The definitions were crumbling and soon the center would go.

I got out in SoHo, but instead of walking to my loft, I walked back to Little Italy. As I walked up Mulberry Street I heard a host of summer memories—children playing, old men telling stories, the gentle laughter of mothers who were always there. I passed behind the old St. Patrick's Cathedral. There in the locked graveyard lay the remains of Pierre Toussaint, born in slavery in Haiti, who had ministered to the poor here in America.

I returned to the happy sounds of the festival of San Gennaro when under arcades of light the saints traveled the streets on the backs of the faithful and the whole neighborhood was a carnival. I could smell the spicy Italian sausages, taste the deep-fried zeppoli covered in powdered sugar, and see the many street stands offering rosaries, nail polish, ashtrays, the Statue of Liberty, the Italian flag, and games of chance. I could taste and smell the sweets of childhood right through the thin winter air, but I could never go there again.

I entered SoHo's empty streets. The ones with no stores, no restaurants, no people, just the small factories that had been turned into lofts by artists back in the days when it was illegal. In the sixties, SoHo had been an artists' Eden where rents were cheap and lofts plentiful. Now only the wealthy could afford SoHo. Behind the Palladian windows and Corinthian columns, I saw another, older SoHo. A SoHo of sweatshops, where immigrants like my grandparents worked twelve-hour days. These days boutiques offered designer clothes, glittering handbags, lamé aprons, cowboy boots, Tibetan jewelry, and the finest art in the Western world. I had bought my way in with Joe's death benefits.

"Blood money . . ." I heard my mother's voice. Was she right? Had I brought the *malocchio*—the evil eye—down on me when I started to buy my way out of my mother's house? I was a lousy widow. I wanted, instead, to start my life over. But tonight, I was suddenly afraid.

The streets were dark and silent. An occasional truck was parked half on the sidewalk. I walked in the middle of the street, knowing my sneakers would make running easier if that's what I had to do. I thought about my demotion, how unspoken it all was —demoted on the inside, not on the outside. That's how it had begun with Jason. Would I be next to move to the basement?

My block was deserted. Above me carved in sandstone were griffins, lions, and winged creatures with human faces. I unlocked the outside door to my building. Inside, it was the color of pitch and I couldn't find the light switch. I stepped into the freight elevator, which was the only elevator. It was very quiet. I felt something sinister, a presence in the darkness. But I was alone. My heart began to pound. I turned the lever. A gear shifted. The elevator began to move. Then it bounced to a halt. I tried to open the door. It wouldn't open. I turned on the overhead light bulb in its socket. I heard the gentle shaking of the filament. The bulb was dead. The elevator rocked a little and so did my stomach.

The elevator was as big as a room, a room with no connections to the rest of life. It was full of emptiness, and then the emptiness was filled by a kind of clanking noise that seemed to originate below me. Was it a crazed lunatic, some rowdy teenagers, or the hand that had tried to push me off the platform? I crouched on the floor, folding into myself, and then I began to scream. After the echo of my screams subsided, there was nothing. Not even the noise downstairs.

"Help . . . help . . . I'm stuck on the fourth floor."

I tried the lever again. The elevator began to move. A moment later I was able to open the gate into my loft. The loft was a jungle of writhing shadows that wove around and into each other as headlights passed below. I stood on the threshold, afraid to enter, afraid that the intruder had preceded me, afraid even of the shadows. Then I heard a piercing electronic shriek that started deep inside the darkness. The telephone was ringing. I moved toward it and took the receiver from its cradle. The voice said, "I'm downstairs. . . ."

At first I didn't recognize it.

"Can I come up?"

Raul. It was Raul.

"You can't," I whispered. "The elevator's up here."

"Well, come and get me."

I put my groceries down, returned to the elevator, and got downstairs with no problem. He stood there obscured in the shadow of the mesh gate. I let him in. "You look like you saw a ghost," he said.

I was glad for his familiar face but I didn't say anything. I just started the elevator. Again, when the elevator got to my floor, it wouldn't open. This time I was more embarrassed than afraid. I jiggled the lever. Nothing happened.

"Let me," Raul said. "I think you passed your floor. Is the fifth floor occupied?"

"No, I'm the first tenant in the building."

The elevator went down a flight. He said, "The other floors are locked; that's why when you overshoot your floor you can't get out."

So there had been no adversary, only my own miscalculation. Once inside the loft, we both just stood there. I was breathing hard, trying not to let it show, hoping he wouldn't notice.

"I know what you're thinking," he said. "You're thinking what is this man doing here? Why isn't he gone from my life?"

I searched for the light switch. "Listen, let's put Florida behind us."

My groceries were in a bag on the counter. I reached in to begin unpacking. He leaned against the counter, blowing into his hands, which were red from the cold, and chose to misinterpret me. "Fine," he said, "let's start over."

"I don't think we can start over."

He reached into the bag and brought out the olive oil. "Let me stay and I'll cook for you." He pulled out onions, tomato paste, the green peppers, and the chicken breasts. "But I need rice."

"I was planning to make pasta. I make a pretty mean sauce."

"I'll bet. But my offer was to cook for you. I didn't say it would be your recipe."

He had his hand on the zipper of his coat. Either I told him now that he was welcome or he was leaving. I did want him to stay, but only because I was afraid of being alone. Everything about him threw me off balance. I put my face into my hands and started to cry.

I felt him move in close and put his hands on my hips. "Now, now," he said, tilting my head up so that he was looking into my eyes. "All that because I want to cook rice and not spaghetti?"

I laughed like a girl, a silly girl. I was so tense, my emotions were changing like quicksilver. He took his jacket off and put my apron on. I wiped my tears.

He washed his hands in the sink and asked for a big pot, a little pot, and a frying pan. Across the loft the shadows had softened. I gave him an unopened box of rice.

He washed the rice. He washed it several times. I asked, "Where did you come from?"

"Is that question cosmic or geographical?"

"What brought you to my doorstep?"

"I had a lousy day. I wanted to be with you."

He peeled the red onion and sliced it in half. Then he went on, "I was trying to get to talk to that old man who was on the steps today, but no go. The cops were very uncooperative. Something weird is up."

As I dropped the oil into the pan with the small blue flame underneath, the comforting smell of olives escaped into the air.

"I've been interviewing people about the shelter fires, and a lot of them mention this old man who was at the Donovan fire. Apparently, he keeps telling people he knows what started the fire. He says he saw it with his own eyes. I think it's the same guy."

He was chopping the onion fast and hard as he spoke, and when he finished, he used the knife to lift the onions into the oil. I took a wooden spoon from the drawer, stirred the onions, and said, "It is. It is the same old man."

Raul crushed a clove of garlic. "What makes you say that?"

The water started to boil over the rice. He cut the flame down and covered the pot.

"I met him the night of the fire. He was babbling. I thought he was paranoid and crazy."

"Why didn't you send him to me? That old man was the story."

"I didn't realize that. Besides, I was mad at you."

"Why? Because we made love or because you liked it?"

"Because you seemed to be enjoying yourself at the fire."

Raul said, "I'm a reporter."

I remembered the children, the flames, the stink of death. He sliced a chicken breast with my best knife. "There's an adrenaline rush when you have an exclusive. I can't deny that. It doesn't mean I don't hurt for those people just like you do."

I said, "I hated that the mayor didn't come."

"He couldn't. He was on his way to Washington."

My eyes said that that was a lie but my lips kept silent.

"Oh," he said, "it's like that!"

I sat down at the empty kitchen table; inside I was falling off that cliff again.

I said, "That apartment of yours looks like a woman's apartment."

"It is. It's a sublet just for a month. . . . Is that what's been bothering you? Is that why you left? Boy, you hold it in. We were just together for four days and you never even asked."

He checked the pots. I started setting the table.

"Well?"

"Well what?"

"Well, why did you leave that first night? Why did you shut me out after Florida? Why are you always mad at me?"

"I just wanted to get home before everybody woke up."

"Why? Were you ashamed of spending the night with me? I guess they didn't know who you went to Florida with?"

"Joey knew."

He looked surprised. Then a smile curved his lips. "But not Mama," he teased.

"No, not Mama."

We went around the bush like that until it was time to eat. The meal was wonderful.

"You're a good cook."

"This is nothing. I can do better, but not without the ingredients."

"I don't know why I get so mad at you. I just can't seem to trust you." A grain of rice caught in my throat. I coughed until I could breathe again. He watched me and then he said, "It's your husband, isn't it?"

"What do you mean?"

"You're stuck in the past," he said, "and determined to stay there."

I looked around at the unfinished loft and the striving for a new life that it represented. "That's not fair," I said softly.

"I understand. I understand how awful it is to lose someone with no explanation. Even with an explanation it's bad."

"I know what happened to Joe," I said. "He was undercover, and an undercover FBI agent on the same investigation shot him by accident."

Pity flickered in his eyes. "Didn't you ask yourself how the department could have made a mistake like that?"

I had asked but I didn't say so. I just waited for him to change the subject. Because he was right. I had never gotten an answer.

After we ate we washed the dishes together. As I put the last dish away he pushed me into the counter from behind. I felt the dampness of his apron. "Let's have dessert," he said. "It'll make us both feel better."

I turned around and took the apron off him. Then I tried to explain that it was impossible. He ignored me. I asked, "Anyway, how old are you?"

"Old enough," he said, reaching under my blouse.

"Really, how old are you?"

His expression soured. "I'm thirty-three, so what? How many hurdles are you planning to erect?"

He picked me up and sat me on the counter, then put the palm of his right hand between my legs. "I haven't stopped thinking about this."

"I just came from work."

"So?"

I made a face.

"You're hung up about that. Let's take a shower together."

We never made it to the shower. Instead he reached under my skirt and slipped my panties down. Then I played with his hair and listened to his tongue in my folds. At first I worried that I wouldn't taste good, but then I just closed my eyes and let go. I felt myself open, open petal by petal, and then one by one, the petals fell. I made some very strange sounds. He looked up at me, his face wet and satisfied. Then he stood up and dropped his pants around his ankles.

"Help me," he said.

I put my feet up on the counter and he slipped into me. He hooked my knees over his elbows. I grabbed his face. He groaned into my mouth. There was that rhythm again, our rhythm, the one we found every time we were inside each other. Our bodies grew damp. I reached down to his firm butt and pulled him into me again and again.

"Shit, yeah," he moaned, "give it to me. *Dame tu leche.*"

My nipples itched and ached. I bit his neck. I wrapped my legs around him, and as everything in me contracted I began to chant, "I love you."

I heard myself say it. I didn't mean to say it. I didn't know if I meant it.

"Say it. Say it. Say it to me."

"I love you."

The room around us fell away and we were all alone in the universe. There was no time, there was no place, there was only us, and this exquisite feeling that connected us. I lay back on the counter. He took my ass cheeks in his hands. I memorized his damp, golden face as his concentration deepened. A powerful pulse beat between us. *"Vente conmigo,"* he whispered. I didn't know the words but I knew what he meant. When he cried out, I let go.

He clung to me and his knees were shaking. We were both breathing hard. He pulled me off the counter. Its edge had carved a ridge across my butt. We laughed. I took him by the hand. "Let's lie down."

"I've got to go soon," he said. "I have no change of clothes and my car's parked down by City Hall."

I lit a small cathedral of candles and placed them in saucers around the futon. We lay down and held each other. After a while he climbed on top of me. This time was slow and gentle and sweeter than chocolate. When we finished, all the candles had grown short. We were surrounded by puddles of paraffin and he turned on the eleven o'clock news.

A reporter was saying, "No response from the mayor so far, but his press secretary had this to say. . . ."

The camera cut to Hunter standing in the rotunda with about twenty microphones pointed at him. "Gentlemen, I can't explain the discrepancy just yet. The official statement we put out after Mr. Isenberg's suicide was based on information provided by the family." He fell short of saying Esther's name, but I felt sure that must be who he was talking about.

"I assure you," Hunter said calmly, "no one wants to get to the bottom of this more than we do . . . and when City Hall knows, you'll know."

The piece finished with an outdoor shot of City Hall behind a small candlelight vigil of the homeless in their rags. Then a shot of the mayor getting into his car. Reporters ran after the Lincoln Continental with the tinted windows as if they were chasing the don of dons himself. The homeless watched like Mary and Joseph shut out of the inn.

The reporter signed off. "The mystery around the suicide deepens as leaked lab reports confirm that Deputy Mayor Isenberg's tumors were benign, while Isenberg's personal physician refuses comment. From City Hall, this is Dominic Vicker for News Four."

Behind him, the big hungry eyes of the homeless peered into the camera as if the answer were on the other side.

Raul turned to me. "That proves it," he said. His voice was

harsh with excitement. "That proves it. There is some kind of a cover-up going on."

"That's crazy."

He cupped my chin with his hands, forcing me to meet his eyes. "Remember what I told you in the Bahamas?"

I shook free of his hand. "What?"

"Isenberg was laundering money."

"That doesn't mean City Hall knew."

"This fake cancer story does. It proves they were stalling for time. Maybe they've known for a while. Maybe that's why he got shot down."

"They would have fired him."

"Not necessarily. Not in an election year. They'd be more interested in keeping it quiet than in cleaning it up. Think of Watergate or Iran-contra. Both times they kept a lid on the truth until after . . . after the election."

On the rooftops across the street lay a gray and melting snow. Below, a garbage truck groaned and crushed metal and glass. I pulled the blanket over my head and hid there in the salty smell of sex. I felt him hover over the futon. "Come out," he said. "Come out and face reality."

I sat up and looked at him. There we were, stark naked on opposite teams. He knelt by the futon. "You could help me, Marie. You could help me a lot."

I was braced for this moment when he would reveal his true intention. I think I had always known it was coming.

He went on, "We both know Isenberg approved a lot of those shelter contracts. We both know that must be where he was getting the graft. I want a list of the companies that got those contracts. If I request them under the Freedom of Information Law, City Hall will stall me for months and then it will be too late. The election will be over and the truth may never come out."

"Is that why you made love to me . . . to get the contracts?"

He didn't answer. He walked to the bathroom. I heard the door close. I felt foolish and fragile and old. How could I have allowed myself to think he wanted me for me? Finally he reappeared dressed and ready to leave.

"Ride me down," he said as if I had insulted him.

I wrapped myself in the sheet. "You didn't answer me."

"Just ride me down."

"I want my answer."

"You're asking the wrong question."

He stood by the elevator, hands in his coat pockets, casual as a man waiting for the operator. I pretended he didn't exist and never had.

"If you don't ride me down, I'll do it myself and you'll be stuck up here with no way to get out."

Arrogant bastard. I hated his guts. I got up and trudged over to him.

In the elevator the silence was icy.

Then he said, "When it comes to me, you believe what you want and it's never positive."

I didn't answer. He wrapped his scarf around his neck.

"You saw the fire. You saw what it did to those people. Don't you care?"

"I can't get the Pulitzer. I can only get fired. Did it ever occur to you that Jason might have been acting all on his own?"

"Unlike some people," he said, "I don't believe in fairy tales. I can't afford to."

"What's that supposed to mean?"

"You decide, Ms. Terranova. You decide."

He slipped into the night. Bastard! How could I have said that I loved him? Sex could make a person lose their mind. I called Esther but there was still no answer.

9

I was in a deep dreamless sleep when the phone rang. The digits on the clock said 2:30 A.M. I picked up.

He didn't bother to say hello. "Look, I'm sorry about before. I know it's late, but hop a cab to City Hall."

I hung up on him. The phone rang again. I picked up. "What for?"

"Trust me just this once."

"Leave me alone."

"Just this once."

I hung up but I went. As if preordained, an empty cab was coming up the block. "City Hall," I said.

The driver laughed. "Don't you know you can't fight City Hall? Especially not at this time of night."

The frozen streets were empty, and in minutes we approached City Hall. At Chambers Street a line of buses and police barricades closed Broadway. "Lady, I can't get any closer," the driver said into the rearview mirror, shaking his head. I paid him and got out. As he drove away I slipped under the barricades. A row of floodlights illuminated the eerie scene in City Hall Park. Tall helmeted silhouettes moved menacingly in front of me. I heard the nervous neigh of the horses and their hooves against the pavement. The cops on horseback wore full riot gear. Bluecoats on foot, also in riot gear, were moving into the park. They slashed at the tents and cardboard-box houses with their nightsticks.

"Wake up. Let's go. Time to move on."

"Into the buses. We don't want no trouble."

The homeless began to crawl out of their makeshift shelters. When they realized what was happening, they clung desperately to bushes, trees, and park benches, trying not to be moved. This enraged the bluecoats. They pushed, pulled, and kicked the homeless toward the waiting line of buses. The older people were tripping and falling. The cops grabbed them by their feet and dragged them over the hard, crusted snow. Every time a homeless person wriggled free of a cop, he or she ran back to the shantytown. This grotesque charade went on until the police shoved the wrong guy.

"Motherfuckers!" a voice screamed into the night.

Rocks and bottles began to fly. The police began using their nightsticks on flesh and bone. Cries of pain filtered through the searching floodlights. A bottle hit a bald head—a cop's head. The head split open. The blood was red, very red; it spread down the cop's forehead like a stain.

"Get those bastids," echoed from behind a plastic visor.

Horses with blinders on began their stampede into the crowd. Hooves on the pavement, screams in the dark, cursing faceless riders—in moments the fragile protestors were surrounded. Then, like cowboys herding steer, the mounted cops chased the homeless into the buses. After that, they silently demolished the cardboard-and-plastic shantytown.

I saw him then. He was leaning up against a building, his hat slanted over his eyes like Dick Tracy. A cop on horseback spotted me. "Get off the street, you dumb bitch!"

"Off the street!" The cop swung his nightstick like a polo player. His horse began to trot.

A terrible anger rooted me like a tree. I screamed, "Leave me alone! Leave these people alone!"

Raul ran toward me. He pulled me out of the horse's way. We fell. Hooves passed inches from our faces. I heard the cruel thud of the nightstick as it hit Raul's back. A few feet away a bus pulled out. People were chanting, "No housing, no peace." Others held their heads and cried.

I looked up at him. The sky was the color of smoke. A drop of blood hung from his nose. "Still say your mayor is a man of the people?"

"Get off me," I whispered hoarsely.

He was on all fours now, still unable to get up completely. I could see the pain in his twisted face. I gave him a hand. We helped each other up.

"How come you're not running for a phone?" I asked as we stood there, surrounded by the devastated shantytown.

"I can't afford to," he said. "If I bring in one more story I haven't been assigned to, Larry Pierce will make sure I get canned. I called all the news desks in town anonymously. But by the time they get down here, it will be over."

"Am I supposed to believe you called the competition?" Anger flamed in me. When would he stop lying?

"Why not? This little raid was timed to avoid press coverage. Tomorrow, City Hall will play it any way they want. Like Granada, no witnesses. The media will buy the party line, and the illusion will become the truth. But you saw for yourself. So you, at least, will know. And right now that's all I care about."

The buses rolled past us like cattle cars. "Why? Why me?" I asked as we walked uptown. It was pointless to try to get his car, which was behind the barricades.

"Because I want you to know the kind of people you're working for."

"You're not exactly working for Saint Peter."

After a while he said, "I'm having a lot of problems with that black bastard I report to."

"Larry Pierce?" Larry was the *Dispatch*'s City Hall Bureau Chief and a crackerjack journalist. "You curse a lot of people in your pursuit of truth."

He shrugged and it made him wince. "Pierce is one of those minorities who thinks there's only room for one."

"You hate so many people. What kind of crusader are you? How can you have it both ways?"

"Don't you?"

I thought about all my troubles at City Hall and said, "I never saw you tonight."

"Then I guess you didn't see what you saw either."

"I can't change anything. I'm not in a position to change anything."

"If you gave me those contracts, we could change it together."

I listened to the cadence of our tired footsteps until we reached SoHo. The night pressed down on us. When we reached my place, the gargoyles looked evilly down. He stopped. In the darkness the dirt on his face looked like a bruise. I said, "I need some time to think."

"I understand that."

"I need you to stay away from me for a while."

He took a step toward me as if he were about to touch me, then changed his mind. "How long?" he asked. "How long do you want me to stay away?"

I opened my hands in a gesture that was something of a plea. "I don't know, a few weeks, a month, I don't know."

He looked so stricken that I touched his dirty cheek and said, "Come on in and get cleaned up. Let's say good-bye like human beings."

Upstairs, as he washed the blood from his face and hands, I asked the question I hadn't asked earlier that night. "I hear you asked Hunter about me. I hear you asked if I called 911 from City

Hall the day that mother threw herself and her baby out the window."

"Hunter told you that?"

"Sort of." Actually it had been Brogan.

"That's really weird. Hunter invited me to an off-the-record get-acquainted lunch. He dropped a hint about you and the 911 call. When I didn't bite, he dropped it."

"They told me that you're out to get me."

"I am, but not that way."

He was thinking, trying to put the pieces together. "They're baiting you, Marie. I wonder why? Do you think we've been seen together?"

"I don't know. I'm not exactly popular on the job either these days."

He looked surprised. "But you're an insider."

"I was."

I handed him a towel. He dried his face and hands. "I never was. People like me have to make our own rules. Even on the inside we're outside."

"Do you make your own rules in relationships too?" I asked.

"In the heat of passion do you lie or do you tell the truth?"

"I hear you're a real Don Juan. That you use sex to get sources. That there's a trail of women you've used from Miami to New York."

He looked at himself in the mirror. "Those women wanted me to use them. They used me just as much. It was no one-way street."

In the mirror I raised an eyebrow.

"All right, true is true," Raul said. "I have been what you say. It's expected of me, Latin lover, you know. It's expected of me. Even at Harvard. People do what's expected of them, you of all people should know that."

"Me of all people?"

"Until me, your whole life was about meeting other people's expectations. You're changing. I can change too."

I said, "You're such a mass of contradictions."

He put his coat back on. "You're not? In bed you say you love me, on your feet I can't be trusted."

"It was the kitchen counter, not the bed."

He laughed. "Still . . ."

Then, as I rode him down for the second time that night, he said, "It would be good if we could separate my flaws from your paranoia."

It was my turn to laugh. But in my heart I promised myself I would stay away from him.

The next morning the homeless were gone. Only the extra barricades and a half-dozen cops on horseback said that they had ever been there. In the light of day the cops wore no riot gear. Inside City Hall, the mood was almost festive. The papers reported that the homeless had been peacefully relocated during the night. A few advocacy groups claimed excessive use of force, but the police commissioner and Hunter had denied it. For the first time in a long time, the mayor was in his office and available. I handed him his coffee just the way he liked it. He looked happily out the window at his antiseptic view. Then, as he took his first sip, I asked, "Did you hear that the Coalition for the Homeless says a lot of people got hurt last night?"

His face flushed and he tugged on his elegant pinstripe jacket as if it didn't fit right. I could see him searching for an answer just like Joey when he knew he was wrong. He picked up his cup and burned his tongue on the coffee. He banged the cup back down with an evil look. "These days it's almost as if you were on the other side, Marie."

"Other side?"

"A campaign is war. Think of it as war. You have to be prepared to make sacrifices."

"I'm confused. You told me Isenberg had cancer but the lab tests show his tumors were benign."

"I told you Jason was nuts at the end. Maybe he lied to me."

"Why did you let Brogan take the schedule book and the call sheet away from me?"

He sighed deeply. I was hanging myself. "Marie, I can't get into personality conflicts. I'm the mayor, for Chrissakes."

"Then why didn't you tell me yourself?"

He tried to hide behind a solid mask of arrogance. I saw through it and he knew it.

"You could tell Brogan to give my responsibilities back to me,"
I said as gently as I could manage.

He got up and walked to the window. He tapped the pane with
his nailless fingers, still trying to hide the fact that he wasn't his
own man, but his discomfort left no other explanation.

I felt something seep from me, drain down my body, out my
feet onto the floor, where it evaporated unseen. All the faith and
hope that I had tied up in him faded. I stood there feeling like I
had felt years before when my mother told me my father was dead.
Finally, when he had gathered himself, he studied me paternally.
"After we've won, it'll be different, you'll see."

The conversation was over.

Rather than sit in my office, I went to the meditation room in
the basement. It was a large room with simple red couches meant
to be a church without denomination, but you could tell that it
was a place of meditation and worship. Inside, I found several
workmen painting the walls.

"Remodeling?" I asked.

One of the men shook his head. "No, this room is being
turned into an office."

"Why?"

"It's a waste of space, no one uses it anymore."

I headed back to the stairway, wondering where I could go for
solace, when I saw a face I hadn't seen in a long, long time. Joe's
partner, Mel Davis. He was coming out of the City Hall police
station but he was not in uniform. His chocolate-brown face was
warm and familiar but troubled too. He stopped. "Hey, little lady,
what are you doing down here in the trenches?"

He offered his hand and I shook it stiffly. The only time we had
ever hugged was at Joe's funeral. I said, "I work upstairs."

"No kidding. I never had you figured for—"

I interrupted, "I'm the mayor's administrative assistant."

An eyebrow went up. "Powerful lady."

"What about you? How's life?"

I started walking again. Mel fell into step beside me.

"Oh . . ." He gestured with his hand in a way that made him
seem just as lost as I felt. "Oh," and then he added, "I left the
department."

I stopped. So did he. I asked why.

"Things change, things happen, people change."

For a moment neither of us said anything. Then he added, "I changed directions after"—he gestured again and studied my face as if looking for a sign—"after . . ."

I finished for him. "After Joe died."

He nodded. We headed up the narrow steps together. "My office is right across the street on Park Row. I run my own little shop now. I'm a PI."

"What?"

"Private investigator."

"How is that?"

"It's okay," he said. In the curve of the stairwell he asked, "Something's wrong, Marie. What is it?"

I looked into his eyes and the past welled up. It made the present seem unbearable. I shrugged because words wouldn't come.

He said, "I'm taking you to lunch, lady—no ifs, ands, or buts."

We sat across from each other in the semidarkness of the Irish restaurant/bar and neither of us knew what to say. My misery seemed to reflect in his deep black eyes. I dressed better than I ever had. I paid more attention to my makeup. So nobody had challenged the illusion that everything was all right with me. And now this man from the past took one look at me and knew different.

I studied the mahogany-paneled room with its dark mirrors, the few light bulbs under red shades. At the bar, cops, bailbondsmen, and ambulance chasers drank in merry camaraderie. The waitress came with the menu. I ordered a cheeseburger with lettuce and tomato. Mel ordered the vegetable platter. I asked for water. Even that was gone now. In New York City you couldn't assume you'd get water just because you sat down in a restaurant. I was thinking about insignificant things like that, I guess because he was making me nervous. He rubbed his hands together, readjusted his athletic frame on the bench, spread the napkin on his lap, and said, "I'm off meat these days."

"A vegetarian private eye! I bet the guys have a field day with that."

The water arrived. We each sipped from our glasses.

"Yeah." He wiped condensation from the outside of his glass with a finger. "In life you gotta do what you gotta do. I'm trying to get back to teaching t'ai chi. But it's hard to make a living that way."

Mel was a t'ai chi master. He had taught Joe in 'Nam long before they became a salt-and-pepper team on their Bed-Sty beat. He had stood by Joe in a neighborhood where it was definitely not chic to like whites. They were both reluctant cops. After Vietnam, unlike WW II, the GI Bill was so severely curtailed that becoming a cop seemed their best option for earning a decent buck. I said, "You and Joe had fun together, didn't you?"

"Big fun."

We both silently remembered.

"Yeah," he said, "we kind of got into that cops-and-robbers shit for a while, but it turned out to be . . ."

He left the sentence hanging, I figured because of the way it had ended for Joe. Then he looked at me proudly. "But you did all right for yourself, Marie. I know the kind of heart that took." He added, "We do it for our kids. We keep going regardless."

I nodded. My hamburger arrived and so did his vegetables. As I fought with the cap of the ketchup bottle I said, "I like my job."

The cap finally came off. I turned the bottle over and waited.

"You don't seem happy, though, Marie."

I slapped the small glass circle that was the bottom of the bottle a few times. He began to cut his broccoli stalks. A lump came to my throat. The lump cut off my air. I watched the ketchup spill out onto the meat.

He took the bottle and put it back on the table. "Listen, I'm calling Anji. You're coming to dinner. I know you can talk to her."

That night after work we met at the Lexington Avenue line and went uptown together. Mel and his family lived in the Shomberg Plaza at 110th and Fifth Avenue. The Shomberg was two thirty-five-story octagonal towers on the corner of Frawley Circle. Frawley had been a state senator and Tammany politician back in the 1800s when Tammany Hall was the most powerful organization in New York City party politics. Tammany politicians had milked the city like a cow. I didn't know how much of the cream, if any, Frawley had drunk.

The two high rises stood like vertical islands in a sea of decay. A lot across the street was piled high in auto carcasses. A mural on the wall above showed workers straining their muscles to build something that disappeared into the darkness. The towers themselves were up on a plaza where bored teenagers killed time while waiting for life to begin or justice to arrive.

I knew I had never been in this building before, but it seemed strangely familiar. "Why do I feel like I know this building?" I asked Mel as we stepped into the lobby.

He pushed the elevator button. "There was a fire in this building. Seven people died. People jumped from their balconies to escape the flames. Maybe you saw it on television."

"I think I did. I did see it on television."

The door slid closed. He said, "It's worse than that because it could have been prevented."

I felt the elevator move upward and asked Mel what he meant.

"This building was a joint city-state venture. Everybody cut corners. Everything was done on the cheap. The architect's plans weren't followed. The garbage compactor chute was poorly constructed, for six years tenants' complaints about the fire hazard were ignored, the sprinkler system didn't work, and yet the building always passed fire inspections. As the fire spread at least twenty-one calls to 911 were ignored."

"How is all that possible?" I asked.

He said, "This is Harlem."

When Anji opened the door, it was like stepping into the arms of an old comfortable friendship. As cops' wives we had shared our deepest fears. She wore a sarong and a silk blouse and her long black hair was pulled back. At forty she still looked no more than twenty-six. There was a warm smile in her Oriental eyes and a smoothness to her brow that belied everything she had been through. I just stood there filling my heart with her beauty until she pulled me inside. I said, "Hello, stranger."

She was still holding me when she said, "Friend, not stranger . . . always friend."

Then she stepped back. "When Mel called to say he saw you, I couldn't believe it."

She took my jacket and studied my new look. "Elegant, very elegant," she said.

"You look pretty good yourself," I told her.

Anji was tall for a Vietnamese and very beautiful. Her cheekbones were high, her face wide, her skin a brown gold, and her mouth perfect like a heart.

"Come sit down." She led me into a living room that looked like a garden. The coffee table was low, the L-shaped couch comfortable, and lush green plants hung from the ceiling. A Buddha carved from stone sat on a lotus.

"Can I get you ladies some wine?" Mel asked.

Anji looked at me. I nodded. "Sure."

"Red or white?"

"Either one."

"That bad?" Anji said gently, and took one of my hands in hers.

I said, "Thank God you weren't home the night of the fire."

She looked down sadly. "Some of our friends were not so lucky."

Mounted on the wall across from me, a young naked girl ran from the fire on her own back. It was a black-and-white photo of the Vietnam War, and I had seen it before. As I looked at the photograph I saw the shelter fire—the eyes, the many eyes, children, mothers, and then I saw Joe's waxen face, silent and still as a statue.

"Why do you have that picture?" I asked.

"So we never forget," she said.

I told her about being at the Donovan Shelter fire and how the suffering I had seen that morning had shaken my faith in City Hall. I looked at our intertwined fingers, and it seemed that all I had ever wanted to do was forget. Forget and run. As fast as I ran, my memories ran faster—always waiting wherever I arrived.

I looked over at the Buddha's serene composure, his hands resting on his knees, thumb and middle finger meeting in a circle. The green plants that hung around us seemed to vibrate, and my heartbeat slowed way down until I could hear myself breathe and the running stopped. Anji held me to her warmth and I began to cry. Somewhere at the edges of my grief, I could hear Mel puttering in the kitchen.

My chest was tight and full and it seemed a long time before the pain was emptied out and there was silence. I reached for the Kleenex on the coffee table and I blew my nose, I blew it several times. The damp tissues I kept in my palm. Mel ambled in with a bottle and three glasses on a tray, which he placed in front of us and headed for the stereo. Billie Holiday began to sing "My Man." Anji shot Mel a look. He grinned sheepishly and said, "How about a little Coltrane?" The music changed to a saxophone that melted body into soul. Anji smiled. "Open the bottle, honey, and join us."

He looked at me. "You sure?"

I took my shoes off and pushed deep into the soft couch. "Absolutely."

Then as I watched how comfortable they were with each other, I added, "It's been almost three years since we last saw each other."

They looked at each other guiltily. He said, "We just kind of lost touch."

After Joe's death, all my married friends had eventually cut me off.

"Mel says you have an important job now."

He filled our glasses. I took mine. "It was good for a while but now it's not so good."

She said, "Nothing stays the same."

Mel sat down across from us. The love between them was like an aura that touched me with its warmth. After the small talk, I opened up. I talked about the last three years. About going to City Hall for an explanation of Joe's death. How could a police officer and an FBI agent be on the same investigation and not know about each other until one had shot the other?

"There never was any answer to that," Mel said.

"The mayor was very kind to me," I said. "He wanted me to feel useful and busy. He personally would call and invite me to press conferences when he declared war on drugs."

"He's been declaring war on drugs every summer he's been in office and twice in every election year. And every year the problem is worse," Mel said, and I could feel him contain his anger. A question popped into my head that I hadn't expected to ask: "Does the police department have copies of all the calls that come in to 911?"

He looked at me oddly. "There's a tape. The department holds on to it for about ninety days."

"Could a reporter get to hear it?"

"Under the Freedom of Information Law, he could. Or if he had a buddy, a source on the inside, he could get it a lot quicker."

Mel shifted his large body in the chair and studied Anji's lovely face. He leaned forward, his voice low and conspiratorial. "Why are you asking about the 911 tape?"

I explained about the call from the welfare hotel and the trouble I was in for having called 911 from City Hall.

"So ironic," Anji said, "so ironic."

"It's no big thing," Mel said. "Just a strange coincidence."

"What?" I asked.

"Mel called 911 the night Joe was shot. He felt trouble coming when they got separated. But there was no response until it was too late."

"I called in a 10-13, officer in trouble. No call is taken more seriously than a 10-13. So I wanted to know what happened."

"I didn't know about that call."

"During the investigation I told about that 911 call but the FBI had subpoenaed the tape."

"How come you never told me?"

"There was an internal-affairs investigation going on. I was sworn to secrecy. Joe and I were on a big drug case and we were just the New York arm of a federal case. I didn't even tell Anji until two years later. Not that it means anything," he said. "It's just an odd coincidence."

I felt trapped between the Buddha and the picture of the child running from the napalm on its own back. Running but unable to escape. I began to wonder about something. And then Mel put the question into words.

"How did you get that job at City Hall?"

A tall, lanky teenager in Reeboks and a running suit came in through the front door before I could answer. Under his arm he held a basketball. His hair was cut into a fez. He was a cross between his mother and his father, golden-skinned and very handsome. He looked at the three of us. "Hello," he said, surprised but very polite.

Mel stood up angrily. "Where've you been? Where do you think you've been?"

"I shot a few baskets in the park. You told me yesterday I could."

They glared at each other, father and son. Then Mel turned to me. "Marie, you remember Kareem?"

"Nice to see you again," I said, not sure that he remembered me.

Mel looked pointedly at his watch. "Shooting baskets is one thing, but I better not find you out there mingling, hear."

"Yes, sir."

The teenager excused himself and went to his room.

I looked at Mel. I was used to him being so gentle. "Wasn't that a little harsh?" I asked.

"I don't have much choice. I have to keep him on a short leash because the pull of the streets is like a hundred magnets."

"Wait a few more years and see what happens with Joey," Anji told me.

I laughed a little. "Joey's already jumping with hormones."

Mel sat down again and leaned toward me. "You don't think this could be history repeating itself?"

I didn't know what he meant and my expression said so.

"I got shot down after insisting about that 911 tape. They had me driving a desk until I quit. I still think that something was wrong with the way that investigation was put together. We were supposed to be eavesdropping on a big drug deal, but some heavy names were mentioned in those calls."

"Like who?"

"The Brooklyn party boss for one."

"Old Vic Milano?"

"Yeah, and the night Joe was killed he had caught another big name, somebody at City Hall. He was on his way to tell me what he had figured out when he got shot."

He stood up, blocking the light from the floor lamp. A shadow fell over the room.

I got up and headed for the balcony. There was a long deadly silence, and after a while I realized it emanated from me. I felt like I had stumbled over backward and fallen off a cliff. Outside, night had fallen. "How come you never told me that?"

He spread his hands as if to say he wished he had. "I was told there was a heavy-duty investigation going on and that it was my job to keep quiet, talk to no one. And back then I believed them. I believed that they were investigating. Now I think they were covering up—what I don't know."

I said, "Let's get some air."

Anji opened the balcony door. We stepped outside. Below us, the city was alive. Headlights moved in all directions. We could see down Fifth Avenue with its glitz and money-is-no-object glitter. Behind us lay Harlem and the bitter passions and desolation of a betrayed community.

"How's your boy?" Mel asked.

"He's still with my mother," I said. "I'm just now getting settled in the loft."

"It's hard raising a kid in this city," he said, leaning forward into the panorama that surrounded us. "Kareem likes jogging and I have to tell him he can't because in this town when the cops see a black teenager running, they get trigger happy."

"I'm afraid for him all the time," Anji said.

We looked at each other, sadly estranged. I said, "I'm afraid for Joey because he's white."

Mel put an arm around his wife. "If it was up to the politicians, we'd be in a race war tomorrow. Maybe we already are."

"What do you mean?" I was just asking now. I wasn't defending anymore.

"Poverty is partners with racism," he said. "Poverty lets politicians squander money on graft, kickbacks, and patronage. Then when nothing gets better because poor people were never helped, racism gets the pols off the hook."

I thought about how he and Joe had been best friends.

"How did you and Joe do it?" I asked. "How did you get around all that?"

Mel chuckled. "When your lives depend on each other, you learn how to get along. When you see a man holding his guts in his hands, you realize we're all the same under the skin."

Anji touched his cheek. "Seven years after the war, Mel had post-Vietnam syndrome. Him and many others."

"What's that?" I asked. A breeze rose out of the night. I was thinking how in life you think you know and then you don't know.

She said, "Delayed reaction, depression, anger, nightmares. He would wake up in the middle of the night reliving battle scenes, sleepwalking. He'd get up, grab the bedpost as if it were a gun. The way he looked at me, I didn't know what his eyes were seeing. Maybe Viet Cong. I was afraid. Afraid he would forget I am the woman he loves and see the enemy."

"The enemy that never was the enemy," Mel said.

Her laughter was sad and soft and then she said, "Americans search for the enemy, but often there is no enemy except inside. Inside the heart."

10

"No, my fault," she said. "Whatever happen no my fault. I told you. I told you he's no good."

My mother stood there, her arms defiantly folded across her chest. In her eyes I saw the fear. Joey's trunk was packed and waiting by the door where I had left it the night before. But Joey was gone. For the third time I asked, "Where is Joey?"

"He bring home trash, trash from projects."

"A friend from school?"

"I tell him no, you send this boy home. He say no, he say boy go, he go."

"How could you do that? How could you be so goddamn stubborn?"

She spread a hand over her heart for emphasis. It got lost in cleavage. "He in my house. He suppose listen to *me.*"

"I told him he could always bring his friends home. We talked about that. That's what homes are for!"

Because I had started yelling, she walked away from me into the safety of her kitchen. I followed.

"This friend no good," she insisted.

"Joey's friends are okay. You know what the world is like out there, Mama. We should thank God he's not running in a gang or using drugs."

She headed for the stove and busied herself checking the contents of the pot that stood on a low flame. "You can't control him. He needs a man to control him."

"I'm a good parent, Mama. I'm sick and tired of your putting me down. That's why I moved to Manhattan."

Tears began running down her cheeks. "He suppose listen to me. This *my* house."

She seemed to fold into herself, and the sobs that racked her fat little body were deep with grief. A terrible wave of guilt washed through me. I felt suddenly weak. Like a child again, a guilty child who had done something bad. Resisting the temptation to comfort her, I asked, "This boy. This boy Joey left with. Did he have a name?"

"Cal," she said, reaching into her soggy pockets for a hanky.

"Cal Scott?"

She nodded. I walked out.

I headed for the Bay Parkway, where the subway rumbled overhead. Under the L, Cadillacs and Lincoln Continentals inched slowly along. Inside the cars, Italian teenagers with slick hairdos engaged in some kind of mating ritual on wheels. The teenagers leaned out of their car windows in animated conversation. Spring was a long way off, but in their T-shirts, skintight jeans, and new-wave outfits, they looked like summer. At the traffic light, whether it was green or red, all the cars stopped. The teenagers climbed out

of their cars, often through the window, to consummate their ne-
gotiations. They kissed, cooed, and rubbed bodies. Some switched
cars. In the neighborhood the suspicion was that these were the
kids of the mob. Who else drove that kind of a car at seventeen?

I passed by the Italian bakery, the Italian grocery stores, and
the *salumeria* with its hanging braids of garlic, mortadella, and sa-
lami. Then I turned off the parkway. Suddenly the streets were
uninhabited. Street lamps were broken. One-family houses stood
abandoned. Dirty snow was piled in crusty heaps. A cyclone fence
told me that this was the demilitarized zone. Single-edged razor
blades on circles of barbed wire sliced the sky. The fence protected
hundreds of dilapidated buses in the Transit Authority depot. The
depot separated the Italians from the Latinos and the African-
Americans.

The Marlboro Houses loomed like a prison compound. Here
most of the people were dark-skinned. On the benches and cement
walkways between the buildings, the few remaining elderly white
couples sat like statues among a lively population of black teenagers. As I passed by I got a lot of tough looks. I stepped up to a
young crowd and asked for Cal Scott. The teenagers looked at me
as if I were a rare species of cockroach. "Never heard of him, lady.
You sure you're in the right neighborhood?"

A pretty young girl studied me as if I had personally created
this rotten world. She glanced up. I followed her eyes to a catwalk
outside the building behind us. Wire mesh lined the sides of all the
buildings. Behind the wire mesh, every floor had a catwalk, like
tiers in a prison. "Cal lives up there in 4-E," she said.

I thanked her and walked toward the building. Behind me, one
of the boys demanded, "Why'd you help that white bitch?"

"Mind your business. I take my orders from my mama, not
from you."

I climbed the outside stairs of the building to the fourth-floor
catwalk. Through the pattern of the wire mesh, I watched nervous,
determined mothers on the ground below. Holding children
tightly by the hand, trying to spot danger wherever it might arise,
these mothers wove their way through drug dealers and users. I felt
like a rat in a dangerous maze. How could anyone live like this day
in, day out?

When I found 4-E, I pounded on the door until Cal let me in. Joey was on the floor, bent over an open book. The only light came from the window. In the corner a toddler bounced in a playpen that shook as if it would fall apart. Joey looked up casually. Cal sat pale and still as a big doll. I had expected him to be black, but he was white—very, very white.

"How could you, Joey? How could you scare us like this?"

He gave me a silencing look and then he turned to the fragile-looking preteen who watched me with dark blue eyes.

"Mom, this is my friend Cal."

"I'm sorry about what happened," I said to Cal.

"That's okay." His voice was soft and slurred.

Joey returned his attention to the book on the floor. I waded over clothes, newspapers, and empty takeout containers to step deeper into the room. The window was so crusted in grime, it seemed to be a part of the crumbling walls. Somewhere a faucet was dripping.

"You transpose these two numbers," Joey said, and then without looking up at me he added, "We're doing our math. We were gonna use my computer but Grandma wouldn't let us."

Outside, a firecracker or a gun went off. Something with a long naked tail slipped behind the stove. The pale boy shuddered. I walked over to the playpen. The child looked up at me, desperately hopeful. I couldn't tell if it was a boy or girl.

"How old . . . ?"

"Linda. She's almost two."

At the sound of her name Linda squealed and stretched her arms toward me. The small dirty face begged to be set free. I picked her up. The smell of urine enveloped us both.

"Where's your mother?" I asked Cal.

He shrugged but didn't answer.

I looked around for a place to sit. A box spring on the floor was covered by a naked mattress. I sat gingerly, the wet two-year-old squirming in my arms. Joey and his friend continued with their homework. The unmistakable staccato of an automatic rose from the courtyard and penetrated the stillness in the room between us.

The door kicked open and she came in, freckled face, wild red hair, shorts, and halter top. She was twenty or twenty-one and slightly pregnant. A paper bag inside a plastic bag dangled from one hand. With the other, she pushed a stroller that held a baby that looked about six months old. The baby hung half-conscious, eyes closed, mouth open, strapped to the stroller in a dirty snow-suit. Its hair was plastered to the little head with sweat. On the girl's right leg hung a four-year-old who was very tired of walking.

She put the bag down on the floor, then looked at me as if I were just another reptile that had wandered in from the jungle.

"Goddamn motherfuckers. You can't walk near the street lamps because they shoot at your shadow for sport." Her accent was undiluted Appalachia.

Then she added, "What the fuck is going on here?" She took the two-year-old from me and put her back in the playpen. The child began a high-pitched scream.

I stood up.

"She's my mom," Joey said. He had obviously been here before. I moved toward the door.

I said, "Nice to meet you. I just came to pick up Joey."

I didn't know if she had heard me or not. She pulled some Rice Krispies from one of the bags. The three girls whined like reso-nating violins. She looked around for a place to sit and picked the box spring I had just vacated.

"My son was helping your son with his homework," I said.

"Let's go." Joey shut me up.

She twisted a bottle cap on a jar of Beechnut baby food, picked up a spoon from the floor, and wiped it on her shorts. Then she shoved a spoonful of spinach into the baby's mouth. The baby was screaming so hard that the spinach dribbled back out. The mother gathered the green dribble from the baby's chin and shoved it back into her mouth. The baby dropped her head into her chest and hiccuped. Then she tasted the spinach. She stuck her fingers into her mouth and sucked frantically. I headed for the door. As I said good-bye the mother poured the Rice Krispies into three bowls and turned on a TV that sat on the floor by the playpen. The screams of the children mingled with the evening news. Joey closed the door behind him.

The narrow, unlit hallway smelled of grease and stale urine. Three men knelt in a circle like campers around a fire. They looked up at me. Blood flowed down the crook of an elbow in a thin red line. The hypodermic needle went from one hand to the other. "I'm next."

"That's not fair, I'm always last."

As I reached the elevator I could feel Joey behind me. He said, "Let's walk."

In the half-light of the stairwell a small female leaned against the wall, her pants pulled down around her knees. She sucked on a glass pipe in which a milky-white substance swirled. Behind her two men were hard at work. One masturbated, his hand motion fast and steady. The other pumped her from the rear. She made no sound at all and neither did we. We just continued on down—over empty crack vials and used rubbers.

In the courtyard of the projects the evening froze into itself and the people seemed as still as mannequins, their dark faces pale as agony. Agony in every shade. Even the young people in frozen laughter seemed impaled on the miserable end of an empty day. The smell of garbage that should have been picked up weeks ago laced the air. Decay sprouted from the buildings, the lampposts, the pavement beneath our feet. In my heart I had no explanation for any of it.

"What are you trying to do—make me crazy? This place is dangerous as hell."

"Cal isn't the only friend I have who lives here."

"Nobody should have to live like this."

He gave me a long look that was deep with contempt. "You work at City Hall, don't you?"

"I wish you hadn't seen that in the hallway just now."

"Why?"

"It gives you the wrong idea about sex."

"I know all about sex," he said.

"How could you walk out on Grandma like that? She almost had a heart attack."

He looked at me as if my routine were pathetically transparent but the anger in his eyes was unmistakable and hardened in a way I had never seen before.

"Your trunk is packed. You knew I was coming to get you today."

We walked past a trio of garbage heads. They were passing a pipe, a glass pipe, crack, the deadliest high of all. A kid with sores on his mouth pirouetted toward me, "Oops," he said, "sorry, lady." His eyes locked into mine. He swayed like a cobra about to strike. Joey grabbed my hand and pulled me along.

"What made you decide to finally come and get me?" Joey asked. "Why now? Why not when I wanted to come with you?"

"Your room is ready now and I've found you a decent school."

He said, "Cal's quitting school."

"He can't quit school. The law says he has to stay in school until he's sixteen."

A coldness in his eyes said that I had really fallen in his estimation.

"He can't get any sleep in that apartment. He's got three baby sisters, his mother uses drugs. He can't get his homework done, so the teachers treat him like shit. The kids hate him too, even though he's a nigger like me."

He shoved his hands deep into his pockets and searched the low narrow horizon.

I said, "We don't use that word and besides he . . . you . . . he . . ."

"You're not with it, Mom."

"I've never heard you talk like that before. You know we don't use that word."

"In my school you're either a nigger or a nerd. Us niggers are the homeboys, we're hip. The nerds get their asses kicked every day."

"Still, we don't talk like that."

Joey gave me a glance that cast the evening in stone. My heart pumped silently. I felt if we didn't reach each other now, we never would. He said, "The word is the problem?"

I said, "Words can hurt."

He said, "Grandma's prejudiced."

"Grandma's scared."

We passed a group of teenagers. Guns bulged under their jackets. A tall thin junkie held a tall thin Doberman on a leash.

"Mom, do you know anything about Dobermans?"

"Not really."

"They're very gentle animals, really sensitive. You look at them wrong and their feelings are hurt. People turn them into killers."

"How's that?" I asked, grateful that he was talking to me.

"They lock the dog in a room and scare the hell out of him. They yell, rattle chains, hit him. After a while the dog turns into a killer. Then nothing can change him back."

"Joey, can we be like we used to be together?"

"I packed my computer," he said.

"That's great. Maybe you'll teach me some of the stuff you do with it."

"I create puzzles, then I solve them," he said, "or sometimes a puzzle just falls into your lap."

"What kind of puzzle?"

He didn't answer. I wanted to ask again but we were already back at the house.

My mother stood waiting behind the glass door that replaced the screen door in winter. Joey climbed the steps ahead of me, shoulders stooped as if he were carrying the burdens of a much older man. I watched him open the door, ready for anything. But now she wasn't angry, she was affectionate. She pulled him to her, shoved his head between her breasts, and sobbed.

"Grandma . . . Grandma," he said. "It's okay."

"You gonna visit Grandma, Joey?"

He hugged her tight. "Of course, Grandma. I love you, *nonna.*"

She pushed him away. "No. You no lova me no more."

A powerful guilt took the shine from his youthful face. I stepped between them. "Mama, we're coming to see you Sunday. Sunday, *va bene.*"

She looked at me with a kind of confused venom. "Joey, help your mother carry your things to the car."

Between us we dragged the footlocker Joey had inherited from his father. In the yard the rope we had bound it with snapped. We picked up the locker and carried it through the crusted snow like pallbearers. In the shadows of the leafless trees I felt a secret joy. Joey's eyes said he felt it too.

Half an hour later, the world's first and prettiest suspension bridge, the Brooklyn Bridge, lay before us, a gateway to our new life together. A gateway built by immigrant sweat. On the other side the city glittered like Mecca. Joey was starry-eyed. He pointed to the Statue of Liberty out there on an island. The Mother of Exiles. She was colossal, regal in her flowing robes, her burnished copper softened to green by the years, her feet stepping forth from broken shackles, the Declaration of Independence in her right hand. In her left hand the eternal flame shone gently but steadily over the dark river that traveled to the sea.

"Do you know the poem that's written on the statue, Mom?" he asked. "The one we learned in school?"

"The one by Emma Lazarus? I know some of it." I recited what I knew of the sonnet: " 'Give me your tired, your poor, your huddled masses yearning to breathe free.' "

Joey studied the lady and then he said, "That's sort of like false advertising, isn't it?"

"Sometimes people have an ideal but it's a long fight before it's really real."

"What do you mean?"

"Well, like when the Statue of Liberty was dedicated in 1886 women weren't invited to the ceremony."

"That's foul," he said.

"A bunch of women rented a boat and circled the men's celebration, shouting at them with megaphones."

He chuckled. "What were they shouting?"

"Votes for women."

"Women couldn't vote then?"

"Nope."

"And now you're in City Hall."

"Yeah, but I don't have much power."

"Everybody has power, Mom. You told me that. You just have to figure out how to use it."

11

It was the middle of February
and winter seemed like it
would never end. Even though I saw Raul in the hallways almost
daily, we had not spoken since the night of the raid on the homeless shantytown, now almost a month ago. And I missed him terribly. Not only that, I was "out of the loop." Nobody talked to me. I
got no phone calls, no perks, and no invitations—no parties, no
press conferences, no weddings, and no work. In a food chain
where I had once been a shark, I had become an amoeba. I had

disappeared. I was about as visible as Abe Lincoln's ghost up there on top of the stairwell.

I sat staring at Jason's painting, feeling that I had become Jason, banished from the inner circle without an explanation. I no longer wondered about that jump he took, I understood it now. I figured he threw himself off that balcony as a kind of salvation. I stared at that painting, thinking about that big red schedule book, trying to figure a way to get it back so that I could hold my head high again, pass security without a check, be a shark among the other sharks. I was brooding on that when I heard a tap on the door.

"Come in."

"It's locked."

I got up and unlocked the door. She didn't look like herself. She was tanned. Her short, dark hair was long and blond. She wore aviator sunglasses that covered half her face. The coat she wore was frumpy and hid her shape. She pushed past me. I stood there stiff and angry.

She grabbed my hand. "Come with me. Come with me right now."

"Where have you been, Esther?"

She took her sunglasses off. Her coat fell back to reveal an expensive leather suit. "My son," she whispered. "My son is gone."

For three months every reporter in town had been looking for her and now she just wandered into my office in the heart of City Hall. I grabbed my jacket. She put her sunglasses back on. "My driver is outside."

A press conference was in progress on the steps. Esther walked past the mayor, Hunter, and Brogan. Not one of those geniuses recognized her. In the cluster of reporters I saw Raul and felt again how much I missed him. Esther and I climbed into the backseat of her BMW. In City Hall Park the branches of the trees were naked and gray with winter, and on the ground below, the snow had frozen into a sooty crust.

She grabbed the wig and pulled it from her head. "Jazz has disappeared. I need you to help me."

"Where've you been?" My voice was wintery too.

She took a monogrammed handkerchief from her Yves St. Laurent bag. "Well, to be honest, since his father died, Jazz has developed a drug problem. I wanted him to come with me to Saint Barts so we could both heal. He refused, so I committed him to Four Winds Hospital in Westchester."

I wasn't sure I had heard right. "Committed?"

She tugged on the corners of her expensive handkerchief like she had that day at Jason's shiva. "To clean up. It's one of the best facilities in the country."

Around us rush hour was beginning. Her driver pulled away from the curb; behind us the press conference shifted into high gear.

"He ran away yesterday just as I was on my way up there to get him. He ran away."

"Why don't you go to the police?"

"I can't do that." She closed the tinted windowpane and leaned her forehead against it. "Jazz can't handle any more scandal. The cops leak like a sieve. Jason always told me that. The press would find out; they'd make our lives miserable. We've suffered enough, Marie."

"Where do you think he went?"

"I have a few ideas," she said, leaning forward toward the driver. "McGregor House."

We headed uptown in silence. On Broadway at Forty-second Street the driver turned left. Now we were in Times Square, where Broadway and Seventh Avenue intersect, a corner that was known as the crossroads of the world back in the days when *The New York Times* had just moved here from Park Row at the turn of the century. The *Times* had succeeded in having the subway stop named after it. Now the Richard Haas mural behind us was all that remained of the Times Tower as it had looked back then. The *Times* itself had moved to Forty-third Street. At the foot of the mural tourists clustered at a police information booth.

Across the street a black Muslim wearing a turban, harem pants, and a wide belt with half-moons and mirrors preached into a portable microphone about the white devil. On the corner the white devil preached about Judgment Day. A little farther down the street, two Jehovah's Witnesses handed out the *Watchtower*,

which placed Armageddon on next Wednesday. Tourists stopped
to watch and listen. The young hustlers who called the strip home
were too busy to listen. Male, female, black, brown, and white,
they scurried like ants carrying a carcass—moving, scratching, calling, and eyeing each other. On the fast track to nowhere and
afraid to miss out. Above them, dirty and broken light bulbs of
half-lit movie marquees offered violence and loveless sex. I looked
for young Jason's face, in a doorway, alone in a crowd.

On the corner of Eighth Avenue loomed the Port Authority
Bus Terminal, a windowless, anonymous way station to commuter
land. Tourists clutched their luggage and nervously walked the
gamut of hustlers to reach a line of waiting yellow cabs. Across the
street, Holy Cross Church was closed, its steps fenced off for the
night. The rest of the block was deserted.

The desolation of the next block was punctuated by the gently
lit mural of a hand holding a dove. The driver pulled up by the
mural and Esther got out. I followed. She rang the bell by the door
and we waited. She rang again. Somewhere inside, a radio played.
The door opened a sliver.

A young brown-skinned man dressed in chinos and a pale blue
sweater stood in the doorway. "Father McGregor, please," Esther
asked.

"The Father's not here right now. Would you like to wait?"

She didn't thank him. She just stepped into the small waiting
room with glass walls. On the other side the glass was covered by
venetian blinds. We sat down surrounded by silhouettes. We
couldn't see the faces. The young man left us there to wait.

I fought the impulse to ask about Jason and the gambling
chips. After a while Esther rested her head on the glass wall and
closed her eyes. Soon her mouth fell open, and through the slits
that were her eyelids I could see her eyeballs moving right, then
left, then right. By the time the priest came, she was fast asleep.

He looked like a football player in a collar, tall, blue-eyed, and
Irish. I stood up to greet him, and as he took my hand I felt that I
had stepped back into childhood. I introduced myself.

"What can I do for you?" he asked.

I studied the little broken blood vessels on his face that formed his ruddy complexion and said, "I'm helping my friend find her son."

"Oh," he said, looking at Esther, almost as if he were disappointed, but his eyes were kind, very kind. Esther's head fell forward. Then she woke up.

"Is my son here, Father?"

He shook his head in a way that fell just short of anger.

"Are you sure?"

"He's not here, Esther, and if he was, I wouldn't turn him over to you."

Esther grabbed my arms and pushed me forward. "Father, this is Marie Terranova. She's the mayor's special assistant. This is no longer a private matter. I suggest you be as helpful as you can."

The priest said, "Esther, the boy needs help and so do you. His sickness began with you, with you and with his father."

The shapes on the other side of the glass seemed to be sitting down to eat. Esther opened the door to the street and some emptiness came in. She pushed on into the darkness. "You'll be hearing from City Hall, Father, and you'll regret this."

I followed her out, mumbling my apology.

"That God-fearing bastard," she said savagely, back in the luxury of the car. I was about to ask a few questions when she nodded toward the driver and silenced me with a look. "Let's try Port Authority," she said.

After the driver's skillful U-turn, I followed Esther into the cavernous building. The shops that defined the main concourse of the terminal were closed for the night. The walls were lined with bundles of cloth and shelters built of grocery boxes. When the rags stirred, I felt the haunted angry eyes on us. We took the stairs to the second level. Breathing was difficult in the stench of unwashed human flesh and excrement. Esther searched the faces as if it were not the first time. Every once in a while a police officer would come along and rouse a sleeping bundle with his nightstick.

"These all seem like old-timers," I said. "What makes you think Jazz is here?" She seemed full of a kind of frantic energy but I was out of breath and out of stamina.

"I guess he's not. Let's try the Salt Mines."

The driver went up Eighth Avenue to Forty-eighth Street,

where he turned left. At Eleventh Avenue the traffic jammed. Suddenly we were surrounded by young drivers in souped-up cars, with blaring stereos. A girl wearing only a corset and garter belt came up to the car. She leaned in for a look. When she saw two women in the backseat, she tossed her blond curls and turned away. But not before her eyes had met mine. For a moment I saw an angry, confused child. Then I found myself staring at her naked butt which protruded from under a white rabbit-fur jacket.

There were eight girls in all. They strutted on their stiletto heels, chests out, heads held high and proud. Leaning into car windows, they joked with the males inside. Most of the cars were full of young men who were only teenagers themselves. There was a carnival atmosphere, as if this were Disney Land or Great Adventure. The girls rolled their hips and licked their lips suggestively. All colors and all sizes, each was beautiful in her own way. I wondered what terrors lay beneath their misguided self-confidence.

The driver took us down Eleventh Avenue to a Department of Sanitation salt dump. He pulled over where a lot of sanitation trucks were parked. Esther got out. I smelled the river, the salt, and the rusting metal of the beveled shack that stood behind the empty trucks. Our headlights illuminated a sad collection of boys, transsexuals, and leather queens on the wharf. The clang of a car door shutting punctuated the stillness. The car disappeared onto the West Side Highway. Esther stood there calling her son's name. No one answered. She leaned in through the car window. "Runaways sleep in these trucks," she told me. "We've got to check them."

I got out. The smell of garbage, oil, and dead fish crammed itself down my throat. I stepped up on a running board to see inside a truck. A man sat behind the steering wheel, his head thrown back, the whites of his eyes staring at the night beyond the large windshield. He groaned. On his lap a shadow moved, bobbing up and down. I jumped down to go quietly. As I stepped behind the truck a tall muscular woman's back blocked my way. She turned. Her blouse was open to the waist. She was so tall that I faced her spectacular breasts. Her hands were pushing something down. From below two hands fondled her nipples. I looked down. A young boy seemed to be swallowing her penis. My horror aroused her deep, angry laugh. I ran back to the car, the laugh ringing in the caverns of my hollow heart. The stench of garbage hovered like a rotting carcass.

I looked at the driver and he looked at me. In his eyes I could see the sickness of it all. Was this my city? In front of us a stretch limo pulled up and two giggling girls got in. I turned to Esther's pale, empty face.

"Find anything?" she asked.

I shook my head. She pointed to an enormous metal shack by the water's edge. "Let's look in there."

We stepped inside. Before us rose a mountain of salt. Crystals crackled under our feet. Again she called her son. Did she really expect to find him here or was this her way of punishing herself? A bundle of rags groaned and lifted its dirty face. I saw the open sores like purple mouths on the young bald head. "C'mon, lady, please. . . ." he said, and lay back down.

I walked to the pier trying to swallow the share of all this pain that was mine. The night-blackened river spat up reflected points of light from neon signs on the other shore. Behind me I heard the swish of Esther's expensive leather skirt. "I guess he's not here," she said. I turned to watch her disappear into the silver BMW.

A few minutes later, I followed. She huddled in the farthest corner of the backseat and folded into herself. The driver headed back to the ivory towers of the East Side, past the glass palace hotels of midtown, past the United Nations, to her Sutton Place home. Before she got out, she touched me with a cold hand. "I appreciate," she said, "I appreciate your coming with me. The driver will take you home."

"Esther, we have to talk—"

"My driver will take you home," she repeated, as if that put the world back into place. Then she turned and walked away. I followed and grabbed her by the arm.

"Esther, did you know that Jason was laundering money with his gambling?"

She pulled away but stayed. "That's absurd," she said angrily. "If City Hall is saying that, it's because Jason's not here to defend himself."

"*I'm* saying it. *I've* seen the evidence."

"I can't believe you believe that!"

She rummaged in her purse.

"What about the cancer report?"

"What about it?"

"It was a lie."

Before answering, she thrust a snapshot of Jazz at me. "In case you can use this," she said.

"What about the cancer report?" I insisted.

She shook her head with irritation. "Oh Marie, City Hall cooked that up with Jason's doctor, Dr. Mintzis," she said matter-of-factly, as if I should have known.

Mintzis. He had been the mayor's doctor for years.

I said, "I don't get it."

"Mintzis and I went along to protect the mayor from the embarrassment of Jason's suicide."

"Why?"

"Because the mayor's father-in-law begged me. I couldn't turn him down. He was Jason's mentor."

She walked into her fancy building with all the dignity of a true martyr—the aura of her agony as thick as stone. Jazz's picture lay in my palm. Her explanation about the phony cancer story was so deceptively simple. It made sense that the mayor's father-in-law had stepped in to protect the mayor. Mendelssohn often did. But would Dr. Mintzis risk his career with such a big lie? On the other hand, perhaps Mintzis had risked nothing. After all, he hadn't gone on the public record. He had refused to talk to the press. His complicity was his silence. Hunter had given out the fake lab reports. Mintzis had simply done nothing. I went back to the car, my thoughts churning.

The driver didn't ask me any questions. He just headed downtown. I guessed Esther had told him where I lived. We cruised down Third Avenue. At Fifty-third and Third we stopped for a red light. Postal trucks lined the side street. In front of us marble, glass, and chrome defined an ultramodern structure with many shiny brown columns. Slim young men stood between the marble and glass, not obviously from the Avenue but as visible as items on a supermarket shelf if you knew what you were looking for. A limousine pulled up. A teenager ambled toward it. I asked the driver to stop.

My footsteps echoed off the marble as if I were at the foot of a temple. Handsome boys leaned on the columns, as still as flies in a web. They seemed not to notice me. I asked a young blond if he had seen Jason and I showed him the picture. He took it, his fingers trembling like an old man's, then he asked me for twenty dollars. I rummaged in my purse. Among the chrome and glitter, the bill was a filthy green. He took it quickly, as if it might evaporate.

"We call him Fleece," he said, "cuz his name is Jason. His father's a big-time politician and Fleece used to be the most expensive piece of meat out here before he got on the needle and the pipe."

"Do you know where he is now?"

He looked down the long row of gleaming columns. "He hangs at the other end. Don't tell him you talked to me."

I walked from pillar to pillar, half hoping I'd find him, half hoping I wouldn't. As it turned out he saw me first. We stood looking at each other, separated by a world of secrets. He came closer.

"You're bad for business, Mrs. Terranova."

"You remember me?"

"Is my mother with you?"

"No."

He watched me silently, his hands thrust deep into the pockets of jeans that fit too loosely.

"Come with me," I pleaded. Across from us a BMW not unlike his mother's pulled up. "I gotta go now," Jazz said, and turned up the collar of his expensive leather jacket.

I hesitated and then I reached for him. In the moment of my hesitation he slipped away and got into the BMW. I ran back to Esther's car. We followed the other BMW onto the FDR Drive, where we lost it. I sat there shaking, not knowing what to do. The driver offered me the car phone. I called Esther. "Forget it," she said wearily. "We'll never catch him now."

But I couldn't forget. I asked the driver to take me back to McGregor House. We were crossing Forty-second Street by the old

Rivoli Theater when I saw the truck with the dove painted on it. The priest was standing behind it holding a stack of paper plates. I asked the driver to stop and walked across the street. A sad collection of young losers held their empty plates and waited for the priest to serve them from his truck.

"What can I do for the mayor's office, Mrs. Terranova?"

"I'm not professional staff, Father. I don't know why Esther said what she said."

I watched him drop some rice onto a plate. He waited for me to go on.

"I saw Jason Junior on Fifty-third Street and Third Avenue, but I couldn't get him to come with me. Is there anything you can do?"

He added some beans to the rice. "You found him almost under his mother's window," he said. "Would you say he was trying to tell her something?"

I didn't understand. "I thought his parents offered him the world?"

"Everything but the time that is love," the priest said. "But you know that."

"What's really wrong with him?"

"He has the same disease all these young people have."

I studied the lineup of lost looks, the faces just this side of childhood, the aged eyes full of emptiness. He handed a child a paper plate.

I asked him to name the disease.

His blue eyes searched the skull behind my eyes. "Hypocrisy," he said. "The children are dying of hypocrisy. Find out what was going on between those adults and you'll understand Jason Junior."

"Jason's father is dead."

"When you know the father, you'll understand the son."

12

Sounds of satisfaction escaped from the press office. I heard laughter and applause. The door was open. The staff craned their necks to see the television that hung from the ceiling like an altar of moving images. I stepped in.

This was Hunter's turf. The counterpart to Room Nine. The place where the mayor's press strategy was shaped and executed. The place where press conferences were scheduled and press releases written. Hallowed ground. Like Room Nine, this was a small room, like Room Nine there were lots of phones and computer terminals. On the television screen, the anchor, a familiar face and voice, was saying, "Live now to One Police Plaza for a special report."

It was Dominic Vicker again. He stood in drizzling rain and stared down at all of us, "Mr, Finx was arrested six weeks ago for assaulting Mayor Nicosea during a momentary lapse of security on the steps of City Hall itself. The charges added today include arson and inciting to riot. Eyewitnesses have connected Mr. Finx to December's deadly shelter fires in Brooklyn, Staten Island, and the Bronx."

"With any kind of luck he'll go to trial just as the campaign heats up," one of the deputies said.

"How sweet it is!" Hunter rubbed his hands together as if he were an Indian rubbing sticks to start his own fire.

"What's sweet about that sad crazy old man?" I asked.

Like an eight-headed Hydra, the group turned to me.

Hunter's eyes flicked over me furiously. "When they bring that crazy old man to justice, the public will be free to focus on the real issues of the mayor's housing program, which just happens to be the most expensive in the country."

"And a very important campaign issue."

What did I have to lose? Nobody ever got fired in a campaign year. Especially not if they knew anything, and even though I knew nothing, I knew too much.

Hunter got to his feet. He grabbed me by the elbow and shepherded me into the hallway. He was biting the inside of his cheek, his eyes were daggers, and he was tongue-tied. The press secretary tongue-tied! That was a kick. I shook him loose and kept walking. He followed me down the hall, and when he still couldn't find any words, he grabbed my arm again. I looked down at his spidery hand.

"Excuse me!" I said stiffly. His hand dropped back to his side. The hatred between us became suddenly so tangible that I felt I could bite it. The poisoned apple.

"I saw the peaceful way you had the homeless removed during the middle of the night," I hissed.

"You what?"

"You heard me."

"I'm surprised you didn't call the media," he said, recovering his sarcasm.

"What are you hiding?"

"What are you implying, Ms. Terranova?" He was good, very good. Still, I could see how much I terrified him.

"Something's going on around here and I think you're in the middle of it."

"Damn right I'm in the middle of it. We're trying to clear the decks so Ken can run a good race. We want to see him reelected, don't you? Whose side are you on anyway?"

That shut me up because I had no answer. Before Jason's suicide the answer would have been obvious. Now I wasn't so sure.

He left me standing there. After he had gone, I turned and walked back out of the building. It was raining. I walked through the central arch on the ground-level colonnade of the Municipal Building. Once a monumental gateway to the melting pot of the Lower East Side, it was now the grand entrance to Police Plaza. The television had shown the old man being taken up the steps of One Police Plaza for his second arraignment. I wanted to see it with my own eyes.

When I arrived, it was over. The old man was walking the gauntlet of reporters back down the stairs. He had grown a beard, his hair was wild like a crown of thorns, and his hands were cuffed behind his back. His feet seemed barely to touch the steps as two officers dragged him by the television cameras, microphones, and shouting print reporters. In the swirling rain the klieg lights seemed to blind him. Then he saw me. He winked like he had known I would be there. "You know the answer," he said. "You just have to remember it."

"Can you explain that?" A radio reporter shoved a microphone in his face.

"No," the old man said. "It explains itself."

The cops hustled him into a squad car and he was gone. In seconds all the reporters had disappeared too. I found myself alone with Raul at the center of the brick-paved plaza. Behind us, rain pattered on the five oxidized steel disks that symbolized the five boroughs.

"They're lining up their scapegoats," Raul said, "and that poor old man is *numero uno.*"

We were silent for a while. Just listening to the rain fall. Then he said, "Now the shoe is on the other foot."

"What do you mean?"

The disk sculpture looked like a propeller that was too heavy to fly. He said, "I've been so critical of you, accusing you of blindly going along with the system. Now it's my turn to go along to get along. Either I report what everybody else is reporting, or I'm out."

I looked across the large empty plaza. The gray air was wet with drizzle. Police headquarters was behind us, the Department of Justice and St. Andrew's Church in front. Across from us umbrellas lined up to buy Lotto tickets.

"If you were able to get the real story," I asked, "that would make it different, wouldn't it?"

"It might," he said, "but it would have to be a hell of a story and my facts would have to be solid, solid as a rock."

I listened to my own heartbeat. He was watching me closely, very closely. Looking back, I think he knew what was coming.

"I'll make a deal with you," I said. "You get me the details of the FBI's findings on my husband's death and I'll get you the shelter contracts."

I don't know what reaction I expected from him then. But I was disappointed. Now that he was going to get what he wanted, he was less than enthusiastic. "It's hard to get stuff out of the fat boys," he said.

"But you have your sources. You told me so."

Neither of us had an umbrella and we were getting wet. In the center of the empty plaza we seemed small. He was looking at me with a tenderness that reminded me of Florida. Florida seemed as innocent as Eden now. And just as unattainable.

"What am I looking for?" Raul asked.

"I don't know. I talked to the man who used to be my husband's partner and he made me want to know what really happened to Joe."

"It doesn't sound like much of a deal," he said. "Even if I get the file, all you find is the past."

He looked at me like he wished I had asked for something else. Anything else.

"That's the deal. You want it?"

He shrugged. His hunger for victory seemed to have dissipated.

"Well?" I asked.

"Okay," he said. "I'll need copies of the contracts and company names. Who worked on those shelters and for how much."

As I walked away he called after me, "Does this mean we're talking again?"

I licked a raindrop from my lips. "Yeah," I said, "we're talking."

He just stood there, his jacket dark with rain, his eyes full of questions. I was headed back to my office, trying to figure out how I could get my hands on the shelter contracts, when an answer rose from the concrete before me. Jason's files. They were in the Tweed courthouse. I had seen the boxes being carried from City Hall's back door.

The Tweed courthouse, ugly, unkempt, and unrenovated, stands behind City Hall, a silent testament to political corruption. During the building's construction, robbing city taxpayers had been refined to a high art. City contractors were told to pad their accounts. The difference between what the work actually cost and what the city paid was kicked back to Tweed and his cronies. If you didn't kick back, you didn't get contracts. The Tweed ring fleeced the city in many ways. But the cost overruns in the construction of the criminal courthouse precipitated Tweed's downfall. Risen from humble roots, he had never actually held office himself. He had been a kingmaker who profited from friends in high places. He died in jail, destitute and friendless. The criminal courthouse, originally slated to cost $250,000, took ten years to complete and cost between twelve and thirteen million dollars.

The Tweed courthouse wasn't a courthouse anymore. It didn't even have a front door. It was just an office building where City Hall housed its overflow. In the fifties the entrance stairway was demolished and never replaced. I stepped from the sidewalk into its tomblike opening. Inside, security was tight. As I prepared to show my ID, I noticed there was a children's art exhibit in the rotunda. Brightly colored paintings from various projects around the city expressed the children's yearning for sun, grass, and flowers.

"I'd like to take a look at the exhibit," I told the guard.

She nodded and gave me a stick-on visitor's pass. I wandered among the paintings until she looked away. Then I headed for the information board to see where I might find Jason's files.

The board listed all kinds of offices, but none seemed the obvious candidate for the repository of Jason's file boxes. I decided to start at the top. The elevator was a cage with an operator. I asked for the third floor. As we went up we saw people and floors pass by. I got out on the top floor almost in front of a staircase that led to a walkway. Hundreds of look-alike boxes covered the walkway. From the walkway another staircase led into the ceiling.

I went up to take a look. I had labeled Jason's files and I was certain I would recognize my own scribbles. The walkway was stacked to the ceiling with old dusty cartons and their secrets. I looked for my own handwriting but didn't find it. I decided to search the small building floor by floor. I peeked into every office. I found nothing.

On the second floor I recognized a name on a door. James Mullhern. Mullhern was an assistant to Brogan. I didn't quite know in what capacity. I stepped inside. It was lunchtime and the office was empty except for one secretary. Unlike City Hall, here there was no artwork, no fancy furniture, just six desks and six phones. The furniture was the kind you often see in government offices, handcrafted by prison inmates who did a careful job but worked with the cheapest woods and fabrics.

The secretary was dressed in a tight straight skirt and a blouse with a little bow at the collar. Her hair was perfectly coiffed, her face perfectly made up, and she had long Chinese-red fingernails. She was feeding paper to the machine in the corner. The papers went in whole and came out in strips. She didn't see me come in. I walked quietly toward her. She turned. "Oh," she said, and stopped doing what she was doing.

"Hi. Remember me? We met at the mayor's Christmas party."

"Hi, Miss T. What are you doing out here with us plebs?"

"I have a little situation." I almost smiled. *Situation* was Hunter's word. "The mayor is asking for a file. I think I sent that damn file over here with the Isenberg boxes."

"That was weeks ago."

"Yeah, I know. Hizzoner's like that. Just when you've forgotten something, he remembers it."

She turned on her very high heels and wobbled across the room. There they were! Jason's boxes. I recognized my handwriting. She opened the top box. Then she stopped. Her face turned pink.

"Holy shit . . ." she said. "Holy shit. I think I already did these." She cocked her head and puffed her hair, searching for a thought that was stuck somewhere in the hairspray. Finally she turned to me. "You're gonna hafta come back after lunch."

"Why?"

She smacked the lid down onto the empty box, buying time, trying not to get caught in a mistake.

I said, "Those are Isenberg's files. I recognize them. I boxed them myself."

Her hands fluttered nervously over the boxes. She broke one of her very long nails. "Aw . . ." She studied the nail in deep distress. "Jesus . . . You'll have to ask my supervisor."

I went over to her and sat down on a box on top of a box and rummaged in my purse. I had it. Krazy Glue! Eureka! I'd bought it to repair Joey's model airplane. I handed her the glue. "This will hold it together till you get a chance to get it wrapped."

"Thanks!" she said, then sighed her relief. She sat down next to me and repaired her nail. First she took off the pin that was the glue's cap. Then, delicately, very delicately, she squeezed one tiny drop of glue onto the crack in her nail.

Together, we watched the glue dry.

"Don't worry about the file. I'll just tell Hizzoner it never got here."

She looked at me gratefully. "These boxes have been standing here for weeks, and just yesterday Denise told me to feed 'em to the shredder because we don't need 'em and they're taking up space."

"Wires got crossed," I said. "It happens. The mayor doesn't have to know."

I took my glue back. "Is anything left?"

She blew on her nail. "I don't think so, Miss T. I think I did 'em all last night."

She went over to the shredder and with her good hand she sifted through the slices of paper in the basket underneath. "I think this was the last of it."

I looked up at the big old clock on the wall. The second hand moved relentlessly. It was 1:45. Her supervisor would be back soon.

"Forget it," I said. "Don't even mention it to Denise. I'll handle the Old Man."

She beamed. "Thanks. Thanks, I really appreciate it."

One of the phones rang. She looked around trying to decide which. As she wandered among the desks, picking up one wrong phone after another, I reached down into the wastebasket, grabbed a handful of paper strips, and headed for the door.

"Thanks again," she called after me. She didn't look up.

Outside, the sky hung over the city's cradle of power like a gray blanket. It had stopped drizzling. On the dampened benches between City Hall and the courthouse, workers took advantage of the unusually warm February day to eat their sandwiches outside. Old men played chess on the tables. I walked back to my office quickly. Once inside, I pulled the shreds from my pocket and tried to align them into a solid piece of paper. But it was useless. The shreds were from many different pieces of paper and there was nothing to decipher. But one memo had gone into the shredder sideways. I was able to read a number.

I sat there staring at that number. Seven digits. A telephone number? The key to Pandora's box. Did I really want to open it? I put my hand on the phone. I'd call the number and see who picked up. What if it was somebody I knew? What if I said the wrong thing? I had a better idea. I called Mel. He picked up his own phone.

"How you doing?"

I could hear the tremble in my voice as I asked him if a phone number could lead to a name. I didn't want to be too direct.

"If I read you right, Marie, you're telling me you have a number and you want to know who it belongs to."

I nodded. On the other end of the line, Mel waited for my response.

"Is that right?"

"Yes."

"Easy," he said. "Use Cole's, the reverse directory. They have one at the public library. They probably have one right there in Room Nine."

I thanked him and then I hung up. Hunter walked in. Had he been listening? He smiled at me as if I mattered. "Marie," he said, "let's bury the hatchet."

I couldn't look him in the eye. I wanted to ask how he knew I had called 911 the day of the suicide-infanticide. And why had he mentioned it to Raul? But I knew it would be a mistake. Instead I focused on his pink tie and mauve shirt. His manicured fingers were wrapped around an envelope. He smiled down at me.

"Chasen and Chasen, the restaurant PR firm, is giving a big benefit for the homeless in the Puck Building tonight. Tickets are five hundred dollars a head and I have several extra."

I waited for the punch line.

"Take these tickets. I know how much you care about this issue. I want you to see the quality of people involved."

He put the envelope down in front of me on the desk, on the spot where the schedule book used to rest. "Take your son with you. There's going to be a live band."

"Thanks, thanks a lot."

As he prepared to leave he stopped to stare at Jason's painting. He turned back to me. "Why are these people all so ugly?"

"They're wearing masks," I said. "It's part of a ritual dance. Something to do with good and evil. Didn't Jason ever tell you about it?"

"Who?"

"Jason. Jason Isenberg."

"Oh yes," Hunter said. "That painting belonged to him. Anyway, we're a team and it's important to remember that, Marie."

When he left, I wanted to leave too. I wanted to go uptown to the library and look up the number I had found. I knew I couldn't go to Room Nine. But as it turned out, Brogan came in and handed me a stack of invitations to decline on the mayor's behalf, and I couldn't leave. So I did the next best thing. I called Jolynne, the commissioner's secretary, my counterpart in the Department of Human Services. Human Services was responsible for staffing the shelters that had been built under Jason's supervision. That meant they were given duplicates of all the shelter files. I had done Jolynne a few favors over the years. She would help me if she could. I asked her if she had copies of the contract files on the shelters. I told her the mayor had requested the files on the qt.

"They're kind of old," she said. "I'll have to see what I have."

We gossiped a bit about City Hall and the coming election. I made everything sound fine. The mayor was great and his victory was a foregone conclusion. That made her happy. "We just bought a house," she said. "I can just imagine trying to make those mortgage payments on just Greg's salary."

"With your skills you can get a job anywhere," I told her.

"I don't know. I'm no spring chicken."

"Anyway, I wouldn't worry about it if I were you. Things will be fine."

"I'm glad to hear that. There's been so much bad press lately. . . ."

Then we chatted about what dirty dogs the press were, like we usually did. But my heart was no longer in it.

I didn't get uptown that day. But that evening Joey and I got dressed in our best and walked down Mulberry Street to the Puck Building on Houston. Over the entrance, which was on Lafayette, stood Puck. Top-hatted, with a devilish grin, the bronze imp looked down at the mayor's entourage as they arrived. We watched from across the street. When we went in, the mayor had joined the receiving line. He looked very handsome in his elegant evening clothes. We walked through and were introduced to the owners of some of the finest restaurants in town. The mayor received me as if I were his long-lost daughter and he made an even bigger fuss over Joey. No one took our tickets.

Then we were inside a large attractive hall. This building had once housed the defunct humor magazine *Puck*, and now it was used for social functions. Pillars reached to the ceiling and tall windows circled the gleaming, loftlike space. In the far corner of the room, a calypso band was setting up. Both sides of the room were completely lined with booths representing all the participating restaurants—Italian, French, nouvelle, Russian, soul, German, Mexican, Caribbean. The booths were staffed by restaurant employees who served miniportions of the house specialties. There was also a dessert booth with *petits fours* and Italian pastries, cappuccino, champagne, and mineral water. The air was fragrant with expensive food and perfumes.

Joey and I picked our way among the booths, tasting this and that. The room became crowded and the music began. It was a trendy crowd, dressed in the kind of casual elegance that is very costly to achieve. As they entered they lingered at the reception line to see and be seen. I went to get a cup of cappuccino and lost Joey. When I saw him again, he was across the room talking to Hunter and Brogan. I elbowed my way over.

"This young man is quite impressive," Brogan said, smiling at me.

"He's a computer whiz too," Hunter added.

Joey looked at me as if to say, "Who are these clowns?"

"Are you enjoying the food?" Hunter asked me.

I nodded. "Very much."

The band struck up a limbo beat. Across the room I could see Raul on the receiving line. Joey saw him too. He left my side and rushed toward him. Fortunately, just then an assemblyman arrived and took Hunter and Brogan's attention. They didn't see Joey embrace Raul, I was certain of it.

I inched my way over. The room was now overcrowded.

"Ready to go?" I asked Joey.

"Aren't you going to say hi to Raul?"

"Working?" I asked Raul.

He shrugged. "If you can call it that."

"Come with us?" Joey asked.

"Can't, champ. I've got to talk to a few people. But I'll be seeing you soon. That is, if Mom says it's okay."

I nodded, sure. But I felt trapped. What the hell was I supposed to say?

We were standing on the corner of Houston Street waiting for the light to change, watching two men dressed in rags wash car windows from dirty water buckets. One was young, the other old. They were annoying the drivers. Nobody wanted their window cleaned by these two slimy-looking desperadoes. But when a car was forced to stop for the light, the pair smeared their filthy sponges over the windshield, then stretched an open palm hopefully at the driver. Most of the drivers stared dead ahead and pretended no one was there. I was watching the younger man, thinking that at least he was trying, he wasn't hitting people over the head to take what he needed. He must have felt me staring at him because suddenly he was headed toward me. The older man followed.

"Can you spare some change for something to eat?"

I handed each man a quarter. The younger man looked at Joey. Joey looked at me. I produced two more quarters. Joey reached into his pocket and came out with the benefit invitations we hadn't used. He handed them to the older man. "They have a lot of food there."

The older man handed the invitation to the younger man, who read it and said, "What's this? Five hundred smackeroos for the homeless?" He patted Joey on the back. "Did you go?"

"Yeah, my mom got free tickets."

"I'll bet," the young bum said, "but me and my buddy would get arrested at the door. You got another quarter?"

I pulled out some more coins. Mercifully the light changed. I grabbed Joey's hand.

"What was that party for, Mom?"

"It wasn't a party. It was a fund-raiser for the homeless."

"All that food we ate was for the homeless?"

"Not exactly. The money people paid to get in goes to the homeless."

He said, "Oh," and stared at me in disbelief. If I had any integrity at all, I would have thrown up right there on the spot.

Joey seemed to have less and less to say to me. That evening, like so many others during those days, he did his homework and then stayed glued to his computer until bed time. I knew now that mere words wouldn't win his respect back. The priest's words kept haunting me. Perhaps he was right, and the hypocrisy was coming between us. That night I dreamed about those seven digits. The next day at lunchtime, I went to the library on Forty-second Street.

The main branch of the New York Public Library sits up on a wide terrace that runs the length of its Fifth Avenue facade. Two marble lions flank the steps, where shoppers rest when its warm, workers eat lunch, tourists study maps, and a collection of New York eccentrics gather. That day a pale winter sun assisted the comedian who was loudly stereotyping the sexual habits of different ethnic groups. People clustered around, laughing. At the top of the stairs, behind a fountain, stood Truth in the form of a man leaning against the Sphinx. On the left, Beauty was a woman on a winged horse.

Inside, under the vaulted ceiling with its marble candelabra, the library was cool and silent. I listened to my footsteps and headed for the third-floor research room. In the stillness, I felt a kinship with the other seekers of truth, beauty, or just a little illumination. I went to the information desk.

"Where do you keep the Cole's Directory?"

She pointed to the center of the room. I whispered thanks.

There among the other reference books was one Cole's Directory for each borough. I started with Manhattan. The number was there. I followed the dotted line across the page to the corresponding name and address. The address was on Attorney Street, the name was Werner Schilling. It rang a bell, but I didn't know why. I went outside to a pay phone and called Mel. Again he said, "That's easy. You make a ruse call."

"A what?"

"Well, you call and say you're calling from UPS. You have a package for Mr. Whatever-his-name-is and your driver hasn't been able to get into the building. What do they want you to do?"

"Is that what detectives do, lie to people?"

He laughed. "Sometimes it's the only way to get at the truth."

I went back to the silence of my office and closed the door. Then I dialed. On the second ring a woman picked up. She seemed to have a slight Spanish accent and she was very friendly. I told my lie.

"That's odd," she said. "Do you have any idea what it is?"

"No, ma'am, I don't. It's a box. Could be a gift."

"Well, Mr. Schilling is my father but he moved to Toronto almost three years ago."

"Should we deliver the package to you and then you can send it to him? Could you sign for it?"

"It would be better," she said, "if you sent it straight to him." She gave me the address. When I asked for the phone number, she gave me that too. I hung up. Briefly, I considered calling Raul. Instead I called for a plane reservation to Toronto that Friday night. The idea was to find out what I was giving up before I gave it up. But it didn't work out that way.

13

Outside the window the propeller created the illusion
of a circle. The night was too dark to see the land below. I felt like
a fugitive. But this time I wasn't running from anything. This time
I was running toward. Only I didn't know what.

We landed on a small island in Lake Ontario. The airport was
just a brightly lit empty room. Two customs officials awaited us. I
approached with my overnight bag.

"Purpose of your visit?"

I handed the official my passport and then realized that hidden in the masculine cut of the uniform stood a woman.

"Pleasure," I lied.

"How long are you here for?"

"Just the weekend."

She compared my face with the face in the passport. "Anything to declare?"

"No, nothing."

She stamped the passport and gave it back. I picked up my bag and headed out into the night.

The Toronto skyline stretched across the curve of the horizon, lower, wider than New York City. The Canadian National Tower, higher than the Twin Towers, pierced the sky like a needle, a beacon of the twenty-first century. In front of me stood the Lighthouse Café, still under construction, where I could wait for the ferry to the city.

I sat down in the café. It was just a shack with an open door on either side. Behind me was the customhouse, ahead the ferry dock on the other shore. I was warming my hands on a cup of coffee that was too bitter to drink when a torrential rain began. The rain rustled like wind in the trees and tapped the tin roof in a tribal rhythm. The air itself began to drip with moisture. I felt the dampness in my bones. Like a swimmer, he slipped through the translucent wall of rain. For a moment, he just stood there, drenched and dripping. Then he came over and sat across from me. A rivulet ran from the brim of his hat onto the table. Where the hell had he come from? No other planes had landed. I hadn't seen him on the plane. Was I traveling with blinders on?

"Why bother to follow me?" I asked brutally. "We already have a deal."

"Joey told me where to find you."

I shoved my coffee toward him just so he could warm up.

He took the cup. "When are you going to tell the truth?" he asked.

"When I know it."

A puddle was forming around him. "I tried to tell you all this is dangerous."

I laughed. "Especially for you, Raul."

He cupped his hands around the Styrofoam and stared down into the cup. He took a sip. His face contorted. I said, "I should have warned you."

"What do you know you're not telling?"

All around us the falling water whispered its secrets. I wondered about the secrets between us. Did he have as many as I did? The ferry touched the dock in front of us like a key fitting into a lock. The sound was cold and metallic. It meant it was time for us to go.

We stepped out into the torrent. He grabbed my hand. "We'll talk at the hotel."

"What hotel?"

"Your hotel."

We ran to the ferry. If we didn't make it, we'd have to wait for another. I said, "I'm not sleeping with you."

Rain raced down his face. "I noticed."

"No, I mean separate rooms."

"Fine."

We huddled alongside the cars on the small ferry and watched Toronto approach. The ferryman pointed across the water. "Those grain towers are going to become condos," he said. "I won't be able to afford them." Then he pointed farther along the shore. "Over there I can't get in because I make too much."

Raul chuckled. The rain kept beating down, slashing across the water. He looked at me. "You think there's a vacancy rate in hell?"

"I thought you were going to give me space. Why are you sticking so close to me?"

He looked down at the wind on the dark water. "This private investigation of yours worries me."

"Why?"

"I told you, it could be dangerous."

The ferry ground into the dock. We didn't speak again until we were on the bus to the hotel, and then he asked, "Who did you come to see?"

I hesitated.

He said, "Schilling?"

"If you know, why are you asking me?"

"Looking for your reaction. To hear myself talk. I don't know."

"Who is this Schilling?"

"You don't know!"

"I feel like I know the name but I don't remember why."

In the pattern of the rain on the window I saw Father Mc-Gregor's eyes. I asked, "Do you think it's true that the sins of the father . . ."

"Are visited on the son?"

"Jason Junior is an addict and he's missing."

"I didn't know that." He paused to watch the rain streak down the windows. "Does this mean you believe I might have been right in Florida? Do you think Isenberg was involved with some kind of drug cartel, after all?"

I was wet and cold and I said wearily, "I'm ready to believe anything."

He said, "Schilling was the first architect of the shelters, but he withdrew from the project before construction started."

"Withdrew?"

The bus stopped. We were at the hotel.

"Yeah, he withdrew his designs."

"So he doesn't know what happened. I've come up here for nothing."

"You could have asked me about him," Raul said.

I just sat there, wet, shivering, disappointed, and angry, angry at myself.

"We're here now. It's worth a try," Raul said. "He may know more than you think."

The door opened with an electronic sigh. The night porter appeared. "Your bags?" he asked.

As the porter walked ahead of us with our luggage Raul said, "I'm taking the room next to yours."

I raised an eyebrow.

"Just in case someone's shadowing the shadow."

I changed out of my soaked clothes and settled into my room. Here we were again, together in a place I had never been to before. The curtains were drawn shut. The room could have been any hotel room, anywhere in the world. Nothing about it was distinctive. I thought about Schilling. I tried to imagine his face. I imagined that he would help me get at the truth—pieces of which had to be lodged in the recesses of my own memory. After all, I had worked with Jason three years ago on the emergency shelter program. Raul came to the door. In his hand he held a Toronto guidebook. "Toronto has really changed," he said.

I sat down on a chair. "You know Toronto?"

"I used to come up here and cover the film festival when I was in features. I'm a bit of a buff. Toronto used to be really homogeneous."

"You mean white."

"Yes. But now it's a nice mix."

I sat there as stiff as a patient in the waiting room. I said, "Let's call Schilling and see if he'll talk to us."

"You call," he said. "This is your trip."

"What should I say?"

"Say whatever you were gonna say before you knew I'd be sitting here with you."

I knew the number by heart. When I dialed, I was calm. The phone rang. It rang and rang. No one picked up. I put it back in its cradle. "What if he's not around?"

Raul walked to the window and pulled back the thick hotel curtain. Outside, the rain had let up. "Don't panic, not yet," he said.

I joined him at the window. We were in downtown Toronto. I could see the very modern City Hall, two curved towers of different heights.

"Let's go out," he said.

I fought the yearning to melt into his arms and let him take me to the end of myself, where I could forget all my fears for a little while.

"Have you seen *Les Misérables?*"

I shook my head. "That's playing in New York."

"It's here too. Only here we could probably get tickets. It's a great show based on Victor Hugo's novel. The musical was originally written in French, but the translation is superb and so is the music."

"You've seen it?"

"I could stand to see it again."

We headed back to the harbor front and the Royal Alexandria

Theatre. Our seats, the last available seats in the house, were high up on the second balcony. The turn-of-the-century theater was decorated with deep red velvet, gold brocade, baroque swirls, and enormous crystal chandeliers. The chattering audience sounded like birds on an empty beach. When the curtain went up, the audience fell silent.

Les Misérables is the story of a man who makes one mistake that changes his whole life. He steals a loaf of bread to feed his sister's starving child. He is caught and sent to prison. I cried from beginning to end. I tried to do it discreetly. Fortunately, Raul had a handkerchief. All around me women were wiping their tears.

After the show Raul watched a parade of blue-haired ladies emerging from the theater. "All these really square people love this really radical story," he said.

"What's so radical about it?"

"It's about social injustice."

He grabbed my elbow to keep us together in the moving crowd. We were standing in front of a restaurant. I was suddenly very hungry. "Let's eat."

We went inside. As he opened the door he said, "The owner of this restaurant made his fortune with a bargain-basement store. He owns this whole block."

We stepped into the most bizarre collection of art and artifacts I had ever seen. Greek statues, bunches of purple glass grapes that were lamps, ornate bird cages, fountains, and even a collection of hand-painted soup tureens that turned out to be bedpans.

"This is a capitalist frenzy and in poor taste too," I said.

He laughed. "Let's not get dogmatic."

The upstairs dining room was lit like a bordello. Everything was red—the walls, the rugs, the tablecloths, the lampshades. We were led to a table in the corner. In the red glow Raul was more gorgeous than ever. He looked at me with fiery intensity. "I'm not going to lose you, am I?"

I didn't know what to say. "I feel like the man in the musical."

"Jean Valjean?"

"Yes. When he said, 'If I speak, I am condemned; if I am silent, I am damned' . . . I feel crazy."

He took my hands into his. "You're not crazy, Marie. Your fears are real. Nobody likes a whistle-blower."

"Then why are you encouraging me?"

"Because the choice you made is the only choice."

I looked at our hands on the table. In the light they were red, not as red as blood but almost. Kitsch dripped from the walls. I was thinking about my own guilt. Where had it begun? Where did it end? "How did I get into this when all I ever wanted to do was the right thing?"

"You let others define you. That's always dangerous."

"I feel like I did when my husband died. Like I'm going to lose my whole life again."

He ran his thumb along the edge of his golden knife and signaled the waitress. "Maybe you'll start a new life."

After dinner we walked back to the hotel. The wet streets were empty. There were no homeless people sleeping on grates or wandering the night. Toronto was a clean city and one that went to bed early. We entered the hotel together, rode the elevator in tense silence, and then stood in front of my door. I had the key in my hand.

"Will you be able to sleep?"

I said that I would.

"When you get inside, unlock the door that joins our rooms. I'll feel better."

I went alone into my room. I knew that if I took him to bed with me, I'd forget for a while, but in the morning I'd be back to square one—panic. I lay on my bed thinking that he was smart to let the trust grow away from the heat of passion. Exhaustion wrapped itself around me like a cloak, and I slept.

The next morning a bright spring light snuck around the heavy curtain and woke me. Raul and I had breakfast together and then I called Schilling again. Again no answer. We decided to stroll around Toronto. The streets were full of sidewalk cafés and leisurely shoppers.

"Let's go see Pellet's Folly," Raul said.

"What's that?"

"Casa Loma. It's a castle that Henry Pellet, who owned Toronto Light and Electric built for himself and his wife. It has a great view of Toronto."

Casa Loma was a medieval-style castle on a hill overlooking Toronto. It was big and gray and didn't look anything like someone's home. A group of French schoolgirls in blue and white uniforms took pictures of each other in the courtyard. Inside, we were each given a tape recorder, which would be our tour guide. We put our earphones on and followed the disembodied tour guide inside.

After each point of interest we heard a drumroll. During this drumroll, tourists were supposed to reach the next stop on the tour. Somehow, I was always at the wrong stop. Finally I just gave up and followed Raul.

Sir Henry had designed his ninety-eight-room castle to become a military museum. The cavernous living room boasted an organ. From a balcony above, Sir Henry could oversee his guests while military marches rose to the rafters. Sir Henry's lady, founder of the Canadian Girl Scouts, had been an invalid. She spent most of her time in a bed that, according to the tape recorder, Marie Antoinette may have slept in.

Raul and I stood in a circle of tourists at the foot of the immense bed. Angels and vines were carved into the bedpost. "Where are you?" he asked.

I saw his lips move but I couldn't hear him. He tried again, louder. Several tourists turned to look at us. I pulled off my earphones. "I'm in the dining room with the three ovens each large enough to roast an ox."

Raul pulled me into the biggest shower stall I had ever seen. Spigots came from every angle. Sir Henry and his lady, who were both seriously overweight, could shower without moving. By this time we were both giggling like lunatics.

"Had enough or do you want to listen to the part where Sir Henry died destitute in his chauffeur's arms?"

"Serves him right," I said because I had had enough.

We walked back through the living room to the front door. Right there on the castle wall, there was a pay phone. Raul handed me a Canadian quarter. "Go ahead, I think you're gonna get lucky."

The phone rang only once before a woman picked up. She had a heavy German accent. I asked for Mr. Schilling.

"Who's calling, please?"

I introduced myself. I asked if I could speak to Mr. Schilling. I explained that I was researching the history of the New York City shelter system. "One moment please," she said.

The rest was easy. In an equally strong German accent Mr. Schilling invited me to come over. "Come now," he said. "We're on Spadina one block north of Bloor."

He gave me the exact address and then I hung up. My heart was pounding. Raul beamed at me. "Are you going to let me tag along?"

"Who will you say you are?"

We stepped out of the castle into the sunlight.

"We'll play it by ear," he said. "This guy has nothing to hide. But don't be disappointed if he doesn't know anything."

A green-eyed cat sat on the porch of the nineteenth-century house. We took the four wooden steps onto the canvas welcome mat and rang the doorbell. Delicately etched flowers ornamented the glass panel of the outside door. Inside, a lace curtain with a swan pattern covered the pane. Through it, I could see her face. It was a good face.

She was small and she tottered just a bit as she stood there with a smile in her chestnut eyes. She wore an apron over her skirt and blouse. Her hair looked like it had just been set and sprayed for the week. "Come in," she said.

We stepped into a room between two rooms. From above, a formidable wooden staircase descended. Sliding doors on either side led to other rooms. On the wall in front of us, a group of watercolors illustrated the Fall of Man, the Birth of Moses in the basket of reeds, Moses and the Ten Commandments, and Moses and Pharaoh separated by a serpent. I stood there studying the serpent. Schilling came down the stairs in his bedroom slippers. He was small and very frail; his skin, hair, and sparkling eyes were pale gray. He pointed to an easel with a pencil sketch on it. "I draw history for my own amusement," he said.

"Your work is lovely," I said.

"Moses convinced the Pharaoh to let his people go. Do you know how he did it?"

"He turned his staff into a serpent."

"Well, yes," the old man said, "as a show of power. The Pharaoh always understands power."

I nodded. Schilling must have been about eighty. In his hand he carried a book of poems by the Chilean poet Pablo Neruda. I introduced Raul, and the old man beamed as if I had brought him a gift.

"Come in, come in," he said.

He opened one of the sliding doors. Beyond was a small room dominated by an enormous Viennese armoire. He invited us to sit.

"You read Spanish?" Raul asked as Schilling put his book down on the table between us.

"Is there any other way to read Neruda?"

"I love Spanish, especially for poetry. I was born in Cuba but I never really lived there," Raul said.

"Of course," Schilling said, "you could not live there because that criminal took over."

Mrs. Schilling brought a tray with a large bottle of Fra Angelico and four liqueur glasses. "Let's drink to Cuba," she said. "We landed there after the war and we wanted to stay until the end of our lives."

"This is the time of day when we pay homage to the hermit," Mr. Schilling said as he filled our glasses with the Italian liqueur. As he lifted the bottle I noticed the number tattooed on his wrist.

"The hermit?" I asked.

"The hermit who lived on the border of Piedmont and Perugia in Italy. Smart man. He kept no human company. From herbs and plants he made divine concoctions." Mr. Schilling handed us our liqueur.

Mrs. Schilling raised her glass in a toast. "To the lovers," she said, "and to their search."

I looked at Raul and he looked at me. We sipped from our tiny glasses. The hazelnut liquor warmed me from the inside. "To Cuba," Mr. Schilling said, "and to anarchy if it ever comes."

"Nobody believed a man who couldn't even speak the language

properly could ever take over the country, but he did," Mrs. Schilling said.

I thought she meant Castro. She rubbed the number on her wrist. I realized she was going further into the past. The skin was a deep red, as if she had been rubbing that spot for a lifetime. She took another sip and said, "Any good-looking actor can lead a people. People aren't led by deeds, they're led by rhetoric. Hitler promised everybody exactly what they wanted."

Raul leaned forward. "My grandparents were in their sixties when they left Cuba. I don't think they ever really recovered."

"That crook. Even his father before him was a crook."

Raul and Mr. Schilling were united in their hatred for Castro.

I took another sip and said, "I guess you don't have much faith in government or even revolution."

"Revolution," Mrs. Schilling said. "I've never seen one work. Perhaps we've had the misfortune of seeing too much. Too many broken promises."

The word *promise* hung in the air like a balloon. I took a deep breath and grabbed my chance.

"Speaking of broken promises," I said, "we really came to ask you what you know about New York City's shelter program. The shelters opened late last year, and in December and January there were three major fires."

Schilling pulled on his chin. "New York City is farther south than it seems on the map."

I didn't know what he meant, but Raul chuckled. Schilling went on: "In the old days in Cuba corruption was so simple, so obvious. You paid a bribe for everything. There were no dangerous illusions. Corruption was simple . . . one, two, three."

"How did that one, two, three work in the New York City shelter program?" Raul asked.

The old man cocked his head. "Ah . . ." he said. "You'll have to figure that out yourself. I left before—"

"Why? Why did you leave?"

Schilling shrugged and looked at his wife. She nodded. He said, "The city wanted me to modify my designs to the point of lunacy. What started out as a plan to provide decent housing for families turned into a plan to warehouse human beings. I couldn't agree to that."

From where I sat, I could see Moses turning his staff into a serpent.

"Who," I asked, "wanted you to modify the designs?"

"The man in charge, Jason Isenberg."

Raul looked at me and I looked at him. Now I knew why the name Schilling had seemed familiar. I had scheduled meetings between Jason and Mr. Schilling. I had even spoken to Schilling. But I had never actually met him. And I had no idea what happened at those meetings. Back then, it hadn't even occurred to me that I should be interested.

"Do you think the fires were accidents or that there is something wrong with the renovations?"

"Do you remember Upton Sinclair's book *The Jungle?*"

I had read it in high school. It was about the meat-packing industry in Chicago at the turn of the century.

"What about it?" Raul put his hands on his knees and leaned forward as if he knew what was coming.

"They processed everything but the squeal. The shelter program was like that. Everybody involved benefited."

"Everybody but the homeless," Mrs. Schilling said, and rubbed the numbers on her wrist.

Mr. Schilling said, "You can be sure that during construction of those shelters all the contractors cut corners. If the architect requested three-quarter-inch Sheetrock, they used half-inch. If the wiring was to be triple-insulated, they insulated once. Then they billed the city according to the original specifications. Profits must have been enormous."

In a pencil sketch, in the corner of the room, Moses parted the Red Sea. I asked, "Do you think the mayor knew?"

Schilling placed a finger over his lips. "Unspoken. You can be sure his benefits were unspoken."

He refilled my glass. "You must be careful when you depose the czar." He looked at Raul. "You can go from bad to worse. You know what I mean?"

Raul wrung his hands. "Batista to Castro."

"We are too old to be afraid. What would be the use? But you
. . . you should be careful. You are dealing with very bad people."

Mrs. Schilling took my hand and joined it with Raul's. Raul
said, "I'm a journalist."

Mrs. Schilling smiled as if to say in and of itself, that was
neither good nor bad. I wove my fingers through his.

"Look for the obvious," Mr. Schilling said. "And remember
the lion."

"What do you mean?" I asked.

"The lion is the king of the jungle but he doesn't do his own
killing."

14

Under the Hudson River, in the Lincoln Tunnel, stuck in bumper-to-bumper traffic, he turned to me and said, "So who is the power behind the throne?"

"You mean who pulls the strings?"

"Yeah."

"I don't think it's one person. Brogan, Hunter . . . Jason was the mayor's right hand from the beginning. Nicosea comes out of the Brooklyn machine. Maybe the party bosses?"

I had come out of the Brooklyn machine myself. I had met Joe licking stamps at district headquarters. Besides church, that was the way to meet people in the old neighborhood.

"Do you think the mayor knew?"

"No, not necessarily. Details were probably left unspoken. You know—deniability," I said.

He nodded. We both knew that the golden rule of politics was to keep bad news from the man in charge. That way he could always say he hadn't known.

Raul touched the accelerator and moved the car forward two inches. Then he said, "You have the capacity to really stir these guys up."

"How? I have no power. You were right when you said I was just a glorified secretary."

"You're close, very close to the power. They're in a tough campaign and you may scare them into hanging themselves."

"Nicosea hasn't even declared."

"So what? We all know he's running for an unprecedented fourth term. Even without Isenberg's suicide and the shelter fires, he's been in office long enough to make a lot of enemies. There's more than one viable opponent on the horizon. He could lose the primary."

We emerged from the tunnel into gridlock, which forced us to turn uptown rather than down. Over the weekend a section of the highway had collapsed and a truck was jackknifed between the upper and lower levels. "Holy shit," Raul said, "it's good to know our tax dollars are really maintaining the roadways."

"I hope nobody was killed."

I was looking up at the *Intrepid,* an aircraft carrier that loomed over the pier. This multibillion-dollar war machine was now a museum. Mothers like me could bring their little boys to see the kind of sophisticated killing they could aspire to. I had heard there were twenty stories inside its huge hull.

"I wonder how many homeless shelters they could have built with the money that thing cost?"

Raul chuckled. "Aw, c'mon, that's a relic. Besides, a country needs national security."

"Why? Because it makes the puppets in charge feel strong and tough?"

"No, because it keeps communism in check."

"It didn't do them much good against Castro. He made a revolution with twelve men."

"Castro is a public-relations genius. He took to the hills, grew that beard, and pretended to be the savior. He didn't just betray the Cuban people, he betrayed most of those twelve men too. Anyway, there were several thousand *barbudos* in the hills, not just twelve. Castro was and is a dictator. The fact is, America fell down on the job."

I had been doing a little reading on his homeland and I had my own opinion.

"The fact is the Cuban people were starving and Batista was milking the country like the shah did to Iran, like Marcos did to the Philippines. And the power behind the throne for all those scumbags was America."

"You just made my point. Did you know when Castro came to the United States after his revolution, he hired one of New York City's absolute top public-relations firms?"

I imagined a guy like Hunter taking a guy like Castro on a press tour and I had to laugh. Raul didn't join me. Traffic was murder and he was tense.

"It takes me months to get you to admit that this mayor to whom you're so blindly loyal is either a crook or a front for crooks. Then in one weekend you turn against the whole country. It's still the best in the world."

"Don't patronize me. The first thing that's wrong with the country is that women have no power."

"Oh, I see."

He started honking the horn as if that would make traffic move. A bunch of other drivers started honking their horns too. An Irish traffic cop came over.

"Cut that out. It's doing nobody any good."

Raul whipped out his press pass. "I'm a reporter and I need to get down to City Hall."

"Well, you're going the wrong way, buddy."

"Maybe I wouldn't be going the wrong way if I could have turned downtown at the tunnel."

Raul honked his horn one more time for effect. The cop turned red. "This is the last time I'm gonna tell you to cut that out." He walked away.

"Bastard. Give a guy a little power and he goes crazy." Raul shoved his press pass back into his pocket.

The monument to national security in front of which we were stuck hid not only the river but the other shore. Behind the *Intrepid*'s planes, radar disks, and turret guns, the wind separated the clouds into a gold-trimmed lace.

"I don't buy it anymore," I said. "I just don't believe all this national security bullshit anymore. Who are we securing ourselves against? All these billions—half my paycheck every week buys overpriced weapons. There's nothing left for the things that I care about. Me and all the other mothers out there. We want good schools, safe streets, day care. That's national security to me. The country went bankrupt over the Vietnam War and what did that accomplish?"

"We need national security."

"How much is enough? Besides, security comes from the inside. Security is riding the subways, walking the streets, and sending my kid to school without worrying about him getting hit over the head by some homeless druggie who's so sick he's dangerous. How does national security protect me against that? National security is a bullshit macho trip and I don't buy it anymore."

"That's okay," he said, "you're mad now. I expected you to go a little overboard when you first got in touch with your anger."

"You're so goddamn superior. Is that because you went to Harvard or because you're macho?"

"You like the sound of that word, huh?"

"I don't like what it implies."

"Look, in Spanish it just means male . . . there's *macho* . . . male, and *embra* . . . female."

"Well maybe there hasn't been enough *embra* power in this world."

The traffic finally started moving. "You wanna stir the shit a little?" he asked.

"Meaning?"

"Next Saturday is the night of the Inner Circle."

"What about it?"

In city politics the Inner Circle dinner held in the Empire Ballroom at the New York Hilton is the social event of the season. The first Saturday in March, the press, politicians, and the public-relations types who serve as their intermediaries paid five hundred dollars a plate to attend the black-tie gala. During the dinner, members of the Press Club present a show they have written—a spoof of the year's political events in which reporters played the politicians. A lot of the reporters were very talented and the show was fun. During dessert, the mayor offered a one-act rebuttal. Support staff like myself were invited to the dress rehearsal the Friday night before the actual show. We'd come right after work and brown-bag it. A lot of people said the dress rehearsal was more fun than the actual show. We'd laugh with the actors as they made their mistakes. But we never saw Nicosea's rebuttal, which was rehearsed in secret. According to the newspapers, the mayor's part of the show was usually spectacular. He was always backed by the cast of a current Broadway musical. In his younger days he had done some acting and it showed. Profits went to the New York Press Club's retirement fund. It was a see-and-be-seen kind of event. I was intrigued.

"I have tickets," Raul said.

I laughed a bitter laugh. What he was proposing gave me two kinds of pleasure. Not only was it at last a public acknowledgment of our relationship, but it would strike fear into Hunter's petty little heart. Not that he would take our relationship seriously, but he would certainly spend a few sleepless nights wondering what kind of pillow talk was going on. Still, I said, "I have nothing to wear."

"Rent a tuxedo."

"What about you?" I asked. "What about your publisher, your editors, the other reporters?"

"It won't hurt me a bit," he said. "They'll assume I'm working you."

"That's nasty."

"It's what they'll assume."

He was right. In the City Hall caste system, reporters might socialize with press types or even politicians but not with support staff. Class lines were never crossed. He added, "The consequences would be mostly on your side. You might want to think about that."

He was trying to make an illegal turn to get back downtown and it wasn't working.

"I should hear about the 911 tape today," he said. "What is it you hope to find there?"

Cars were honking at us from all sides. I said, "You'd better watch where you're going."

He sighed. The river glowed with reflected morning light.

"I want to know why my husband died."

He took his eyes off the road to squint at me. His eyes said, "Your husband's death is old news," but his mouth kept silent.

When I pretended not to notice, he pulled at his collar and rolled his window down. A gust of wind slapped my face.

"Is it because of your job? Do you think your career was somehow bought by his death?"

"Could you close the window?"

He rolled the window up. I looked at my watch. Then I answered his question with a question. "Why did the mayor hire me? I never even used my secretarial skills after I was married."

"Do you ever look in the mirror?"

Our eyes met. I said, "We can't both just ask questions. Now and then, somebody has to provide an answer."

"You're a great public-relations gimmick, Marie. Not many widows are as articulate and sexy as you are."

"But I'm an excellent secretary."

The car inched forward a foot. "I don't doubt it, that's why you lasted."

"I'm fast and efficient."

"I know."

He was tired of this conversation. Still, I wondered how guilty that efficiency made me. How much had I rubber-stamped in the mayor's name? A feeling washed over me as if I had been here before. Something had slipped. I had made an irreversible mistake. Now I was waiting, waiting for my punishment to arrive. But the punishment wasn't coming. And somehow that was worse. The feeling was so familiar it took me back.

On my mother's mantel stands an old Florentine clock. My

mother inherited it from her mother, who inherited it from hers. The Roman numerals on its face surround a very pink, fat, naked woman who lies in garlands of roses. Next to her is a keyhole. The hole is for the key to wind the clock. My mother keeps the key in a secret place. She never winds the clock. I daydream about winding the clock. I climb on a chair, rest my chin on the mantel, and study that keyhole until my mother yells at me to get down.

One day I take the brass key from its hiding place to wind the clock. I struggle with its glass face and the clock slips from my hands. It hits the floor.

The fat lady's face cracks and slides off. My mother is on her knees, staring at the missing face. I wait for her to cry, to slap me, to yell and send me to bed without dinner. But she doesn't even look at me. Gently she picks up the clock and puts it back on the mantel. Stooped-shouldered, she returns to the kitchen. Her silence lasts weeks. I go to my room, crawl under the covers and cry. I wait for her to bring the punishment, but she never does. I am alone. I cry until my misery becomes sweet and delicious. Now I have a companion.

I remembered crying after I was married too, hiding under the covers, loving my misery because it was mine. Joe was a lot like my mother. His weapon was silence.

"Could you return to the present?" Raul was pissed.

I realized how much I liked Raul's anger. It was up-front, tangible, we could fight, and then it would be over. "Men wear tuxedos," I snapped.

We bickered until he dropped me off a few blocks from City Hall. He said he didn't give a damn what I wore. I should just decide whether I wanted to go or not. I said, "All right, goddamn it, I'll *go*," and slammed the car door shut.

When I got to my office, a large interoffice envelope lay in the center of my desk. It had a rubber band around it, and although it wasn't sealed, it was held shut by a string that twisted around a tiny cardboard circle. I walked around my desk. I took off the little silk scarf I wore under my coat to keep my collar clean. I took off my coat. I hung it up. Finally I pulled the rubber band from the package. The band slipped and snapped against my wrist. I began to unwind the string. It went around and around that damn circle. Finally there was no more string and I opened the flap.

Inside, there was a note from Jolynne at the Department of Human Services: *This was all I could find. Is it what you were looking for? Call me. J.*

I ran my hand over the one folder my request had yielded. Before actually extricating the file from the envelope, I got up to lock the door. I cleaned off my desk completely. Then I opened the file.

The file was not what I had expected. It was five years old. On top was a memo from Jason to the Human Services Department. He was asking the department to evaluate the possibility that a vacant office building at 49 Sherman Street on Staten Island could become a temporary family shelter. Human Services administers shelters and welfare hotels. So it would be up to them to decide whether a facility was feasible. Nothing indicated how the site had been selected. The city's lease with the landlord was attached. The lease included an option to buy.

The next memo, dated about a month later, was Human Services' preliminary review of the building's feasibility for conversion to a shelter. According to the engineers who inspected it, the building had only one bathroom per floor. After listing problems with the roof, bathrooms, floors, and electrical wiring, the memo concluded that the building was less than ideal for a family shelter. A return memo from Jason requested a second opinion.

The second HSD review concluded that the building could be adapted by adding one kitchen per floor. The last memo in the series showed that a company called Riley Inc. had been hired to do the renovations. Their address was on Staten Island. Riley Inc. had subcontracted the electrical wiring to a company called American Enterprises on Mott Street in Chinatown.

Then there was something interesting—an anonymous letter attacked the city's "unconscionable plan" to provide two bathrooms and one kitchen for every twelve families. This was tantamount to a "health hazard," the letter said. The letter also charged that the city was leasing the Sherman Street property at twice its purchase value. The rest of the file seemed to be a Department of Investigation review. The DOI review had been triggered by press inquiries. Each reporter in Room Nine had received a copy of the anonymous letter.

The review was a paper review. No DOI investigator had ever actually visited Sherman Street. DOI investigators met with Human Services personnel to review the Sherman Street files. DOI did not comment on the question of unsanitary conditions—that was strictly a Human Services determination to make. On the other issue, DOI concluded that the city had been forced to pay a higher price for leasing the building because of its own cumbersome purchase process, which no landlord would tolerate without the incentive of extra money. The only thing DOI questioned was the fact that the contractor, Riley Inc., was actually a subsidiary of the landlord. DOI issued a press release concluding that the city had been under duress because of the enormity of the homeless crisis, but that the city had done nothing illegal.

A month later, the city's lease with the landlord expired and the building still had not been purchased. Renovations stopped. The city had spent two million dollars only to let the site revert to the landlord. A final memo showed that only eight weeks later the landlord had leveled the building. If the press had noticed it, there were no clippings to reveal it.

I went through the file a second time. I found a personal note from the mayor that had been stuck to the back of another memo. It seemed to have been misfiled. Not only was it dated two years after the first set of memos, but it referred to a different location. The note urged the human-services commissioner to expedite Deputy Mayor Isenberg's request for purchase of an empty lot on Staten Island for construction of a temporary shelter. It pointed out that a housing emergency had been declared and normal approval processes were suspended. The lot was at 12 Liberty Street. That was the address of the Donovan Shelter.

It was an informal note signed informally. Just *Ken*. I studied that casual signature. It was my imitation of the mayor's scrawl. From day one, forging these informal notes had been part of the job. The mayor would dictate the notes and I would sign and send them. That way his busy schedule didn't slow down the correspondence. On formal letters, as usual I used the auto stamp to imitate his signature. But informal notes were supposed to look like he had signed them personally. So I signed for him. It was a task I had always performed with great pride—after all, it showed how much he trusted me.

But this particular note was dated during the time that I was still working for Jason. Jason had often asked me to sign letters and memos for him. Occasionally, when the mayor was out of town or very busy and Jason was in a hurry, he'd ask me to sign for the mayor. This memo had been one of those occasions.

It was March and a deceptively springlike sun flooded the room. From my window I looked out at the lawn between City Hall and the Tweed courthouse. The crust of snow was gone, but underneath the grass was a dead frozen gray. I thought of Raul's warning in Florida. He had been right after all. I was a perfect scapegoat. On impulse, I went to Room Nine.

The reporters were all hard at work at their computer terminals. I walked the very narrow isle between the desks and leaned down to whisper to Raul. "I need to talk to you."

He looked up sheepishly; everyone else in the room was staring into their monitors, but I could feel their attention on us.

"I'm filing a story," he said. "I have fifteen minutes."

"After that?"

"I have to be here for the fact check."

Larry, Raul's boss, was working at the next terminal. I could tell that he was listening.

"When do you get off?"

Raul was glancing at me now with a pained look. I whispered into his ear, "Meet me at the Staten Island ferry at six-thirty." Then, feeling Larry's eyes on me, I walked out.

It was lunch hour. I headed for American Enterprises. The Manhattan Savings Bank with its red pagoda-style roof loomed over Chatham Square, where traffic was congested around the Kim Lau Memorial dedicated to the Chinese Americans who died during WW II. I passed a colorful movie marquee advertising an import from Hong Kong called *Poison Rose and the Bodyguard.* I headed for Mott Street in the heart of Chinatown.

As I entered the narrow cobblestone streets the sights and smells of Chinatown embraced me. Although only a block from Mulberry Street, the center of Little Italy, this community's heart beat to a different rhythm. Instead of mozzarella, mortadella, and Gorgonzola, glazed ducks and dried fish hung in shop windows. Vegetable stands offered exotic roots and spices. In the noodle shops and rice houses people ate fish or vegetables over rice or noodles, moving their chopsticks with expert precision. The bakeries offered sweet dim sum, almond cookies, buns, and steamed sponge cakes. I felt a pang of hunger.

The address I was looking for housed a Chinese apothecary. I studied the scrap of paper in my hand. Had I copied the address incorrectly? I stepped inside; a bell chimed lightly over the door, and as it closed behind me the three other customers peeked at me and looked away. Behind the counter, a very old man concentrated on a miniature scale he balanced on a pencil in his right hand. He was measuring the weight of a piece of bark against a handful of dried flowers. When he had assured himself that the scales were balanced, he dropped the contents onto a piece of paper on the counter. When he folded the paper, a drawing emerged—yin and yang. His three women customers watched intently. In their hands they each held scraps of paper like mine, but theirs were prescriptions.

Behind the pharmacist was a cabinet with hundreds of small drawers that were labeled in the mysterious drawings that are Chinese writing. The woman took her prescription and paid the pharmacist. The old cash register rang as the door chimed to her exit. He turned to the next prescription. I wandered to the back of the store, where glass and ceramic cookware shared the shelves with dried and canned foods.

The pharmacist began measuring out a larger, more complicated prescription, which included dried roots, dried leaves, bark, dried antler, sea-horse skeletons, and a few tiny starfish skeletons. When he had finished that prescription and the next, he turned his attention to me. Now we were alone with each other.

"Doctor send you?"

I shook my head and showed him my slip of paper. "I'm looking for this company, American Enterprises."

He studied the scrap impassively. "This right address."

"What about the company?"

"Never hear name."

"Did they move?"

"This my address for ten years," he said. "Nobody else. You from Office of Professional Discipline?"

"No, why?"

"They arrest acupuncture doctors. White people no understand Chinese medicine."

His face told me he hadn't the remotest idea that his address had been used by some phantom company to bilk the city. But he did sense that I was trouble. I wanted to buy something to let him know that I was all right and that I liked his store. He turned back to the drawers that contained his ancient remedies. He didn't want my money.

As I returned to City Hall I wondered where American Enterprises had disappeared to. Had it evaporated like all the premises on which I had based my life? Or maybe it had never existed at all. I saw my reflection in a store window. My eyes were hollow, my face a shadow, I had only one hand. I stopped to look at my undefined self. Was I like that because I had let others define me, choose my loyalties for me? Was Raul right? The world had turned into a hall of crazy mirrors where everything was twisted.

When I got back to City Hall, a press conference was in progress, one of four scheduled that day. Now that the homeless were no longer camped outside, Nicosea had switched gears. He was in the campaign mode. Not that the mayor had declared yet. The longer he could put off declaring, the longer he could work the media without worrying about equal-time considerations. He could pretend that all the flimflam was just business as usual, while his every move was calculated to build momentum for the day when he finally did announce his intention to run for a fourth term.

I peeked into the Blue Room. Raul sat up front with the other reporters. The rest of the room was stacked with City Hall types so that it would look packed for the television cameras. It was like a play; everybody knew the staging and everyone knew their part. Only I seemed to have forgotten my role. I retreated to my office through a sea of looks that said my lunch hours were getting longer and longer. But no one had the authority to challenge me and no one did.

For the next several hours I wrote notes politely accepting invitations for the mayor. I signed them Ken, the way I always had. It seemed a little late to protest. These days he was accepting almost everything. Brogan and Hunter were making the decisions. At six I grabbed my jacket and headed for the Staten Island Ferry. I wanted to get a look at Riley Inc. I hoped Raul would meet me at the ferry.

In the crush of commuters I couldn't find Raul, so I boarded without him. As an early dusk settled I stood outside and watched Manhattan drift away. I was staring down into the water when I heard him say, "Why so glum?"

"I thought you weren't coming."

"And miss another ferry ride with you?"

His hair was blowing wild in the wind. He leaned on the rail next to me, held it with both hands, and looked down into the water where I was looking. "See any answers?"

"It's too turbulent. There's nothing down there, not even a reflection of you and me."

"You're pissed that I didn't pay more attention to you when you came to Room Nine."

"I never go to Room Nine."

"I know you never go to Room Nine."

"Is that the way you plan to acknowledge me at the Inner Circle?"

He put both his hands on my arm, the one that was near him, and stroked me. The wind was cold and brutal. "Don't be insecure about me," he said. "Please don't be insecure about me. This is a very sticky situation; we have to trust each other."

I watched the trails of tugboats and barges disappear in the choppy gray surface of the river. Finally I let my eyes meet his. Since Toronto I had known that I had meant my words that evening on the kitchen counter. I was in love with him. Outside the bed too. I said, "Easy for you to say. What have you got to lose?"

He shrugged. "I can't make you believe in us."

I changed the subject. It wasn't safer, it was just different.

"I got a file today. One file. It's not even about the construction of any of the shelters. It's the previous history of a Staten Island site where an office building was going to be adapted into a family shelter. It didn't work out, though."

"Why go to Human Services for construction files? Isenberg headed the shelter initiative. Can't you get his files?"

The metal rail we clutched was now so cold that I thought my hands might be stuck. A wave slapped the ferry and sprayed salt in our eyes. He squinted. "What happened to them?"

"They were shredded."

He didn't react, so I thought my words had been lost in the wind, but an intense fire lit in his eyes. "You didn't . . . you didn't . . . tell me you didn't."

My hair completely covered my face and then the wind pulled it back like a veil. I said, "I didn't."

We both went back to contemplating the water. Finally I said, "But I might as well have. I boxed them. I cleaned out his office. I even brought some of his things to the widow."

"Oh no," he said, "oh no."

Manhattan was moving away like a dream out of reach. The ferry hid whatever approached us from behind. The Statue of Liberty didn't shed much light on the water. On the other side, Ellis Island loomed like a dark and brooding memory of misery. Inside the ferry, through the window we could see the tired commuters clutching briefcases and small purchases.

Raul began to pace in that small space at the end of the ferry. He looked around at the water on all sides and talked to the wind. He refused to look at me. At first I thought he was talking Spanish but then I realized it was mezza-mezza, half Spanish, half English. Finally he hit his forehead and came over to glare at me. "I don't believe it. I don't fucking believe it. Who had you do that?"

"Does it matter?"

His voice got higher, not louder really, but higher. "No, actually, actually it doesn't. It doesn't matter. Your ass is cooked, that's all."

"I was just doing what I was told to do."

The wind slapped the words back in my face.

"A lot of people explained the Holocaust with that line."

Then it was quiet between us. There wasn't a whole lot I could say.

Two teenagers joined us at the rail. One lit a joint. We looked out at the water. They began a long passionate kiss. Raul grabbed me by the back of the neck. For a second I thought he was going to kiss me too. "I just wish you had told me, Marie. I wish you had told me before I dragged you into all this."

"Would that have stopped you?"

We both knew it wouldn't have. He stepped back and looked out onto the river, which was losing its shores to the darkness. I said, "It was Nicosea himself who asked me."

He walked inside. I followed. Hundreds of tired-looking workers were squeezed together on the benches, each pretending to be alone, dozing in their seats, glancing at their watches, or chatting with the few they had chosen to acknowledge as fellow travelers. I felt claustrophobic. I grabbed Raul by the hands and led him into the ferry's belly, which was like a floating parking lot. We stood there surrounded by cars. The metal floor beneath us seemed to shift.

"In Miami you warned me that I could be cast as the City Hall scapegoat. Why are you so surprised now?"

We walked between the cars toward the front of the ferry.

"It was abstract then," he said. "This is real. And now the conflict of interest is real too."

A gigantic cement dock that led into a tomblike garage approached. To our left spanned the magnificence of the Verrazano Bridge, connecting Staten Island to Brooklyn. Ahead, Staten Island seemed uninhabited.

"What's the conflict?" I asked.

"What you just told me nails the mayor. If Nicosea personally asked you to pack Jason's files, he probably knew how dangerous they were. You should have said no."

"I had no reason to suspect anything then."

"And if you had suspected, would you have turned him down?"

"Probably not."

Then I explained what the file I had gotten earlier that day did contain—the history of an office building at 49 Sherman Street on Staten Island. I told him about the anonymous allegations that the building was inappropriate for a family shelter and that the city was paying twice the market value in rent, about the DOI whitewash and the two million dollars the city had wasted on a building that was ultimately razed.

"When was all this?"

"Five years ago. The memos are from Jason Isenberg to the human resources commissioner."

"What are we doing out here?"

"Two companies were named in the file—a contractor, Riley Incorporated, and a subcontractor, American Enterprises. I went to look at the subcontractor this afternoon. It looks like American Enterprises never existed. So I wanted to see the contractor. I figured you would too."

The ferry bumped the dock and the commuters began their rush to shore. We followed. It was chaos. There were no cabs. From a pay phone I called a car service. We waited for twenty minutes in the shadows of that huge tomb of a garage. Finally the car arrived. The driver was an Italian old enough to be my father. He took us deep inside the island, past poorly maintained one-family houses, past low-rise apartment houses, past every fast-food franchise in America—Burger King, McDonald's, Wendy's, 7-Eleven, Red Lobster—past several communities of well-maintained town houses. The whole time he was blasting my favorite opera, Verdi's *Aïda*.

The arias reached that bittersweet melancholy I carried around inside me. Raul reached for my hand. Finally he said, "Listen . . . listen." At first I thought he meant the music and then I knew better. He had something to tell me.

The music was so loud he had to talk right into my ear.

"I got some information today too."

The tenor was telling Aïda that he would love her forever.

"My snitch in Florida, the one you saw, I asked him for a lead on the FBI operative who shot Joe."

"And?"

"He refuses to talk about it on the phone. He wants me to come back down there. I think he knows something and he wants cash before he talks."

We were driving through a new development of cul-de-sacs; the houses that were finished all looked the same. The circular drives led one into the other. Finally we reached what seemed to be the last circle. Here the houses were just frames against the sky. They looked like skeletons of houses that had been. But they were frames of houses that were yet to be.

"This is it," the driver yelled over the music.

I didn't even bother to ask him if he was sure. I figured he knew his island. Raul leaned forward. "Could you wait for us?"

We got out and approached a fence. Behind it stood a mountain of garbage big enough to block the sky. Aïda's pure soprano floated over the stench. *"La fatal pietra sovra me si chiuse."*

I felt sick. Obviously, that mountain of garbage hadn't grown overnight. This had never been the site of a construction company. This trail too was a dead end.

"Will you still go to Florida to find out about Joe?"

"I promised, didn't I? I'm going the Sunday after the Inner Circle dinner. I have that Monday off."

I nodded, swallowed a bitter taste, and got back into the car with him.

Aïda and Radames were saying good-bye. *"Si chiuse . . . si chiuse."*

"What is that?" I asked the driver.

"Is Juan Ponce sing Radames."

I said, "No, I mean that dirt mountain."

"Isa dump." He spread his hands like "whaddaya want from me." "They say they gonna clean but I no believe."

I asked him to take us back to the ferry.

Raul added, "Please drive by Sherman Street on the way back."

"No problem," he said. "Is onna way."

Just two blocks from the ferry we entered a neighborhood of older, poorly maintained single-family houses that had been converted for commercial use and now housed the Chase Manhattan Bank, the Staten Island Chamber of Commerce, and the city sanitation-department garage. A couple of co-op conversions were in progress. I couldn't see a street sign, but it all looked very familiar. At the end of the next block stood a wrecking crane and the two remaining walls of a fire-ravaged roofless building. On a twisted pile of broken bathtubs and half-melted refrigerators lay a headless doll. The crane said that soon this eyesore would be gone and with it the entire history of corruption that had built it. It took me a moment to realize that this monument to agony and death was the gutted Donovan Shelter.

"This isn't Sherman Street, it's Liberty Street," I said.

"Sherman is around the corner. This is Liberty."

We turned the corner. The Donovan was so big, it covered the whole corner of the block. It had entrances both on Liberty and on Sherman.

"This is unbelievable," Raul said.

We stared at each other, silently reaching the same conclusion.

"It's the same lot, the same goddamn lot," he said.

"It can't be."

"It is. It's a corner lot, so they gave it two addresses."

"It's worse than even Schilling imagined."

"The mayor and his cronies exploited the homeless situation from every possible angle. First they milked the renovation on Sherman Street. Then, after they demolished the Sherman Street building, they began again with the empty lot on Liberty Street. But it was the same property all along."

"All along," I echoed.

On the way back to Manhattan, the stone-and-glass city rose before us like a testament to human accomplishment. We held each other tight because the wind was brutal. After a while I said, "That file I got today. There was one more thing in it—a note from Nicosea to the human-services commissioner asking him to expedite the purchase of the lot at 12 Liberty Street."

His eyes lit up. "So we know the mayor was definitely in on at least some of it."

I nodded. "You and I know that. But the signature on the note is mine. His name, my handwriting."

This time Raul just put his arms around me. His body shielded me from the wind. "Do you still want to go to the Inner Circle? It could backfire. Maybe it's time to leave well enough alone."

I thought about Nicosea and how I had trusted him. How I had blindly, efficiently obeyed his every command. A flash of rage shot through me like heat lightning. I felt myself grab onto it and hold it tight—the rage.

"I can't turn back now. I don't want to."

I left the shelter of his arms to look down into the dark river.

Reflections of the city's lights danced below us and made pictures of the past. Raul touched my cheek. I could feel myself torn between his warmth and the deep, frozen anger, down inside me, down there with the betrayed loyalties of a lifetime.

"Before Joe died, things weren't very good with us," I said. "We were kids when we got married and we grew apart. Inside . . . our marriage was dead."

"I'm alive and so are you. There's no sin in that."

15

In a room small enough to be a closet, I was surrounded by costumes and uniforms for every profession and occasion—from celebrants at Mardi Gras to guards at Sing Sing and everything in between. I found my way through several centuries of military uniforms to the tuxedos. Of the six on the rack, one was designed for a woman. I am an average size. It fit.

Everything about it was like a man's tuxedo, except that it was tailored to the smaller waist, the wider hips of the female form. It had an extra feature too. The usual ruffled shirt was replaced by a

black chiffon blouse with see-through sleeves and back. Wearing a
bra would be out of the question. I put the tuxedo on and stood in
front of the fading old mirror. With the jacket, I was one of the
boys. When I removed the jacket, I became a woman. A wild
woman. A woman I was just getting to know.

That Saturday I took Joey to spend the night at a friend's
house. Then I went home, climbed into a hot bubble bath, and
just lay there. In the steam that rose around me I imagined Raul's
hands, his touch. My body came alive with yearning. Our lovemak-
ing was always so good and I had always given him the credit for
that. But as I lay there in the hot water's caress, I began to credit
myself too. It was a fifty-fifty proposition. He took his pleasure
from mine just as I took mine from his. I tried not to imagine the
evening ahead so that I wouldn't be disappointed if it turned out
differently.

By the time Raul called up to my window from the street, I was
dressed. I leaned out the window and threw the key down to him.
A few moment later, I heard the elevator begin to move. In sec-
onds it locked into place on my floor. Raul stood behind the gate.
In the shadow that separated us, I thought I was looking at myself.
He gasped with what I recognized as the same sensation. I had put
my long hair up so that it looked short. He pulled the gate back.
"Your car awaits, madame."

He had rented not a limousine but a tasteful Lincoln Continental. As the driver held the door for me I thought that except
for the fact that the windows weren't tinted, this car was just like
the mayor's car. Once inside, Raul looked at me like a kid in a
candy store. "I was kidding about the tuxedo."

I thought he was saying he didn't like the way I looked.

"I'm nervous."

"It doesn't show. And you look great."

We didn't talk much for the rest of the ride. I felt like an actress
conserving energy for a performance. As we pulled up in front of
the Hilton he kissed my cheek and squeezed my hand. "Mazel
tov."

I laughed and felt more like Molotov, as in cocktail.

The driver opened the car door for me. I stepped directly under the hotel awning. Raul followed. He grabbed by elbow. My heart was pounding.

We passed through the glittering hotel lobby and up two long escalators. The area in front of the grand ballroom was crowded. The women were dressed in spectacular floor-length gowns. I was the only woman in pants. I fit in with the boys, who looked kind of funny, all in the same outfit. I watched several couples pass quickly by the reception table where stacks of seating charts were piled up. Raul grabbed my hand. I pulled it back. I didn't want to be led around like a child.

"Let's go get a seating chart," he said.

I followed him over to the table and picked one up. I opened it. The attendees' names were listed two ways, alphabetically and by table. Once you found yourself alphabetically you had your table number. Then you could look at the table listing and see who else you were seated with. I couldn't find my name. Raul grabbed the chart from me.

"Don't study that. It makes you look insecure."

"My name isn't on it."

"I gave your name to the PR guy who handles the chart, but it was too late. It had already gone to the printers."

I felt erased. People would look for my name, and when it wasn't there, they would know I didn't matter. I was an interloper. Raul gave me a deep hard stare. He was reading my thoughts again.

"You're the mystery guest," he said.

My strength would have to come from inside me—not from some fancy piece of paper. I folded the seating chart in half and held it with my evening bag. As I did I noticed other couples making a quick, furtive study of the chart. When they found themselves, some looked relieved, others pained. It was important to be seated at the "right" table but it was more important to act like it didn't matter. Raul was either so self-confident, so arrogant, or such a good actor that he didn't even look at the chart. He just said, "Hang on to that. It will come in handy later."

With an elaborate gesture he offered me his arm. "Allow me to escort you to the cocktail reception."

The reception was jammed with media stars, public-relations types, assemblymen, state senators, borough presidents, city-council persons, and of course, reporters. Nobody stood alone. Everybody was talking to somebody. I stood there on the threshold, my feet rooted to the floor, wondering what the hell I was doing there. Raul had this evil smirk.

"Well, let's elbow our way through and let the people know we're here."

The room swayed before my eyes, the people moving like marionettes, their strings too well camouflaged to see. Like an actress remembering her part, I remembered my mission. I was going to start talk, talk among the people who would no longer talk to me, talk that might lead to some truth slipping out, talk among the men to whom I had once been so loyal. I unbuttoned my jacket.

Raul's eyebrows went up. "Holy shit," he said. "Tongues are going to wag."

Across the room I could see Hunter talking to Larry Pierce. This was going to be fun. I put a hand on Raul's shoulder. "I'm ready."

People stood in little clusters. Everybody held a glass in one hand. The first cluster we reached was the Staten Island borough president and several people I didn't know.

I smiled. "Hello, Mr. Luzetti."

"Marie, Marie Terranova. How the hell are ya?"

"I'm fine. This is my friend Raul Vega from the *Miami Herald.* He's at the *Dispatch* now."

Luzetti's face muscles tensed. His eyes flickered over Raul. "I've seen the byline. You wrote about that terrible shelter fire that happened in our borough."

"It was a tragedy," a woman in the cluster said. The sequins on her gown sparkled as she turned to Raul.

The borough president introduced her. "Raul, this is Dina Dansk. She's with Brooklyn Union Gas."

"You should come by sometime. We have a lot of good stories," she said to Raul.

"He's not interested in good news," the borough president said. He was joking but he wasn't.

Raul grabbed me by the elbow. "Nice meeting you folks. Hope you enjoy the show."

Everybody nodded. As we moved on they huddled closer to-gether. The gossip had started.

The room had two entrances. We worked our way from one to the other. Raul introduced me to the news types and I introduced him to the political types. Each time we passed through a cluster, we could feel the shocked stares we left behind. By the time we got out of there, I was giddy from all the power play.

On our way back to the ballroom Raul asked to see the seating chart. He found the table number next to his name. He didn't bother to see who we were seated with.

Our table was pefectly situated, close to the stage but not too close. The table itself was crowded. At its center in a sterling silver stand stood the table number, big enough so nobody could miss it. Each place setting had two plates and three glasses—water, red wine, and white wine. I sat down. Over me hung a chandelier that could have killed six people.

Raul stood and looked around. We hadn't seen any of the City Hall crowd we had come to be seen by. I knew the mayor and his entourage would wait until the last minute to arrive. The mayor wouldn't be caught dead standing around waiting for something to begin. His time was too valuable for that. Larry Pierce came and sat down next to me.

"Hey, lady, good to see you."

I took a drink of water. "Nice to see you, Larry."

"You sure you're at the right table?"

I didn't have to answer because, just then, both Larry's wife and Raul reached the table. Raul sat down next to me. Larry's wife sat down next to him.

"Hey, buddy, meet my wife, Jasmine."

Raul turned to me. "Jasmine, meet Marie."

Larry looked like he had just been stabbed in the back. "Your date for the evening?" he questioned stiffly.

"You did tell me to bring a date."

"Yeah, buddy." But the tone was tentative.

"Who's going to be joining us?" Raul asked Larry.

"You must be jiving. This is Whittaker's table. All the brass are at this table."

Whittaker was the *Herald*'s publisher. Now even Raul looked a little concerned. "Since when do I rate?"

Larry slapped him playfully on the back. "New boy in town."

"I'm not a boy."

"You know what I mean, buddy. Hispanic byline."

"The word is Latino and I like to think I do some good work now and then."

"Yeah, that too."

Someone caught Larry's eye. "Back in a minute, honey," he said to his wife. Then to us he said, "I see somebody I wanna catch up with."

As he got up to walk away he leaned down to my ear. "Is this relationship news? Should I tell Page Six?"

Page Six was the *New York Post*'s infamous gossip page. "Not just yet." I smiled. "Hold that thought for now."

Raul squeezed my knee under the table. "You're good at this," he said, leaning in closer.

"I haven't been the palace guard for three years without learning a little something about something."

He laughed.

In the back of my head I heard the haunting melody of the Act Two finale of *Aïda*—the big production number, the elephants, the camels, the captive slaves, the dancers, and of course, the doomed principals themselves.

Just then we were joined by two couples. I didn't know who they were, but the wives were wearing lots of money. Raul leaned into my ear. "The managing editor and the publisher."

If he was intimidated, he hid it masterfully. Raul introduced me to Whittaker, his publisher, and McDermott, the managing editor. They were both Ivy League, Whittaker silver-haired and sleek in his fifties, and McDermott, blond and athletic, and about ten years younger. They introduced their wives. They were a smooth foursome. Smooth as old money.

When they sat down, the table became a magnet. A steady stream of people happened by to pay homage to the publisher and the managing editor. I recognized two borough presidents, a congressman, half a dozen commissioners, a lot of PR types, and Howard Mendelssohn, the mayor's father-in-law. A lot of them knew me. Over the years they had all needed me. Only I could put them on the mayor's schedule. A lot of the people who knew me didn't recognize me. For them I was so unbelievably out of context they literally didn't see me. The ones who did see me made a show of kissing me, talking to me, some even knelt at my chair. Obviously, none of them knew that I no longer kept the big red book. The mayor's father-in-law looked right at me. I could tell that he recognized me and chose not to acknowledge me. Mendelssohn lingered for a moment with Whittaker, then moved to his own table, not far from ours.

As the appetizer was being served, Whittaker turned his attention to me.

"What do you do, Ms. Terranova?"

"I'm the mayor's administrative assistant."

"Hizzoner is a lucky man," he said. "How is he to work with?"

"Probably no different than you."

Whittaker cocked his head as if to indicate that he wasn't certain he had heard me correctly.

I smiled sweetly. "He's a busy man. I take it you are too."

He raised his hand to signal a waiter. "Touché! Are you always this reticent?"

A waiter came right over. He was wearing the same outfit as every other man at the table.

"Dom Pérignon," Whittaker requested. "Two bottles."

There were already three bottles of wine on the table. The waiter nodded and disappeared into the crowd.

"Well?" Whittaker turned his attention back to me. "Since your boss and I are so much alike, I insist you have a glass of champagne with me."

Larry pretended he wasn't watching but he was. I felt him wonder how all this would affect his standing with the big boss. Raul put an arm nonchalantly on the back of my chair and murmured, "Kick him under the table."

"Which one?" I whispered.

Raul turned to Whittaker. "Even Dom Pérignon won't induce this lady to talk."

I felt myself blush. The waiter returned. He showed the dew-covered bottle to Whittaker. The publisher nodded his approval.

The waiter popped the cork. Whittaker filled our glasses and toasted me. I brought the exquisite champagne to my lips. Was hemlock this good?

Just then Darnell Smalls, the mayor's personal bodyguard, walked into my line of vision. He was the head of a human triangle; Hunter and Brogan completed the geometry. The triangle pushed through the crowded room—the mayor safely in the middle. Last year that group would have included Jason Isenberg. Hunter, whose job it was to make sure the mayor greeted all the right people, scanned faces as he passed. When he saw Whittaker, he said something to Smalls, who then headed for our table. I was mesmerized by Jason's absence.

Whittaker stood up. So did McDermott. They huddled with the mayor, Hunter, and Brogan while Smalls kept a lookout. As the mayor was about to move on, his eyes met mine. He looked at me long and hard, as if making a decision. Then Brogan and Hunter saw me. By now the whole table was tuned in. Even though Hunter was the last to see me, he was the first to recover. He bounced toward me like Ulysses finding Penelope.

"I almost didn't recognize you," he said, smiling stiffly. Over his shoulder Brogan watched me but said nothing.

I stood up. The mayor kissed my cheek. He whispered in my ear, "Watch out for that guy, Marie. Don't let him use you."

I sat back down.

The entourage moved on. Now they were clustered two tables away from us with the mayor's father-in-law and several other men I didn't recognize.

"Who are those guys?" Raul asked.

The cacophony around us provided a kind of privacy for our own conversation.

"One of them is Mendelssohn, the mayor's father-in-law; the others are Wall Street types."

"What does the father-in-law do?"

"He's with Northeast Bank and Trust . . . a VP, I think."

"A banker," Raul said, "that's very interesting. That whole table must be movers and shakers."

The show shifted from the ballroom floor to the stage. The first act was last year's news, a falling bridge, schoolteachers and principals indicted for drug abuse, the cultural-affairs commissioner in a love affair with a convicted felon—light stuff. The audience loved it. Act Two was a parody of Mayor Nicosea trying to get into City Hall and being taken hostage by the homeless. I had turned my seat slightly to see the stage better. I felt myself being watched. It was him, Nicosea. He looked away. I watched him, the smile, the booming laughter. He was sitting with the governor and the attorney general. I saw through the mask to a portrait of agony. Raul, Larry, and their bosses were getting a big kick out of the show. None of it was funny to me. I turned to the plate in front of me and pretended to eat. Raul seemed totally at home. He bantered with Larry, Whittaker, and McDermott. Whatever subject came up, Raul had knowledge and an opinion. It was a long meal and a long show. Between acts the actors on the floor of the ballroom went table-hopping.

It was after eleven before dessert was served. We were waiting for the lights to go down on Broadway so that the actors from whatever show the mayor had chosen to work with this year could take their bows and get to the Hilton. Raul excused himself and headed for the back of the room. I stayed put. I was on my third glass of champagne when a fragment of a conversation drifted to my ears. "What kind of game is this, pal? Whittaker's not going to say anything tonight but he's going to want to know."

It was Larry's voice. I twisted slightly in my chair and then I saw that he was talking to Raul. They were standing behind my chair. Raul seemed very uncomfortable. Over Larry's shoulder Raul returned my gaze. I thought I heard him say, "It's no game."

"Enjoying the show?" Whittaker asked me.

I nodded. The curtain was about to go up on the mayor's rebuttal. Raul and Larry returned to their seats.

The mayor was a great song-and-dance man. He danced with the two members of the cast of *Cats*, and then he sang "Memories," but the lyrics were all about his memories of the days when the press still loved him. He was very funny and even I had to laugh. But I wondered how he felt inside.

When it was finally over, we said polite good-byes to Larry, Whittaker, and the others, and then Raul said, "Let's get the hell out of here."

On our way down the long escalator I noticed how tipsy I was. Almost everybody seemed to sway a bit. By the coatroom a very elegantly dressed woman leaned on the wall and threw up.

"Thank God I'm not driving," Raul said as soon as we were in the car. "I can barely see straight."

I leaned my head on the cool windowpane and watched as we drove uptown to Washington Heights, where Raul had a new sublet. He couldn't seem to commit to a lease in his own name. It was about 1:00 A.M. as we passed near the foot of the George Washington Bridge. Traffic was backed up like rush hour.

"The Jersey crowd is on a shopping spree," Raul said. The driver laughed.

Cars were stopping for entrepreneurs who sprang from the shadows to transact business through open car windows.

Raul said, "Like McDonald's drive-in counter. Only the customers are buying crack, smack, and weed."

At 138th Street the driver dropped us off. We climbed five flights to Raul's sublet. It was unfurnished and therefore almost empty. Raul had added a table in the dining nook, a compact-disk player on the living-room floor, and an empty bookcase along the wall. Boxes stood around waiting to be unpacked.

I went to the bedroom and sat on the edge of the bed. From the apartment below a salsa beat vibrated in the floorboards and pulsed around me.

"Why did you pick this neighborhood?" I asked him. "It seems kind of borderline."

"It's Latino. I'm trying to broaden my horizons. As you love to point out, we Cubans can be pretty insular."

I kicked my shoes off. I had chosen SoHo because the old neighborhood was choking me. Now I felt dislocated. He was looking for his roots and I was trying to escape mine.

He knelt at the foot of the bed. "You were magnificent tonight. You can handle yourself anywhere."

"You were very supportive." I pushed a lock of hair from his forehead. "But I don't know if we accomplished anything." I helped him out of his tuxedo jacket.

"Maybe not. Time will tell," he said.

He helped me out of my jacket and blouse. I said, "We need to talk."

He unbuttoned his shirt. "It's been so long."

We unwrapped our cummerbunds. We unzipped our pants and climbed out of them. He came up onto the bed. I felt the weight of his body on mine. I wrapped my legs around his back and felt him hard against my belly.

"We need to talk," I repeated.

"You're right," he said, "we do need to talk." He sighed. "I'm going to have to write something about Isenberg soon."

"What?"

I writhed out from under him and left him there on all fours, the dirty dog. I pulled my knees to my chest. He turned to sit next to me. "I got myself in more hot water than I expected tonight. Larry's out to get me. I have to come up with something good. Either that or give him something."

"What are you telling me?" I got up off the bed, folded my hands across my naked chest, and went to the window.

"Just that I'm sitting on a lot of information and I can't sit on it forever."

"You haven't done your part of the deal yet. You haven't told me anything new about Joe's death."

"But I will. I will as soon as I get back from Miami."

"What if you don't get anything?"

"What if I don't?"

I marched out to the empty living room. He followed. I said, "Then our deal is off."

"Okay, but I have plenty on Isenberg I didn't get from you."

"You always have just one more goddamn secret. Always one more twist." I was yelling now.

He stood there in his underwear, his hard-on fading fast. "I thought you wanted me to be honest with you."

I started digging in the open boxes. They were all full of books. I put a few on a shelf.

"You're going to clean my house now?"

We stood there glaring at each other until he moved to the CD player and put on a classical disc.

"What's that?"

"Mozart. The man who was living proof that Freud's theories of sublimation were bullshit."

I slammed more books on the empty shelves.

"Freud said that art was the product of sublimation of the libido. But so many of the greats were promiscuous."

"Is this some kind of a rationalization of your past?"

He laughed. "Mozart, Picasso, Bach . . . well, Bach wasn't exactly promiscuous, but he did father twenty children."

"What are you leading up to, Vega?"

"Am I ever gonna get another whiff from you?"

I was laughing when he came over to me. His hands wandered over my body. We kissed there in the dark and somehow we wound up on the rug. I laid my head on his shoulder, listened to him breathe, and watched the play of light and shadow on the ceiling as headlights passed below. After a while I crawled over to my little sequined evening bag to get the Inner Circle seating chart. I crawled back to Raul who was still directing the concerto, flat on his back. I started reading out loud. I read the names—I read by table—like stanzas of a long poem.

Raul said, "Mendelssohn and the guys at his table. They interest me. How close is Mendelssohn to the mayor?"

"Mendelssohn is probably the only person whose calls Nicosea always takes."

Raul turned to me. In the background the concerto was winding down. He put his arms around my waist and his face close to mine. Somewhere a window was cracked. His breath smelled of champagne. Even though the air above us was chill, my body temperature rose.

"Do we have a deal or not?" he asked.

I took his cock into my hand. I said, "Mendelssohn's rich."

"So? The rich like to get richer and the only thing they like even more is power."

Then, as our lips touched, I remembered one more thing. "Jason worked at Mendelssohn's bank before he joined Nicosea."

16

The next morning we were both hung over. Raul made us quick cups of coffee and then we went to get Joey. He had spent the night at the house of a new friend just a few blocks from home. Joey was thrilled to see Raul but seemed a little angry with me.

"How was the party?" he asked as we stood waiting for Raul to buy the morning editions.

"Kind of silly," I said, looking at the many publications the little newsstand offered.

Joey asked, "What did you do after?"

"I stayed at Raul's."

Joey turned away from me. Raul came back with three newspapers under his arm. "You gonna read all those?" Joey asked.

"Gotta keep up with the competition, champ."

Joey nodded. He seemed relieved not to have to talk to me. We started back toward the loft. Somehow I drifted behind.

When we got home, they cooked breakfast together while I read the papers. After pancakes, eggs, and three cups of coffee, I lay down for a nap. I was tired from last night and tired from trying to keep up with their sports talk. Raul looked tired too, but he seemed determined to please Joey. After they had done the dishes, they went to shoot some baskets in the school yard. I fell asleep.

In my dream I followed them. I followed them to the school yard. Then I was the ball. Joey held me in the crook of his arm. After a while he started to bounce me. By the time he and Raul reached the school yard, they were tossing me back and forth. They were talking. I could hear but I couldn't understand. I was jealous.

Suddenly I was in front of them. I was the girl under the hoop. Raul disappeared. Joey smiled at me. I heard the pitter-pat of the bouncing ball. I was young enough to be his girl.

I woke up to another rhythm. A quiet little tapping somewhere in the loft.

"Don't you think you should tell your mom?"

"You promised. . . ."

I got up and followed the sound to Joey's room. They were facing the computer screen.

"Nice nap?" Raul asked without turning around.

"Uh-huh." As I reached the computer a document disappeared from the screen into the computer's mysterious memory. For a moment I thought Joey was deliberately excluding me. But then I figured it was just my jealousy. I put a hand on his shoulder. "Ready for the museum?"

Raul gave Joey a long look that seemed to communicate many messages. "What do you say, champ?"

Joey brought the document back up. "All right," he said, "but she's gonna be mad."

"No she's not." Raul winked at me. "Promise not to get mad?"

I didn't want to but I promised. I looked down over their shoulders at a screenful of numbers. Every time Joey hit the page-down button, another screen appeared.

"What is that?" I asked.

They looked at each other. "Go ahead," Raul encouraged Joey.

"Those are all the numbers the dead guy circled on his calendar."

"You kept that calendar?" My voice was an incredulous whisper.

I recalled that day in the dead of winter when Joey and I had packed Jason's things. The picture that fell, the frame that broke, Joey's finger cut on the fallen glass—and the desk calendar. Joey had taken that desk calendar into Brogan's office, the desk calendar with the circled dates. The dates he had entered onto Brogan's computer. Joey flipped to another screen. It was full of initials and numbers.

"The kid is ten steps ahead of either of us," Raul said.

"You had no right to take that calendar, Joey."

I glared at Raul. He said nothing.

"You could get us all into big trouble, Joey," I said.

Joey looked at Raul. Raul looked at me. "You promised not to get mad."

I said nothing.

"Maybe he shouldn't have done what he did. But what he has here is very, very important. It could be the answer to a lot of our questions," Raul said.

"Do you still have that calendar, Joey?"

He reached into the cabinet under his computer and handed me the calendar. I flipped though it.

"This is a simple binary code," Raul said. "It tells how much he got, from who, and when."

"It tells *who?*"

"Well, not exactly, but it gives initials."

"I wish you hadn't taken that calendar," I said.

"Why, so you would never have to know about corruption in the Big Apple?" Joey challenged me.

"No, because you were working on it on Brogan's computer and he knows you're a computer whiz. So you might be in danger."

"I don't think so, Mom. I've had this thing for months and even you didn't notice."

He flipped to yet another document. The screen read *The lion is the key.*

"This is what the circled dates in December say." Joey pointed at the screen. "That month is different from the others."

The three of us stared at the screen. I thought about all the lions in the city—stone, marble, brass. Finally I whispered, "What's that supposed to mean?"

Joey shrugged.

Raul asked, "Are you sure you got it right?"

"Positive."

Joey closed the document. I just stood there. We were reflected on the computer screen as if we were trapped in there just like Jason's message. A message from the grave transmitted through a child. A chill went through me.

"Are you mad now?" Joey asked. "Does this mean we won't go to the museum like you promised?"

Raul gave me a look that seemed to be a warning. Being mad now would be a mistake. So even though I was mad, I kissed Joey's cheek and said, "C'mon, let's go."

On the way to the museum Joey pointed out the cast-iron architecture he was learning about in school. It was created to imitate stone. Some of the columns were grooved to look like marble or limestone. Many of the buildings were designed to make you believe you were in ancient Rome. The Medusa-head keystones looked down at us. Several of the buildings had lions' heads engraved over the windows. I kept hearing Jason's voice. *The lion is the key.* What the hell did it mean? We took a wrong turn and wound up on Canal Street.

Canal Street was a bazaar of nuts, bolts, spare machine parts, Plexiglas, and Lucite that spilled onto the sidewalk from one store after another. It seemed like you could buy pieces of anything here

but nothing complete. There was no logic to what you might find
in any given store. We passed a hardware store with a collection of
rubber monster heads. I put one on. I was Frankenstein. Raul and
Joey turned. Through the slits that were my eyes, I saw their laughter. They pulled plastic monkey masks down over their faces. We
danced around each other and made weird noises. People stared at
us. Behind the mask I felt better. Finally we found the Museum of
Holography on Mercer Street. Inside, it was dark and cool. Joey
was in a hurry to see everything, so he went on in while we were
still buying our tickets. I watched my son's enchanted face out
there among the exhibits—three-dimensional people created by
mirrors and light. Was it possible that this child had stumbled onto
the truth of the lies behind this administration?

"I have an idea," Raul said. "You could do a title search on the
Sherman Street/Liberty Avenue lot while I'm in Miami. It might
give us some leads."

"I don't know how to do that."

"Yes, you do," he said. "You can figure it out. Just go to the
Registry of Deeds. I'd be curious to know who held the mortgage
on that renovation that went nowhere."

"What do you think 'the lion is the key' means? The key to
what?"

We stood at the threshold of this strange museum where beams
of light created illusions. The visitors to the museum stood among
the holograms, and it was hard to tell which was which.

"The key," he said, "the key. The key to this thing is there is
no key. No one answer. The corruption is all around us and as
subtle as two men swapping favors over breakfast at '21.'"

"Where do I fit in?"

"You're the tool, the facilitator. You push paper, answer
phones, and execute deals you never dreamed were cut. People like
Mendelssohn and his cronies handpick guys like Nicosea. He's a
puppet that allows them to execute their schemes. People like you
are grist for their mill."

"What makes the paper you push so much loftier than the
paper I push? Your publisher is a rich developer. Imagine the deals
he cuts."

I put my hand into a beam of light, thinking that the flat iron building it created would fragment. But it didn't. The three-dimensional picture remained intact. I said, "Just because you have the power of the pen that doesn't make you more of a human being. I've seen you do your share of compromising."

"Like how?"

"Like with me. You compromised your ethics. Now you justify it by saying you're in love with me, but you didn't start off so pure."

He sighed. "How many times are we going to have this argument? Are you going to do the search? I could do it myself but I'm too busy compromising with my bosses."

I knew what a title search was because I had recently bought the condo. A title search shows the bank that it's okay to lend you the mortgage because if you can't pay, the bank can take the house or the land you're buying and they haven't lost anything. A title search shows that property is free and clear. No other bank already has a mortgage on it.

"Be careful, though," Raul said. "If New York is anything like Miami, you'll have patronage positions in the city clerk's office and you don't know who they talk to. Your poking around there could tip someone off that we're onto them."

A hologram reflected off a mirror and created the illusion of Mayor Nicosea. Mesmerized, I stood in front of it. Joey came back. "Hey, your stinky boss. Did you know that the whole world might be a hologram?"

I walked away from Nicosea. Even though he was only a fragment of light, he gave me the creeps.

We moved on to the next hologram which was a gray-haired, vibrant little man playing timbales.

"Tito Puente, the King of Latin Music," Raul said. The illusion of Tito was accompanied by a salsa tape. Raul took me into his arms and danced a few steps.

"I don't know this. . . ." I started to protest.

"Just follow me," he said.

"That's the problem, you learned to dance and I learned to follow."

I laughed but I wasn't really joking.

"You were right the other day," he said. "We men have made a mess of it. There has to be a better way."

I stopped dancing. "You mean women in power. Real women, not women like Maggie Thatcher."

"What's wrong with Maggie Thatcher?" he teased.

"She's a man. A man who carries a funny-looking pocketbook and wears a skirt."

He laughed. Now we were in front of Mozart. "Hey, here's your buddy. Any more theories?" I asked.

"Chiaroscuro," he said. "Mozart was a master at it. The bittersweet. Maybe that's the answer."

"Chiaroscuro is a term from painting. What's it got to do with music, or for that matter politics?"

"The interpenetration of opposites . . . men and women together . . . shared power, Yin and Yang."

"Why not just give it up? Give it up for a while. Let us women have it."

"You're talking to the wrong guy, Marie. I don't have it to give up. I'm a so-called minority male. Out there in the power structure, that puts me in the female position. Maybe that's what draws you to me. I'm your natural ally."

"Think so?"

"Yes. I think so."

"It's a good line anyway."

"Thanks. Thanks a lot."

"It's just that I'm not always sure I can trust you."

He stepped in close. "That's because of all the heat between us."

"How did you get Joey to tell you about that calendar?"

He looked hurt. "I didn't get him to tell me anything. He sprang it on me. He was dying to tell. I did get him to tell you, though."

There in the darkness of that museum where reality and illusion seemed inseparable, my anxiety dissipated. I let myself feel the possibility of the warm arms of a new family, a family that didn't diminish its members but made each stronger. That afternoon was the magic moment outside time, the motionless moment; the wave had reached shore and gravity had not yet begun to pull it back. We were happy.

None of us knew how fast the change would come and how far into the abyss we would soon be pulled. That evening Raul left for Miami. He would be back the next day. In the meantime I would attempt the title search.

The statue of Justice in front of the New York County Courthouse was a woman. I wondered why. We had so little say in the halls of power. The sun gleamed from the golden pyramid that crowned the Municipal Building. I crossed Chambers Street to the Surrogate Court Building.

Inside, it was like a temple. From the domed ceiling a winged lion with a human face looked down on me. Beneath me the marble floor stretched in all directions, shiny, cold, perfect. Globe lamps cast a warm light over the rotunda. Time, the wreathed clock with the Roman numerals, flew in the claws of an eagle.

I took the elevator to the second floor and followed the curved hallway to Room 203, the Registry of Deeds. Behind the old wooden door, neon illuminated crumbling walls and filthy windows. Half a dozen people stood pale and still as wax. They were lined up in front of two clerks behind a counter. Everyone spoke in low tones.

I stepped up to the counter and waited my turn. The clerks went back and forth from the counter to the carousel file of color-coded cards. The history of every building in Manhattan was recorded here on microfilm.

The people in line ahead of me all held slips of paper that they handed the clerk when their turn came.

"I'd like to check the history of a building," I asked when I had reached the front of the line.

"Do you have the address?"

"Yes, I do. I have two addresses."

The clerk pointed behind me to another room. An open double door led to dozens of stacks of oversized books. Rows of people sat in front of microfilm viewers and peered into their eerie light. "Do you know how to use the plates?" he asked.

"Could you show me?"

He lifted the part of the counter that becomes an exit and stepped through, closing it behind him. I followed him to the other room. Directly behind the double door a collection of glass plates hung on hinges like the pages of a gigantic book.

"Each plate has a section of the city; block by block, lot by lot, everything is numbered. Find the block and lot number and come back to me."

I thanked him and stepped between the pages as if I were walking into a book. Each giant page was a map of a part of the city. I searched until I found 49 Sherman Street and 12 Liberty Street. They were on the same lot. I copied the block and lot number and brought it to the clerk. He handed me a slip of paper. "Put your request on this."

When I had filled it out, he took it to a computer, keyed in some numbers, and came back with, "This lot is owned by the city."

"I'd like to do a title search."

He looked at me like a doctor studying an X ray. Was he memorizing my face? Was I paranoid? "What for?" he asked.

"A course I'm taking."

He went over to the microfilm carousel and pushed a button. It began to turn. After a while he stopped it and removed a stack of cards. When he handed them to me, I saw the little microfilm windows. There were about forty of them.

I went back to the other room and found a microfilm viewer that was not in use. I sat down. Under the viewer were two glass plates, like the plates under a microscope but much larger. I inserted the first card. Nothing happened. I turned the screen on. A document appeared. The writing went from right to left. I removed the microfilm and turned it the other way.

I was looking at a negative—white print on a black page. Like an archaeologist digging through layer after layer, I read document after document. The room was quiet and stuffy. I read for hours. I read until my eyes watered and my head ached. I began to feel that I had fallen through a hole in time, that I was trying to decipher hieroglyphs and that the answer was doomed to elude me. I was seeing something but I couldn't believe that I was seeing it. It should have been impossible. While the records clearly showed that the two addresses were the same building, there had been construction mortgages on both 49 Sherman Street and 12 Liberty Place. Both were from Northeast Bank and Trust. Every once in a while I felt the clerk's eyes as he passed by. I copied every name that appeared on every document, even the notary public's. All the while I doubted what I was seeing.

I was still reading when the light left the screen. I looked around to ask for help. Every other viewer in the room was out. Even the overhead lights were dark. I looked at my watch. It was four o'clock. When the bureaucracy shut down, it shut down.

"I'll need those back," the clerk said. "Find what you were looking for?"

I answered with a question. "Who are all these people?" All around me they were packing briefcases with the precision of an old ritual.

"Most of them are free-lancers," he said. "Some work for title search firms. There's only two big ones."

As I walked under that winged lion on the ceiling there was no longer any doubt at all about the corruption I had been a part of. I thought of all the others like me who followed blindly, spreading misery with well-intentioned efficiency. In the sad cadence of my footsteps I heard a whisper. A question. How had the difference between right and wrong eluded me?

17

I stood on the corner of Chambers Street as dusk settled over the Tweed courthouse, and it was as if time had stood still but nobody had stopped to notice. The sidewalks were full of rushing people and on the street traffic was hopelessly snarled. I stepped off the curb in the direction of the subway. Two men stepped off with me. One was tall and elegant in a three-piece suit, the other short and fat in polyester. In an almost absurd synchronized motion they flashed their badges, flipped them closed, and stashed them, the tall one in his breast pocket, the fat one in his back pants pocket. Their names were Kennedy and Plank.

"FBI, Ms. Terranova. We'd like to talk to you."

"I'd like to talk to you too."

The short fat one registered surprise; the other registered nothing but leaned toward me as if to see deeper into my eyes.

"What do you know about the death of Police Officer Terranova at the hands of one of your own?"

Kennedy didn't blink. "We know he was your husband."

"Is that all you know?"

"That's not the case we're on."

I started walking again. "Well, then we have nothing to talk about."

The fat one blocked my route. I started to walk around him. It was a chore because he kept shifting his bulk. "Do you have a subpoena?" I demanded.

"No, but it would be in your best interest to come and talk to us. Otherwise, we could . . ." The threat itself Plank left unspoken.

"You understand you don't have to, Ms. Terranova. You don't have to do anything," Kennedy said. He looked like a Kennedy, a young John Kennedy, fair-haired and handsome.

They escorted me to their office high up in 26 Federal Plaza. We went through the metal detector, waited at the elevator bank, and took a local elevator which stopped at half a dozen floors that looked exactly alike. On the thirty-second floor we followed a maze of cubbyholes to an office that looked like a cell. It wasn't even a real room, just a plasterboard box in a maze of boxes. The windows were so far away I couldn't even locate them in my imagination.

Kennedy flipped a switch, and the room was bathed in a cold fluorescent light. It wasn't like in the movies. No high-intensity desk lamp to shine in my eyes, just a small table, three straight-backed chairs, and a blackboard on the wall. Next to the blackboard a long thin wooden pointer ended in a jagged broken tip. On the table lay a manila folder.

"Have a seat," Kennedy offered. "I'll be right back." I watched him leave. I watched the door close and then I looked at Plank. A sadistic little smile played on his thin lips. He turned to the blackboard, and his broad back hid its surface. He picked up a piece of chalk and consciously did violence to my nerves as he scrawled on the board. Then he turned to me. I still couldn't see what he had written.

"During the American Revolution more men died on prison boats that were anchored in New York Harbor than were killed in battle. Almost eleven thousand men. Not too many people know that." His tone implied the whole thing was somehow my fault.

He bounced a piece of broken chalk in his pudgy little hand. "All that because of one little whore," he said.

What was I supposed to say to that? He went on.

"Mrs. Loring was having an affair with General Howe. Howe was responsible for feeding the American prisoners. But because he was fucking her, he let her sell the good food on the open market at two-thirds its value and replace it with cheap rotting food."

He leaned in closer. I could smell the garlic on his breath. "Things like maggot-infested cattle heads."

My stomach rose up and turned. This guy was really crazy. I straightened and crossed my fingers like I figured a lawyer would do if I had one and said, "You're blaming this one woman for most of the deaths in the Revolutionary War?"

"It's not the woman," he said. "It's who she was fucking."

He stepped aside. I saw the big letters and the neatly printed words. *NIGHT IN CONNECTICUT.*

He watched my face as it sank in. Then he pulled something from his inside jacket pocket. It fit in the palm of his hand. He brought it to me. I blinked at it stupidly. How had it come to exist? I remembered the day Joey and I had cleaned out Jason's office. One of Jason's framed family photographs had slipped through Joey's fingers. Behind the broken frame I had found a second photograph. I had ripped it and tossed it in the wastebasket. Then I erased the memory of its existence.

As I studied the photograph a night emerged from the recesses of memory like vapor from melting snow—like a decomposed body from the waters of long ago. Who had witnessed that night? The interrogation began to feel like an interrogation.

"Do you remember when this photograph was taken?" Plank asked. I could see the sweat on his upper lip. The room was hot and there wasn't much air in it.

"Offhand, I don't," I said. "I don't exactly remember when that was taken. Offhand."

"You do recognize yourself, don't you?"

I took the picture from his hand. "Yes, of course I recognize myself."

"How about him . . . know who he is?"

"You were following him?"

"I'm asking the questions," he snapped.

I continued to study the picture in the palm of my hand. He leaned down to me. "Are you the reason he killed himself?"

We were eyeball to eyeball and then I said, "Of course not. That's crazy."

"What were you doing impersonating Mrs. Isenberg in the Bahamas?"

"I heard Jason was a compulsive gambler and I wanted to find out if it were true."

"You knew he was laundering money?"

"I figured it out."

The look of satisfaction on Plank's face frightened me. So I added, "I figured it out after. After he was dead."

He slid his fingers into the manila folder on the table, then slid them back out along with an old memo. The same one Jolynne had found at Human Services.

"Recognize this?"

"Of course. I signed it."

"So you admit you were in on the scam with Isenberg."

"No, I don't admit that."

He picked the chalk up and scratched the blackboard some more. My teeth ached. "It would be better for you if you did admit it."

"Even if it's not true?"

Plank leaned on the plasterboard wall and tapped his fingers as if he were playing the piano. Then he came and sat down across from me and repeated, "It would be better for you if you admitted it."

"I don't think so."

I wondered if they knew about Jason's shredded files. Was I going to be blamed for that too? In the fluorescent light, the air took on a greenish hue, and as he brought his face in close, he turned slightly purple at the edges. I began to feel light-headed, dizzy.

Kennedy walked in. He had the clean-cut look of a savior. In his hands he carried a white paper bag. He set two Styrofoam containers and two sweet rolls on the table and crumpled the bag. The third cup he handed to Plank with no roll. Plank must have been on a diet.

"Coffee?"

I nodded gratefully. Kennedy handed me a cup. Plank took a chair and retired to a corner. He turned the chair backward and straddled it. I listened to Plank slurp his coffee and looked into Kennedy's handsome face with misplaced gratitude. I opened the coffee.

"Sweet roll?"

I had no appetite but I said yes just for something to do. Then as I sank my teeth into a mouthful of glaze and dough Kennedy's blue eyes met mine.

"Tough time for you," he said, "huh?"

I nodded and kept taking little bites and carefully chewing them.

"Those three shelters went up in flames because everything was built below standard. We can prove that, Ms. Terranova. Everybody was paid off, from inspectors to carpenters. Where do you fit in?"

I thought about the title search, the names in my purse, Jason's calendar at home, and hoped he couldn't read my eyes. "I don't," I said.

"You expect me to believe that?"

"I'm just a secretary."

He took an elegant sip of his coffee and studied me over the edge of the cup. A picture popped into my head, a haunting picture. Thaddeus Finx the night of the shelter fire. Thaddeus Finx, soot-stained and warning me that my eyes were closed. Thaddeus Finx, the scapegoat in handcuffs.

"What about Thaddeus Finx?" I asked.

"Who?"

"The old man who's being charged with burning the shelters down."

"What about him?"

"He's no arsonist."

"I guess not." He took a bite of his sweet roll.

"So he should be released."

"What? And blow three and a half years of undercover operations?"

He wiped the corners of his mouth delicately with the cheap paper napkin. My heart pounded with revulsion. I felt my face flush.

"This is a major investigation, Ms. Terranova. It involves a whole administration, not just one crazy old homeless man, and we're not ready to go public just yet. Soon, but not just yet."

I watched the blue of his blue eyes.

He said, "I've told you too much already. But I know you're in no position to talk." He paused. "So who was in on those contracts? Who paid kickbacks to Isenberg?"

"I don't know."

"Does your reporter friend know?"

"I don't know. How would I know what he knows?"

"You seem to be pretty tight. He was with you in Florida."

I wove the fingers of one hand into the fingers of the other and listened to the blood rush through my veins. Plank stayed in his corner. Eventually, Kennedy spoke again. "So tell me what you *do* know, Ms. Terranova."

He said my name like a kiss.

"Not much. Everything was so rushed. The mayor wanted something done about the homeless situation and fast. I worked late every night for months."

"How were the selections made?"

"Isenberg made them. I just processed the paperwork. I had no idea."

"But you do now. You have an idea now."

I had a few ideas. One of them was the calendar, which gave initials and amounts. The other idea was not to speculate within earshot of the Federal Bureau of Investigation. A taut silence stretched between us. Then Kennedy leaned in close. "There's a lot of evidence against you," he said. "Enough to present to a grand jury and ask for an indictment."

My heartbeat echoed in my ears and reverberated through the boxlike room. Suddenly Kennedy's elegant blue eyes, his expensive suit, just faded, and he looked every bit the reptile his partner was. He sipped his coffee and watched me as if I were under a microscope. I was trying not to breathe too loudly when he surprised me again. "On the other hand . . . if you cooperate with us, we'll get you immunity."

"Cooperate?"

"Wear a wire to City Hall and get some conversations going with Deputy Mayor Brogan and the mayor. Do you know the mayor's father-in-law?"

"Not well."

"You sure about that?"

I breathed deeply. I said, "I'd like the advice of counsel."

As his disappointment sank in he stretched his arms across the table. I thought he was going to take back the half-empty cup of coffee and the half-eaten roll. Instead he put his head down. When his head came back up, he was showing his teeth. He reached into his inside jacket pocket and produced a wallet that contained a business card. "When you get a lawyer, Ms. Terranova, tell him to give me a call."

Just like that it was over. With the mention of the word *lawyer*, all questions died. Kennedy was playing by the book. He must be ready to turn his information over to a prosecutor. For a while I just sat there missing my center of gravity, and so I wasn't sure I could get up. "I'll walk you to the elevator," he offered.

I had to accept because I would never have been able to find my own way out. I followed him through the eerie stillness of the maze of cubicles. All the lights were out; whatever natural light

had filtered through these arid spaces was now gone. In the real
world night had fallen. I went back to the subway studying the
faces in the crowd. Which one was watching me?

"What's wrong, Mom?" Joey asked me over dinner.

"Nothing."

"I hate it when you do that."

"What?"

"Say it's nothing when it's something."

I felt hollow and young. How could I protect him when my
judgment was so questionable? I thought about that stupid night in
Connecticut and felt ashamed. He asked, "Are you still mad about
the calendar?"

"I'm not mad."

"Yes, you are, you're mad."

"I'm not."

"Then what's wrong?"

"It was my mistake, Joey, not yours. I should never have taken
you into that office. We weren't supposed to be there."

The look in his eyes told me I was in real trouble.

He got up and came around the table. He let me hug him but
not for long. I knew what he was hiding. Like the oyster makes the
pearl, he had covered the pain of losing his father with an exquisite love for me. Rather than show his fear, he began to comfort
me.

"It's gonna be okay, Mom. I know it is, because you haven't
done anything bad."

"I know, Joey. I know."

But neither of us was really sure. We held each other and remembered the past—so neither of us trusted the future. I stood
up. "Gonna help me with the dishes?"

He chuckled. "Taking advantage while I'm soft."

"You bet."

After that, he did his homework and I pretended I was reading
a book. My mind kept wandering. Where would I get a lawyer?
How was I going to tell Raul about that night in Connecticut? At
nine Raul called up from the street. I went down to get him. We

hugged briefly but he was tense, very tense. I felt more bad news coming on. "I came straight from the airport," he said.

"What did you find out?"

Before he could answer, Joey was taking his overnight bag from his arm. "C'mon, tuck me in," Joey said.

Tuck me in? I was never allowed to tuck Joey in anymore. They walked off to Joey's room discussing the latest basketball scores.

" 'Night, Mom," Joey said without looking back. I returned to the kitchen. I scrubbed the counters, started a load of laundry, tidied the living room, and made tea. Still, Raul didn't come out. Finally I peeked in.

They were both snoring lightly. Joey was under the covers with an open book on his chest. Raul lay on top of the covers, one of his feet rested on the floor. The worried look was gone from Joey's brow, his face content, no nightmares, just sleep, just dreams. I took the book from my son. Then I pulled off Raul's shoes. As I shoved Raul's leg up onto the bed he opened his eyes, smiled, then drifted off again. I tiptoed out.

I showered, slipped under my own blankets, and surprised myself by falling asleep.

"That night . . . how do you explain that night?"

A bright, intimidating light shone into my eyes. I couldn't escape it. Then I was standing in front of my own pupil. The interrogator's voice was thin, cold, metallic. St. Peter's beard hung from my eye. He stepped out of my pupil. It was Joe. He was angry because I had betrayed him. As he came closer he was Raul.

Before I was awake, his silky skin touched mine. He was naked, warm, tender. With his hand Raul separated my legs. I pulled his face to mine. His mouth opened and his tongue came down my throat. Below, I took him in.

He slid a hand under my ass and I pushed up. He rose onto his knees and I felt him move inside me. His breath was hard and fast, and I tasted the salt in it. One by one, my vertebrae unhinged and my backbone connected with his; like poles of a magnet we clung, me, him, us. Amid sweet, low, murmurings, our bodies came home to each other. When it was over, I lay with my face in the pillow, trying to catch my breath while the universe skipped a beat.

The afterglow glistened around us and then a deep tension ate it up and darkness enveloped us. He turned on the lamp by the bed. I shaded my eyes. He sat up. I could hear him pulling the rubber from his dick.

"What did you find out about Joe?" I asked.

He sat there holding the condom. In it I could see the translucent gel that makes babies.

"Are you sure you want to know?"

I didn't answer. Because of his tone, because of my guilt, I got very scared. He got up to dump the rubber in the toilet. I heard it flush. He came back. Water was still rushing into the bowl.

"Sometimes I think I have a sixth sense," he said. "I seem to know the right question. When you ask the right question, you get the right answer." There was a long pause. I think he was waiting for me to say something but I didn't. Then he added, "My informant knew about the case Joe was on."

I pulled the blanket up around me and sat up. The light from the lamp cut my body on the diagonal. "What did he say?" I asked.

He tried to straighten the small lampshade. It slipped from the bulb. The naked light hit my eyes. He said, "It sounds complicated but it's simple. It started about four years ago when the FBI began investigating Milano."

"Old Vic Milano? The Brooklyn party chairman, old Vic Milano? He's retired."

"Still, that's who they were investigating."

He tried to get the shade back on the lamp. "Milano's name came up on a wiretap in a trailer at a mob-affiliated construction site. There was going to be some kind of meeting at his house in Brooklyn."

"The mob and the party boss?"

"That's right. So the FBI got a court order to wire Milano's basement for a certain twenty-four-hour period when the meeting was scheduled. That twenty-four hours changed a lot of people's lives."

The clamp of the lampshade screeched as it fit around the hot bulb. He asked, "Are you following this?"

I nodded. I knew all too well how twenty-four hours can change a life. He continued, "Isenberg's name came up at that meeting. It seems he was the administration's point man when it came to repaying party bosses for their political support. He made sure a lot of city contracts went to companies the bosses favored. Many of those companies were mobbed up. The FBI started to look at Isenberg."

"I asked you about Joe and you're talking about Isenberg."

"It's all connected," he said. "Milano connects to Isenberg and Isenberg connects to Joe."

"How?"

"Brogan found out the FBI was onto Isenberg."

He paused to look at me. I nodded to indicate I was following.

"Brogan used the city Department of Investigations to keep tabs on the FBI investigation. About six months ago he must have figured the shit was about to hit the fan, so he pushed the mayor to demote Isenberg. Isenberg had been the administration's deal maker from the moment Mendelssohn gave him to Nicosea back during Nicosea's first run for mayor."

"What about Joe? I don't see how he fits into this."

Raul played with the base of the lamp. "Brogan was covering the administration's ass. To do that, he had to stay a step ahead of the feds. He needed to know what was coming so he could control the release of information, a kind of on-the-spot damage control. Two cops were assigned to work with DOI. They thought they were wiretapping big-time drug dealers when really they were wiretapping the feds. The NYPD had these cops believing that they were on a top-secret joint task force with the feds. Meanwhile, DOI buried the investigation so deep the FBI didn't know about it. That's how an undercover FBI agent wound up shooting an undercover cop."

I felt that I had returned to the mirrors and lights of the Museum of Holography. The things that looked real weren't. The things I should have seen, I didn't. "Joe was on the Isenberg case?"

He nodded. There was a short silence in which the betrayal sank in like a stain into fabric.

"Are you saying Nicosea knew why Joe was killed?"

I thought again about coming to City Hall to get at the truth about Joe's death. And how instead I had walked out with a job, a job I desperately needed, a job better than any job I had ever had. I heard my footsteps on the marble floor and saw the mayor's hand shaking mine. How miraculous it had all seemed. Then I came back to the darkness of my own room and heard Raul say, "You add it up."

I clutched the sheet to me. Through its pink shade the lamp covered my hands in a reddish hue. I tried to rub it off. I thought of the numbers on Mrs. Schilling's arm, the soot on Finx's face the morning of the shelter fire. It took me a long time to get the next sentence out. "Hiring me was part of the cover-up."

"In a way."

He sat down next to me. "When people are grabbing for power, they don't usually have time for compassion," he said.

I laid my hand on the wetness between my legs where he had just been. He shivered. The room was cold. The light from the lamp fell on his penis and his balls that had gone into hiding. That's what I was looking at when I whispered, "That makes every-thing else so much worse."

There was a long dead silence during which the room got colder. In the half-light my guilt sat between us like a shadow. Raul seemed to be studying the floor.

"What do you mean?"

"The FBI brought me in for questioning today. They've been looking at me ever since I worked for Jason."

He stood up, seeming suddenly pale as as specter. "What!"

Looking back, I guess neither of us wanted the conversation to go where it had to go next. I got up and got the notes I had taken earlier in the day at the Registry of Deeds. I handed them to him.

"What's this?"

"The title search. Mendelssohn's bank had mortgages on both lots . . . the real one and the imaginary one."

"That's not possible," he said.

"There's only two companies in New York City that do title searches. He must have paid somebody off. I bet if you match some of these names with the initials on the calendar, you'll have some answers."

He let the papers slip from his hand. They wafted to the floor. "I don't want any more answers," Raul said. "Every answer is worse than the one before."

There was a long silence, because basically I agreed with him. But it wasn't like I had a choice anymore. Finally he said, "You're gonna hate me after this. You're gonna hate me."

"Maybe you'll hate me too," I said, thinking about that night in Connecticut.

"I told Larry about the FBI investigation into Isenberg. I told him he could write it. I thought I was buying time. It never occurred to me that I was leading him directly to you."

I was suddenly so angry that my next line slipped out almost casually. But my hands were shaking.

"I slept with Isenberg once. The FBI knows about it."

"It was just one of those things," he said. "I had to get him off my back."

I said, "It was a mistake. It never happened again."

He turned; he studied me; my words were sinking in. "You didn't," he said. "You couldn't have."

I wanted to tell him about the good parts of Jason, the parts I had admired. "Jason wasn't completely evil. There were other sides to him. That was what I saw back then."

"Other sides? The man was *married*, Marie."

He pulled a blanket from the bed, and as he tried to wrap it around his torso he knocked the lamp off the night table. The bulb shattered, the filament sizzled, darkness settled around us. In his eyes I saw an evil glow. He grabbed my wrist hard. "He was a sleaze, a total sleaze, why don't you admit it?"

I pulled my hand away. "I'm not going to lie just to satisfy your fragile ego."

"They wanted to be sure they had you," he said bitterly.

I slapped him hard. He pinned me to the mattress. I bit his shoulder. He yelped in pain. I kicked my knees into his ribs. Then, as I undulated under him, he pushed into me.

"Was it good?" he demanded. His voice was savage, the voice of a stranger. "Did it feel like this?"

"Get off me. Get off me. . . ."

He wrapped his fingers in the hair at the nape of my neck and jerked my head back. "Like this?" he demanded. "Was it like this?"

"Please."

He pulled out abruptly. I lay there shuddering.

"You bastard," I whispered. "You bastard, sex isn't a goddamn weapon."

"They used you all around, didn't they?" He said it as if any two-bit whore had more dignity than I did.

"So you decided to join in."

He picked up his chino pants and began to put them on.

"How many times did you sleep with him?"

"That night?"

"How many times?"

"He's dead," I said, and thought about that other ghost between us, the ghost of my husband. And for that split second I felt that Raul's jealousy was about Joe and not Jason at all.

"I've never had sex like I have with you," I said.

He pulled his undershirt down over his head in a few deft moves. In the process I saw the curve of his chest, the blue-black hairs around the honey-dark nipples. When his head emerged, he looked at me as if he was no older than Joey. "You mean that?"

I shrugged because I didn't want to debase myself completely. He came over and took my head into his hands. He touched my neck so lightly with his fingers that I felt goose bumps rise and fall and a cool rush right under the skin.

"I don't mean what I say when I'm hurt, Marie. I'm jealous, very jealous."

"You haven't exactly gone through life as a celibate saint," I said.

He got up from the bed and stood there in a wide-legged, arrogant stance. In the half-light the sheet gathered around me like a shroud.

"It's different," he said.

"Since when?"

"Since the beginning of time."

"I don't think so," I said. "I don't think so."

I could see him calculating the implications, implications to his ego when this thing went public.

"They want me to wear a wire and get all the heavy hitters on tape . . . Hunter, Nicosea, Brogan."

I started to cry. He let me sob for a while; then he sat down next to me where I lay facedown. He stroked my back. I just cried. After a while I felt his tears on my back. I turned to see his face. He took me in his arms. "Forgive me. Can you forgive me?"

Without the anger and the fighting, I spiraled downward to the dead center of a dark pool of anguish. Down there I was very alone. When I looked at him again, it was as if there were water and not air between us. We looked at each other across the abyss like strangers into a mirror. I didn't see him, I saw myself. He didn't see me. He saw the sum total of his life. We had chosen each other. We had chosen this moment. We had both always known it would come to this.

He said, "You need a lawyer, a good lawyer."

We were both quiet for a while, not judging each other, just both wondering where it was all going to end.

"Half-truths are so much worse than lies," he said. "They have the sound of truth and we believe them. A simple lie is so much easier to see through." He stopped and looked at me and then he went on. "You can spend a lifetime stuck in the mire of half-truth. I'm good at that myself."

What was he leading up to? He picked up his jacket, put it on, and repeated, "The mire of half-truth, no place to be."

He performed a ritual with his tie that turned out to be a knot. Then he made yet another confession. "I knew who you were. I've always known. I knew you used to work for Isenberg."

I got up, went to the window, and looked out at the city that had long since been claimed by night. "What are you telling me?"

"I thought you knew more than you did."

"Is that why you wanted me to go to Miami with you? Because . . . ?"

"Because I'm a shit," he said. Then he came to stand beside me at the window. In the dark neither of us had a reflection. On the street below, a couple passed arm in arm. They were laughing. We couldn't hear them. I walked back to the bed. He followed. "I fell in love with you," he said. "It changed everything."

We sat down on opposite sides of the bed, our backs to each other. Neither of us was innocent and we both knew it.

"I wouldn't go back to City Hall if I were you," Raul said.

I felt it then, the cold breath of the punishment I had been waiting for. It was close now, very close. I said, "I have to go back."

18

The crush of commuters closed in around me. The lucky few who had gotten seats were reading the morning editions —*News, Post, Times, Dispatch.* The train barreled through the tunnel, emitting the high screech of metal on metal. Hot air blew from the vents, sweating bodies pushed against me, a heavy foot crushed my toes. One of the *Dispatch* readers glared up at me. Then she looked back at her newspaper, then back at me. I leaned forward to see the paper on her lap. There I was, upside down. The train rumbled on.

When the train pulled into the City Hall station, I went straight to the newsstand. The headline read ALLEGED ARSONIST HANGS SELF IN CELL. According to the article inside the front cover, Thaddeus Finx had managed to hang himself in his Riker's Island cell using his own trousers.

"You gonna pay for that paper, miss?"

I paid.

I just stood there reading. On page three across from another picture of Thaddeus Finx a much smaller headline read MAYOR'S AIDE PROBED. Under it was a tight head shot of me that seemed to have been cropped from a group shot. I could hear the rustle of the paper as it trembled in my hands. Behind me a train ground to a halt and people pushed out.

The article, written by Larry Pierce, was about the FBI's long-standing investigation into Isenberg. Only the last paragraph mentioned me. "FBI sources confirmed that the mayor's administrative assistant, Marie Terranova, who was Deputy Mayor Isenberg's administrative assistant during the inception of the shelter program, is also a target of the probe." Mercifully, the night in Connecticut was not mentioned.

It was the height of the morning rush hour and the platform was crowded with people. One man seemed to be paying particular attention to me. He too was reading the *Dispatch.* He seemed to be watching me over the edge of his paper. He kept pushing the Mets' cap he wore down over his eyes then pulling it back up. I wondered if he were following me. Behind me a mother with a sleeping infant strapped inside a stroller looked up at the long climb to the street. I grabbed the front of the stroller. She smiled. Together we carried the sleeping child up the stairs.

The man in the cap followed me through City Hall Park and into Ellen's Café. In the crush of the morning coffee line he stood a few people behind me. When my turn came, I ordered my coffee but then didn't wait for it. Instead I left by an exit that led into the lobby of 270 Broadway, the State Office Building. When I stepped out into the street, he was gone. I crossed the street to City Hall. As I started climbing the steps I recalled the thrill of that first day on the job, the almost erotic power exuding from the architecture itself. I remembered how special it made me feel that I would now be among the people who governed the city.

I was about halfway up the steps when something different floated up from the deep waters of memory. I saw Joe sitting at the breakfast table so stressed out that he couldn't talk straight and me screaming at him, wanting to know where what we had between us had gone. I saw the two of us arguing about badly cooked eggs because neither of us really understood what was happening to us. I recalled Joe's pride the day he first stepped into his uniform. The man in blue, ready to be New York's finest. How miserably City Hall had used him. How confused and sad he must have been during that last crazy secret investigation. Thaddeus Finx was right. I had been blind. Had Nicosea been blind too? Or had he been a willing participant? And in the end, weren't we responsible nonetheless?

There are only thirty-two steps to the portico. I felt a sadness so deep that the climb was difficult. But, as the pieces fell into place, I felt a stillness inside. And in that inner stillness I opened the door.

All around me I felt the cold marble and then I saw him, Jason, the ghost of Christmas past, carrying his burgundy briefcase, passing through security without a check. As my purse went through the metal detector a low human thunder seemed to roll toward me.

From the legislative wing the Room Nine press corps rushed toward me. At the same time Hunter ran from the executive wing yelling to the guard. "Let her go. Let her go!" On the monitor the skeleton of my purse appeared, all the contents revealed in outline. When the purse itself reappeared, Hunter scooped it up as he grabbed my elbow. I heard the voices from Room Nine saying my name, first, last, in lots of tones. I did not see Raul.

"Recognize this?" a reporter yelled, sticking a piece of paper in my face.

It was the same old memo, the one I had signed. The one Human Resources and the FBI had. Hunter tightened his grip and pulled me along.

Ahead of us was the gate. The gate to the executive wing. It looked like St. Peter's gate, ornate and golden with regal lions worked into the elaborate filigree. A white-gloved guard stood behind it. No one crossed that sacred threshold uninvited. Least of all the press. Hunter's eyes spoke to the guard.

"Sorry, folks," the guard said to the reporters. "You can't come through here."

The gate clanged shut behind us and the reporters grumbled their dissatisfaction. Some cursed under their breath. Hunter hustled me to my office. He slammed the door behind us and leaned on it, panting as if we had just escaped a wolf pack.

"I tried to call you," he said. "I tried to call you as soon as I read the paper. Why didn't you get in touch with me?" His usual icy calm had cracked.

"I saw the paper just now on the subway."

"You must have known it was coming. You must have known you were being looked at. You could have warned me."

He glared at me as he aligned his cuff links in an apparent attempt to steady himself. As I watched that wild crazy look in his eyes I began to wonder if he knew less than I did.

I said, "I need to talk to Nicosea about that memo."

Hunter took the newspaper from my trembling hands into his and opened it. As he stared at the article about the FBI probe he said, "What you need is a good lawyer."

I repeated, "I need to talk to the mayor."

"If you're as loyal as you profess to be, you won't want to jeopardize this administration by talking to him about this."

I put my hand on the knob of the door that connected my office to the inner sanctum. It was locked. I headed for the other door, the door to the hall. Hunter stepped in front of me. "Look," he said, "the press are like dogs, wild dogs. Right now, they're on the trail of blood, your blood. Don't you think you should protect yourself with the advice of counsel?"

"I thought you leaked that memo to keep the dogs on me and off Nicosea."

"I've never seen that memo before."

We circled each other until he stopped and looked dead at me. "You're so mistrustful you're dangerous to yourself." He smiled cynically, "I know we've had our little friction but I'm not crazy enough to undermine this administration with a move like that."

"As a diversion," I said, "to keep the press focused on Jason's grave and me . . . anything but Nicosea."

"Nicosea has nothing to hide. He's an honest man."

"Then let me talk to him. I want to talk to him."

"If you believe he's innocent, you don't."

I stopped pacing to take a closer look at him. His Yuppie face was inscrutable. Who was he? I had always hated his arrogance, but I didn't really know him. I asked, "What are you trying to say?"

His eyebrows went up and down. "You know what I mean."

"Maybe if people weren't so busy keeping bad news from the mayor, he'd know what was going on around him."

Hunter sighed. "Look, Nicosea's a figurehead. Nobody wants him to know too much, but without him this administration tumbles."

My mind was on the title search and what it showed, but I couldn't risk mentioning it. If Hunter was in on the corruption, he could make the records disappear. If he wasn't, he might have the records destroyed anyway, just to guarantee the election.

"Who's the lawyer?" I asked. "Anybody I know?"

"Blanchy, Knopff and Oman," he said. "Strictly big time. They do corporate and criminal. We want to help you. We're not going to let you sink. Did Jason ask you to sign the mayor's name to that memo?"

I didn't answer. After a while I asked, "Who else does that law firm represent?"

"I don't know exactly, big shots. I know they represent the mayor's father-in-law."

I sat down. Even though I was still wearing my jacket, I was cold and I felt very small. Like an insect, I felt the web surrounding me. I could almost hear the wolf pack down the hall, the footsteps of the FBI with its ubiquitous agents, Milano's insidious clubhouse power, the mob with its long tentacles, Mendelssohn counting his money. And I began to feel that I could never stand up to all of that. I said, "I'll go."

Hunter perked up. He walked along the four walls and then he stopped in front of the desk where I sat.

"Then listen very carefully, Marie. You're going to have to stand up to the press."

"How?"

"You're not going to make it out of here without running the gauntlet again. They're out there waiting for you. Everybody wants this story. Tough it out, walk right through them. They can't actually follow you. That's harassment."

"What are you saying?"

"Get out there and no-comment them to death. Just keep on walking."

"I'm not supposed to defend myself?"

"You'll just dig in deeper."

"Where's Nicosea?"

"In his office, I guess."

"I need to see him."

"I don't think that's a good idea."

"I'm not going anywhere till I see Nicosea."

He stared at me, caught somewhere between anger and despair. Finally he said, "Wait here. I'll see if he's available."

When Hunter had gone, I sat down at my desk. Even the blood in my veins seemed to tremble. My eardrums pounded with the echo of a wild rushing like the stampede of a herd. After I sank fully into my terror, a calm returned. Like the shutter closing on the eye of a camera, I turned inward. I stared idly at Jason's painting. The lion looked back at me from behind his grimacing mask. I got up and walked toward him. The lion's mane had a golden luminescence. And then I heard Thaddeus Finx say, *You know the answer. You just have to remember it.*

My mind wandered to the day I had signed that memo and the night that followed. Jason and I had been working late every night for weeks to complete the paperwork that would allow the emergency shelter program to move ahead on schedule. That night we finished. To celebrate, Jason had invited me to dinner in a country inn about an hour outside of New York. I had said yes.

On the ride up he joked with me about the variety of egos that populated City Hall. Jason was a great mimic and could assume the mayor's, Hunter's, or Brogan's persona at will. I laughed so hard my sides ached. Joe had been dead all winter. Sitting beside Jason in the car, I longed for Joe's touch.

After a cozy dinner by a fireplace we walked toward Jason's

nearby cabin. The snow was several inches deep. We made our way along the path between the trees. We reached a clearing. Except for the deer tracks and their droppings, our footprints were the first. A small brook had frozen in its fall over the rocks. The moonlight reflected there in a faint rainbow. Jason talked of New York City's greatness. "Only two hundred years ago, New York had no safe drinking water, the population was constantly decimated by plagues and disease, the city kept burning down because there wasn't enough water to fight the fires. Now it's the cultural and financial mecca of the world. A vertical city with vertical dreams. A city where a guy like me whose father was an alcoholic bum can make it to the top."

The glass arms of the low-hanging branches framed us in magic. I was filled with admiration for him. He generously made me feel that my work of the last few weeks had been an indispensable contribution to the city and its people.

I had frozen there on the bed in the log cabin. Jason wasn't much of a lover and I don't think he even noticed. I didn't sleep that night. Instead I listened to the branches of the trees crack under the winter's weight. I snuggled up to Jason's back and closed my eyes. But it didn't help. The night stretched ahead of me, long and indifferent.

I watched the Connecticut hills become violet shadows against a pink dawn. By the time we left, the icy brances of the trees covered the hills like giant cobwebs; Jason and I had returned to work as if that night had never happened. We never spoke of it again. Soon after, I went to work for the mayor.

The dancers, the foliage, the monkeys, and the drums were pulled out of the darkness of the canvas by the light of the painter's strokes. I saw Jason standing in front of this very same painting and I heard him say, "Unlike us Americans who think corruption is a thing you root out once and then you're done with it, the Balinese know that the struggle between good and evil is eternal."

He had brought his hand up to the canvas and pointed to the benevolent-looking animal with a golden mane and spindly human legs. "The lion is the heart of it all," I heard him say.

I studied the picture. I studied the frame. At the upper left-hand corner two pieces of the handcarved wooden frame didn't completely meet. There was a little crevice there just like the crevice of memory I had just entered. Hidden in the crevice was a slender metal object.

With a nail file from my purse I extricated it from its hiding place. It sailed to the floor and landed with a tiny toll that reverberated in the back of my skull like one hand clapping. A key. I picked it up. It looked like a standard locker key, but the bulky top, the part that served as a handle, had been filed down. A number was scratched on the key itself—GC 78639.

The door opened, the side door, the one directly to the mayor's office. Hunter stepped in. "I was wrong," he said. "Nicosea's not here. He's speaking to the Staten Island Chamber of Commerce."

I slipped the key into my pocket. "When will he be back?"

"I don't know, about eleven."

I just stared at him until he admitted that he knew what I wanted.

"Okay," he said, "okay. I'll talk to him. I'll ask him if he wants to talk to you. But that's all I'm saying. I'm not saying anything else."

I wanted to get out of there and get it over with, so I asked, "If I just say 'no comment,' doesn't that imply that I'm guilty?"

Hunter sat on the corner of my desk. "Marie, trust me. It's just a tactic . . . a delay tactic. Sure, you want to defend yourself, but anything you say now will lead to a follow-up question. It'll be like opening a Pandora's box. If I were you, I wouldn't want to open that box until I had a good lawyer at my side."

I tried to read his inscrutable face. I wondered what he knew. Then I got up and walked toward the door.

"It won't be easy," Hunter said. "Most people can only take but so many questions before they start giving some answers. Reporters know that. One thing those bastards know," he added, "is human nature."

For what I was about to go through, I was remarkably calm. He seemed calmer yet. For a moment I actually felt that we were allies. Then he said, "I'm not going with you. My going with you wouldn't serve your best interests."

"Why not?"

"I would be just one more target. And when the press secretary starts stonewalling, everybody knows the trouble is real."

"You'll talk to the mayor," I reminded him as he opened the door for me.

He nodded. "Call me after you see your lawyer. I should have an answer for you."

I stepped out into the hallway. I walked past the mayor's office and past the Blue Room. Then I turned toward that golden gate with its filigree lions. There were no reporters at the gate, but by the time I had reached the rotunda they had gathered like filings to a magnet. This time one of them had a Xerox of the photo, the one the FBI had. The photo of Jason and me in Connecticut. A television cameraman ran backward in front of me. The camera peered into my face like a giant eye. Klieg lights blinded me.

"Ms. Terranova what was your relationship with Jason Isenberg?"

"Where was this picture taken?"

"No comment."

"Can you confirm that this is on Isenberg's Connecticut property?"

"No comment."

"Aw, c'mon, Marie, this isn't like you."

"Have you met with the FBI?"

I was walking as fast as I could, but the pack was all around me. I began to understand what Hunter had meant about sticking to an answer. I was getting angry and it was getting harder and harder not to fight back. I just kept repeating myself while keeping my eyes on my feet as much as possible.

The reporters and the cameras—there were two cameras now —followed me down the steps. Then, except for the camera crews, they all stopped. The camera crews followed me all the way to the street as I hailed a cab and even aimed their lenses through the cab's mud-splattered window. The driver screeched away then studied me nervously in the rearview mirror. "Where you go?" he asked in a heavy accent.

I gave him Esther Isenberg's address.

"We take FDR?"

In the rearview I nodded yes.

On the drive I kept looking back to see if the press or the FBI were behind us. But on the busy highway it was impossible to tell. It took us almost an hour to get uptown. I got out, paid the driver, and headed for Esther's building.

Esther's doorman studied me carefully.

I said, "Isenberg, Apartment 2315."

As he dialed on the intercom phone he watched the panel of black-and-white television screens that monitored the hallways and elevators of this mammoth high rise. I watched reflected shadow images cross his white shirt, his badge, his belt buckle. "Who shall I say—"

"Marie, Marie Terranova."

He spoke my name into the mouthpiece and then listened. A moment later he handed me the receiver.

"Marie . . . Marie, I don't feel up to company just now. Why didn't you call first?" Esther asked.

"I need to—"

The guard pushed his hat back and studied me more intensely.

"Can we make it tomorrow?" Esther asked.

"It's urgent, very urgent."

"All right, give the phone back to the guy."

I handed the guard the phone. He put it to his ear then nodded. "Yes, ma'am," he said. Then, as he put the phone down on its cradle he shoved a clipboard and pen toward me: "Sign here."

As I signed my name he watched his monitors. He was still doing that when I walked around the corner to the elevator bank. An empty elevator stood waiting. I stepped in. The door closed. Musak was playing. Above me hung a camera. Through its electric eye I could feel the guard watching. Overhead the numbers of the floors lit up in sequence. Then the elevator door slid back. Another camera followed me to Esther's door. I rang the bell. I heard it chime but no one answered. After a while I heard a noise inside like a mouse scurrying over a chain. Then Esther opened the door and I saw one of her eyes through the crack. "What's going on?" she whispered.

I leaned toward the eye and said, "Let me in, Esther."

The pupil seemed to get bigger. I moved in even closer. "It's life and death, Esther. Let me in."

In the lock the chain rattled a little as she pulled it from its socket. She stepped back just enough to let me in. I was in a hall of mirrors. The sheets that had covered them during the shiva were gone. I became many arms and legs, a doll in a row of cutouts. Esther was there too. The two of us were reflected so often, we were a crowd. In the mirrored hallway I followed Esther's reflection to the living room.

When we got to the sparsely furnished living room, I searched for a place to begin. Two mirrors on opposite walls doubled the size of the room. I took the key out of my purse and showed it to her. She grabbed it from my hand, then turned from me abruptly. Because of the mirrors, I could still see her face.

"Where did you get this?" she demanded.

"Jason left it hidden in his Indonesian painting. The one he had in his office."

"How long have you had it?"

"I found it just now."

"How do you know Jason put it there?"

I stepped around her so that we could really look at each other.

"He left a code, a code on his desk calendar. The code led me to the key."

She hurled the key at her face in the mirror. I heard the mirror crack. As I turned to look a spiderweb seemed to be growing around us.

"Silver, or was it gold?" she asked.

"What?"

"Judas, when he betrayed Christ, was it for gold, silver, or designer clothes?"

"Silver. Thirty pieces."

"Yes"—she chuckled wildly—"betrayed with a kiss. That's the scandal of it all. Judas sold himself and it wasn't even for gold. Greedy, greedy, greedy just like me."

Her self-accusation echoed back from the mirrors. What passed was a short time that seemed long. She was breaking. She took her face into her hands as if it were an object, an object with no other place to go. Her body began to heave, but the sounds of her grief were silent. When she looked up again, her eyes were wild with memories. "I didn't want to feel poor ever, ever again. I wanted to be on the inside, not the outside. I never had any decent clothes, I lived on the wrong block, everybody hated me . . . the Italians . . . the Jews. Even my father hated us. He said my mother's people killed his God."

I felt consumed by her nightmare. Her hazel eyes had crazy yellow specks in them. I whispered, "Esther, you were very popular."

Her voice dropped. "You don't know how much time I spent on my knees to get that popularity, Marie. And I don't mean in church. I sucked off practically the whole goddamn football team to get that popularity. I worked at that popularity just like I worked at all this." She waved her arm around at the cold elegant apartment.

"You knew about the kickbacks?" I whispered.

"I didn't care where the money came from as long as it came. Jason, poor schmuck, he took it where he could get it."

"Where was that?"

"The water contracts, the shelter contracts. He was making so much money for the campaigns, for Mendelssohn and Milano, I guess he felt he had a little taste coming to him."

"What do you mean?"

"He always greased the skids for Mendelssohn and his crowd, and they always gave generously to the campaigns."

"Do you think the mayor knew?"

She shook her head. "No, but Brogan did. He got a cut and he helped keep it from the mayor."

"Did Mendelssohn know?"

"He didn't care as long as the campaign coffers were full so that Nicosea could keep winning elections. As long as Nicosea's in office Mendelssohn and his cronies make out like bandits—mortgages, shady real-estate deals, money, money, money, all the goodies government has to offer."

"How could all that be going on and Nicosea not know?"

She spread her hands. "He's well insulated. You know that."

"Still . . ."

"I guess he's not that different from us."

"What's that supposed to mean?"

"He didn't *want* to know."

I was quiet for a long time. So was she. This not wanting to know, it was a quality we had all shared. Finally she turned to me again, this time with a cruel grin. "When Jason tried to get out, they murdered him."

There was another moment during which I wasn't sure I wanted to hear the rest. Then I asked, "What are you saying?"

"Jason didn't commit suicide. Two men came in here and threw him off the balcony. I saw them. They said if I talked, my son would be next."

She was watching my reflection now, or was it her own? The web covered the room. In the light of the chandelier the cracks in the mirror seemed to hold us like wet glue. If there was any air in the room, I couldn't feel it. Then she laughed. "You don't believe me, do you, Marie? You think I'm nuts."

I couldn't speak.

"The priest was right. Secrets fester. Secrets kill. I should have told, I should have talked, but it's too late now."

"It's not too late," I said. "Jason left behind a lot of evidence."

Suddenly she was quiet, very quiet. I felt her search the past for the exact moment of her first fatal choice. She headed for Jason's study. I followed. She opened the balcony door.

"Right here, here is where they tossed him over. He didn't even scream for help. It was like he knew it was coming."

She grabbed my arm. Her thumbs bit into me. "There were two of them. One was big and tall and bald. The other was shorter with a lot of sandy hair. I let them in."

"Why? Why would they kill him?"

She shuddered, "Because Jason was the nexus. He gave city contracts to the mob, and when he turned on the administration, the mob couldn't afford that."

"What made him turn?"

"On his last trip to the Bahamas, Jason found out that the money he was taking, the kickback money, was drug money." With a gesture her hands encompassed the expanse of the city below. "The dirty money, all the dirty money, it's all from one pot. By that time Jazz had a crack problem, and he felt like he had been dealing to his own son. It almost killed him. He decided to wear a wire and nail them all. Even himself."

She looked down at the ground twenty-three stories below as if she could undo time. "Just before they grabbed him, he held me and whispered to me that he'd left a record, a record somewhere, but I don't know . . . that key must be . . . he said End-of-the-World Station. He said it twice."

"That's Grand Central," I said. "That's what New Yorkers called it when it was first built. Back then it was so far uptown, it was out of town. Jason told me that. He was always talking about the history of the city."

She studied me for a long sad moment. "How close were you to Jason?" she asked.

I didn't know how to answer that but I guess my face said it all. I tried to explain. "Jason and I . . ."

She raised her hand to stop me. "It's not important," she said. She picked the key up off the floor and placed it in my hand. "Use this," she said. "Make them pay," she said. "Make them all pay."

"You may have to testify."

"It can't be any worse than it has been," she said. There was no emotion in her voice.

After that I took the subway to Grand Central. I walked upstairs to the information booth to ask about the lockers. On the vaulted dome all the constellations except Orion were painted in reverse. As I walked through this reverse universe, where the sun would rise in the west and set in the east, the smells of misery surrounded me. The homeless were everywhere. They flanked the ticket booths, lined the walls, and obstructed travelers from all over the country and the world. On any given day, I had read, there were seventy-five thousand homeless women, children, and men in New York City, and Grand Central was one of the places where they gathered. Fifty million commuters a year passed through this place, and as uncomfortable as it was, none of them seemed to ask why or how it could be that in the richest country in the world, grandmothers and babies were forced to turn this commercial hub into the world's biggest bedroom and bathroom.

I rushed through the terminal, through the promenade with its network of banking, betting, and eating places, past the ticket windows, to the information booth. The Kodak billboard and a dozen others were suspended over the golden-brown marble. At the information booth I asked for the lockers.

"There's no lockers, lady. The MTA ordered them taken out. Bums were living out of 'em."

My heart began a violent beating. Then I had a thought. If the MTA were as disorganized as the rest of government, maybe I still had a chance. I read the woman the number on my key. "Where would this locker have been?"

"On the lower level," she said, bored. "But it's gone now."

I elbowed my way through the crowd and went underground. My footsteps echoed in the forgotten depths of the terminal. There in the semidarkness I felt that I had returned to the primordial caves where human beings banded together to seek refuge from other, wilder animals. But this tribe sought refuge from other humans. The walls of the underground tunnel were moist, the air dank. The homeless had organized their turf into neat little squares that were defined by blankets and shopping carts. Water dripped down from leaking pipes, and I tasted rust in the back of my throat. A young mother with a baby strapped to her chest squatted over a hot plate plugged into a naked socket and cooked some rice. Behind her on the wall of the tunnel someone had painted a palm tree, a piece of ocean, and the sun. I wondered how long before even this wasteland was taken from them. Down here there were rows and rows of lockers that had not yet been ripped out, most of them battered and pried open. I wandered among the dispossessed, showing them my key. They pointed deeper and deeper into the interlocking tunnels. The smell of urine, feces, and unwashed flesh made my knees buckle. Finally, at the end of a dark empty hallway, I saw the wall of lockers I was looking for. I walked toward it slowly.

A grime-crusted old woman pushed a shopping cart toward me. She stopped and rattled some change in a cardboard cup. Her eyes peered through a filthy rug of gray hair. She opened her mouth to reveal her missing teeth. "Please," she said, "please."

She was old enough to be my mother. I studied the numbers on the lockers on the wall. "Please," she said. "I'm hungry."

The locker I was looking for was gone.

The old woman rattled the loose change in her cup. I searched my pockets. I found only a quarter and several tokens. I handed her a token. She studied it carefully.

"God bless you," she said. I followed her back toward the light.

I looked at my watch. It was the middle of the afternoon. I walked to the nearest pay phone and called Joey. I told him to pack Jason's calendar in his book bag and to meet me in City Hall Park.

19

In City Hall Park, the trees were blurred with buds and the air was full of the bittersweet hope of an early spring. I told Joey what he had to know. There was a calm determined anger in him that left no room for fear. Above us the statue of the lady they called Justice seemed to balance the pale sunlight that washed over lower Manhattan.

We stood at the foot of the stairway that led to the portico, admiring the facade. Many considered it the most beautiful City Hall in America. The marble-and-limestone whispered of the immense power contained inside these doors and of the rich and turbulent history that had consolidated it. We climbed the steps.

Joey and I headed for the security guard just inside the front door. Apparently he didn't read the papers because he didn't give me as much as a second look. We stood for a few moments in the magnificence of the rotunda. Joey had his book bag on his back.

"I'm going into my office," I said, "and from there through the side door into the mayor's office. I want to talk to him. If I'm not back in fifteen minutes come on in."

I walked quickly toward my office, hoping to make it inside without being stopped. But as I turned into the executive wing I saw them—Hunter and Brogan, standing just inside the gate. Hunter, elegant in shades of gray, and Brogan, as always, conservative in a blue three-piece pinstripe suit with the mandatory red tie. They were deep in conversation with Raul, who stood just outside the gate. Raul was casual in black denim jeans and a blue blazer. From a distance it looked like business as usual.

As I stepped up behind Raul I heard him say, "I'm asking you for a reaction to this title search. We're going with it, and in the interest of fairness I'm offering you a look. This copy is for you." He offered Hunter the copies.

"We have no way of knowing if these Xeroxes represent actual documents," Hunter snapped, and stepped out of Raul's reach.

"C'mon, let's not play games." Raul turned away to emphasize his contempt.

"We'll get our own copies, then we'll get back to you."

Hunter saw me. His shock was so obvious that Brogan and Raul followed his eyes to see what he was looking at. Hunter quickly opened the gate. Raul blocked my way. "Marie," he whispered, "Marie."

I stopped just to look at him. It was as if time were a strand of pearls coming undone. I felt the knot that separates one pearl from the other loosen, and then, like heavy drops of water, the pearls fell. In the space created by that undoing I again felt everything that had passed between us. All the moments. They added up to this, this which was coming now.

I said, "You were more right than you know."

"I don't understand."

Brogan reached for me. His fingers bit into my arm as he discreetly tried to pull me through the gate. I resisted. But as my body slid past Raul's I said, "I'm coming to Room Nine to make a statement as soon as I've talked to the mayor."

Hunter and Brogan froze. Still as statues, they stared at each other. Raul took a deep audible breath. "Anything for the record now, Marie?" he asked.

Hunter added his grip to Brogan's. Together they pulled me through the open gateway. Then Brogan slammed the gate shut.

"Not just yet," I told Raul.

My feet barely touched the floor as Hunter and Brogan escorted me up the hallway away from Raul. When we reached my office, Hunter kicked the door back with his foot as Brogan pushed me inside and shoved me down into my chair. "Have you lost your sanity?" he hissed.

Hunter closed the door.

Brogan loomed above me, the sweat on his pale upper lip solid as blisters. "What the hell do you think you're doing?" he shouted. I got up and pushed past him toward my personal entrance to the sanctum sanctorum. I rattled the doorknob. It was still locked from the other side. As Brogan pulled me from the door I sensed a terrible violence in him.

I swung around to face him. "Stay away from me," I warned him.

"Please," Hunter urged, "keep it down."

Brogan stopped. We glared at each other, panting. He cocked his head. I heard it too. Behind me a lock turned. The mayor stood in the open doorway. He too seemed stunned. Brogan shuffled his feet. I couldn't take my eyes off Nicosea. His skin was gray and ashy, the profound shadows under his eyes betraying a host of sleepless nights. "Marie," he asked. "Marie, what's going on?"

My throat was tight. The words came out pinched and slow. "Can I talk to you without them?" I moved my hand vaguely in the direction of Hunter and Brogan.

Nicosea ran nervous fingers through thinning hair and studied me. For the moment he seemed to have forgotten the others. "That memo, that memo," he asked, "why did you sign my name to it?"

Before I could answer, Brogan attacked from behind. He brought his hands roughly over my breasts and pulled me to him. Nicosea stood like a witness to a mugging, mesmerized. Through my silk blouse I felt the dampness of Brogan's hands. His breath brought a wave of nausea upward from my belly. I kicked one heel viciously into his shins, the other I ground into his toe. He groaned but his hands kept searching. When he didn't find what he was looking for, he released me.

Hunter's face was white. "You're losing it," he said to Brogan.

"I had to be sure she isn't wired."

"You didn't have to do that. You didn't have to do that to her," Nicosea said.

As I straightened my blouse and skirt Nicosea studied the lapel of my suit jacket, and a terrible nostalgia distorted his features. "That's the brooch," he said, "the one . . ."

"The one you gave me at Christmas—at Christmas when you asked me to pack Jason's files."

"Okay, she's not wired, but she's desperate, there's no telling what she's up to," Brogan interrupted. "She may try to implicate you."

"Once you've been alone with her, it'll be your word against hers," Hunter chimed in.

I said, "Those files have since been shredded."

There was a silence during which Nicosea's eyes traveled from my face to Brogan's and back again. "Come on then," he said, and led the way into his office.

"This is against my best advice," Brogan called after us fiercely.

I closed the door. The urgency I felt clashed with the lush stillness of the room and the tranquil aura of the antiques that furnished it. I felt like a child on my first train ride. The room was the train. It semed to be standing still while the world outside moved. We looked at each other for a moment that was much deeper than it was long. Now he was not the patronizing father, he was just a guy who was scared, very scared. Even the founding fathers in their frames seemed to be worried about what I had to say. Nicosea pointed to the chair in front of his desk where for three years now I had sat. "Sit down, Marie."

Then Nicosea took his place behind his desk, the same rich

mahogany desk that generations of mayors had used. As he ran his hands over the elegant blotter I felt him search for the rituals that would reestablish our roles. In front of him rested his golden letter opener with the lion handle. It lay there like a miniature double-edged sword. He ran his thumb along its edge and cast me a glance that seemed to contain a plea not to tell him more than he wanted to know.

I told him what I was about to do and why. I told him about Isenberg and Joe. He listened like a man being slapped into consciousness. He clenched his fists, his knuckles were white, finally he just got up and went to the window. I kept talking. As I spoke he fiddled with the blue velvet curtains. The velvet's sheen alternately absorbed and reflected the sun, so that he seemed to be surrounded in deep blue flames. "I didn't know," he said. "I swear to God I didn't know."

"It's not enough, Ken, not enough to feel regret."

"I didn't know," he repeated.

"Why, why did you hire me?"

"You needed the job. I felt bad about what happened to you."

"You can't bring Joe back. But you can do the right thing now."

He rubbed two fingers between his eyebrows. "Against Brogan's advice; I hired you against Brogan's advice. Even Jason was against it at first."

"I can give you all the evidence I have. Verify it any way you want, then go public. You can clean house. You can stop this."

His face seemed to set into a mask, an ancient mask, a mask of terror. "After the election would be better," he said.

"That means you'd become a participant, an active participant in the cover-up."

He looked at me as if the exact reason why Brogan hadn't wanted him to be alone with me had just dawned on him. "Was Brogan right about you?"

"I don't know. Is life a choice between loyalty and integrity?"

He turned away from me, back to the window. "I was the first in our family to go to college, Marie. The day I passed the bar my dad threw a party for the whole block. My parents had a dry-cleaning store in Brooklyn. They worked ten, twelve hours a day so that I could have a better life. Dad was always so proud of me. My folks, they were true believers, true believers in the American dream."

"It's a good dream," I said. "Worth saving."

"It all went sour." He sighed, full of self-pity. Outside the window the branches of the trees glistened with sunlight. "Soon the cold will be back and all those buds will die," he said bitterly. There was a tap on the door. We both knew who it was.

I said, "Tell them not to come in yet. There's still a lot I haven't told you."

He looked at me as if he were peering into the darkness, trying to identify shadows there. As he wallowed in his indecision Hunter and Brogan stepped in. "Ken, Howard Mendelssohn's on the phone for you," Brogan said.

"I . . . I can't talk to him now."

"I think you'd better, Ken. I've briefed him on the situation and he has some very illuminating information for you."

Nicosea stepped behind his desk. He picked up the phone. His hands were trembling. He cradled the phone to his ear and listened intently. "All right," he said, "all right. Yes." I watched Nicosea as he slowly put down the phone. Then I looked at Brogan. His eyes were full of a mixture of relief and satisfaction. It was as if an atom had split, there in the room between us, and we were bound by an evil energy. We glared at each other. The look on Hunter's face was different, though. Somewhere along the line he had begun taking me seriously and he was worried.

"I'm going across the hall," I said.

"That's been your plan all along, hasn't it?" Brogan said bitterly. "That's what you told Raul Vega on your way in here, isn't it?"

The mayor turned to me then, his eyes feverishly bright. "You're sleeping with that reporter, aren't you?"

"Is that important now?"

He ran his thumb along his letter opener. He said slowly, "It's clearly conflict of interest."

I studied his face, his eyes, his jaw. He seemed rigid as a marionette. "Didn't you hear anything I said? Jason was murdered because he was about to expose everything that's been going on around you here at City Hall. My husband died because of a cover-up he didn't even know existed."

Slow ripples went through the room. I could feel everyone holding their breath. As if that could stop us from having to move into the next moment. Hunter was the first to speak. "C'mon, Marie, this is City Hall, not Sicily."

"Do you know what she is talking about?" Nicosea asked Brogan.

"Of course not. Are we going to let ourselves get sidetracked by a hysterical woman with no political experience?" Brogan turned to me patiently. "It's important the media realize Isenberg operated in a vacuum. We can help you prove that you didn't know what he was up to. It will be difficult because everybody knows you were sleeping with him too. You'll need the mayor's backing. Without it, you'll definitely wind up behind bars, Marie."

Did everything that went wrong in this world hinge on my tortured sexuality? I was so angry, I was cold to my fingertips. As I searched for a comeback the door from my office opened and Joey walked in.

Brogan wiped his brow with a monogrammed handkerchief. "What are you doing here, son?"

"I'm not your son," Joey snapped. He came to stand at my side.

Brogan turned to me. "We know Isenberg tricked you into signing that memo."

I said, "Isenberg worked for all of you."

"I'm afraid not. Isenberg abused our trust. He fooled us just like he fooled you."

"What are you saying?"

"Properly handled, your reputation can be salvaged, Marie. It's delicate but it can be done. Especially if the mayor says that Isenberg tricked you into signing that memo."

I turned to Nicosea. "Come across the hall with me."

He shook his head sadly. "Marie, you're so painfully naive."

"It's all going to come out anyway. The FBI was onto Isenberg."

"Isenberg's dead. He can't do any more damage," Brogan said.

Brogan and Nicosea's eyes touched. If the truth had ever had a chance with Nicosea, it was gone now. I felt an unspoken agreement take shape as an old pattern took hold. In their eyes I saw the greed and fear of old, old men, clinging to their power as if it were life itself. Brogan stepped in closer to the mayor's desk. "Sounds like you've thought this through," Nicosea said.

Joey put his hand in mine. His eyes were rich with hope, expectation, and a pure, clean faith. Together we walked out.

"Where the hell do you think you're going?" Brogan called after us.

"Room Nine?" Joey asked.

"Yes," I said, "Room Nine."

ABOUT THE AUTHOR

Ms. Santiago served five years as Deputy Press Secretary to the New York State Attorney General and two years heading the New York press office for the State Comptroller. She has contributed to the *Daily News,* the *Village Voice,* the *New York Post,* G.Q., and *Penthouse. Room Nine* was written while she was a Charles Revson Fellow at Columbia University.